DARK SHADOWS

Tor Books by Lara Parker

*Forthcoming

Lara Parker

DARK SHADOWS

The Salem Branch

TOR®

A Tom Doherty Associates Book
New York

DARK SHADOWS: THE SALEM BRANCH

Copyright © 2006 by Dan Curtis Productions, Inc.

A Tor Book
Published by Tom Doherty Associates, LLC
175 Fifth Avenue
New York, NY 10010

www.tor-forge.com

Tor® is a registered trademark of Tom Doherty Associates, LLC.

ISBN 978-0-7653-7002-0

First Edition: July 2006
Second Edition: April 2012
First Mass Market Edition: May 2012

Printed in the United States of America

0 9 8 7 6 5 4 3 2 1

FOR MY FAMILY,

Jim, Rick, Miranda, Andy, Celia, and Caiti

with love

Acknowledgments

A novel takes a great deal of painstaking effort on the part of many to bring forth a final product. I could not call this book finished without thanking Jim Pierson, who, in his never flagging devotion, has kept the spirit and the integrity of *Dark Shadows* alive and secure for all these years. I am deeply grateful to my patient and perceptive editor, Caitlin Blasdell, for her keen insights and continuing support as Tor waited—and waited—for the manuscript. It is difficult to fully convey my indebtedness to fellow writer Debbie Smith, and to reader Roy Isbell, for their many hours exploring the story and their invaluable contributions to both character and plot. I am indebted as well to Vera Marano, for her copious pages of research, and to Ray Isbell, who suggested the book's title, *The Salem Branch*. I would also like to boast of my good fortune in having such gifted mentors in the Creative Writing Program at Antioch University in Los Angeles. Dodie Bellamy, Marcos McPeek Villatoro, Nancy Zafris, and Jim Krusoe led me through the labyrinth of the long form, and—on a vampire novel—graciously shared their literary skills. Most of all, my love goes to my husband, Jim Hawkins, who has an instinctive feel for horror stories and talked me through the scariest parts. I am beholden to them all.

I met a lady in the meads
    Full beautiful—a faery's child;
Her hair was long, her foot was light,
    And her eyes were wild.

I made a garland for her head,
    And bracelets too, and fragrant zone;
She look'd at me as she did love,
    And made sweet moan.

She found me roots of relish sweet,
    And honey wild, and manna dew;
And sure in language strange she said,
    "I love thee true."

She took me to her elfin grot,
    And there she gaz'd and sighed deep,
And there I shut her wild wild eyes—
    So kiss'd to sleep.

And there we slumber'd on the moss,
    And there I dream'd—Ah! woe betide!
The latest dream I ever dream'd
    On the cold hill side.

I saw pale kings, and princes too,
    Pale warriors, death-pale were they all;
Who cry'd–"La Belle Dame sans Merci
    Hath thee in thrall!"

I saw their starv'd lips in the gloam,
    With horrid warning gaped wide,
And I awoke, and found me here
    On the cold hill side.

—FROM "LA BELLE DAME SANS MERCI"
    BY JOHN KEATS

If you take away my life, God will give you blood to drink.

SARAH GOOD, FROM THE SCAFFOLD,
Salem, Massachusetts Colony,
July 19, 1692

Dark Shadows

Prologue

Salem Village—1692

That autumn, as she rode in the wagon toward Gallows Hill, Miranda du Val was not thinking of the babe in her arms they had given her to suckle one last time, nor was she thinking of Andrew Merriweather, whom they had already broken and banished to the forest, nor of Judah Zachery, whose head was far from his body. She was thinking of her bright farm aflame with the Devil's torches, the fiery maple trees against the sky, and the ribbon of stream that beavers had backed into a pond. She had let them have it, finally, when she had decided a pond was as good a thing to have as a wood lot.

She had no fear of what was to come. It would be only an instant, then darkness. Hanging was little more than humiliation. Burning witches, as they had done for centuries, was the only way to rid the land, and even that not always successful. Fire would have been something to remember: the faggots at her feet, heat rising, smoke swirling into breath, as the trees she loved returned her to her beginnings. Hanging was child's play. But these townspeople were children, their reason as primitive and as spiteful as a child's.

The wagon shifted in the ruts of the road and she fell against the rail. She could feel the life in the new pine at her back. She could ask it to pull itself loose from the nails, collapse over the wheels, or even burst into flame. But she was bound to the boards by her chains, chains she had been obliged to purchase—along with the hangman's fee—with the meager sum they had offered for her land. She was weary of them all, this town of Salem with its hypocrisy and its hardheartedness. Better to go elsewhere now.

And she would have her revenge. All the sermons from all the pulpits in New England would not hold a candle to the benediction she would deliver from the scaffold. There were many things to empower a curse, but the blood of a child was the spell-caster's delight.

One

Collinsport—1971

The Bentley throbbed down the dark road through a long corridor of overhanging trees. Wet with a late evening rain, the pavement mirrored the headlights and sucked the speeding vehicle into a whirlwind of new-fallen leaves. Barnabas Collins loved the feel of this car, the muscle of it, the singing hum of the engine. It was one of the few things in his life that gave him pleasure. Since he had learned to drive, he had found solace in the hardened shine of black enamel folded like wings about him, enclosing him like a carapace—or a coffin.

"You ain't gonna believe it, Barnabas. It don't make sense. I mean when you think about it." Willie sat in the passenger seat, leaning back against the leather, staring out the window. His hay fever had returned with the goldenrod, and his breathing was a shallow wheeze. Barnabas glanced over at Willie's hands clutching the corners of his jacket, nails bitten to the quick.

"I can only assume she found an original set of plans."

"No, that's not it. It's not just the same rooms and the same stairway. It's really old; it's hundreds of years old. Where are the plans for that?"

"That's the purpose of a restoration, Willie. To produce as authentic a replica as possible."

"Yeah, well, you ain't seen it." Willie extracted a filthy handkerchief from the pocket of his jacket and blew his nose.

"What were you doing wandering around the Old House anyway?"

"Roger sent me to check on them hippies living in the woods back behind the cemetery. He wants them out."

"Hippies?"

"Down . . . down by the stream, living in tents. She lets them live there. She even sleeps out there with them."

"It's her property."

"Roger thinks they're smoking, you know, heroin or something."

"I advised him against selling her the wreckage."

"Yeah, I can see why you don't like her, Barnabas." Willie blurted a noisy sneeze into his handkerchief.

"I did not say that. I never said I didn't like her."

"She looks an awful lot like that painting of Angelique."

"Really? I hadn't noticed."

Barnabas gripped the wheel, and his arms tingled with a peculiar pain as if they had fallen asleep. Although he had not spoken with the woman who had bought the Old House, had intentionally avoided her since that morning when Roger had introduced them in the study, she had nevertheless become as close to him as the rhythm of his breathing, the ebb and flow of her presence fixed deep in his brain.

She did not only resemble Angelique; he was convinced his old enemy had returned.

"They got a camp," Willie was saying. "The whole thing's set up. Hammocks between the trees, a fire ring, a big pickle barrel for water."

"You mean these people are actually living . . . in the woods?"

"Swimming in the river. Naked. I saw them."

"Amusing . . ."

"I came back along the bluff and saw the Old House. All the scaffolding was down and there wasn't nobody around so I—"

"So you decided to have a look."

"Even before I opened the door I was feeling funny. And when I saw the inside . . . it was like something was crawling around on my scalp."

Barnabas stepped on the gas and the car exploded into the gloom. Hulks of trees flew past and heavy branches reached down with leafy fingers, as torrents of leaves lifted by the force of the moving vehicle tumbled in its wake.

"The thing is . . . I got no idea how she did it so fast."

He braked as they came over the bridge. Off to the right, in the headlights, the columns of the Old House glowed a sickly yellow. Barnabas pulled the car into the circular drive, cut the engine, and sat listening to Willie's panting, aware now of his odor—what was it?—oil, wood smoke, damp unwashed corduroys. After a long moment, during which he tried to calm his nerves, he forced himself to turn and look up at the mansion where he had lived out his sentence. It had been six months since it burned to the ground. Yet, here it was: the enormous columns, the parapets, the thick moldings. Catching sight of the chained globe hanging above the door, he felt a chill. Where had she found such a perfect replacement?

He turned to Willie. "Now what?"

"Just come on. You got to see this."

The night was still and completely black; clouds obscured

even the stars, and, feeling the October cold, Barnabas pulled up the collar of his cape. Willie had brought a large club-shaped flashlight, and its beam splayed and jerked across the lawn and up to the knoll where the house sat waiting. The ground was carpeted in spongy leaves and drifts had blown up on the long porch. Once again he had the sense of being weightless, of flying, as he had in the Bentley, as though the earth were far beneath him. And yet he heard the sound of his own footsteps like old newspaper crumpled in a box. He smiled at the foolishness of his fancy. Remembrance of flight was not enough to spirit his mortal body away from this despised place.

The light flickered over the three rounded steps; a layer of leaves obscured all but a glimmer of the crumbling brick. Moss crawled across the chipped masonry like spilt blood. Barnabas hesitated, reluctant to go further, not because he believed Willie's warnings, but because he thought he heard a human cry, deep within the house.

"Does it occur to you that we are trespassing?"

"Nah, nobody's around this time of night."

It was the squeak of a baby owl perhaps, or the mouse its mother had found for food. Barnabas rested a hand upon one of the thirty-two massive pillars which surrounded the exterior. These had remained standing after the fire. The new owner could never have found trees with trunks so broad and tall, the supports of a mansion that had been over two hundred years old when it burned. Willie's light revealed the peeling paint, the cracks in the round footings; then he cast the beam up to the pediment, which was new and now intact. The wedding cake cornice was perfectly restored, held aloft by the Doric columns and crowned with the intricate filigree of the parapets framing the roof. Barnabas was suddenly wary of what lay within.

As it is with ancient doors whose wood has swelled with age and which now sag on rusting hinges, the heavy portal was difficult to open. It dug into the hardwood floor, and the light illuminated a curved scar in the oak, which Barnabas remembered had always been there. Pinpricks of muscle spasms began in the back of his neck and spread across his shoulders.

The shadowed vestibule opened to the staircase, and the flashlight flickered across the wallpaper and moved on. Barnabas seized Willie's arm and returned the light to the wall in front of them. The green hand-blocked pattern, with its stylized irises and running band of leaves, was identical to the one he had admired hundreds of times in the past.

"I told you," Willie whispered.

When he entered the drawing room and saw the huge fireplace of chocolate marble—Rosso Francia marble from Italy—and the swell of the Empire mantel, a sense of the familiar came flooding forth. He remembered kneeling on the hearth less than a year ago and, with trembling fingers, lighting the first match of the conflagration that was to follow, Angelique's laughter echoing in his brain.

Placing one hand on the graceful swirl of the stone to steady himself, he studied the carpet on the floor, the louvered doorway into the study, the crimson damask at the window. His thoughts reeled, and he had a sudden sense of deceitful remembrances invented by his unconscious. As he gazed around the drawing room in amazement, he recognized the same leaded windows, the parquet floors bronzed with aging varnish, the tall arched hallway door, and the stairs rising from the foyer up to the landing. He had a feeling of overwhelming bewilderment. What trick was this? Had the house never burned? Had it all been a vision of desperate rancor, the phantom flames against the sky a mirage? It stood as it always had: heavy, maimed, thick with ghosts.

"What did I tell you, Barnabas? Spooky, ain't it?"

He reached for Willie's torch and cast it over the sconces on the wall—already laden with dripping candles, up to the heavy chandelier, along the crown molding. His mind was playing tricks with him now, teasing him to seek further examples of a stunning replication that seemed to border on the macabre. The only item out of place could be the carpet. He remembered the old Tabriz well, an antique treasure the color of blood. Focusing the flashlight on the ruby nap and the creamy fringe at his feet, he was reassured to see that it was actually a new rug. So, he thought with grim satisfaction, Antoinette has not achieved perfection.

Now he was intrigued, eager to discover other variations. A portrait in a gilded frame hung in the gloom above the mantel. In a faithful restoration of the Old House, the portrait would be that of his beloved Josette. Where would the new owner have found a duplicate? And if she had, would she have made the decision, obviously one that would inflame her pride, to hang it there? He hesitated before shining the light behind the delicate French clock—which, he had to admit, was a faultless rendition of the one that had ticked away his time—and he anticipated the joy he would feel at the sight of Josette's gentle eyes. But, just as he had suspected, it was not Josette. It was instead, a portrait of Antoinette in a scarlet gown; or, to be more precise, it was Angelique, smiling down at him with those same knowing eyes.

A nagging suspicion had been hovering just below his level of awareness, but resisting its import, he had pushed it back into the depths of uncertainty. He turned to Willie.

"Have you been downstairs?"

"No, Barnabas. I got as far as the stairway and I couldn't take any more. That's when I came to find you, to tell you about all this."

"Well, let's have a look."

"You sure you want to do that?"

"We must see, at the very least, what lies in the basement."

If it were there, then it would be proof undeniable. In the basement, in the room where he had slept, if his casket was there, then he would know that not only had she come for him, she had made preparations. All this she had done to rip away any shred of sanity he had gleaned from ten months of normalcy. Why else would she have recreated this pageant of their life together? How, in fact, could she have known how to do it at all?

At that he felt light-headed, as if sleepwalking. After all, he had been lying to himself since he had first seen her, denying suspicions huddled in the corners of his mind. Of course she had come back. All this time, when he could have been finding a way to challenge her, to resist her, instead, like a fool, he had left her to her plans, and she had almost completed them.

Opening the basement door, he whipped the light across the fire-blackened stone of the foundation and the old brick that supported the chimney. As his foot fell upon the stair, Barnabas heard the familiar clink of a loose brick, the same that had betrayed his step hundreds of times when he had returned, each daybreak, satiated from his nightly forays. He thrust the beam into the blackness, and it washed across the masonry arches. Cobwebs clung to the heavy joists that supported the floor above. They hung in tattered remnants, as if time itself had shriveled into a sticky tangle of gauze. Yes. There it lay, covered in dust, as though undisturbed for months. His coffin.

He handed the flashlight back to Willie, who held it nervously, the light playing across the carved mahogany.

"Let's see if I am here."

"Jeeze, Barnabas. It's gotta be empty. That ain't your coffin anymore."

His fingers left glossy smears in the dust as he lifted the lid. How many times had he performed this weary gesture when the moment had come to escape the dawn? The squeak of the hinges was the music he remembered, inviting him to sleep. He pushed back, and Willie cast the light into the interior.

It was empty. The blue satin of his inner sanctum bore not even a faint silhouette of his slumbering form.

"What's that?" Willie whipped the beam around. "You hear that?"

At first Barnabas thought it must be the sound of the sea, just beyond the cliff where the wide lawn tumbled to the rocks. He had often heard the rushing of the waves and the churning of the surf echoing through the chambers beneath the house, lulling him in his daylight dreams. But there it was again, nearer, within the room, a gasp and then a gurgling moan. Barnabas breathed in. There was the smell of newly sanded wood, paint and lacquer, but beneath it two familiar odors intermingled: the reek of a predator and the stench of prey.

"Barnabas . . ." Willie sounded panicked. "Someone's coming. . . ."

"No. He is already here."

"Where?"

"Just . . . under those tarps."

A pile of painters' cloths, stiff and dried, gave evidence that construction had taken place in the house. Barnabas approached the cans of paint and paint thinner, rolls of wallpaper, and hardened brushes cluttering the floor. Reaching down, he pulled back the canvas.

The man was still alive. He stared up with the helpless gaze of a dog struck by a car in the street, crushed inside but still breathing. From his heavy work boots he looked to be one of the laborers, left to clean up perhaps, after the others had gone home. He was jowly and unshaven and wore overalls and a flannel shirt which was soaked with blood. He sighed, and soft, sweet bubbles formed on his lips. It was a messy kill, careless and cruel. Wasted blood pooled on the floor beneath the man's head.

The ripped flesh laid bone and sinew bare, exposing the faint flutter of an artery, and Barnabas resisted an old urge as he lifted the man's head, and gazed into his terrified eyes. He leaned closer, breathing in the scent of blood and saliva.

"Who did this to you?"

The man tried to speak but could only manage a wheezing, "Sh-h-h . . ."

Was the man warning him to be silent? Was the attacker still close by? A chill crept between his shoulder blades as he looked around slowly. But he heard only his own breathing, and Willie's asthmatic pant, and the rasp of the dying man who shuddered now as his eyes glazed over.

Willie tugged at his sleeve. "Barnabas . . ."

"Help me lift him . . . roll this tarp around him." He pushed the body on its side.

"You crazy? What for?"

"He must be moved. The last thing we want is for the authorities to come snooping around here and suspect something."

"But we got nothing to do with it."

Barnabas suppressed the impulse to strike Willie. Always his dim-witted servant opposed the simplest instruction, the most obvious choice of action. He was ruled by cowardice. But Barnabas had no one else he could trust, no one who knew of his past and still remained loyal. He strove for patience. "As you have shown me, Willie, the house is now perfectly restored, and this basement room was—"

"Okay, Barnabas, okay, we'll take him to the cliff and—"

"No, Willie, better the woods. We'll bury him in the woods."

The corpse was light, like a sack of paper rubbish. Willie wrapped the body in the drop cloth and tied it with a length of rope. Then he and Barnabas carried it out to the Bentley.

The clouds had passed and faint starlight shone down. A new wind lifted the branches of the great oaks, and flurries floated to the ground, swirling around the two men. Leaves brushed by their heads and scraped their faces, and Barnabas tasted dust and debris.

It was first necessary to empty the trunk of the two carpets Barnabas had recently purchased to add to his collection. They had arrived that morning and he had not yet taken them to the shop. Rolled and tied with taut string, they were bundled like the dead man, but heavier, bulkier, and Barnabas dragged them across the gravel and struggled with their weight as he shoved them into the back seat. The corpse fell easily into the boot, and one arm tumbled out of the wrapping and over the bumper. Barnabas picked it up gently and placed it against the body. The bones of the wrist were still pliable, and he felt for the faintest pulse, but there was none; it was death, final and forever. Another unfortunate had perished that a beast might live to hunt again.

After searching for a deserted area close to the river, Barnabas turned off the road and drove in jarring lunges through sparse undergrowth in among the trees. There they found a place. Even though Willie had brought a shovel and a pick, he was incapable of digging the grave alone, and the two of them hacked the unyielding earth for the better part of an hour. The leaves were the problem—leaves that lay in knee-high drifts, concealing rocks the shovel struck with a harsh ring—dry leaves that once raked away, blew back into the grave as though utterly depraved, a whirlwind of leaves, filling the hole up again with insidious purpose as though they would make the tomb their own. In the end, he and Willie dragged the body into the shallow excavation and covered it over with rotting compost. Most difficult to bury were the worn, paint-spattered boots, protruding out of the mulch.

As Barnabas walked back to the car, the residue of physical effort triggered a surge of nausea. At first he thought he was going to faint, or be sick to his stomach. These, he remembered, were the first signs of the unpleasant symptoms he had been experiencing since his cure. New blood, manufactured within his own bones, rushed through his arteries and ricocheted into the ventricles of his heart like a flashflood tumbling into a dry gulch. The vampire's silver stream and the cool, tensile strength in his limbs were gone forever. In their place were spasms that doubled him up in pain. Throbbing began in his temples as though his heart was burdened with blood too thick for his veins. Dizziness ensued and he began to pant for breath.

Willie looked over. "What's the matter, Barnabas? You okay?"

"It's the cure again," he muttered. "At times, it's unbearable." As he spoke he felt his legs grow numb and crumple beneath him. His hands were charged with an electrical tingling, as if they had been asleep, and blood was flowing back into them with a slow dull ache. Heat rose out of his core. He wondered whether diabetics or epileptics also learned the signs of convulsions coming on, and waited for them to begin, knowing nothing could stop them. He reached for Willie and gripped his shoulder.

"Barnabas?"

The blood heat began and grew steadily. A volcano stirred, bubbled, expanded; his breath came in gasps, until his whole body pulsed like coals fanned in a grate. A mist settled over his skin, and in seconds he was bathed in clammy sweat and reeking of his new human smell. Breathless and exhausted, he began to shiver—always the inevitable aftermath of the reaction—and he drew his cape about him. He looked over at Willie's face, which was shadowed with concern. "I'm fine," he whispered. "Let's forget all about this place."

"Yeah, right, Barnabas. Tonight never happened."

Later that night Barnabas sat by the fire in the drawing room at Collinwood. His arms ached from digging, his hands were cramped, and blisters reddened his palms. Now he remained deep in thought. Had Antoinette placed his casket in the secret room? Had she known about the body? Was she aware of a vampire on the loose? There must be some connection. Perhaps she herself . . . no, but still, if she were actually Angelique, nothing was beneath her.

If she had returned, if this so-called Antoinette were truly she, then she was a living connection to his past. He felt a sudden twinge in his throat. He despised her. But he had been certain she had died by his hand, forever, lost to him but for the memory of her insatiable love.

And if that were not sufficient torment, he now faced a new and even more formidable opponent. Just as he had relinquished all supremacy, another vampire had entered his domain.

Two

Salem Village—1692

The madness had begun early in the year, but it was only a matter of weeks since Miranda du Val had first begun to suspect she herself was in danger. That spring day she had been on her way to her farm, the walk being over an hour along the forest path, and she had warned herself to stay fast to the ground. Never let them see her in the trees, never give them cause. They had hanged a woman in Topsfield for reading books not the Bible, and another in Marblehead for giving birth to a deformed child. The day would come when they would saw off Judah's head in Bedford, and bury it far from his body, that he might not ride the night. Little did they know.

She remembered that she must use the utmost care, never let them see her fly, nor give them any reason to imagine she was peculiar. Two were in prison in Salem Village waiting trial: one an old hag who deserved to die, vile and dishonest; another a sharp-tongued woman with a questionable reputation. Neither of them witches.

They had drowned a girl in Whethersfield, proving that she was not a witch, which Miranda could have told them, even though the girl was first stripped and searched for marks. The pure water never released its grasp on her struggling body, and she died to defy their sentence. What beasts they were. Loathing women. Desiring women. Ashamed, resentful, full of hate.

She had watched them as they moved out of the meetinghouse that morning in their tall hats and black waistcoats, their faces grim above starched lace, their eyes darting, judgmental, fearful. She had listened to the sermon: *"The Devil hath been raised among us and his Rage is vehement and terrible, and when he shall be silenced, only God knows. We must cast out the impure. Let no aberration exist among us."* And she had read their inner thoughts: *And mine own un-Godly covetings, I must repress.*

That sunny morning, as she struggled through the tasseled grasses towards the forest, her heart ached to be at her farm again, though she knew it would be sadly overgrown, and to see the wood lot and the broadsided house built by her father, with its faded red paint, the tint of blood. It had been six weeks since she had seen it. Careful she must be that they not take it from her.

As the forest grew darker, and she moved across the dappled shadows into the caves of green, she thought of the many nights she had spent in these woods as a child, living with the Wampanoags, before the Reverend Collins found her and took her back to Salem Village. Often she had slept high in the trees, rocked by the wind. Moths sometimes clung to her eyes, and one dawn a spider spun its web across her mouth. Another morning she woke to a sparrow building a nest in her hair. She was so at home in the trees her fingers were often stuck together with sap, and the bottoms of her feet grew rough as bark. She flew easily through the branches and across the canopy.

ooleawa, the Wampanoags called her. *Sisika.* "Tree Flying Girl."

When small birds began to follow her, she knew her farm was near, just beyond the rise. A woodchuck whistled in the eaves, and when she saw the snake her heart lifted, the pattern on his skin more intricate than clock springs. She followed his path through wild strawberry, and his design blended with the old leaf shapes, crimson and pale yellow and deep, brackish brown. The whispering sound he made, though faint, gave way to another, a broken twig, and then a silence came more quiet than a duck's swimming, as birdsong ceased. She broke a vine across her path, and in the ruffled green she saw the doe's eyes. With her was a strong fawn, out of spots, mossy antlers newly sprouted. Her farm was shining through the shadows of the last trees pouring gold and green across the hills.

The men of Salem Village would take her land if they could; they despised a woman owning land, held fast to their resentments. All the recitations of the commandments could never cleanse their hearts of coveting. It was the meat of their thoughts. Old Bartholomew Gedney, that schemer, for certain had an eye on her farm, and her benefactor, Benajah Collins, would stop at nothing had he any inkling of her true nature. But her father had cleared the fields and built the house. It was in her name: a wood lot newly grown, a fast flowing stream, a meadow with bog, and the great forest all around. She would marry Andrew Merriweather in the spring, and they would farm his land together. Somehow she would hide from the world her secret wickedness. Andrew loved her and suspected nothing. He was a simple, kindly man.

She was crossing the field of flax, thick now with young weeds, when she felt water seep into her shoes. She looked down and saw the field was flooded all the way to the stream. The beavers had been at their work again. She half-waded, half-leapt through the marsh, flies buzzing in her eyes, and when she reached the waters she saw at once the damage they had done. The dam was already two feet high, a tangled mass of sticks and larger limbs piled in a messy heap that backed the flow of the water into her best wood lot, turning it to swamp. The small trees were dying, and others had been downed by the beavers and already wedged into the dam.

Flinging off her shawl and wading waist deep into the cold water, she began to tug at the branches and to tear away weeks of the beavers' toil. The sticks clung to one another; mud and leaf mulch held them fast. A large, rust-colored rodent rose to the surface of the pond and waggled his slick head at her before he turned and slapped the water with his tail. The beavers had woven a hillock of trunks and branches, cleverly interlocked and glued together, firm enough to stop the water from flowing. She labored for over an hour, tugging and dragging the branches to the side of the stream. And the irate beaver came more than once to the surface to chatter at her and swim back into his marshy kingdom.

She did not see them before she smelled them, a man's pungent odor along with his horse's, drifting over the water. She was hauling a branch up the bank when she saw them on the opposite side, two townsmen from Collinsport she recognized. Deodat Larson on his Morgan, and her master, Reverend Benajah Collins, on his sickly mare. Behind them was Judah Zachery, the schoolteacher from nearby Bedford, riding his mule. She felt a sour taste rise in her mouth when she saw Judah, because she knew at once that it was he who had brought them and, of the three, he was the one she feared.

"Good day, my child," said the Reverend. "What brings you out on the Sabbath?"

"I was to meeting, sir, and, this being my free day, I have come to tend my farm."

"Have you no work to do at home for Goodwife Collins?"

"She has stayed this day in the town, sir, and given me leave."

"Would it not be better to spend the day in prayer and thanksgiving for all of God's many bounties, or in the quiet contemplation of the scripture?"

"God's beauty and His bounty are here, sir, and this woodland is as holy as any church."

Reverend Collins's horse pulled at her bit as he held her too firmly. When he spoke again, his manner was one of warning—hesitant, but not unkind. "Aye, Miranda du Val, we were just admiring your farm, as you do so call it yours, although it sorely wants care."

"I will care for it, sir, as soon as I can," she answered.

"Oh, we are certain of that eventuality, my child, but your indenture is not up."

"Within the year."

"But now is the time to plant. And what of debts promised by you for board and clothing? You must sign on for another year, must you not? Meanwhile this good land languishes and turns to marsh."

"I was clearing out the stream, sir, when you arrived." She thought of telling them about Andrew, who would have a hand in her release, but at that moment decided to hold her tongue except to say, "What calls you this way, sir, so far from the town?" They wanted something, and it was best to hear them out.

"We have rode out to see this property for Sir Isaac Collins," said Deodat Larson, smiling down from his saddle. "You must know he is a wealthy merchant in the shipping trade, and he wishes to make you a respectable offer."

She shivered from her damp clothes and turned to the Reverend. "Sir Isaac Collins? And would that be your kinsman, sir?"

Benajah jerked his horse's head away from the grass. "He is my brother, and has plans to be . . . an absentee landlord—"

"You may tell him the land is not for sale, sir, and that is the end of it."

"And when will it be planted?"

"Soon."

The schoolteacher's voice was hard. "But what of your lessons, Miranda?" His legs hung low on his mule.

"Indeed they are all well mastered, sir. Would you think otherwise?" The hint of defiance in her response was not lost on him; she could tell by the cast of his eye, but he spoke to her in another tone, more intimate, that made her throat tighten and her teeth go numb.

"This is rude toil for such a tender girl. Need you not a man to help you?"

"Nay, Judah Zachery." And then she added, if only to spite him, "And my days at the schoolhouse are numbered. I have learned all I care to know from you."

"But have you mastered your commandments, Miranda?" The Reverend spoke. "And the Lord's Prayer. Can you recite it by heart?"

"Of course. I am not a child. And many verses of scripture have I set to my memory."

He paused. "Then you must know it bodes evil to speak with a sharp tongue."

"I did not mean to do so, sir. I only meant that I have learned all Judah Zachery has to teach me."

The men looked down on her as she stood in the water, her dress clinging to her body, her hair loose from her cap. Judah Zachery looked the longest. Then they turned to one another and muttered among themselves. She felt the fool, shivering beside a beaver dam with her apron floating on the still water, and so she gathered her skirts and moved back up the bank as though to take her leave of them. But even as she climbed she heard a splashing sound. She turned to see the water bubble through the place she had cleared of debris, and the stream tumbled out, silver and murmuring. They all were amazed that she had man-

aged it alone, and stared a long time at the clearing ripples, thinking their evil, suspicious thoughts.

Then Deodat Larson called to her. "Take care how you
conduct yourself, my child. There is witchcraft afoot and many
are suspect."

"I have naught to do with witchcraft, sir."

Once more they looked at the stream she had released, and
they turned their horses to go.

Miranda stood on the bank and watched the water flow, as
the shallow pond sank slowly, and the tips of reeds and wilted
grasses began to emerge into the air. When she saw the dis-
gruntled beaver waddle into the trees, she wondered whether
she had been wrong to destroy his home. Walking back through
the forest, she began her search for roots and herbs; and she
thought again of her time as a child with the Wampanoags when
enchanted mists hung among the dark trunks, and mysterious
winds whispered in the branches of trees as friendly to her as
the bear, the raccoon, and the skunk.

Metacomet, who was called King Phillip by the English, had
kept her in the wigwam with his other children. When she asked
what had happened to her family, he told her that her father left a
dead cow, bloated and reeking with larvae, across the stream
above the Wampanoag camp, and it poisoned the water. Many
took sick and died. Later he admitted the deaths might have come
from blankets the settlers brought and traded for beaver pelts. He
never spoke of the two years of war, of the land stolen from his
people, and the Puritan attacks that killed his own sons. He
should have known she had not been too young to remember.

She woke one morning when she still lived in Salem Village, and she was barely three years of age. Hearing loud cries,
she looked from her attic window and saw several barns ablaze.
When she first saw the Indians, she did not think they were
people at all but animals without fur. She saw her uncle run

from the house only to be shot down by a group of redskins lying on a hill behind Willard's barn. Her mother fled up the stairs, gathered her up in her quilt and, running, thrust her into the hayloft and told her to bury herself and lie still. But the screams and moans drew her to the dovecote, and from her hiding place she saw her mother's brother struck on the head, then dragged out into the yard where the howling savages stripped him of his clothes and split open his belly. She saw a leaping red beast with only her aunt's long golden hair in one hand, a bloody knife in the other. The naked men danced around with torches, set fire to the buildings, and she heard bullets spray against the door like stones. She crept to the top of the ladder and looked down into the barn where the Indians were stealing the family cows, and saw her father trying to stop them with a great hay fork. An Indian shouted gibberish and stove him through with a spear. Then they set fire to the barn, and the flames came up through the floor and caught the hay on fire, and her quilt began to burn. She jumped, and tumbled into the manure pile, where she was scooped up by her mother just as another wailing Indian covered with feathers and paint grabbed them both and pulled them on his horse. Her mother held on to her so tightly she could not breathe. And that way they were carried off, but not before she had time to look back and see her father stagger out the door, the spear still in his breast. Another Indian knocked him down with a club, lifted his head by the hair, and cracked his skull against a rock.

Miranda shook the memory from her mind. The visit from the townsmen had disturbed her, and she knew the time had come to bind Andrew to her forever. She had only to make him lie with her, and his goodness was such that he would never forsake her. She tried not to think of his silent ways, how he would go dumb when spoken to, and remember only his strong arms and solid back.

She looked over at the forest trees, flowering now in the

season before the heat, magnificent clouds of pale green and emerald and gold. Metacomet once told her that in the time before the snow, when the trees turned scarlet, the Great Bear in the sky was wounded by the Hunter, and his blood dripped down on the leaves. But another time he told her the trees drew the blood from some other kingdom beneath the earth. As she tugged on the snowapple root, she smiled as she thought of the great sachem. Metacomet was wise because he could admit he did not know all things. He made long talks at council and all others were silent when he spoke. Often he said one thing as it pleased him, and then at another time another, but he was greatly respected. He once told her that he regretted the killing of her family, but that the Wampanoags suffered much because of the settlers. He said that he had stolen her for ransom, or to make her a slave, but when he saw that she could fly, he let her stay, and kept her as one of his own. His hope was that she would become a great Medicine Woman one day.

She pictured him now, with his russet skin and deeply lined face, telling the children the story of the beaver. The largest beaver pond he had ever seen lay across the great valley, and he had journeyed three days there to set traps. He spoke of a lake that could swallow the moon, a great water that stretched from rock outcropping to marsh meadow, and the dam as long as a morning's walk and taller than two men.

The little beaver pond she knew from her childhood was near the Wampanoag camp, and always held the sky in its surface; fleecy clouds flew across it like flocks of white birds. Metacomet told the children who sat with him by the fire and listened to his tale that many things came to them because of the beaver's work: the moose and her calf to feed, the duck with the bright green head, the darting fish, and all the reeds and berries. Then he laughed because he said the beaver made a home for all these things not because it was generous, but because it could not bear the sound of rushing water.

Miranda searched through rotted mulch and new green sprouts for what she needed, nightshade for virility and lavender for courage, yarrow to banish negativity and wild rose to bind the spell. Soon she would have Andrew in her power. She remembered it had been sport for the children to swim the underwater tunnel to the beaver's home. Those who reached the hidden sanctuary had dancing eyes when they spoke of it. The first time Miranda dove into the murky water and down through leafy branches at the surface, she saw roots imbedded in an underwater forest floor, and the trunks of saplings stored for food; but she came up, sputtering and laughing, and certain she would never find the secret passage. The beavers hid their tunnels deeper than she could dive.

Then one bright morning a young beaver splashed, and she followed his paddling feet and the flag of his tail waving in the gloom. She was sucked into a burrow of branches that slid their long fingers along her body and scraped her arms and legs, but urged her on with tender nudges. When the beaver disappeared, and she saw the ruby light glowing in the distance, she doubled her efforts. She pushed through the tangled sticks and slime, poked her head through the narrow hole, and gasped for air.

She was inside the hut. A dome of twisted limbs and twigs above her head was woven like a huge basket, and the floor was dry and strewn with shavings made by the never-ceasing teeth. All was glowing with the rosy light of sun slivers piercing the canopy, and the odor was fresh as cut bark. She saw the beaver children huddled in the corner, five of them, with twitching noses, rounded ears, and dark and frightened eyes. She waited, still as the water, until the small rodents forgot she was there and began to groom themselves, dragging their long claws over their heads and through their fur. Miranda thought that finding the beavers' den was like being born.

It was growing dark and she still had a long walk home. It

was too risky to fly, even in the night, and Miranda trudged through the woods. How to make Andrew long for her? Several times when they had been alone together, she had laid her hand on his, or moved her body close to his warmth, but he had always gone mute and pulled away and shyly returned to his work. It must happen soon, for she needed a champion.

Three

Collinsport—1971

The next morning Barnabas rose, dressed hurriedly, and stole down into the kitchen before the rest of house awoke. The keys to the Bentley were on a hook within a key safe by the door, along with keys to locked rooms in the basement, outdoor sheds, Rose Cottage, even keys to the Old House, useless now, and gathering dust. She would have her own locks soon. His hands were trembling, and he hesitated, remembering Julia's admonition to eat more often. But after decades of dining on blood alone, his craving for food was minimal. He drew a sweet roll out of the bread box and forced himself to take a bite of the sugary icing. His stomach heaved, and he threw the rest in the trash.

He paused at the front door and glanced to the wall on his right at a magnificent portrait in a gilded frame. Everyone in the present family assumed it to be the likeness of his ancestor, the first Barnabas Collins, said to have left Collinwood for England in 1795. Often Elizabeth or David would comment on its uncanny resemblance to the Barnabas who now resided with them. The high cheekbones and deep hollows enhanced a face handsome as a Roman emperor's, with dark eyes gazing out from beneath a curling fringe. The ringed hand rested on the silver wolfhead of the cane he no longer carried, for he had put it away when he ceased to walk the night. The sight of his likeness gave him a sense of bemused reassurance; it always comforted him to know that his years as an immortal had left him unaltered and, since as a vampire he could not see his own reflection, it had served as his looking glass. Abruptly curious, he turned back for the first time to the small mirror beside the tall torchiere at the foot of the stairs.

He was shocked at the change. It was as though a stranger looked back at him. The youthful vigor and arrogance he had come to expect had vanished. Instead the skin was drawn, the hair dull, and the dark circles under his eyes had swollen into bags. His ivory complexion was soiled by a blotched ruddiness. As he stared at his image, he had a fleeting thought that this was the type of victim he would have once pursued. In only a few months, years had taken their toll.

He hurried to the garage. He was obliged to meet with a traveling rug dealer that morning, and he was not looking forward to the appointment, this particular breed of human being the one he despised the most. It was lamentable that they dealt in the most beautiful handmade objects on earth. As he backed the sedan out of the driveway and headed down the road, he felt his pulse quicken. He was determined to see the Old House again in the daylight and reexamine what he was certain was a factory-made carpet. He realized he was risking an encounter with the new owner of his old estate, but he was willing, eager even, to chance it. It was ludicrous that the woman now called herself Antoinette Harpignies, since, aside from the style of her hair and wardrobe, she resembled Angelique in every way.

His fingers clenched as he imagined digging them into her shoulders or grasping her neck, and he shuddered to think how strong was his desire to destroy her. If she threatened him, he might lose his temper, his feelings being so close to the surface. Consequently, he had decided it would be judicious for their first meeting to be early in the day, with no one else about, perhaps in the drawing room of the Old House where he would feel in control, and where he could demand from her an explanation of why she had returned.

As he drew near the Old House, Barnabas noticed several battered pickup trucks parked in the drive. The workmen had arrived, and Barnabas, who had expected to see no one, stopped the Bentley and watched the activity for some moments: the unloading of tools and lumber, light fixtures, and cabinets for the upper rooms. Two young men greeted a third with good-natured banter, hooting at some rude remark, and their raucous voices and harsh laughter floated over the lawn. He wondered whether they had missed their murdered coworker, since they gave no outward signs of alarm.

As Barnabas watched them tussle with a large box of wallpaper and heard their sounds of jovial camaraderie, a wave of despondency weakened his resolve. This energetic scene only served to deepen his sense of loneliness. His life, in comparison, was without purpose—buying and selling Oriental rugs being a shabby substitute for his past adventures. He thought of the dead man who only a day earlier had worked with these tradesmen, exchanging a joke over the ladders and paints, sharing a beer after work, returning in the evening to his family. Now, for the first time in over a hundred years, he, Barnabas, was facing death, inevitable, and all the more terrifying in the wake of a fruitless life, a life without accomplishment or merit of any kind.

He felt unable to meet the workers, but instantly rejected this attitude as cowardly. He got out of the car and strode across the lawn towards the steps, nodding to the crew in a businesslike manner, as though he had every right to be there.

Once inside the foyer, Barnabas experienced the same eerie sense of the past metamorphosed. Beams of sunlight sliced the somber interior of the drawing room, sun motes spinning lazily in the air. Once more he was struck by the perfection of the restoration, the precise selection of furnishings: a Baroque statue of a rearing horse, a decanter of sherry and crystal glasses on a tray, a crocheted antimacassar with a small tear few would have noticed on the back of a chair. But he had not been mistaken about the rug. The garish colors of metallic dyes betrayed its cheap pretense. It was stiff and thick in pile, and he turned back a corner to see the weave, which was, as he expected it to be, tight and uniform, woven on a factory loom. Nothing about the fold of the carpet characterized the supple artistry of a handmade rug.

Back again in the Bentley, he remembered that he had forgotten to go to Julia's room for his injection. His early departure had swept it from his mind. Lately he had begun to muse on the small and irritating changes which being human had brought. Forgetfulness was not the least of his annoyances. While a vampire, his mind had resembled a set of surgeon's tools in a case, precise, finely tuned, and designed for the task. Over the years he had become accustomed to clarity of forethought, a photographic memory, and absolute confidence in his perceptions. Now, with his brain addled by conflicting sensations, he found that stern focus eluded him and the simplest tasks required a supreme effort at concentration. He drove the road with care. The Bentley glided over a carpet of autumn leaves which formed a tapestry on the pavement. The bright colors glittered in shades of ruby, emerald, amber, citrine, and bronze, like a thousand jeweled eyes.

hen Dr. Julia Hoffman opened the door to her room back at Collinwood, Barnabas could see she was upset. She had been waiting for him. She was dressed for the office in a rust-colored suit, one that he admired since it complemented her fine brown eyes. But she was paler these days, thin and drawn. The gloss had leaked out of her copper hair, and her bright eyes, the most attractive thing about her, had grown muddy. She must have forgotten her makeup this morning, for her skin was sallow.

"Barnabas, where were you? I have missed my first appointments."

He hesitated to tell her about his discovery the night before. "Please forgive me, Julia. It was thoughtless. I rose early and went for a drive." He resented her impatience, which was more evident these days, the result of bruised feelings from what she must assume was disdain for all her efforts.

"Yes, I came to your room." She opened her valise and removed the hypodermic needle and the serum. The nausea that proceeded the injections flared in his gut. "Must I remind you again . . . the cure is still uncertain. Without the injections—"

"Please, Julia, don't. I'm quite aware." He found her halting manner of speaking more irritating than usual this morning, and silently chastised himself for such ungenerous feelings. "I returned to Collinwood the moment I remembered, before going to town. I'm grateful to you for waiting."

"If we were sleeping in the same room, this would not be a problem," she said, and lifted the vial. He watched sun from the window catch fire in the claret-colored liquid as it drained into the tube.

"Of course, my dear. And I assure you that it will be soon." His mouth felt dry. She had expected him to marry her by now. It was autumn, and he had proposed to her in the spring when the cure first took effect. She was a brilliant physician, and his admiration for her was unbounded. The formula she had invented, and administered every morning, kept him human. He knew her expertise had given him a new life, the life he fervently desired, and only her vigilance sustained him. But he was so completely dependent on her—not that she would ever abandon him. He decided that it was her vaguely critical air that annoyed him.

"I was thinking," she said as she approached him with the needle and rolled his sleeve, "perhaps we might reveal our intentions to the family this weekend."

He tensed. "It's not too soon?" Searching for a means of escaping further discussion, he thought of the mangled body of the worker. A killer on the prowl would force them both to reconsider their plans. Words were forming themselves in his mind but he faltered, wary of her mood, and only said, "You just warned me you are not certain that the change is permanent."

"I am certain. As long as I am here to care for you."

"And if you are mistaken? Would you relish being wedded to a monster?" He was suddenly ashamed of what he had found in the Old House basement, of his kinship with its killer. The urge to tell her his secret evaporated.

She looked up at him quickly, her bronze eyes widening. "I love you, Barnabas. And I'm not afraid."

After she had administered the injection, he sank back on the bed. He closed his eyes and waited. Bright shards of light danced behind his eyelids. His fingertips tingled as though electricity radiated through them, and he groaned. He could feel Julia's hand on his arm.

"I know it's painful," she said, "but each time it will get easier, I promise you that." She rose, and he could hear her rinsing the vial in the bathroom and replacing it in her valise while he followed the fiery journey of the medication through his veins. This time, more quickly than he had expected, the heat began in his core, like a pile of radiant coals urged into flame by pulsing bellows, and flowed rapidly through his body. His breath came in gasps, his throat swelled shut, and stabs of pain pierced his muscles, wrapped themselves like white-hot brands around his bones, until he was coiled like the springs of his bed, as new blood bloomed.

The family had withdrawn to the drawing room at Collinwood to enjoy an after-dinner liqueur, but Roger Collins's Shakespearean rant was disrupting any pretense of tranquility. As the family patriarch, responsible for the preservation of the estate, Roger had become more irritable of late. Often Barnabas suspected that the aggravation was aimed in his direction. At first Barnabas had been treated with high regard, as he had been perceived to be a cousin from England with a fortune who would restore the Old House and the woods nearby. Welcomed into the fold, as was the tradition in fine old families—he was, after all, a Collins—he had sensed that, in recent months, he had fallen into disfavor. He strove to remain composed in spite of Roger's sharp staccato echoing in his skull.

"It's your responsibility, dammit, not mine. I want them out of my woods! And the sooner the better." His silver blond hair lay perfectly combed over his bald spot, but his aristocratic face was flushed with annoyance. While his sister Elizabeth poured his sherry, Carolyn, her daughter, golden hair shining in the firelight, sat curled on the stool beside the grate, blue eyes focused on a large jigsaw puzzle spread out on the coffee table. Opposite her on the floor, Roger's son, David, was also concentrating on the reproduction of an impossible Manet, all leaves and dappled sunlight. Together they ignored their parents' bickering and gave all their attention to the puzzle.

"Roger, dear, you must try and keep your temper." Elizabeth

Collins Stoddard's patrician tones were soothing as she handed him a cordial. "What possible good can it do to become so distressed?"

Barnabas was keenly aware that this time the tempest was for his benefit. "Why is it my responsibility, Roger?" Barnabas asked. "I wasn't the one who left the gate open for this particular invasion you find so distasteful." The remark was pointed, and Roger chose to acknowledge it with a sniff of his brandy before he answered.

"Because, Barnabas, you seem to forget the Old House was under your care."

Quentin Collins entered the room and quickly searched the liquor cabinet for a bottle of whiskey. Supposedly another distant relation, but of suspect genealogy, he had been enjoying the family's hospitality for several months, taking full advantage. Finding a label to his liking, he turned towards Roger. "Oh, what harm do they do?" Quentin's heavy sideburns framed an angular face, and the twist of a smile played upon his lips. "They call themselves 'flower children,' and their makeshift commune they call 'Paradise.' I think it's all rather innocent."

"Paradise!" Roger sputtered. Barnabas was surprised to hear Quentin, whose opinions of others often bordered on the contemptuous, defending the campers in the woods. Was it that he was tempted to antagonize Roger for amusement, to prick his bubble of self-satisfaction?

"Look, David," cried Carolyn. "I've found that piece. Now the whole corner is finished."

"Yes, but we will never figure out all these trees," David said, as he stared down at dozens of speckled green shapes.

Roger's upper lip quivered. "You call them *innocent?* Using the forest floor for a latrine, bathing naked in the river, coupling incessantly and . . . indiscriminately—probably with the dogs as well as one another."

"Roger!" Elizabeth's hand flew to her mouth and she frowned, nodding in the direction of the children. But Roger ignored her. His chiseled features abandoned for the moment their finely hewn perfection, and he grimaced with indignation. "I want them off the property!" With that he drained his glass and set it down on the mantel with such vehemence that they all heard the crystal stem crack.

"But it's not your property anymore, Uncle Roger," said Carolyn, teasing him in an attempt to lighten his mood. Her amethyst eyes hinted of mischief and glowed in a delicate heart-shaped face.

"Well, get rid of them nevertheless!"

"How exactly do you expect me to do that?" Barnabas asked patiently.

"I suggest you go over there and tell them in no uncertain terms that they are to pack up and leave. Without question, they are a disgrace to the neighborhood: undermining property values, polluting the stream, risking a conflagration with their cooking fires. They are the talk of Collinsport. Filthy, long, tangled hair—Good God! Perverts and degenerates—disgusting. They have absolutely no right to be taking up residence in an area of historic homes. Think about the tourists!"

David chimed in. "It's only a camp in the woods, Father, and they can't even be seen from the road."

"You stay away from there, young man!"

"They make a lot of music. Some of them play the guitar and sing. I've heard them."

Roger turned to Barnabas. "You see? They set a horrible example for the young people in the town." He glowered at David. "I forbid you to go anywhere near that area."

"Why?"

"Because they are the worst sort." Roger drew himself up, shoulders rigid, and his stern jaw quivered when he spoke. "The worst sort."

Barnabas felt a glow of warmth for his young nephew, who shrugged, but did not seem resigned. David was fifteen years old now, and a bright, articulate youth with a curious mind. His nut brown hair was a gleaming cap that curved around his ears, and his freckled cheeks were smooth and honest. At this moment, his hazel eyes glowed with defiance. "Well I certainly intend to visit them if I like. And you can't stop me, Father. Even if they are so objectionable, why wouldn't it enlighten me to see them for myself? I should be allowed to draw my own conclusions about them, shouldn't I?"

Barnabas realized with a start that David had already been to the camp. Right under their noses the boy had been making friends with their new neighbors.

Carolyn sighed. "David, I think Uncle Roger's just mad at himself for selling the Old House, and he doesn't know how that lady talked him into it."

Roger turned to his son with an attempt at forbearance which cost him a great deal of effort.

"David, they are consuming drugs. And drugs are illegal. Marijuana and heroin and . . . and—what is it—mushrooms! Anything they can get their hands on. It is against the law. Do you understand me?" He drew in a breath and turned to Barnabas. "I have no idea why you care about them one whit, but if you do have your reasons—"

"I have no desire to protect them."

"Then perhaps you should take these matters into your own hands and convince them it is in their best interest to leave. Otherwise, I intend to call the sheriff and have them forcibly removed." With that he turned and marched out of the room.

"Well, that was an uncalled for display of bad humor," said Quentin, pouring himself another drink. "Roger's contempt for the peasant classes knows no bounds. As for myself, I must say, I think the Harpignies woman is rather attractive."

"I don't think she is a peasant," said Barnabas. He watched

the movements of Quentin's lean body as he moved to a chair by the fire, and grudgingly admired the French tailoring of his dove-colored suit. Quentin raised his glass, peering at the color of the liqueur.

"No, she is not. She seems to have resources. I would say a trust, or access to a large bank account."

"You would say? Have you become acquainted with her?"

Quentin tipped his head forward and glowered at Barnabas from beneath dark brows and a mass of curly black hair. "I've taken her to dinner," he said, and then added after a pause, "several times."

Barnabas was surprised by the irritation that swept through him. Quentin resided at Collinwood when he was between adventures. An inveterate bachelor, he was the sort of philanderer whose façade, Barnabas knew, hid the soul of a man who secretly feared and despised women. He charmed them with ease, and abandoned them just as quickly once he became bored with them. And he made no apologies for his behavior. An elegant exterior hid an empty shell, callous and compassionless.

"I happen to know that she is not to be trusted," said Barnabas.

Quentin's eyes lit with interest. "Really? How do you know that?"

"Because I . . . I have done some investigating."

"And you have discovered exactly what?"

"Why . . ." He hesitated, searching for words. "I've heard that she has a shady past, that she was once involved in the occult, and that she is rather promiscuous."

"Sounds like my type."

Their conversation was particularly irritating to Barnabas because it was a sham. Quentin and Barnabas both knew of one another's secret. But the charade was necessary while the rest of the family were present. What's more, Quentin had been acquainted with Angelique in another life. Surely he had noticed the uncanny resemblance.

"Quentin, I am quite serious. I don't think she is of the caliber of women who would be welcome at Collinwood."

"What bloody foolishness."

"I'm merely trying to warn you, for your own benefit, that I believe a relationship with her would be ill-advised."

"And I think I am old enough to take care of myself," said Quentin, chuckling, and he drained his glass.

Elizabeth sighed and murmured her disapproval. She had dressed, as was her habit, for dinner. Her gown of black silk was well cut over her trim bust line and complimented her dark hair, which was beautifully coifed and pinned with bright clasps. Her face, though lined, was still lovely, with large emerald green eyes. Her great-grandmother's diamonds glittered at her ears, but Barnabas noticed with dismay that her carefully-applied lipstick had run a bit into the tiny crevices around her mouth. How sad it was to age, inevitably, against all efforts at preservation, and Elizabeth had access to the finest creams and facials. Yet there it was, time's caress.

"Roger is overwrought," she said. "You're right, Carolyn. He is horribly upset with himself that he sold the property to that woman."

"Elizabeth, she is completing the restoration as she promised," Quentin said in his nonchalant tone.

"But she is one of those *hippies*." Elizabeth mouthed the word as if she were describing a creature from another species. To Barnabas it was strange to hear something that hinted at bigotry coming from a matriarch whose family hid unspeakable secrets within a deteriorating mansion and who had very little contact with the people of the village. Even members of the social register had not been entertained for decades. However, financial straits had encouraged the Collinses to open the house for monthly tours through the summer when other fine homes of the area were on public display.

Carolyn looked up. "What do you think a hippie is, Mother? Some kind of a monster?"

"Darling, don't you realize who they are? They are spoiled young people who have made up their minds to sneer at social conventions and reject all our moral standards. They refuse to work."

"What work do we do, Mother?"

Elizabeth sipped her sherry. "Flippancy does not become you," she said with a sigh. "You know perfectly well Roger manages our affairs at the Cannery, and he and I maintain both Collins Enterprises and our other investments." After a slight pause, during which she adjusted her position on the settee, she spoke again. "The point is, these hippies assume that anyone who has earned an income is a greedy materialist. At the same time, most of them come from fairly good families and are supported by their parents. They are simply silly adolescents who only rebel because they have nothing better to do."

Carolyn pulled her knees up under her arms. "I thought they believed that all we need is love?"

Elizabeth's face took on a melancholy expression, and she turned and looked into the fire.

"There," cried David. "There's the crooked piece that fits that branch together."

Four

Although he did not relish a long conversation, Barnabas could not go to his own room before he had knocked on Julia's door. Her response was quick, but her voice was softer than he expected. "Come in."

Her room was dark, with only one light by the desk where she was reading. She looked up without smiling, and a mouth with no lipstick was lost in her pale face. He was surprised to find her room untidy, as he knew her to be a disciplined person. The comforter was crumpled on the unmade bed, and books and papers were strewn over the carpet. She had not joined the family for dinner, and Barnabas assumed it was because she was embarrassed to intrude too often until she legally became a Collins. She had come to Collinwood five years earlier to research a book she was writing, and had never left, becoming, over time, a true companion to all the family members, and devoting herself to helping them in various medical and personal matters. As the family doctor, she had been given lodging in payment for her physician's duties; and when she had discovered his abnormality, she had dedicated herself to its cure.

"How are you feeling tonight?" she asked.

"Well."

"And dinner? Were you able to stomach it?"

"A little."

Her hands were shaking and her face was drawn. The high cheekbones, which had given her the haughty look he once admired, now, to his distress, were protruding, and her temples were blue as bruises.

"Julia, you are the one I am worried about. You must be ill."

"I'm just very tired."

"I'm so sorry. Have you taken cold?"

"I'll be fine."

He strove for compassion. "How can I be of help?"

She did not respond for a moment, only gazed at him with liquid eyes, then said, almost as an afterthought, "Barnabas you must try to eat."

"I had some cake. I only seem to be able to stomach sweets."

She nodded, sighing. "I know it's difficult, but you must make the effort if you expect your system to adjust. The transformation is not complete, and—"

"Julia, I beg of you, don't scold." He was sorry the moment he said it, because she looked at him with such an expression of reproach that he was flooded with guilt.

She came and stood beside him, and he considered, with a growing sense of helplessness, her anemic complexion and her thinning frame. How much she had changed. As she leaned close to him, a stale odor rose from her hair, and he realized she must not have washed it for days.

"Will you hold me, Barnabas?"

He hesitated a moment, then reached for her and pressed her body to his. She was stronger than he had expected and

seemed to gain energy from his embrace. She responded in her
jerky way, encircling him with her arms, and he was unable to
pull back for fear of insulting her. She lifted her face to look at
him and he knew she wanted to be kissed. Overcoming an
awkward feeling of aversion, he brushed her cold lips and tasted
her thin mouth with his own. Finally he withdrew, all the
while wondering how much of his reluctance she had sensed.
Then, in an attempt to distract her, he blurted out, "I have some
rather unsettling news."

"Oh?" Her eyes flickered with worry.

"You must try not to let it upset you, but I think you should
know."

"What is it?"

He hesitated, then turned away from her. "I have reason to
believe there is another vampire. In Collinsport."

She made a faint, whimpering sound. "Another . . . ?" She
sucked in her breath. "How do you know?"

He walked to the window and stared out into the night.
A melon moon stared back at him through dark branches.
"I found its victim."

"Where?"

He realized he had led himself into a trap. He had not
meant to divulge the fact that he had gone to the Old House.
Julia had insisted that it could have a dire influence on the suc-
cess of the cure. Nevertheless, he was now compelled to admit
his folly.

"Where did you see it?" she insisted.

"I . . . at least Willie and I . . . were looking over the Old
House . . ." He turned back to her, but he could not meet her
gaze. Instead he stared at her hands, which were twitching
together. "I know . . . I know you don't approve, but Willie
insisted on showing me the restoration. Which is very impressive, by the way." He forced himself to look at her. "And in the
basement—"

Her mouth gaped. He saw her stiffen and clutch the collar of her blouse. "You went to the basement of the Old House?"

He nodded, feeling suddenly ashamed.

"And there you found . . . ?"

"A slain worker, with the telltale marks on his neck."

"You are a fool," she said. Her eyes glowed with renewed fire. "Don't you realize that nothing would be worse for you than an encounter with . . ."

"Julia, be calm. You forget that only I would recognize the signs, and only I have the skill to track—"

"Barnabas. Stop it! Don't say such a thing. Don't even think it. Those days are over. You are neither the protector of this family nor, God forbid, an exterminator of . . . of . . . creatures who would easily destroy you." She was shaking, and with a wild wrench of her arm, she clutched the back of a chair to steady herself. "Don't you know how much I have sacrificed to bring you back? How can you possibly think of confronting a fiend? Say you won't. Please."

He could not bear the look in her eyes. "Yes. All right. Let's not talk about it any more. I'm sorry I told you. Don't upset yourself further."

"Give me your word." Her eyes implored him. "Say that you will stay away."

"Yes. Very well. If that is your wish." He touched her gently on the shoulder. "Try to get some rest. Good night, Julia."

And he left her standing in the middle of the room.

Barnabas walked quickly back down the stairs and out the kitchen door. It was just past midnight, and this would be the vampire's hour on the prowl. Perhaps, if nothing else, he might catch sight of a suspicious individual down by the wharves.

The steering wheel damp beneath his palms, Barnabas concentrated on keeping the car firmly on the road as he drove hrough a deeply wooded section of ancient oaks. Huge black imbs hung over the road, and great mounds of fallen leaves lay long the borders like crouching beasts. Caught in the whirl-wind of the tires, flying leaves sprang up and struck the wind-hield with such fury he thought they might scratch it. Barnabas had a fleeting thought that the leaves were hostile. The piles mounted higher until, a short distance ahead, he saw a giant mass stretched across the road, completely blocking his way. He braked, and the Bentley struck the mound with a thud. In-tantly he was blinded by a shower of debris. He wrenched the car onto the shoulder, and switched the gearshift into park while he panted from a rush of adrenaline which left him limp. His pulse raced, and for the first time in over a hundred years he was terrified. Had the mound of leaves attacked him? Ri-diculous. Still, they seemed to have come to life, like furies out of the dark. He stared into the night. Caught in the headlights was a vibrating, breathing carpet of crimson, magenta, and gold.

Shuddering as he pulled back on the road, and gingerly negotiating the piles, he headed towards town. Attempting to calm his absurd speculations, he allowed his thoughts to turn to Antoinette. She was here in Collinsport, and living in a small apartment, he had discovered, in the Collinsport Inn. She drove a battered Chevy truck that she used to carry furnishings and materials to the Old House, as she was constantly involved in its restoration. Even though he could feel her presence, at first he had done everything in his power to avoid her. At the same time he had waited in a state of anxiety for her to appear un-expectedly, or to attempt correspondence or a phone call. The innocuous letters on the hall table each morning mocked him, and the telephone's infernal chime had played upon his nerves.

He caught a glimpse of her once, dashing out of the thrift shop in Collinsport on a hot summer afternoon, and he had rec-ognized her gait—a kind of bouncing walk—before he had re-alized it was she. Her costume was peculiar and almost deceived

him, a long lace petticoat and a sheer camisole—the delicate
undergarments of another period in time, perhaps the early
1900s—worn without the dress which was meant to cover them.
Her pale hair was loose and long, falling about her shoulders,
and she wore sandals, her legs bare. Such wanton apparel would
never have been chosen by the Angelique he had known, who
had been so fastidious and vain.

He learned that she had become an amateur folksinger, an
odd choice he would never have predicted, and that some nights
she sang at the Blue Whale. Once, on a whim, he waited outside until he could see her through the window. She was seated
with her guitar on the small stage beside the bar, and, his heart
racing, he had eased himself into a chair in the shadows where
he could watch her and not be observed. She played rudimen-
tary chords, kept appalling rhythm, and her voice had a tendency
to go sharp. Yet her material was appropriate for Angelique. She
sang Childe Ballads of love and abandonment, mountain songs
of lovers who murdered their beloveds, and of faithless wives of
noble gentry.

> *"She step-ped up to Matty Groves, her eyes so low cast down,*
> *Saying 'Pray, oh pray, come with me stay, as you pass through*
> *the town . . .'"*

Her voice had a tinny twang, but she was something of an
actress, and she captured her audience's attention. She possessed
the performer's knack of looking into the eyes of those watching, and focusing a moment on one individual as if to send a
silent message.

> *"Lie down, lie down, little Matty Groves, and keep my back*
> *from cold.*
> *It's only Lord Arlen's merry men, callin' the sheep to fold . . ."*

Her gaze fell on Barnabas, and his heart pitched. But there as never a flicker of recognition, and her eyes moved on. Dis-mforted, Barnabas rose and slipped out, but not before he eard the last grim words of her song.

"Lord Arlen took his fair young bride and led her to the hall,
And with his bloody beaten sword, he stove her against the
    wall . . .
He stove her against the wall."

After ten minutes or so Barnabas was driving down the main oroughfare of Collinsport. Fog had come in from the sea, and e street lamps hung in the gloom, each within a capsule of olden mist. The darkened storefronts reflected his headlights as moved slowly, the lone car on the street, sliding like a low-ung animal with gleaming eyes. At last he turned towards the ocks.

Passing shrouded warehouses, he spotted the lights of the lue Whale glittering in the harbor beyond the wharf, and cars rked in front of the tavern. The bar was still open, even at this te hour, and he heard music and laughter coming from within. e might go inside, if only to pretend to have a glass of wine, d then continue his search. No one would know him.

He was parking the car when he braked, and froze. Antoi-ette dashed out the front door of the tavern. She was carrying r guitar case, and she seemed to be in a hurry, because she mped into her truck and pulled away without looking back. npulsively, Barnabas decided to follow her. But she steered onto e main road heading out of town, and drove at such a break-eck speed that he nearly lost her. He was struck by the coinci-ence of seeing her, of how strange it was on this night of all ights, to come across her. As he accelerated to keep her taillights ithin view, a plan formed itself in his mind. When she stopped,

he would stop as well. When she got out of her car, he wou
confront her. He was no longer a vampire. Nor was he a you
and romantic youth too easily blinded by her charms. He h
changed; and, if he was not mistaken, she seemed changed
well. He might convince her to leave Collinsport. He would off
to buy her out. The Old House should never have been sold in t
first place. It was part of the estate. Surely there was some leg
angle. He would call the lawyers in the morning. Obviously, s
had manipulated Roger into selling it to her, and she could avo
a long involved court battle if she agreed to leave quietly and ta
her hippie friends with her.

Watching her taillights and thinking more clearly now, l
cautioned himself that when he spoke to her, he must exercise t
utmost tact and not threaten her. Then, if she refused to coope
ate, he would seek another recourse, one more devious. As soc
as this thought crossed his mind, he laughed out loud. Of cour
she would refuse. Wasn't that her nature? Perhaps it would be
mistake to speak to her. Would it not be wiser to observe her, a
he was this evening, to follow her unnoticed, discover her habit
where she went and with whom?

Suppose, if he accosted her, she became spiteful and insulte
him? If he made demands, she might treat him with scorn; l
could already see the fire in her eyes and hear the contempt in h
voice. He felt his rage mounting, his fury at her obstinacy. Sh
had cursed him once to eternal darkness, and she would not hes
tate to make him a victim of her whims a second time. Withou
question, her return foretold his destiny. The murdered worker i
the basement of her house exposed her duplicity, proved beyon
doubt that she had a vampire in her service, and that she intende
to exercise her revenge at this moment in time when he was mo
vulnerable. Minutes flew by with the miles as he followed her o
the dark road.

He decided what he must do.

To his surprise, he saw her turn signal blinking, and sh

slowed and pulled into the main gate of Windcliff Sanitarium. She drove directly to the front of the building and stopped where a portico was brightly lit. Extinguishing his headlights, he eased the Bentley into a spot within the shadows of trees. But before he could make a move to get out of his car, she parked and rushed into the double front doors.

Waiting for her to reappear was singular torture, and Barnabas was conscious of a perverse desire to glimpse her from afar even as he was determined to approach her unawares. In fact, there had been a certain satisfaction in following her without being seen. But when, after half an hour, she failed to reappear, he began to lose heart. The cold air seeped into the interior of the Bentley, and his breath fogged the windows. More than once he wiped the condensation off the glass as his agitation increased. He felt a fool waiting there in the middle of the night.

Slowly he opened the door of the Bentley and stepped out. He moved beneath the trees towards the building, his footsteps muffled by dry leaves clinging to his ankles, their stems like tiny claws. Windcliff loomed beyond the main gates, the lone light glowing at the entrance. The building had once been a seaside mansion built in the Italianate style, and even though it had been painted institution white when it became a private hospital and ugly red-brick additions had destroyed its elegant lines, one could still make out the marble pediments above the windows and the stone cornices of an imposing façade. It had been notorious as the state lunatic asylum until it was rechristened as a hospital for the mentally ill. The high dormers of the roofline stood silhouetted against a sky lit by a pale gibbous moon, and Barnabas reflected on those tortured souls who had looked down from those windows, longing for escape even if it meant leaping to the stones below.

How many times in his other life had he stalked an unwary prey, found its sanctuary, and waited until it reappeared, self-involved and oblivious. She would never see him or hear him;

nothing would alert her as he moved with the stealth of a predatory beast. Beside this lonesome building, in this wooded place far removed from town, with the mist rising off the sea and the moon a pale witness, he would end this uncertainty and frustration before it drove him to the brink of insanity, and beyond.

But when he approached the doorway, he saw within the foyer a night guard seated behind a desk. He pulled back into the dark, his pulse racing. Noise would be a problem. If she should scream, he would be discovered. He crept past the lighted area and drew up against the side of the building. He decided to wait in the shadows beside the portico where he knew Antoinette would exit, his back against the wall, his body tensed for springing. The brick was clammy under his palms as he inched away from the glow and hovered beneath the darkened windows. Gauging the distance to her car, he thought he might wait until she was almost alongside before striking; and then it occurred to him to actually conceal himself in the back seat. When she had driven a short distance down the driveway and braked at the entrance to the road, he might seize her from behind.

From one of the windows above his head, he heard voices. He recognized Antoinette's fake English accent, her hysterical inflection. Moving closer, he heard her say, "But why? They know it doesn't work."

She was answered by the soft murmuring of a young girl, speaking in a pleading tone. He heard Antoinette say, "I never, never gave permission for that . . . it's so cruel." After that came the sound of weeping.

When Antoinette spoke again, he could make out few words, but she sounded determined. He heard her say, "Leave that. It's not important," then ". . . tell me I can trust you . . ." and, after another murmur, ". . . never mind . . . I have no choice." There was the sound of scuffling, a door closing, and all was silent.

Barnabas stared up at the moon, now scuttling between streaks of pale clouds. He heard metallic sounds at the side of the building. Moving quickly to the corner, he glanced towards a fire escape that ratcheted up the wall, and saw beneath it a heavy fire door standing open. Antoinette waited while a young girl slipped out and together they raced towards the truck, Antoinette holding the girl close, running as if they were one creature. Barnabas saw her glance back over her shoulder towards the portico, obviously worried should the guard become alarmed, and he shrank into the shadows. As soon as she had her charge in the passenger's side, she ran around to the driver's seat, jumped in, and started the engine. Dumbfounded, Barnabas watched them drive away.

Five

Salem—1692

Morning, and she must be careful not to wake the children. Miranda opened the door to the back step to retrieve the dough, hoping wild yeast had infected the biscuit, and she was buffeted by a blast of wind that struck her with such force it blew her hair loose from her cap and the tin from her hands. The trees bowed and tossed, and she could hear them moan. She spoke to them and they quieted. She reached the woodpile and gathered an armload as the wind roared about the house. This time she hoped there would be no stones.

After a long winter, there was little wood. They had burned what was owed the Reverend by the parish—three full cords a year—and a man with a heart as hard as his would let his children freeze and eat raw food before he would buy one stick with the paltry stipend he received. Back in the kitchen, she tossed a handful of pine needles in the grate and stirred the cinders, lowing softly, but the wind funneled down the chimney and ashes flecked her cheeks like dark tears.

When the tinder caught, she carefully laid on the firewood, whispering to each, *only a short time, only a little pain.* Extracting a small ember, she went to light the grease lamp so as to see to form the biscuits, and turned the dough out on the wooden slab. Soot from her hands blackened the round shapes, and she could tell by the damp feel of it that the dough would not rise. Still the chores to do in this wind. To feed the chickens would be a waste of precious grain, as it would take to the air. Back in the barn, the sheep pushed against the rails, and the cow lowed. Her hands warmed on the teats but when she reached the last one and felt the scab, her chest tightened. She almost turned over the pail in her haste to return to the house. She found the salve in the cupboard. A sore on a teat was witches' work.

Only later, when she had brought water from the well, and left the cream to rise, and set the gypsy kettle on the iron hook above the flame, did she allow herself to think on the night to come.

The girls had asked her to join them. It was the first time they had reached out to her. Their curiosity had gotten the better of their fears and they had decided to befriend her. She knew they laughed behind her back, said cruel things, but she had let her loneliness delude her into thinking they would draw her into their circle, and she could become a normal village girl.

Their parents, like the other townspeople, were suspicious of her, growing ever more so. There were whisperings, as when a bird flew too close to her shoulder or when she heard the sound of snow falling.

Witch they whispered, then turned away and feigned a false silence, and she hated them for their pinched faces, tight lips, beady eyes. What was so different about her? Nothing remained solid—that was the trouble. Nothing remained clear, but drifted into another world, the world of spells and secrets. When she looked at Martha Corey, she saw roaches crawling on her skin, and she knew Goody Easty only pretended to rock and croon to a new grandchild. She saw it for the imp it was as she suckled it to a shriveled breast.

Witch they whispered, and they knew something, but they knew nothing at all of what she saw when she woke in the night and Sarah Good still stared directly down at her from the scaffold, her eye a firebrand and her tongue a lizard leaping from her mouth. "You. You are the witch. Can you say the Lord's Prayer?"

Of course. I know nothing of the Devil.

There were signs unmistakable, as that morning she could see, before she pulled on her heavy shoes and climbed from her casement, the apparition of a girl floating in the bare branches of the trees under the crescent moon, white petticoats lifted by the wind. She heard it—the choked cry—this was not meant to happen—the sound of crashing.

The first time suspicion had ebbed around her like a slow rising tide was after the terrible blizzard when the ewes dropped their lambs in the snow. Outside, the air was a tumult of roiling snowflakes swirling against the sky. The field was obliterated, the fence invisible, and the bleating ewes, dumb in their woolen cocoons, eyes lashed by sleet, chose this night of all others to drop blood and lamb to the frozen ground—unaware of the gift they gave, too cold, too confused to nudge a tiny creature to its feet. Slogging into the stinging blast, Miranda had gathered two tiny babies in her arms and carried them inside. Sitting on the bed, she rubbed and dried them. She puffed warm breath into their black snouts and willed them to live. It seemed a fine thing she was doing. Reverend Collins brought in more lambs and placed them in her lap. She wrapped them in rags and, not sleeping all through the night, she fed each one with fingers dipped in milk. Once he looked in with his lantern and caught his breath.

'Miranda, thou art like our Lord's holy mother—sitting there with the lambs about thee."

Better they had frozen in the snow since the next morning the ewes would not take them, and only a few could be coaxed to suckle with swollen teats lambs they knew were not theirs. And once again she tugged and caressed each mother, gathered the smell from its hindquarters and smeared it on the lamb, though she had never been a herder and had no experience in these matters.

Only later was the scene reflected upon in the parish—that she had saved thirty lambs in the blizzard and wielded a power not of this world. Dead they were, frozen stiff and unseeing when he deposited them on the bed, and they had bleated into life, moving their sharp little hooves, batting at her fingers with their tiny mouths. Out of blood and death came the odor of new wool, and mewing was heard in the room. A slip of a girl should not do these things and, although they gave her praise at first, among themselves they whispered the Devil had come to her aid.

This had been her sorry life since the Reverend had brought her home from the Indian camp. The townspeople bore her ill. If a sow took sick in the hog pen, she was blamed, since she had slopped the pigs that morning; and if it recovered, she was suspected of black arts. If a cow's udders grew thick with blockage, she was the cause; and if they mysteriously drained, it was not natural. In her heart she knew it was her silent ways, her quiet defiance, that antagonized them.

School was no kinder. Friendless, she kept to herself. The other girls avoided her, and the boys feared her with some intuition they failed to understand. Only Andrew, who was a fine lad, though a bit slow, seemed not to notice what the others said about her. As grateful as she was to him for his attentions, she did not love him, and rejected his offer of marriage, until she began to see how much she needed him.

Judah Zachery stood at the front of the classroom with the cherrywood switch in his hand. He tapped the lectern as the children recited their sums. When they finished the twelves, he laid down the rod and nodded his head. "Quietly, ye go." The children bounded for the door, but he called after them. "Remember, ye hath been made in God's image. Conduct yourselves with decorum and humility."

As she passed him by, Miranda felt the heat of his gaze. "Stay Miranda," he said. Silently she watched the other children run over the meadow towards the river. "I have my eye on you," he said, his voice a low rasp in her ear. His hand on her arm was the claw of a vulture and when she looked up at him, she saw his vulture's eyes, red ringed, and his mouth a raptor's beak.

"Can you tell me you are pure and without taint?"

"I know not what taint you mean, sir."

"Why, stealing off with Andrew Merriweather."

"I have not, sir."

"Mind yourself, Miranda. I see you." And she knew he did. For he was closer to her kind than she dared to admit. She knew of his coven in Bedford.

They stood at the door of the schoolroom and the children's laughter floated over the field. Close by, birds twittered and mewed in the bush. One, a swallow, had a song so piercing she imagined it was meant for her, and she let it flow into her heart. Once more she looked up at Judah Zachery. The beak was more pronounced, and his neck was red and mottled where it rose out of his untidy white ruff, which sat like a feathered collar around the naked skin. His face was ruddy and round, with hollow eyes and haggard cheeks, and although the top of his head was bald, his hair hung in filthy locks to his shoulders and his ears protruded from the greasy strands. His nose was a fleshy hook and his beak of a mouth showed yellowed teeth. Slowly he drew the

cherrywood wand between his fingers, caressing its narrow
flute, the long finger bones ending in nails unclipped and sharp.
A moldy odor hung about him as though he often soiled himself. Back and forth he drew the rod between his fingers and it
quivered, still green beneath the bark.

"Choose," he said. "A whipping, or the closet."

She sucked in her breath. "The closet."

"Impudence!" He seized her by the arm, shoved her into the
darkness, and locked the door. Now she was alone. Sometimes
he left her there for hours, until the children had departed for
home, their bright voices silenced, and only the sound of his
breathing on the other side of the panel. How long would today's
punishment be? If he kept her through the night, she would miss
the meeting in the forest, and the girls had asked her to come with
them.

As she sat curled on the floor, she sighed to think that for
a little while longer he controlled her, and she knew she had no
recourse but to obey him. But she did not fear him, for she knew
him. She knew he whipped her to see her bared thighs. His hand
shook so violently, the blows were more glancing than painful;
and when he forced her over his knee, she could always feel the
bulge in his trousers. What's more, she had seen his Devil's ways.

One night she had flown to the clearing in the field behind
Bedford and, from her branch, looked down on his imbecilic rituals. The widows and spinsters of his coven, dim-witted women
driven mad by lust, cavorted in the moonlight. They drank blood
and screeched, and some opened their thighs and rubbed themselves against him while he stood like a great vulture, holding his
book. How willingly they signed, scrambled over one another to
sign. Did any of them care what they had done?

She waited until her eyes became accustomed to the dark.
The crack above the door and another at the floor gave light
enough for her to amuse herself with his books. And Judah
Zachery had many books—books he had brought with him from

England, printed on coarse paper, nearly all in Latin or French. She could not read them, but the illustrations enthralled her: the intricate drawings and foreign designs. They were books that would shock the people in the town were they to see them, they so reeked of heresy. Books of anatomy showed naked bodies stripped of their skin, the muscles pulled away from the bones, the organs hanging out of the stomach cavity, the sex exposed. There were books of astrology depicting the creatures who lived in the heavens—a goat, a bull, and a giant scorpion. She drew Hooke's *Micrographia* into her lap, and marveled at etchings of insects as large as lobsters with ratcheted claws and jaws, and studied drawings of prehistoric beasts: a lion with wings and a pig with a man's head. She shivered at sea monsters with long tentacles, unicorns, and dragons. She knew it was all blasphemy, but that did not trouble her. She only feared that Judah might catch her looking at his books and punish her for not standing silently in the dark.

But she could not resist. Some of the names she had learned from his teaching: Galileo, Copernicus, and Kepler, all known heretics, for Galileo said the earth traveled around the sun, which seemed impossible, although Metacomet once told her it was probably true. But she was incapable of understanding the circles and triangles and the numbers and symbols. Hours passed as she studied a book on mechanics and pored over diagrams of an air pump and a telescope, a camera obscura, a thermometer, a crossbow and a catapult, something called a chastity belt, and the awful rack and the Halifax Gibbet, which severed heads—all scientific instruments, and the last three designed to thwart the Devil. She found a book in English and read a profane treatise on the mortal soul perishing with the body, of atoms that swerve in their path by free will, and conversations with spirits. She found a pamphlet entitled *The Art of Swimming* that delighted her with its drawings of naked men floating in a river. Another called *A History of Ethiopia* showed ferocious barbarians in horned headdresses wielding spears and clubs. Their unclad bodies excited her and she stared long and hard at the organs hanging between their legs.

Miranda reached into the back of the closet for the wooden box, opened it, and drew out the mask. She knew it for what it was, and shivered to think what power it possessed. The mask was crudely fashioned of gold and encrusted with jewels: fat rubies surrounded the eyes and sapphires studded the mouth. A crown of laurel leaves and a beard of dangling fronds were of beaten gold. Gingerly she placed the mask over her own face and felt its heat on her cheeks, but only for a moment. Then she hid it away again and settled down with her favorite book, Milton's *Paradise Lost*. She loved to look at the paintings of the poor souls in hell writhing in the flames, spitted on long spears by magnificent angels. When she heard the key in the lock, she quickly replaced the book and stood, head bowed, like a contrite child waiting her release. This day he let her go without a word.

Midnight, and moving through the dark of the barnyard, loath to rouse the rooster with his clamoring cry, Miranda felt a cold hand on her heart and shivered. Dread weighed on her like a stone as she hurried through the stalls, her fear so humid she could smell it with her tongue. The hogs stirred, and she dared not look at their grunting bodies, the listless sheep with their vacant eyes, or the placid cows swinging their udders, as all could turn into monsters, but kept her eyes on the ground and crept out into the night while the damp gathered around the edge of her petticoat and the cold seeped into her shoes.

The forest where they were to meet loomed beyond the field. Tituba had told them they would see their future husbands in the swirl of egg white, and they would dance, and conjure up

Goody Larson's dead babies again, and tonight they would all fly. But Tituba was an island woman, a voodoo-practicing slave brought over from Haiti. She could not save them from their foolishness. Only Miranda could do that.

She could see three of the girls coming from the village; they clung to one another, whispering softly together, eager to be devilish. They seemed one dark body with many limbs, and she felt envy's sting. She had no friends, and even if they let her come with them to the forest, she knew they were frightened of her.

Behind their path stood the last house in the village: a hard edge of clapboard, a dark shape, a black chimney, dead wood, dead stone, fashioned from the living trees who still cried when they were cut, and from the stone that sobbed when it was pulled from the earth. Men shouted, sawed, pounded, and another grove of rippling saplings was forced into service of these walls, so straight and plumb. Sometimes she would run her hand over the gray clapboard hoping for a splinter, a sign that life still frisked in the boards nailed to that unyielding frame.

She knew she must not think of these things tonight because if she allowed her mind to slip, she might see beyond, see the end of things, and the fear crept up from her damp boots and gathered around her calves. Her skirt was soggy from trailing through the leaves, and in the fabric she could still smell the sheep from the barn, the wool of her dress never rid of that reek, and quickly she stopped herself before she thought of the ewes dying in the blizzard and the new lambs on her bed.

Foolish Tituba, who said they would fly. She tried to imagine them, shapes against the moon, petticoats loose and lifting. Perhaps after they ate the rye bread tinged with red and drank whatever concoction Tituba stirred in the kettle, and after they danced, they could come home certain they had flown, even if they had not. But the dark wedge of a thought, empty except for the cry of surprise and the sound of branches breaking, forced its way into her brain.

When the forest closed around them, they came together and Tituba was leading them. Miranda relaxed a little. Reverend Collins said the forest was where the Old Deluder hid, but she knew it as God's cathedral. How wrong they were about everything. Surely God was among them and would protect them, not her perhaps, with her deceitful ways, but a group of mischievous girls. Running, they were running now, and her sodden skirts were heavy with wet, her boots filled with water. There was no way they could fly, these silly girls, and yet, would Tituba make some spell? She must find a way to stop them, but they did not like her, would not listen if she tried. *You fly,* they would say.

How close were they now to the place Metacomet, the Wampanoag chief, had taken her to live with the tribe? Her heart shrank when she thought of her father's head shattered against the rock, her mother's blood-soaked dress. Reverend Collins had spied her playing in the stream and returned her to Salem Village. There he had dressed her in a woolen skirt, capped her hair, and forced her bare feet into dark stockings and boots, compelled her to sit in meeting and to go to the schoolhouse where her tormentor, Judah Zachery, raised the whip against her. With the evil that coiled in his own heart the schoolteacher saw her mysterious ways as wickedness.

Then one day Abigail Soames had told her she heard her own father say that the three cleared fields and the farm at the end of Litchy Road belonged to Miranda. No one spoke to her of it. But, begrudgingly, or perhaps spitefully, the Reverend had shown her the name Edmund du Val in the book of property.

The girls reached the clearing, and Tituba already crouched at the fire ring, her heavy body splayed over her fat knees, as she blew the tinder to flame. The girls stared at her, waiting: Lucinda Whaples with her yellow curls, dull Betty Parris, and brown-eyed Abigail Putnam, all children under twelve, and Mary Walcott who already had breasts like a cow and who was old enough to know better than to cast spells. But she, more than the others, wanted to see her husband's face in the cauldron. Into the liquid went bits of beetles and lizards. Tituba kept a sack around her neck, from out of which she drew something as red as blood, and then, as the brew began to boil, she dropped the egg white and swirled it on the surface.

"There! I see his face," cried Lucinda, and they all shrieked, the forest echoing their cries. "It's Samuel!"

"No, William! It's William Basset!"

"You are the silly one for I see Samuel."

"Miranda," and they were sing-songing now, "I see your darling Andrew. Come and see."

Could it be they envied her her beau? Or did they only think he was simpleminded?

After they drank the potion, Tituba began beating her little drum. The girls formed a circle and, with clumsy steps, they began to dance. They grabbed their petticoats and lifted them over their heads. Stockings fell in the grass, shifts and pantaloons. Giggling as if tickled in the bed covers to frenzy, they hugged themselves, shivering, then threw out their arms to show themselves to the fire, to the somber, waiting trees. The rhythmic song of the drum taunted her, and finally Miranda joined them. She twisted her body in rakish thrusting motions until she was dizzy, then collapsed exhausted into the grass.

Tituba's drum pulsed in the dark, and she sang in a slow voice odd consonants of an island dialect, a haunting chant. The girls were naked now, and Miranda caught a sweating arm, brushed against a cool, round bottom, or turned and turned like a wound up top. They were graceless dancers, but they savored the metallic taste of freedom, like blood from a bitten tongue. They touched one another, then licked, then prodded in shameful places, and shrieked with glee.

"Stop," she cried out. "We must stop. Someone might come."

"Who?" cried Lucinda. "The Black Man? Let him come. I dare him to show his face to me." The other younger girls shrank back at this blasphemy, but Lucinda glared into the trees. "Come for me!" she cried. The girl they drowned in Whethersfield with their dunking had pleaded for her life; the only evidence had been a pudding that broke in the pan and a cow that died in the coldest week of winter. But she was a wanton girl who had spoken once with Miranda. Perhaps it was better she was gone. Tituba's drum grew louder. What madness this was, dancing in the forest, risking at the very least a whipping in the square. The girl had been called Constance, and she was uncommonly pretty. Perhaps the burghers wanted more than anything to strip her of her clothes and search for a devil's teat. Constance was willful, but innocent. Even if no teat was found, they still gazed on her helpless nakedness and carried their visions to their beds.

Panting, Miranda leaned her bare back against the trunk of a hickory, and ran her hands over the rough bark. She could ease into this tree, become one with it, and disappear into its leaves. She looked up at the faint shapes of the gray beeches and ghostly birches glimmering among the older, darker trees, and she longed to rise, to float upward. Had the girls seen Andrew's face in the cauldron? Would she have seen him? He was dazzled by her, she knew that. A strapping lad with muscular arms. He would make a good husband, a good father to her children.

She must make them stop.

"Tituba!"

Miranda was holding Betty's hand, and for a moment the girl anchored her to the earth. When they saw she had jumped but not landed, they stared at her feet six inches above the ground. She could not control herself and slowly she tipped horizontal, hovered a moment and then, like an expelled breath, flew into the trees. While she looked down at them from her branch, the girls leapt and cavorted, giddy as idiots, and flapped their arms. "Whist! Whist!" they cried.

Lucinda called them towards the cliff and Miranda felt fear clutch her heart. They looked to her. "This way! Come, it's time!"

No, no. She flew down to stop them and she turned to see them coming, their eyes rimmed with red. They ran, flinging out their frail arms, twittering bird sounds and, at the edge she grabbed for them, caught them, all but Lucinda, who hung a moment at the lip of the rock then flung herself out over the gorge. There was a cry, as a wild thing taken by the throat, and the sound of snapping branches. The other girls gaped stupidly down into the dark.

Six

Collinwood—1971

The morning was crisp and the air so cool and clear, Barnabas decided, in spite of Julia's fretting, to walk the half mile to the Old House. David, who had begged to accompany him, strolled by his side for a few hundred yards, then in a burst of youthful exuberance, jogged ahead down the path. The trees were resplendent with hues Barnabas found astonishing, and he amused himself by imagining that they were girls at a ball, each clothed in a different gown: amber, magenta, and aubergine. Each flirted for attention, each demanded admiration, each claimed the crown of beauty as her own. Fallen leaves lay in scarlet pools beneath the gray maples, or in yellow ponds beneath the elms with their black trunks, and Barnabas laughed at himself for thinking such beauty could ever harbor evil intent.

Ashamed of his actions the night before and the tangle of emotions that had ensued after his hotheaded pursuit of Antoinette in the dark, he had resolved to have nothing more to do with her other than treat her as a neighbor with a problem in her woods. Likewise he had made up his mind to respect Julia's wishes and not search for the vampire. As she had said, those days were over. Instead he had decided to be of service to Roger. Undoubtedly Roger's tarnished opinion of him needed some polishing. He knew that the older man saw him as lazy and unproductive, living off the family's good will and making no contribution to the coffers. His intention this morning was to follow Roger's instructions and find some way of ridding the estate of the hippies.

Regressing to the rambunctious boy he had been only a year ago, David leapt into the drifts, nearly burying himself. Then he bounded to his feet, straightened his shoulders, and loped down the path and out of sight.

Barnabas mused on the light low in the sky, the long shadows across the green, the feathery grasses lit like spun glass. He breathed in the perfume of fading roses and rotting mulch. Autumn's dying light, he thought—it had been so many decades since he had seen it. The forest was burning itself out. He wondered how the blood red leaves came to their color, claret and grenadine flowing up from the earth, as though the banners of his sinful years were flung in condemnation all around him.

It had been many months since his cure, and still the light of day was for him a miracle to behold, the sun a golden orb, buttermilk skies with clouds as soft as clotted cream. The first sight of spring had tormented him with its beauty: flowering trees, new grass, and the silken air fractured into rainbows. He would often sit and stare at nothing else, only the air, and the prisms of light dancing within it. But during the height of summer, the unbearable heat of his cure drove him back into the coolness of his dark bedroom with curtains drawn, beneath the canopy of his bed, as though he were once more within the tomb. Now autumn had arrived with all its splendors, and its heartbreaking hues.

Barnabas was eager to show the house to David. It was

pleasant to be in the company of this teenager who was so intelligent, and his heart warmed to the boy. Perhaps he should become involved in David's education, even take him on a trip. He began to imagine a drive to Newport, Mystic, or Salem, a trip of several hundred miles to the south, with himself behind the wheel of his powerful car.

"David," he called, "how would you like to go on an adventure?"

"Where?"

"To see the museum at Salem?"

"You mean with all the goblins and ghosts? That would be cool!"

As they approached the back of the Old House, the tall columns rose up before them. Recalling their clumsy maneuvers with the corpse in the trunk of the Bentley, Barnabas remembered that he and Willie had been forced to remove two of his carpets—a faded Sarouk of a blood red color, and a hundred year old Serapi—and place them inside on the back seat. It had been more to avoid Roger's disapproval of his idle days than out of any real need for income that he had hit upon the idea of collecting and trading Persian carpets. During years of travel and exposure to the great houses of England and America he had developed a sophisticated knowledge of antiques, and he possessed a keen appreciation of objects which had lost any true purpose in the modern world other than their enduring beauty. Exquisite detail and fine materials inspired him. He might have chosen rare wines, or old silver, but nothing excited him more than an antique carpet. Woven long ago by women and young girls on primitive looms in rock-strewn villages above Afghanistan, in the Caucasian hills of Armenia, or on the wild plateaus of Persia; carried on camelback over vast deserts; they were fashioned to grace the marble floors of palaces or to soften the sand beneath royal tents. Even the names of the towns were mystical and jarring: Isphahan, Ardebil, Kazak, Kerman, and Qum.

Together he and David entered the foyer. Dust motes floated through the cold rooms which had always been filled with odd treasures. It was difficult to believe that this maddening woman had replaced them all: the coat rack, the Chippendale looking glass, the mahogany table by the stairs, the brass chandelier. His practiced eye analyzed each object as he tried to decide what had been salvaged and what had been meticulously replaced. She must have shopped at every roadside antique store between Collinsport and Boston, and, of course, Roger had sold her many of the furnishings which were removed when the Old House was destined for demolition . . . before the fire.

But it was the fake carpet he had come to see. A Tabriz as old and valuable as the rug which had once graced the drawing room did not exist in this country any more. He remembered being fond of the rug and recalled the hours he had spent by the fire, gazing at the miraculous detail, searching out the carefully included mistakes in the pattern. Islam dictated that only God was perfect, and anything made by man must be intentionally flawed. Even though the original carpet in the Old House had been one of the family treasures, it was thought to be too threadbare to be moved to Collinwood when the new mansion was built in 1795. His untutored relations had failed to realize that the worn nap made it even more valuable.

As he had done the day before, he knelt by this rug and once again turned back the corner to inspect the warp. The fact that the rug was a fake had an odd effect on him and seemed to prove that the entire restoration was simply that and not, as Willie had insisted and he, Barnabas had feared, something fiendishly, even magically devised.

David, on the other hand, was thrilled with every new discovery. Each recreation struck him as clever rather than grim, and he exclaimed over the marble mantelpiece and the old wavy glass windows. Curious about a room where he had played when he was a small child, he dashed for the foyer.

"Come on, Barnabas, let's see what's upstairs!" Barnabas hesitated, his attention caught by a mistake in the parquet flooring, an irritating jog in the pattern. Why had she chosen to duplicate that? David's voice echoed from the hallway. "This part's not finished up here!" Barnabas climbed to the landing and looked down the long corridor where bare lumber and scaffolding revealed work still in progress. "Here's that old playroom!" David's voice came from around the turn in the hallway. "Hey! It's locked!"

"What's that?"

"The door to the playroom. It's locked!"

Barnabas heard the sound of an engine and walked to a casement window. A battered Volkswagen bus stopped in front of the house and a young man got out, lugging a toolbox and a small electric saw. He disappeared around the side of the building, and Barnabas had an odd sense of being invaded. He checked the door to the playroom with David and ascertained that it was indeed bolted.

"I wanted to know if my toys were still there," David said, looking down at the driveway. "Hey, let's go talk to that guy."

By the time they reached the side porte cochere, they could hear the hum of a generator starting up. The man, obviously a carpenter, had set up a work space with sawhorses and power tools, and was sorting through pieces of clear pine.

"Good morning," Barnabas said, a bit reluctant to disturb the man.

The worker, who wore dark sunglasses, looked up. He was young, probably in his early twenties, dressed in dirty jeans, a T-shirt, and sneakers; his long legs were scrawny, and a worn leather tool belt hung loosely across his bony hips. His stringy black hair would have fallen well below his shoulders had he not pulled it back into a ponytail, and a hand-rolled cigarette hung from his mouth. He gave Barnabas a desultory glance and nodded, "Hiya doin'."

David, curious about the tools the carpenter was using, approached the saw. Barnabas felt he should introduce himself. "We were . . . that is, we're the Collinses. This is my nephew, David, and I am Barnabas Collins."

"Oh-kay . . . ?" The man drew the word into a question as if to say he had no particular interest in this information.

"We're the family that once owned this house," Barnabas explained.

The carpenter broke into a sly grin. His four front teeth were slightly crowded together by incisors that were thick and pointed. "You the people who burned it down?"

"That . . . why, no. It was a rather unfortunate accident."

"Yeah? That's not what I heard." Carefully, he slid his hands over a flat board, as though searching for rough areas, before settling it on the plate and placing it against a metal guide. "I heard the family torched it for the insurance."

David looked up at Barnabas. "That's not true, is it?"

"Of course not."

The man stood looking at them, his hands held lightly on the saw, one shoulder raised higher than the other and one knee slightly bent, as his body assumed a casual posture Barnabas found annoyingly nonchalant; still, he wondered if young girls would find it appealing.

"I don't believe you told me your name."

"Jason," he said. "Shaw." His sunglasses reflected the sun, and a vague smile played about his curled lips. He sucked on the cigarette, then balanced it on the edge of the table.

"Well, Jason," said Barnabas, "I don't know where you get your information, but I sincerely hope you have not been listening to idle gossip in the town."

"Actually, I think Toni told me."

"Toni?"

"She owns this place. You know. Antoinette." He said the name softly as though caressing it.

Barnabas started. "Well, she couldn't have been more mistaken."

Jason shrugged. "Hey, man, it's nothin' to me. Thanks to that fire, I've had one hell of a six months." He smiled as though a pleasant memory had flashed through his mind.

Barnabas's irritation was now magnified by a rank odor that he recognized as grease. A sack with the logo of red letters and yellow circles lay beside the saw and exuded the smell of meat and fried potatoes.

Jason seemed to read his mind. "Want something from McDonald's?"

Barnabas felt his gorge rise, but David said, "Sure!" and reached for the sack, extracted some fries, and stuffed them in his mouth. It occurred to Barnabas that Jason might know something about the dead workman.

"I assume you're the carpenter who's done all this remarkable renovation."

"Well, I have a crew," Jason said slowly, "but I call the shots."

"I must say I am amazed at the verisimilitude."

"The what?"

"It's . . . so very much like the original."

"Yeah, well, that's Toni for you. She's got tons of old photographs, and she's, uh, how shall I say, very . . . demanding." He laughed softly to himself and shook his head. He took another drag from his cigarette and held the smoke before releasing it.

"And the furnishings?"

"Antique stores, man. Every day she brings in more stuff, she and Jackie. That is until she took her kid away to the loony bin." Jason flipped the switch on the table saw, set the piece of wood, and the scream of the blade pierced the air.

Barnabas shouted over the din as the spinning saw whirred to an annoying whine. "And where is . . . Toni? Do you know?"

"Over at the camp. Or maybe she's gone to Salem. She spends a lot of time there. Doing her research in the library."

Completely fascinated, David watched Jason turn the board. "What kind of saw is that?"

"Actually, it's a shaper."

"What's it do?"

"Come here, and I'll show you." David leaned in and both heads hovered over the twelve-inch vertical blade. "See, this is where you cut the piece to measure, and this . . ." he gestured to a smaller steel plate, "has a kind of mother router underneath. What it does is carve out the raised panels. Like this." He reached behind him and held up a finished cabinet door.

"Can I try it?"

"David . . ." Barnabas was feeling nervous about the saw, and he could not help but resent David's immediate connection with Jason.

"Sure." Jason extracted another board from the stack of lumber and measured it with the yellow tape in his tool belt. Then he stood behind David and ran the wood up against the guide. The blade screamed and sawdust flew in the air.

"Watch out for your fingers," he said. David grinned as Jason placed his hands on top of his and pressed the wood into the shaper, inching it slowly along. The pitch of the screeching saw was excruciating to Barnabas.

David held up the piece and displayed the side he had cut; he beamed with excitement. "I want to do another one."

Jason lifted both palms and stepped back. The saw shrieked and purred as David fed the pine into the hungry blade. "This is fun!" He looked up at Jason. "Hand me another piece."

David placed the wood against the blade. "Do you like living in the woods?" he asked. Barnabas suddenly realized that Jason must be one of the hippies.

"Sure. Been there all summer."

"How long do you plan to stay?" asked Barnabas.

"Got no plans, got no plans," Jason answered.

"Barnabas, can I go hang out with Jason?"

"Your father wouldn't approve."

"But why?"

"Now, David, you know perfectly well why." He turned to Jason. "Am I correct in assuming there are illegal substances being consumed?"

Jason hesitated a moment, then laughed. "You got something against smokin' a little grass?"

"I'd rather you didn't discuss such things in front of the boy," said Barnabas, at the same time realizing he had blundered upon an opportunity to carry out Roger's wishes. "Are you in any way a . . ." he searched for the correct term, ". . . a decision maker for the group?"

Jason laughed. "What do you mean by that?"

"It has come to our attention that the campers in the woods are breaking the law, in fact, trespassing. My cousin, Mr. Roger Collins, would like to see the camp removed."

"Now wait a minute. We have permission to be there. It's fine with Toni and she owns the land."

"But it is not . . . fine with the neighbors. There are restrictions against outdoor toilets, for instance. And I understand there is nudity."

Jason laughed again, a low chuckle. "So you and the other uptight neighbors can't stand to see anyone have a little fun." He paused, then turned to the boy. "Hey, David. Wanna go on a magical mystery tour? We got some Owsley we're gonna drop this weekend. It's gonna be beautiful, man."

Barnabas could restrain himself no longer. "I must warn you, Mr. Shaw, I won't have anyone consuming illegal drugs anywhere near my property, or around anyone in my family, for that matter. And I suggest you return to your . . . tent, or whatever it is you call home, and explain to the others that they must clear the area."

Displaying unexpected charm, Jason only grinned, lifted his right hand, crooked it into a gun, the index finger cocked at

Barnabas, and said, "Gotcha!" His dark glasses danced with reflected light. Then he seemed to relax a little, and he shrugged. "Sorry, man. I didn't mean to come on so strong. Everybody's got a right to his own opinion. But you know, you're way out of line. We're not trespassing. You got no say about what goes on in Toni's woods." He laughed again, his soft cynical laugh, then he picked up new board. "I, uh, got to get back to work."

Barnabas and David turned to leave, but as they trudged across the wide drive, Jason called. "Hey, David?" David turned, and Jason tossed him the McDonald's sack. "Have one on me." As they started down the path, they could hear him whistling to himself.

David finished off the fries and stirred the bottom of the sack. "There's brownies," he said. "Want one? Do you like McDonald's stuff? Father never lets me buy any." He handed a brownie to Barnabas and said, "I have a confession to make. I've been to the camp already."

"I gathered that."

"I don't think Jason was convinced. Maybe you should go talk to them."

"Yes, I think I must. Roger seemed adamant."

"Are you going to tell them to leave?"

Barnabas looked over at the boy with his irrepressible smile, his sandy hair and eyes with glints of gold. Once more he warmed with the affection of a guardian for his ward, and he had a sudden desire to share with David his own rather profound knowledge of the world, its wonders and curiosities. At the same time he realized how impossible that would be. "I intend to discuss it with the owner."

"Oh, Toni. Yeah, I met her."

Barnabas's heart skipped a beat. "What is she like?"

"Crazy. Really crazy."

"And who is Jackie?"

David looked away. "I don't know. Maybe her daughter?"

They walked along the edge of Widows' Hill and looked out at the sea. Gulls careened over the murky water, and seaweed lay rotting as the ebb tide sucked at the grimy sand. With a start Barnabas realized why his interest in David had become so pleasurable. He was reminded of himself at that age, when all his life lay before him. He nibbled at a bit of the brownie but found it dry and tasteless. Remembering Julia's admonition, however, he decided to eat it anyway, no matter how unpleasant it might be, and he forced himself to take another bite. At least it was sweet.

"The camp is just over there," David said, pointing, and ran towards a faint clearing. They could hear the roar of the creek. At that moment the gloom of the forest was shattered with brilliant beams of light flickering and flashing from tree to tree. The campers had hung dozens of cheap wood-framed mirrors on the tree trunks, and each reflected the forest, played catch with sunbeams, or captured a blue piece of the sky. The mirrors swayed in the soft breeze like snapshots in the forest. Barnabas caught his own reflection in one of the mirrors—his dark hair and spiked bangs, his heavy brows and his sunken cheeks—and he was shocked to see his face, now so white and grim, in the riot of copper and scarlet.

Stepping into the clearing, he saw a small settlement of tents, domed and triangular, varied in color and shape, scattered beneath the trees like a collection of kites. Odd belongings—books, sketchpads, pieces of clothing, socks, and hiking boots—lay about in the leaves. In the center there was a large dirt area where a ring of flat rocks and fallen logs served as benches. Wide stumps acted as tables where empty Coke bottles held bouquets of wild flowers.

On one stump sat a green plastic barrel with a water spigot attached. It said STOKES PICKLES in black letters across the side. All was quiet except that flies buzzed and small birds scurried in the brush. Logs from a campfire extinguished in the morning mist had burned to ash, and the odor of stale smoke hung in the air.

Three colorful hammocks were strung between the trees, and in one of them two girls were sleeping, their bodies entwined. Barnabas squeezed his eyelids shut and shook his head. He thought something was affecting his vision. He almost failed to notice a third girl seated in the shade of the largest tree. At first she seemed to be entirely composed of dappled light, her dress painted with watercolors and tied with ribbons and bits of lace. Her long brown hair hung down over her face as she concentrated over a small tray; but when she heard their footsteps, she looked up and smiled.

"David! Come see what I made for you." She rose and moved with such languid grace, her dress floating over the leaves, that Barnabas thought she was a mirage. She approached, raised her thin arms, and placed a necklace of glass beads around David's neck, then stepped back to admire him.

"Gee. Thanks," said David, a bit bewildered as he looked down at the necklace. "Cool." She turned to Barnabas, and David said, "This is my cousin, Barnabas Collins. Barnabas, this is Charity."

Barnabas was about to speak when the girl lifted her body against him and kissed him on the mouth. "Welcome to Paradise," she said in a husky voice. She was not so pretty up close; her skin was freckled, and the pupils of her eyes were huge and very black. But she turned and took David by the hand, and Barnabas was mesmerized by the twinkling of her dress. It seemed to be made of prisms.

"Are you making necklaces?" David asked her.

She answered in a slow drawl, "Beads and brownies. Makin' brownies and beads." She closed her eyes and reached for David's hands and spun him with her, her hair thrown back, her bare feet patting the dirt, her skirt flickering, as she chuckled with sounds of her own mischief. Barnabas stood in a stupor watching them.

"Everyone is down by the stream." She led them into the trees. They hiked down the long steep slope toward the water, where Barnabas saw the naked flower children sunbathing on the rocks or wading in the rapids. He could not make out which one of the girls was Toni, but after a moment he saw that David had joined them to laugh and play in the water with a young girl. They had removed their clothes and were holding hands as they walked unsteadily across the low rapids. Her body was like a dancer's, softly curved, with firm muscles in her legs. Her long dark hair fell over her breasts.

Time seemed to be shifting, moving in jerks. To Barnabas, the campers were like nymphs and druids as they frolicked in the spangled light. He sat alone on the bank of stream and watched, suddenly weary. Lulled by the music of the falling water he glanced up into the thick of the forest, at the endless gray trunks. All around him in the air, leaves were gently floating, fluttering, clinging to branches and twigs. Below by the stream, the woods were aflame with vermillion, and Barnabas lay back and gazed deeper and deeper into the unfolding amber, and then, he imagined, into the golden iris of the eye of God. He closed his eyes and fell into a deep sleep.

When he woke it was dusk and he was alone. He sat up and stretched his cramped body, then rose to his feet. Everyone had vanished. The creek still gurgled over the rocks, but the forest was shadowed and still. The trees loomed above his head, their color drained of light, and the leaves beneath his feet rustled under his step. His first thought was of David, but he decided the boy must have gone back to the camp. He felt a chill. The night air was damp and, with no sun to heat the forest, smelled of winter snows. A scurrying sound in the leaves made his heart jump, but he realized it was only a squirrel or a small bird. As he trudged up the steep incline, the sound of the creek subsided, and he could hear sparrows in the bush twittering themselve to sleep. In the dying light between the trees, the forest ros around him thick and restless.

He heard no sound before he felt the creature leap upon hi back. It clung to him with claws that pierced the fabric of hi coat, and hot breath burned his cheek. Alarmed, he arched an grabbed for whatever was glued there, spinning to get hold c it, but it dug in and rode him. Then he felt pain such as he ha never known: razors ripped at the back of his neck, his scal stabbed his cheek and tore the skin, and something hooked t the flesh of his back and pried his collar loose with its claws. Th sharp pain flooded his body again. He roared an oath, and batte at his back, thrashed about in the air, as the jabs moved into hi hair. Terrified that his eyes would be next, he doubled over an rolled on the ground. But the fangs were in, and deep, and what ever it was rolled beneath him.

When he heard the sucking begin, he shuddered, then quiv ered, then fell into the dark.

Seven

He woke with a longing for blood, with a thirst that thickened his tongue, parched the inner layers of his cheeks, and burnt his throat raw. The hunger was deep in his body as well, as though his limbs were traversed with thousands of tiny empty rivulets. He lay with his eyes closed, and on the backs of his eyelids he could still see the bright red leaves tossing in restless patterns against the pale sky. Their color came out of the bowels of the earth; or was it, as the Indians taught, from the great bear in the heavens who was wounded and rained his blood into the trees.

How long had he lain there, the damp earth rising up through his clothes? He could feel the cold of the leaf mulch invade his body and creep into his bones. He longed for the warmth and comfort of blood.

The loamy earth gave forth a sweet odor of decay as he rose on all fours and staggered to his feet. Instantly, he swooned,

and the tall trees splintered and reeled. He reached and caugh
a low branch to steady himself while the forest around hi
bowed and swayed.

He felt his neck inside the collar of his jacket and, with
sharp intake of breath, found the two jagged wounds, tend
and swollen. Barnabas breathed a long sigh. That was the rea
son his body felt so light, as if burned to ash, and why his hea
throbbed with a leaden timbre behind his eyes. He looked u
towards the road. Would he be able to climb the hill? Forcin
himself to move slowly forward, he fell against a rock outcrop
ping, pulled himself up, then lunged drunkenly through th
smooth trunks of beeches. When he heard his heart rattling i
his chest, he was too frightened to go further, and he collapse
again in the leaves.

He dozed, but woke to a scurrying in the underbrush an
froze, not breathing. It was some animal—a rabbit, or even
raccoon. He wondered what sort of creature would be active th
time of night. What nocturnal being worried the dry leaves an
scratched toward the smell of blood he knew he reeked of? Som
curious beast who was hungry as well, sniffing and searchin
bright-eyed and drawn by the long taut wire of instinct. Th
scratching came nearer, and Barnabas prayed it was not a skun
or a porcupine, or even a badger, but he braced himself for th
sharp teeth and claws he knew it would use to defend itself. H
concentrated on the sound of the scurrying, little twigs breakin
and earth flying, and then he could hear it breathing near hi
face, the quick, jerky clicks of a wild animal, now panting besid
his ear.

He was amazed at the speed of his own hand as he grabbe
it, and his fist closed on writhing fur. A high-pitched screec
told him it was only a wood rat, small and terrified. Barnaba
glimpsed its beady eyes shining into his own and saw its rounde
ears twitch, and for a moment he was amused that somethin

so small could have made so much racket. He sank his teeth into its belly.

Julia found him and, with Willie's help, carried him back to Collinwood. How they managed to transport him in secret through the back entrance, down the hall and up the stairs to his room, he never knew. But he remembered how Willie had wiped the blood from his face and shouldered him when he could not walk, and dragged him when his legs collapsed, while Julia, his arm across her thin waist, murmured encouragement.

Once he woke and saw the golden needle in the lamplight, hovering and quivering, bright as a diamond, before Julia gave him his injection, and the battle for his body began anew. He lay in a chasm of pain, too deep for consciousness, but when Julia placed the cool compresses on his wounds, he roused and saw her face looking down at him, skeletal and drawn, her eyes dark pools of worry.

He thought she asked, "Who did this to you?" just as he had asked the poor fool in the cellar of the Old House. And he tried to answer her but his mouth was too dry to speak.

Twinges and spasms rent him all through the night. It all returned: the sweat, the stench of his body in the sheets, his skin crawling with the pricks of fire ants, stings of scorpions, stabs of ratchet-legged centipedes. When he drew close to waking, he thought, how many have suffered in this way because of me? He was tortured by the memory of the many times he had hunted and fed on innocent waifs and homeless creatures in dark streets down by the wharves, and he shuddered with remorse. But when he was deep in dreams, he felt in the fiercest part of him that he longed to return to that life. How could he have found the vampire's existence so barren, when it had been so vivid and defined? All those years when he had felt trapped, he had in reality been able to see clearly, for desire for blood had been his life's sole purpose. That, and secrecy. How simple life had been.

Julia kept the curtains drawn, since once again he feared the sunlight, the searing pain in his retinas. He tossed in the sheets, despising his weakness; strength and courage were buried away in the past. There were times he woke to the sounds of his own moans from the waves of heat or the horrendous cold, and shame washed over him.

At times he heard the murmuring of the family outside his door, and once David came into the room and knelt by his bed and whispered.

"Cousin Barnabas, I'm awfully sorry. I'm just so sorry. I feel so bad that I left you in the woods. But you know what happened, don't you? Those brownies, well, you know what they had in them, don't you?" He leaned in closer. "It was pot. The girls made them with pot, and they got us both really stoned. That guy Jason didn't tell us what was in them and we ate them. I don't remember anything except that I couldn't find you, and I must have gone home without you. What attacked you? Was it a wild animal?" Then David spoke to Julia. "He's going to get well, isn't he? He's going to be okay?"

"He's going to be fine. Don't worry."

"Barnabas," David said, "You have to get better. You still want to go to Salem don't you? For Halloween?"

"Just leave him to rest, David," said Julia. "Come back and see him tomorrow."

Later he woke and saw the sun streaming in his window and Julia standing there in the bright light, her back to him, leaning over the table. She had the needle in her arm, and he saw her draw back the syringe and her own blood flowed into it. He lurched up and reached for it, startling her. She jerked back and dropped the hypodermic, and stood there staring at him, her face ghostly white, her arm hanging by her side, the needle dangling, still in the vein, and he could see the blood pumping through the tube and flowing into the vial.

These waking moments were few and fitful, but his overlapping dreams were more intense. The window blew open and a bat fluttered over him and flew at his face. He heard its plaintive squeaks, and saw its ruby eyes. It came for him, again and again, and he lay there, paralyzed, his arms refusing to move, and he could not ward it off, was helpless to protect himself. He heard Angelique's voice, her fury like an icy blast that wrapped itself around his body and pinned him to the bed.

"You wanted your precious Josette so much. Well, you shall have her! But not in the way you would have chosen. For you will never rest. And you will never be able to love anyone, because whoever loves you will die."

The curse echoed through his brain as down a dark cavern, and then he saw her sorrowful face and heard her begging him to forgive her. He had wooed her, and loved her, and then he had abandoned her for another, for Josette, her charming mistress, in sun-drenched Martinique, when he had been a brash, romantic soldier just beginning the adventure of his life. How long was he meant to suffer for his callousness? And yet, after so long, was not this other, darker existence now his truer self? Was it really possible that Julia could cure him again?

Once, he grew terribly cold, and he did not know who it was, but a woman lay beside him and pressed her body against him, giving him her warmth while he shivered so violently he thought his bones would shatter. She drew the quilts over them both, and he felt her naked stomach against the skin of his back, and her breath on his neck. He panicked and struggled to escape, but again he was helpless and could not move his body so weighted down, as with lead, and she wrapped her arms around him and would not release him and warmed him with her fire.

Eight

Salem Village—1692

In the schoolhouse, as the children were leaving, Judah Zachery caught Miranda by the wrist and bade her stay. She felt her skin shrink like pig's tripe and the hairs on her scalp lifted.

"Where were you the evening last, Miranda?"

She stood in stony silence and glared at him.

"You were there, were you not? You bewitched young Lucinda and she fell to her death. Your wickedness has found you out, Miranda, and I shall go to the magistrates." She tried to pull away, but he held her in a grip like a vise, until she thought the bones in her wrist would shatter.

"Answer me! We are alone in this room, and I will have the truth."

"How could my wickedness reveal to you any truth? If I am so wicked, as you say, then all my utterances must be false."

She saw him redden, then falter, and his body sagged. "Why

lost thou treat me so, Miranda? Have I not been fair with you?
Why this contempt I do not deserve?"

"You know why."

"I wish to make you my wife someday."

"Death would be my choice over a life with you."

She saw his face darken. "Answer me now. Were you with
he Whaples child in the woods last night?"

"I need answer you nothing. I am neither wife nor consort
of yours, nor in any sense your property. You have no rights over
me, Judah Zachery."

"You are all to be whipped in the square, even little Betty.
Shall I show you what is to come?" Again she tried to free herself, but he turned and dragged her to his desk, opened the
drawer, and took out the cherrywood switch. She pulled away
but, still holding her by her resisting arm, he sat heavily in the
chair and twisted her body across his knees. She smelled the
grease on his clothes and his stale odor. Grasping both her wrists,
he pinched them together, pressed them hard against her back,
and with the whip hand, he tugged at her skirts until they were
up and over her head and she was smothered in woolen folds. She
tried to wriggle free, her body rigid, but he pressed the bones of
her wrists together until they seemed ready to splinter, and with
clumsy jerks he loosened her pantaloons and drew them off.
She writhed when she felt his body buck a little and his back
straighten. The switch sang in the air before she felt its scalding
snap, and she arched, and she could hear him grunt. The bulk
of him rose more beneath her pelvis each time she cringed and
shrank against him. She did not cry out, but wrenched her
hands until the tendons of her wrists stretched to wires, and she
squirmed to flee the blows, knowing her every movement gave
him pleasure. Finally a silent scream—not of pain but of fury—
cast a cloud over caution. There slipped from her lips a muttered
rune and the cherrywood listened and caught fire, turning in
his hand to a burning rod. With an oath he flung the whip in

the air, and stared at his hand where the switch had left a mark more vicious than any it had inflicted on Miranda, a welt of swollen blisters across his palm. With another curse he jerked her body free of his. She fell to the floor and pulled her clothes about her. Judah gaped at his scalded palm and back at her in disgust.

"Witch," he said as faintly as a breath.

"Aye. And best you remember it. For I know you, Judah Zachery, and see your wickedness as clearly as you see mine."

He glared at her, eyes blazing. "Thou art what I've always known thou art. A witch and a demon."

"Beware who you speak to of this," she said. "You have committed the sin of lechery."

He grimaced, and then spoke in a raw whisper. "Then wilt thou sign the book?"

"Never."

He reached for her and grasped her behind the neck and pulled her to him. His breath was hot on her face and she could smell the bile from his stomach on his breath. "I will have you," he whispered, "even if I have to kill you. The Court has already called for you to be examined. You will come to me begging for support."

"I will not."

"But who will protect you, Miranda?"

Miranda knocked softly on the entrance to Andrew's hut. A soft rain was falling, the hour was late, and when he opened his door, he left only a small crack for her to see into his room. He showed a scowling face above the oil lamp he held in his hand.

"What brings you here at this time of night, Miranda?"

She shook the water from her hood, lifted it back over her hair, and spoke as if to scold. "Such a sharp greeting, Andrew. Does it not please you to see your betrothed?"

He opened the door a bit wider, but his large frame loomed in the space, and he answered in a halting voice. "In truth it is a pleasure, but you cannot be in this house alone with me."

"And will you refuse me comfort from the storm?" She placed her hand on the rough wood and looked up into his broad and ruddy face. His small hazel eyes were set deep under heavy brows and his beard was reddish in the firelight, as was his shoulder-length mass of hair.

"'Tis unseemly, lass, and that you know better than I."

She lifted her chin and smiled. "The banns will be published in the fall. Even if someone were to see us, they would think no ill on it. Let me come in."

"Nay, girl, I cannot." He glanced nervously over her shoulder. "I am expecting yeomen to come any moment, and if they were to find you here there would be shame on it. I beg you, be on your way and I will see you on the morrow."

She thought he must be dissembling. Surely there would be no visitors at this hour, with the wind whistling and the rain flying about. "Hush, Andrew, and take heart. No one has followed me. I am shivering and wet through, and I have brought you a cake made by my own hand." She pushed by him, and with a helpless whimper he stepped aside, leaned out and swiveled his head around in the dark, then quickly drew back and barred the door.

"What sort of cake?"

"Huckleberry and molasses—your favorite, is it not?" She smiled at him and pulled off her damp cloak and laid it on the bench. He stood dumbly watching her, and she was uncertain how to proceed. After an awkward moment, she took his hand. "Come, sit with me by the fire and I will give it you." When they were settled on the hearth, she reached into the bodice of her dress and watched his eyes while she extracted a small package. Holding it in both hands, she presented it as if it were a bag of wampum, or something equally precious. He took it and unwrapped the cloth. The cake was perfectly round and nicely browned and still smelled of the oven. Disguised by the cinnamon and molasses were the odors of potent herbs, lovelorn and lavender, and the thimbleful of her urine. Andrew broke off a piece with his fingertips and placed it in his mouth. Soon he was chewing happily, and Miranda saw once again with dismay in her heart that he was only a simple man.

As she listened to the smacking sounds Andrew made while he ate, she looked around the hovel. The floor was dirt and the walls unpeeled pine logs with mud daubed in the cracks. The rafters were cedar saplings and the woven rushes that covered them were thick enough to keep out the rain, which was falling now with a drumming sound on the ground outside. The hut did not leak, but it breathed in such moisture the atmosphere felt damp and cold in spite of the fire that spit and crackled, but offered little comfort. Still the hut was a tidy enough place. The room smelled of Andrew's leather clothes and his slab of venison that hung from a hook on the wall. She also could sniff cooked fish in a pan, or was it eels? Andrew would be fine on her farm, a man at ease with the earth.

On his rough-hewn table, a tin cup was turned over in a cracked porcelain basin that she thought he might use to wash his food, or himself. Then she saw his musket lying on the large bench and the metal parts spread out on a rag for cleaning. The horn was filled with powder and his good deerskin coat hung on the back of the chair. The golden hide glowed and the turned-out seams were as pale in the firelight as tassels of flax.

"What are these preparations?" she asked.

"The farmers from these parts are coming for me tonight and we are banding together. That is why you must away."

"You don't plan to join the militia?"

"Aye, that I do, and we conduct a raid early tomorrow." He wiped the crumbs from his mouth. "This time we mean to kill them all."

She watched him in the firelight as he devoured the last of her cake. Now she had only to wait for its sorcery. When he felt her eyes on him he looked up, and she smiled and said, "What do you see when you look on me, Andrew?"

"What say you?"

She pushed her hair back from her face, and sat tall. "Am I comely to thine eye?"

He blinked, not grasping her meaning. His mouth hung open and she could see crumbs of the cake inside. "Aye, lass."

"Tell me what you see."

"Why, dark hair with a shine on it and pale blue eyes. A fair face." He let his eyes roam over her body. "And a fair form."

"And do you think that you will have enjoyment with me as your wife?"

His eyes clouded and he looked at the cloth in his hands. Then he ate the last crumb, saying nothing. She saw his face redden beneath his beard; his curly brows fairly flew out into the air.

"Do not go and battle," she said. "We are at peace with the Naumkeag."

Rising to this subject as though relieved to be done with the other, he answered. "King Phillip's sons have returned to the river valley and joined with the Narragansett."

"Andrew, this is foolhardy. I fear for you grievously. There is a peace. Signed by the Wampanoag and our governor."

"But still they burn small farms. It is better to go after them where they lie than wait until they attack us here some night in our beds and kill us all, scalp us, and take our clothes."

Hearing him mouth the words he had learned from older, wiser men made her weary and she rose, walked over to where he sat, and placed a hand on his shoulder. "Andrew, I beg you, do not take part in more killing. The great sachems are dead."

"What knowledge have you, a mere jade?"

"I heard the Reverend tell Goody Collins that Canonchet,

a chief of the Narragansett, has been beheaded. Their villages were burned, their children scattered. He said they go to join the Algonquin in the North."

"That is only what some would have us believe."

She sighed. He was dull-witted and stubborn, a dreadful combination in a man. She felt desolate when she looked at him, but where else could she go? And now he was out to kill himself. She knelt at his feet and placed her hands on his knees. "These people were once friendly to us. You remember, do you not, when the two warriors brought you seeds?"

Embarrassed by her forwardness, he rose heavily and began to pace. "Friendly? That is in the past. The Indians are not human beings. They are only bloody creatures who sin against God." He stopped, picked the crumbs from the front of his vest and ate them. "You don't know the truth of it, being only a woman. They have no respect, they harrow and saw our soldiers, inflict the most terrible of deaths." He lifted the little cloth wrapping to his mouth and licked it. "They are demons. Sent to destroy our Christian settlement. We have sufficient light from the Word of God for these proceedings." He filled the room with his bulk, a giant hovering over his small windows, where rain spattered and brought a misty vapor to the panes. They reflected his shadow and flickered with a dull light from the fire. He has no mind of his own, she thought, but needs must follow the will of others, and he reminded her of a great sheep with wide eyes and fear in its heart that would leap with the herd off a cliff. She was glad for his strength, but she trembled to think of him forcing himself on her. Any minute now. She had only to keep him engaged. He folded the piece of cloth and walked to his pinecone mattress and stared down at it. Her heart fluttered. Then, reaching under the ragged bedclothes, he drew out a long knife with a bone handle.

"Andrew, thou must not go on this raid."

He turned to her. "Girl, you are ignorant of these things,

and would best hold your tongue. We are the instruments of Providence! Divinely appointed to claim the New World from Godless people!" He had learned his lessons well. She searched for a retort.

"Should we not as Christians have mercy and compassion? Disease has already killed so many."

"The sickness that comes upon them is not our doing. It is God's way of clearing the way for us." He stopped and stared at her as though he had only then discovered her in his room. "Shush! Be gone, Miranda, before the others come."

She rose and went to the door, then turned, feigning helplessness. "In this storm? Andrew, pray let me tarry 'til the blast has calmed."

He spun on her with sudden anger, perhaps the first sign of the spell, and spit out his words, but only to once more repeat the opinions of others. "We face a grand conspiracy of tribes," he said, and she grimaced at the memorized phrase. "Algonquins and Pequot, newly gathered. A farm was burned last week near Twicksbury." He wiped the knife with her piece of cloth, and shook his head as though to clear it. "Still, it is difficult to dominate a people so rebellious and so free—" He caught his breath as though something had struck him, and gave her a look of surprise, his eyes bulging. He stifled a sob. "Wilt thou leave me now, Miranda?"

Instead she chose to taunt him. "Do you plan to attack the women again in a cowardly manner while their men are away hunting? How can you bear so many lying on the ground, gasping for life? I beg of thee, do not join this madness."

He threw the knife on the bed in exasperation and it bounced to the floor. She could see his body dueling with some demon of its own. "I cannot turn the good yeomen away when they come. What would they think of me?"

"The same as I think of you. That you are sensible."

He struck at the air with his giant arm. "You know what

they will say if I do not go. That I am weak, that I have not loyalty to Salem Town."

"You might tell them you will soon have a new wife. That your loyalty is to her."

Confusion flooded his face and he stood with arms dangling, hands opening and closing, and a shudder traveled through his body. "Wilt thou have them say I am not a man?" She could see the cake was stirring in his blood. His chest heaved and he stared at her from under his brows, while he shifted his weight back and forth. A violent heat came off him. She felt a pulse of fear in her belly. She must find a way to gentle him.

Rising, she walked to the center of the room and stood before him in abject meekness and smiled at him sweetly. "Andrew, we are to be wed. Why do you not take me in your arms?"

Quickly he cast his eyes to the floor and curled his hands into fists. "I pray you girl be gone. I fear humiliation for us both if they find you here."

She moved to him and leaned her body close. "What you fear they will ask, Andrew, I will ask you the same. Art thou a man?"

He glared at her and his eyes bulged and his face grimaced with pain. He whirled away from her, grabbed the back of the chair where his coat was hanging and hunched his shoulders. "Go!" he said, "Before I strike you! Out of my house! Get thee gone!" His face flushed to such a shade of purple she panicked and saw at that moment he might injure her.

"Very well. As you wish." She struggled to maintain a calm demeanor. She reached for her cloak and shook it over her shoulders, the damp folds falling to the ground. Then she pulled the hood over her hair. Fearful of looking into his scowling face, she moved slowly, drawing the tie at her throat. But she could not resist one last insult. When she spoke she allowed anger to creep into her voice.

"You have answered my question well enough, Andrew.

Thou art not a man. Thou art only a boy, or worse perhaps, a brute, with all the heart for killing and none for love."

She saw the hair on the backs of his hands, the thick hair on his heavy forearms, his fingers gripping the deerskin, opening and closing. For the first time she noticed how round were the toes of his boots. She waited until he looked up, and caught his eye.

"I will not marry you, Andrew, for you have shown me you do not care for me, and no longer wish to come to my farm with me." She lifted the latch and turned to see his face, contorted with fury as he leaned over the chair and gripped it with all his strength, before she let herself out the door.

Miranda imagined she was moving inside a giant chimneystack, as the night was a sooty black that obscured even the trees. The ground was as wet as a streambed; her feet sank into the mud, her shoulders ached from bending over to spare her body the rain, and her heart was heavy from the failure of the cake. Too strong, and yet too weak. She had not counted on the vehemence of his resistance. If he had struck her, he could have broken her neck.

She would revisit his hut on the morrow and pray that he had returned from the skirmish unharmed. Then the spell would be in full bloom but tempered somewhat, and they would do the deed lovingly. It must be soon. If an attack on the Indians had not been planned, she would have already been summoned before the Court. Goody Collins had told her the girls were crying out they had been abused by witches, and they were being threatened with a whipping if they did not name the ones who afflicted them. She said they had screamed and crawled under chairs like dogs and Abigail tried to fly out the window. Betty now lay in her bed and refused to speak, only stared at the ceiling with unblinking eyes. Goody Parris was beside herself with worry. The threat of a whipping for dancing in the woods had caused them all to begin this shameful pretense, this ridiculous acting out. It was saving their own hides they were after.

In the darkness, she tripped on roots and creepers, and branches across her path struck her in the face. She blundered ahead, her hands held out in front of her, but the sucking sound of her own footsteps in the mud frightened her, and anger began to stir in her that this brute of a man would send her out into such a night with its blackness and its relentless rain. The wind moaned, and branches splattered her with huge drops whenever she moved under a tree.

Her stomach clenched in shame at the thought of Judah Zachery and the humiliation she had endured. Still, she had been wrong to burn his hand. Now he was sure of her. She shivered and drew her cloak about her, suddenly exhausted, and plunged ahead. She made many twists to avoid the trunks, but always turned back and tried to keep to her route, until she saw a dim light ahead and thought she must be at the edge of the village. But as she drew nearer, she heard voices and saw the shapes of men and Andrew's hut lit up from within. Blundering through the dark, she had walked in a circle. Dismayed, she drew back, but she could hear arguing and loud murmuring voices from the farmers, and realizing the foolishness of her quest on that night, she thought to wait in a tree until morning. Or better still, she might fly up, pierce these low clouds, and sail with the moon. The tempting thought tugged at her flagging will as well as her sodden cloak dragging the ground. Biting her lip in annoyance, she recovered her sense of direction and struck out for home.

Again the darkness and the dense thickets made her way difficult. She pleaded with the trees for help and her path grew clearer. Then she was certain she heard footsteps other than her own, a brutal stamping, unless it was the echo of her shoes slapping the mud. But no, there was something breaking through the brush, snapping twigs and falling against a thorny briar or tripping on a root. It might be a bear, although animals were not fools to wander about in bad weather, or possibly the black man everyone spoke of with his infernal book. She thought she heard a crash and a curse, or a cry of pain. But she could have been mistaken. The spattering of the rain and the whine of the wind could mimic voices of all kinds.

Finally the fear and confusion took their toll on all resolve and she looked upward for a clear opening in the trees, saw one, hovered a moment, then left the ground. But in that same instant something grabbed her ankles and jerked her back to earth. A man's strong arms came from behind and caught her. He was soaked through as well, his clothes wet and cold, but she felt the thick deerskin coat and its heavy seams as he crushed the breath out of her body.

"Andrew, Andrew, stop! You are hurting me!"

She was surprised by his brute force, and knew it was the strength of the spell and all her own doing, and she was ashamed as well to think of the torture he had endured, but his hands were furious under her dress and his fingers tore the skin inside her legs. She wanted him to stop, to let her go, and at the same moment an inner voice said this was the better choice for her, and to endure it. Now the rain roared again like the sound of a deer's hooves when it is surrounded and chased into a trap with no way out. She jerked back her head to breathe and her mouth filled with water. She twisted in his grasp, he was hurting her, cruel and unmindful of her struggles. She wrenched round in the darkness, pitched forward, and caught hold of a young beech tree. She wrapped her arms around the smooth trunk and held on, thinking; he is too strong for me, and doesn't know his own strength and will surely kill me, so crazed is he by a spell. She pressed her body against the beech tree, clung to it for strength, hugging for all her soul something rooted to the earth. She heard the clattering rain and her own heart pounding, and she could taste the sap from the bark, and blood from her mouth where she bit her own tongue, and her own salty tears, even though the sky's weeping washed over her face. She clung to the tree, straddling it, but he bent them both, and lifted her hips and forced her from behind.

Nine

Salem—1971

Salem is a city built around its history, a maze of diagonal one-way streets, twists, and rises. As soon as Barnabas pulled off Highway 114 and on to Bridge Street, he was lost. A poor sense of direction was but another of the many infirmities plaguing his human condition. How effortless it had been to glide above the rooftops under the cloak of night, following his keen hearing to his destination. Now he was trapped in a labyrinth.

The roundabout, encircling a barren green, spit him onto Summer Street and, seeing a sign at Essex Street that read OLD SALEM, he turned. To his dismay, Essex stopped at a barricade with the street closed to traffic, and he was forced to make his way slowly down a large thoroughfare called Washington.

He turned to the sleeping form beside him. "David, we're here. I just have to find the hotel." David only moaned. Barnabas eased the car forward in the darkness until he spotted another sign reading HISTORICAL CENTER, pointing back in the direction from which he had only just come. Annoyed, he turned onto a dark street lined with tall white clapboards which stared down at him through their leaded windows like disapproving parishioners.

Signs with Old English lettering leapt out from brooding buildings: New England Pirate Museum, Witch Trials Museum, Vlad's Castle. Another sign pointed to a hill above the pavement and indicated the Old Burying Ground. Intrigued, Barnabas rolled down his window and craned to see the ancient markers; but instead of tombstones, he was greeted by an elaborate display of dangling, white-sheeted ghosts with carved pumpkins for heads. Eerie music, alternating with peals of fiendish laughter, blared from loudspeakers in the trees while grotesque orange grins gaped and glittering eyes leered at him.

Meanwhile, David slept soundly in the car seat, his head thrown back against the window, his mouth hanging open. They had driven for five hours after leaving Collinsport, covering small stretches of road interspersed with towns, each embellished with an interminable stoplight, as though the little villages sought to hold them captive. More than once he had taken a wrong turn and found himself on yet another dark, tree-lined street. Lying so close to the sea, the area was densely settled and wrapped around bays. Once, when he was forced to stop and turn around, David woke and, yawning, said, "Where are we now?"

"Lost again. I just need to get back to the main road."

David stretched, and looked out the window. "I guess that's why Father didn't want me to go on this trip. He wasn't sure you were up to it." He chuckled and Barnabas knew he was teasing. "Hey, why don't you let me drive for a while?"

"You want to?"

"Sure. I've got my learner's permit."

A lonely stretch of road seemed a safe spot, and soon David was grinning with excitement behind the wheel. Barnabas felt a rush of pride to have been the one to give him this opportunity, and to be both his instructor and protector. But David exuded confidence. "Father would bust a gut if he saw me," he said laughing.

"Probably, but you seem to be doing fine."

"Why does he always act like such a jerk?"

"Oh, Roger's not a jerk. He worries about you, that's all."

"He doesn't trust me. He thinks I'm still a little kid."

"But he does love you." Barnabas was surprised to hear himself say this, and to suddenly realize, with acute awareness, that his own love of this family had been the one constant in his long and ageless life. More than anything else, even his immortality, it defined him. Being a Collins was a source of enduring pride, and the history of his ancestors, even from long before the curse, had always fascinated him.

"You do realize, don't you David, that your family boasts an impressive genealogy which can be traced all the way back to the founding of the New England colonies?"

"I know, I've been told that about a hundred times."

"Sir Isaac Collins founded Collinsport in 1660. The main reason I wanted to bring you to Salem is that another branch of the family settled there. Isaac's brother, Benajah Collins—"

"Benajah! Oh wow. What a cool name."

"Benajah Collins—who was a Reverend, by the way—purchased a small farm outside Danvers. He died mysteriously, probably at the hands of the Indians, but Isaac sold the land for a good price and with that capital he was able to finance his first schooner. That was the beginning of the family business."

"You mean shipping,"

Barnabas nodded. "The Collinses have always been in shipbuilding and trading back and forth across the Atlantic." Barnabas decided to omit the facts about dealing in slavery, but he added, "They amassed a fortune in those days, the fortune you stand to inherit."

"And I'm the only surviving male of my generation. Everything depends on me, right?"

"You should be proud of your heritage. Very few of your schoolmates could boast such a lineage. Think about it when you are in Salem. In some ways the Salem Branch was the beginning of the Collinses wealth. I'm sure you've heard about Benajah's father, Amadeus Collins, who was a judge. You come from a long line of lawyers and thinkers as well as shrewd businessmen and merchants. There may have been disagreements in the beliefs and opinions of Collinses down through time, but there is one thing we all have in common. We are a special family. We are all leaves on the same tree. And we know and accept that. Our ancestors are always with us, watching over us."

David was silent for a while, and then he said, "You can drive now, Barnabas, I've had enough for one night."

Still in a weakened condition from the attack in the woods, Barnabas hit upon a trick to keep himself awake while he drove the final hours to Salem. He decided to compose a list of all the ways he found becoming human despicable. First, there was the physical weakness, and the inability to lift or leap. He was living as a prisoner in a cramped body. Each day his shoulders were more slumped, hands more veined, neck more slack. He was plagued by emotional malaise as well, the tendency toward self-deprecation and an unexpected timidity in public. Humans, he realized, were irrational, and often reversed perfectly reasonable decisions on a whim. They were unstable, and quick to anger or place blame. He now possessed all of these contemptible qualities. As a vampire he had known guilt and obsession, but he had never been in the throes of embarrassment, and he had never been intimidated by the supercilious attitudes of others. It had a great deal to do with his physical appearance.

Vanity had been his inclination, and unable to inspect his

image in a mirror, he had seen himself reflected in the admiration he found in others' gazes. He imagined a magnificent countenance: clear, pale skin, aquiline features, black hair which glistened in the firelight, and dark, luminous eyes that shone with the intensity of a two-hundred-year-old soul. As with anyone who cannot truly see themselves, in his mind's eye his likeness was rendered in the great paintings of kings, in the busts of Roman emperors, in the youthful charioteers from the Parthenon frieze. Captured forever in art, their beauty was immortal, as, he believed, was his.

He was always impeccably turned out, with the best tailors to manufacture his wardrobe, since any exclusive haberdashery was available to him in the night. He often chose the finest gabardine for his suits, a brocaded vest of scarlet silk, a loose charmeuse shirt with lace cuffs, and a wide voluminous velvet cape of midnight blue with a scarlet lining—a cape that brushed the ground. He carried a cane that bore the silver head of a wolf, and his leather shoes gleamed, even on the soles.

Now, since shopping had become difficult, he often wore the same suit for days at a time. The clerks were lazy and treated him with indifference, as though he were just another insignificant member of their bossy and overbearing clientele. He avoided mirrors, as the shock of his appearance offended him. A haggard visage with skin grown rough from shaving—another new and tedious necessity—bluish bags beneath his watery eyes, and a dingy gray in his hair and eyebrows—these were not the only signs of a loss of vitality. He was astonished to discover how easily he bruised. He worried about decay in his teeth, cracked nails, odd rashes that bloomed in peculiar spots.

He was, quite naturally, disgusted by his bodily functions, and food was repellent. His taste buds had yet to regain their keenness, and even when the crisp piquancy of a fresh apple or the rush of rare meat juices charmed his mouth, the ensuing digestive process was agony. At one time his body had been lean and tensile, like a tuning fork that vibrated to one pure tone. Now he felt the food he consumed left him contaminated.

But his problems were more than physical. He found that sometimes in conversation he became distracted, or seemed to recall something that had no connection to the topic at hand; and he would blurt out some awkward remark, resulting in embarrassment. Inadvertent mental leaps into the past would leave him confused and he would forget what he had meant to say, only to be left staring into the baffled face of his listener. Consequently, he avoided social contact as often as he had when he had been a vampire, and that old pervasive loneliness had its grip on him still.

Never in his former state, however, would he have mused on the lack of love in his life. He had always only to fix his gaze upon a woman to draw her to him. Young girls had been eager for his company, desirous of his embrace. They had loved him too much, to their own detriment, of course; but he had rarely spent a day without some tender and attentive female companion at his disposal. Now the thought of approaching a woman excited him, but it also left him feeling panicky.

So at last he had arrived in Salem, and the final mortification was that, driving lethargically in ever-widening circles, he was baffled by a city that seemed to have no grid but only streets that crossed one another like the tangled scrawl of a child. His mind refused to focus; the synapses were sluggish. Then the heat began.

His fingertips tingled, as though they had been asleep, and his hands gripping the wheel contorted as if worms were crawling under his skin. Almost at once he felt fatigue in his limbs and nausea in the pit of his stomach. It was heat from the blood made by his own marrow, thick and raw, flowing through his veins like rising lava, and it played havoc with his temperature. Most of all he hated his sweat, which reeked of rotten leaves, and he could not help but wonder whether anyone near him would be able to bear his odor—like the inside of a vase where flowers have wilted and died. Breathing heavily, he slowed the car, rolled down the window, and drank in the night air. David woke again to his sighs, stretched, and lifted up to look out the window.

"Are we there?"

"Yes, finally. This is Salem."

At that moment they passed a huge Gothic mansion of purplish granite. An enormous triple-arched leaded window of great intricacy was lit from within with a crimson glow, and a signpost displayed a swinging placard that read SALEM WITCH MUSEUM, 1692. Carved deeply into the wood was the silhouette of a witch holding a broom and wearing a tall conical hat. In her arms she held a black cat with yellow eyes.

"Cool," said David. "Look at that. Can we go there?"

"Tomorrow, perhaps," Barnabas answered with difficulty. "But first we must find Winter Street. Our lodgings are at the Inn at Winter Street, and I have circled the town and seen nothing by that name."

"I'm hungry. Let's stop and eat, and we can ask somebody."

"That's a grand idea." The thought of food was detestable to Barnabas, but he was determined to be a cheerful companion.

"How about that?" David said, pointing to the lights of the Derby Fish & Lobster just ahead. Barnabas found an empty parking space and, still feeling dizzy, sat for a moment and rested his head against the steering wheel. But David clambered out of the car and made for the door, forcing him to follow.

The restaurant was noisy and crowded with young people, smoking, drinking wine, talking in shrill voices, and the glare of the lights was a shock after the long dark hours in the car. There were no tables available, but the waiter told them they could order food at the bar. So they found themselves seated on stools and staring past gleaming bottles of wines and liquors into the kitchen.

While David buried himself in the menu, Barnabas made an effort to calm his nerves. Paranoia gripped him, and he had the sudden impulse to flee. With some effort he listened to bits of conversation around him mingled with the sounds coming from the cooking area. He was always sad in public places. Under the clatter of dishes in the sink, he heard, "I have no limits in my life," from a dark-haired girl leaning over her cigarette. "You're a guy I could have a relationship with," she said, a gold bracelet glinting on her arm, "but I don't like the baggage you come with."

Then came a burst of laughter from across the room. "It's simple!" someone shouted. "He has to be garroted!" A serious young man at a table close by stared mournfully into his partner's eyes. "I finally read your story, and it really upset me," he said. As Barnabas gazed around the restaurant, he became painfully aware that everyone seemed to be part of a couple, intensely involved in the grip of some intimate problem.

Two pretty boys worked behind the bar, and they were in the process of assessing their lives as well. "Do you want to end up like our parents?" said one. Barnabas wondered if they were gay, as both were very good-looking in a thin, fragile sort of way, especially the blond boy with well-shaped arms and delicate hands.

After reading the entire menu, David ordered a hamburger, and Barnabas felt obligated to choose the house special, clam chowder, although the name and the thought of its ingredients repulsed him. The odors of fish, garlic, and butter filled his nostrils, and he pushed the leaden nausea back into the pit of his stomach. David wandered off to the bathroom and Barnabas glanced over the crush of people. The tables were bright with food, silver, and glittering goblets, and each displayed a Halloween centerpiece, a black witch perched on a pumpkin. Copper chandeliers festooned with spider-filled cobwebs cast a honeyed glow over the room.

Then his heart jumped. He saw, at a far table on the other side of the room, what he thought was a familiar silhouette. Her back was to him and her blond hair fell in loose tendrils over the collar of a white lace blouse: There was something about the shape of her head, the lift of her shoulders, and the way she leaned in when she spoke to her companion that he was certain he recognized. Then he remembered the carpenter, Jason Shaw, had mentioned that Antoinette often came to Salem.

David returned with a fistful of brochures and slammed the stool when he climbed on, scraping the tile floor.

"Guess what? It's a weekend of thrills and chills—Ghosts from the Gallows!"

"Really? Whatever is that?"

"Right now, in Witch City. Salem has this huge Halloween celebration. There's all kinds of stuff we can do."

"Well, I suppose that explains the crowds," Barnabas said, glancing at the woman's back again while making an attempt to sip his wine. David read from the flyer.

"Listen to this! *'Salem's Haunted House! Salem's oldest and largest! A trail of ghoulish chambers filled with vampires and other creatures of the night.'* Wow! Vampires! Let's go there! *'Nosferatu rise from their graves looking for victims to feed their insatiable hunger. If we don't scare you, you must be dead!'*" David laughed and pressed the flyer on Barnabas, who scanned it in dismay. "See, it says, *'Innocent victims of the diabolical Witch Trials come down from Gallows Hill to walk the streets of Salem.'*"

His eyes sparkling from the bar lights, David teased, "I need to see it all, Barnabas, for my educational experience."

"But then, of course you must," said Barnabas.

"Listen to this," he went on, "this is so cool. *'Haunted Footsteps Ghost Tour.'* Whoa! *'Eerie, lantern-light walk resurrects Salem's frightful past. Hear true tales of documented hauntings, chilling murders, and colonial witchcraft.'* Far out! Oh, and get this. *'We offer a spirited,'* duh-h-h, *'perspective on Salem's bewitching history!'*"

David was giggling like a little kid. "'*Group rates available. Visit our unique, gift boo-tique.*' Oh, man, this is great. I can't wait."

"I knew a witch once," said Barnabas lightly, still watching the woman whose back was to him.

"Oh, yeah?"

"As a matter of fact, I knew her quite well."

"A real witch?"

"Absolutely."

"Could she cast spells?"

"She cast one on me," said Barnabas, and to his amazement, he caught himself smiling as though it had all been a great joke.

David gave him a wise look. "Oh, I get you. You fell for her, right?"

Before Barnabas could answer, the boy with the well-shaped arms brought their food. He looked at David with some interest. "You folks from around here, or are you tourists?"

"Actually, we just came to see the town," said David.

"At Halloween?"

"Did we pick a bad time?" Barnabas asked.

"Well, there'll be hundreds of people here this weekend. The witch dungeons and pirate museums will be bursting at the seams. But you will be able to buy a vampire cape for about a hundred dollars, a twenty-five-dollar love potion, or a ten-dollar T-shirt that reads, 'Born-again Pagan.'" He smiled at David. "It's Hysteria Time in Witch City."

"Isn't anything real?" asked David.

"Hm-m-m-m . . . that's a good question."

"What about the cemetery?" Barnabas added.

"Oh, the Old Burying Place? Sure, that's the real thing. The problem is it's surrounded by second-rate wax museums with decaying exhibits. But, you know what? There's a local Circle Ceremony tomorrow night. You can dance with some real live witches." David laughed, and the young man drank him in with his eyes.

"Maybe the one you used to know will be there, Barnabas," David said slyly.

"And every Sunday there's a séance. Attend that only if you are not afraid of going back in time."

"Oh, wow! I'm not!" David's excitement was contagious, but the young man turned his head and looked for the briefest instant into Barnabas's eyes. It was a look of contempt, and Barnabas shuddered.

Directions to Winter Street took them along the harbor, where they could see the lights on the water, and then into the darkest part of town, past the Common. *This would be the place to hunt,* thought Barnabas. The "French Victorian B&B" was not what he had expected; it was rundown and dismal. The house was locked, with only a porch light, and they knocked for some time before an old woman, looking out of place without a nightcap and candle, opened the door to a tiny entrance hall decorated with a floral carpet. She led them, carrying their own luggage, up three sets of steep and narrow stairs, to a disappointing suite which was small and dark and bitterly cold. It boasted a fake leather couch that consumed the whole of the sitting room. A cramped bathroom built of particleboard had been forced into one corner of the eighteenth-century bedroom, where no bathroom was ever intended to be. It contained a plastic shower unit, and Barnabas was annoyed to find it had one of those noisy fans that came on, and stayed on, with the light.

But this was, nevertheless, their home, and David was soon to bed and covered up with an orange polyester quilt. He was asleep in no time, but not before he had exacted a promise from Barnabas, who was also looking forward to the experience, that they could go to the Witch Trial Exhibit first thing in the morning.

Barnabas stared for a moment out the grimy window at

shingled dormers silvered in the moonlight, then glanced back into the bedroom at David sleeping peacefully. The boy's charm and good looks moved him, and he thought again of taking him to Europe or Asia, showing him the world. What a treat that would be, Barnabas mused, sharing his wisdom with one so young and impressionable. How much David reminded him of himself at that age, brash and enthusiastic, full of humor and curiosity, at the threshold of life. He was beginning to notice that David admired his knowledge of history and, more than anything, he was struck by the comfort the boy's companionship brought him.

But his mind drifted back to the restaurant and the woman at the table across the room. Why did she come to Salem, and who was the girl she had secreted out of Windcliff? What, if anything, had Antoinette to do with his recent difficulties? And what of the vampire on the loose in Collinsport now threatening those he loved? Who knew the ways of a monster so intimately, could catch its metallic scent, or hear the velvet silence when it was near? Everyone in the town was vulnerable: his family, the hippies sleeping in the woods. And how could he, in his weakened state, find the cunning and the courage to drive a stake through its heart? He trembled at the thought. How many mornings had he closed the lid of his own casket, wondering whether this dawning day was to be his last? And how many years had he lived in fear of the vengeance that was now his calling to seek?

He felt the sway of the trees beside his window, and branches heavy with withered leaves beat against the glass. A pale moon glinted on warped rooftops, the leaning chimneys, and sagging gutters. Thin clapboard with no insulation allowed the chill to creep into the room. He was disappointed in his lodgings but excited to be in Salem. He anticipated reliving the story of the Puritans—the hardships and deprivation, and the stalwart faith that had sustained them—still in the spirit of the place. As he ooked out on the dark roofs, he hoped the greed of tourism had not sucked away all the fascinating history.

He wondered whether he had journeyed to Salem as a child and he thought he surely must have, with his father in the business of building ships—his cover for being a slave trader—and the port of Salem so accessible. From his window he could see the lights of the harbor and he strained to hear the ships' sounds: the cries and commands, the snap of sails, hulls groaning against the docks. Pondering once again the branch of the Collins family in Danvers, which had been Salem Village, he imagined an earlier century when the town was chartered: the crash of falling trees, the sweat of sawing and shaping, the meetinghouse raised for worship with its black-robed parishioners, so devout and inflexible, and the struggles with the Indians. Were their ghosts still here?

At last dullness came over him, and then a great weariness, and he lay down beside David and fell into a deep sleep.

Ten

Saturday, Halloween, dawned bright and windy. Barnaba
and David decided to walk to the Witch Museum severa
blocks away. The streets were teeming with people in costume
witches and vampires, of course, with the odd mummy or Frankenstein thrown in. There were modern-day monsters as well.
zombies, ghouls, and skeletons with shredded flesh and danglin
eyeballs. It seemed that blood was the theme of the day. A prett
Juliet had a knife in her chest and blood dripping down her
bodice. The headless horseman approached sporting a neck complete with extended arteries spraying crimson liquid. A Roma
soldier brandished a sword, and his mangled arm was cut off a
the elbow. Salome had the blinking, breathing head of John the
Baptist on a silver tray. It was all so silly, and so delighted Davio
that Barnabas experienced a dizzying sense of euphoria.

Just as they were approaching the museum, they saw an old
woman coming towards them. She was a true hag of the town.

with her hooked nose, her wrinkled skin, her protruding skull, and a dangling cigarette in her slack mouth. The hood of a cheap black ski jacket covered wispy white hair and she hunched over a shopping cart filled with junk; she moved with effort, dragging her feet. Barnabas had often noticed how a subtle combination of features seemed indigenous to a certain part of the country. This old woman so favored the paintings and woodcuts of Salem's witches, she could have been their model. Was she born to the breed? Or the last of the line, he wondered. Where else but in Salem would such a hook-nosed, beady-eyed hunchback be found? Then something happened that Barnabas found odd. She looked up at him as they passed, and caught his eye with a cold, accusing glare. An icy stab found his bones.

Eager to see the presentation, Barnabas and David squeezed behind a tour group into the Witch Museum. The crowd gathered into a cavernous room and stared in a dim-witted stupor at the vivid dioramas on the four walls, which were enhanced by a blaring recording that told the story of the famous Witch Trials. In the Puritan kitchen, awkward mannequins of bored young girls were hard at work: weaving, candle-making, and sanding the floor. The children stole away to the forest, cast spells in an iron pot, and danced in the moonlight. In the courtroom, misshapen dummies representing the afflicted girls babbled in tongues and crawled about on the floor like dogs. Spectral evidence was dramatized by projected shapes of ghosts flying about the room. David watched mesmerized, but Barnabas was disappointed in the trite dramatization, and soon became restless, shifting his weight on the bench as he looked out over the crowd, searching, inadvertently, for a golden-haired head.

The pentagram in the center of the floor came to life and glowed crimson as the mock trial began. Black-robed judges intoned the accusations, and dummies of women with arms outstretched, their hair flying and their eyes wild with terror, pleaded their innocence from a tinny loudspeaker. In one of the scenes a

robust settler refused to testify for fear of losing his propert
and he was crushed to death under an enormous pile of rocks
"More weight!" he shrieked, and the crowd laughed. In the las
image they witnessed the pièce de résistance, the hangin
scene. Limp and broken-necked bodies swayed against a bloo
red sky, their little shoes peeking from beneath their black skirts
their recorded moans pitched over the music.

The rising heat within his body drove Barnabas to the exit
Breathing heavily, he wandered into the gift shop, and, stiflin;
a desire to vomit, he tried to focus on the objects for sale: sacks o
fresh herbs and incense, magic potions designed *To make you
love grow stronger* or *To cure a broken heart.* He took up a packe
and read on the cover. *Powder to chase away Vampires—of th
spirit, of course. To rid you of those cruel persons who suck you dry c
your dreams.* He held the envelope containing the herbs betwee
his fingers, and stared at the crude drawing of a grotesque ma
with canine incisors.

A flyer caught his eye: *Visits from the Afterlife. Hauntings
spirits, and reunions with departed loved ones. Identify and enhanc
your own psychic abilities, speak to those who have crossed over.* I
was an advertisement for a séance from something called the
Witch Education Bureau.

Grimacing with disgust, he moved into another room empty
of tourists where he was astonished to find three glass cases tha
held life-sized wax figures of witches. Supposedly displayec
in their natural surroundings, they were so realistic he though
they might speak. The first, a black-robed crone, clung to he
broom and rode the wintry sky with the moon and her cat
she could have been the old hag he had seen on the street that
morning. The warted nose and pointed hat might easily have
belonged to that humpbacked creature who had glared at him
with such temerity. This wax personage stared at him with perfect contempt as well. How alive she seemed. Turning away, he
walked slowly to the second case. In the forest with the Devil,

who was unmistakable with his raven cape and blood red eyes, stood the vixen witch as he knew her, capricious and venomous, caster of spells. Her golden mane and flushed cheek only enhanced her knowing countenance. She greeted him with a look of cool disdain, and the stark trees towered over her as she displayed the book where she had signed away her soul. *That is she,* he thought with rancor, *my tormentor.*

But the third witch caught him by surprise. Radiant within an autumn woodland, a Mother Goddess gazed down at him. Wavy, copper-colored hair hung softly below her shoulders, and her dress was a weaving of grasses and wildflowers. The trees behind her glimmered with scarlet and gold, and the ground at her feet was strewn with herbs and sparkling dust. Her eyes were of the softest blue, and so kind he thought she poured out her soul in love only for him. WICCA the sign read, FIRST, DO NO HARM. Barnabas was transfixed. The resemblance was there; it was not her portrait, but in many subtle ways he thought she favored Angelique. As he stood entranced by the figure, he heard a sound behind him, a whispering and fluttering, and the hair stood up on the back of his neck. He turned to find the space as empty as before.

The old burying ground was a tiny plot in a rise off the street and surrounded by tacky shops and museums. A loudspeaker blared haunting music mixed with absurd sound effects of shrieking wind and howling wolves. An iron gate swung on rusted hinges. But once within the low stone wall, nothing could diminish the quiet power of the place. Fall foliage shrouded the little graveyard with clouds of amber and rust, as though the trees were flowering with fire, and a carpet of leaves littered the ground. An old oak tree as large as a ship towered over the oldest graves, its gnarled arms reaching out as if to shelter them, its chocolate leaves clattering in the wind.

"That would make a good hanging tree," David said.

Barnabas agreed. The spot was haunted. "But alas, no witches were hanged here," said Barnabas. "Their place of execution was Gallows Hill, and I read it's now a housing tract outside of Salem."

"But some of their graves must be here."

"Unfortunately, not even that. There are no ghosts of witches scurrying around our feet, you may be sure. This was a church-yard, and no witch could be buried in hallowed ground."

"Where were they buried?"

"They were cast into shallow graves, I'm afraid, near where they were hanged. Sometimes human limbs were exposed by heavy rains."

"Ugh, that's awful," said David. "And they were all innocent, weren't they?" He looked at Barnabas, his hazel eyes flecked with gold.

"That's what they say. But I have always wondered, what if the elders were right?"

"What do you mean, right?"

"That there were real witches."

"No way."

"Do you believe in reincarnation?"

"Maybe I used to be a tiger or something."

"Do you believe there is a God?"

"Sure. But not a Devil."

"But you are in Salem, David. This is where the Devil resides." David merely snickered. "Wait a minute," Barnabas continued. "Have you considered the possibility that the Devil was alive and well in 1692, and the magistrates were wise in conducting a witch hunt in an effort to wipe him out?"

"Oh, come on Barnabas. That's stupid."

"But you remember it was a new country, tempting for a deceiving Old Soul. And the forest full of wild beasts and Indians lay just outside the town. It was a terrifying place." David's eyes glazed over and he wandered off to read tombstones.

"Seventeen twenty-one," he shouted. "Sixteen seventy-three! Look! Here's a little baby, six months old, with a tiny plaque."

David ran from tombstone to tombstone reading off the dates. Then Barnabas noticed a young woman who stood at the other side of the cemetery looking down at one of the inscriptions. She was tall and wore what at first seemed to be a costume, a cape of sky blue velvet which fell over her shoulders and a hood hiding all but a wayward lock of her golden hair. As he watched her, he thought she could have been from another century, with her straight back and slender form. She seemed to be at home in the Old Burying Ground, a breathing statue marking the grave of some poor girl who had met an untimely demise.

Then he heard David's voice from behind.

"Barnabas, look. There's Toni." His blood rushed to his face. David seemed equally surprised at her appearance. But they both hesitated to approach her, and stood apart among the tombstones, checked by her mood, for she seemed wrapped in a veil of sadness. Like some penitent, she bowed her head, and her shoulders quivered as though she were weeping. She looked up, and straight at Barnabas, and his breath stopped in his chest. He thought he caught a flicker in her eye. Then she turned and walked through the gate of the cemetery and climbed into her car.

Barnabas moved over to the grave where she had been standing. It was a small stone, worn to the softness of snow. It had fallen to one side and the inscription was barely legible, but he was able to make out: INFANT OF MIRANDA DU VAL.—BORN OCTOBER 29—DIED OCTOBER 31, 1692.

Now that he had seen her, Barnabas felt certain he would find her again. The rest of the day he searched for her, and every venue was imbued with her presence. Once he thought he had tracked her down. He had convinced David that the Moby Duck Tourmobile which plunged into Salem Harbor could wait, and they had resisted the Pirate Museum with its rubber-masked employees dressed as Frankenstein and Dracula. However on the same street, alongside its tawdry entrance, Barnabas noticed a carved oak doorway bearing a copper plate on which was engraved in small letters WITCH EDUCATION BUREAU. A slip of paper fluttered from a tack and read: *Circle, midnight tonight*. Barnabas hesitated, then, unable to resist, pushed open the door and peered inside. He saw curtained walls and a polished floor, but the room was empty.

Exhausted now, he and David drove to the site of Gallows Hill, almost hidden in a tasteless subdivision, where, out of a sense of respect, they forced themselves to read the names of those who had been hanged as witches. The final words of the accused were embossed on a weathered plaque.

Rebecca Nurse. Hanged March 23, 1692. *I am innocent as the newborn babe.*

George Jacobs Jr. Hanged May 10, 1692. *Well, burn me or hang me. I stand in the truth and say I know nothing of these lies.*

Miranda du Val. Hanged October 31, 1692. *If you take away my life, God will give you blood to drink.*

Barnabas stopped and stared long and hard at those words. *God will give you blood to drink.* A cold shudder ran down his spine. Who was this Miranda du Val and what sort of innocent victim had she been? What a vivid and remarkable thing for her to say. *God will give you blood to drink.* Of course, it was a curse! From the gallows, in her last breath, she had cursed those who hanged her.

Barnabas had almost given up on seeing Antoinette again when at last he thought he caught a glimpse of her walking up the steps to the library of the Peabody Essex Museum. If it were she, it would be a perfect spot for a meeting, far away from the crowds. Without allowing himself a moment to lose his nerve, he sent the boy off to view a film on Salem's seafaring history, and he dashed across the square.

He opened the door to a large hall, but she was not there,

nd he climbed the divided staircase to an upper gallery lined ith books. Long cherry tables reflected the globes of four rass chandeliers, and white Corinthian columns with gilded aves encircled the reading area. The room was empty of all but handful of readers.

Pretending to peruse a section on family genealogies, he took own several books and read the names: Phelps, Pickering, Rice, Reed, Randolph, and Sacketts, scanning their dates of landing n New England and the property they acquired. Some were nerchants, or craftsmen; others were farmers. It was difficult to oncentrate, and he walked back to the balcony and checked he entrance again, wondering where Antoinette, or the woman who resembled her, could have gone, before he returned to the ooks.

Marriages and children were listed, and times of death. He ead a bit about John Alden selling powder and shot to the Indi- ns and then lying with their squaws. He found a piece about assing a baby through a Witch's Tree on Proctor Street to save it rom spells. All the time he expected to see her at any moment.

A small pile of books and notes was strewn on one of the ables and, still seeing no one about, Barnabas wandered over nd looked down at an open page. He was astonished to see his own name—*Collins.* It was a book very much like the one he ad been reading, and it was open to his family history. Copi- us notes were scribbled on a yellow pad and they drew him ike a magnet. Her handwriting was cramped but he could nake out: *Miranda du Val signed the book of Judah Zachery. Trial y water. Stolen farm.*

He leaned in to read further: *The Collins family curse began he night Miranda was hanged. Among the judges at the proceedings vas Amadeus Collins, patriarch of the line of Collins which stretched ack to Salem, actually Danvers, and before that to England. He lied of internal hemorrhage—choked on his own blood.* Barnabas vas so engrossed he never heard her walk up behind him.

"Excuse me, but those are mine."

He jerked back, alarmed to see her standing so close. She smelled of pine trees, and he stared into the eyes he could never forget, pale turquoise with dark rings around the irises. He tried to gather his resolve, but he could not speak, and it was she who broke the silence.

"You're Barnabas Collins, aren't you? What are you doing here?" After a long pause during which he was helpless to answer, she said in a low tone, "Are you following me?" Now he could see her clearly, and examine her mouth, her cheekbones, her brows. It was the face of Angelique.

"I was, yes." Could that have been his voice? He covered his mouth and coughed.

"Oh, and why?" The familiar lilt.

He steeled himself, and the words felt awkward. "You know perfectly well why."

"Oh-h-h, I see . . ." She smiled now, and in that smile he recognized the vagaries of mood Angelique so often displayed, a taunting cut of the eyes, the mouth slightly open, humor and contempt mingled in a wicked gaze, impudent and challenging. And yet, something was different, something he couldn't define.

"Perfectly well? And how would I know that?"

He was taken off guard. What did she mean? She had merely repeated his words and grinned, and he saw the very human crow's-feet at her eyes. Her hair was pinned up but tousled, and limp tendrils clung to the sides of her face. Her lipstick was worn away on a chapped bottom lip. He was not prepared for her to be so modern. She wore a sheer blouse through which he could glimpse the shape of her nipples, and at least seven necklaces of colored stones and beads around her neck. Earrings that could only have been made from—were they actually peacock feathers?—peeked at him from behind her hair. He had put the moment off too long, and he blurted out, "I must have a word with you."

She shrugged, then smiled again, her eyes dancing. "Well, kay." She turned to gather her papers. The down on her arms reflected the lamplight. "You want to go have some coffee?"

"My dear, I have no desire to make this a social engagement."

She hesitated, then stopped and looked up at him. Her expression was one of easy amusement. "My goodness, you are in hurry. I didn't realize you had been thinking about me in . . . hat way. Why didn't you let me know?"

It was annoying to see her treat his remarks as a joke. So that was to be her game. She had her own wiles, that was certain.

"How can I help but think about you, as you say?"

She smiled as though he had complimented her, and shrugged, "It's only that I would have expected more genteel behavior from an . . . uh . . . *English Gentleman.*" She placed the epithet in verbal italics, her tone sardonic.

At last he recognized the Angelique he knew, a woman who eased to be cruel. He felt his head swim, and he reached for the able to steady himself. A wave of profound irritation swept over him. He had approached her for only one reason: to discuss the sale of the Old House, to entreat her to leave, to abandon her plans, however fiendish, to once again give him peace. But now he stood helplessly on the other side of the cherry table, looking into her azure eyes, aware of a heavy line of black mascara on her ids. She tilted her head to one side, her expression amused.

"I'm afraid," she was saying, "as attractive as you are, I need a little more time. Not that I'm not intrigued—" and she laid her hand on his. A shot of blood rushed to his face. "But," and she was almost coy, "you have to admit we hardly know each other."

"How can you say that?" His voice was harsh and something in his tone made her smile vanish.

"How can I say that? Because I have met you only once, in the drawing room at Collinwood."

"You know, of course, I am not speaking of this life. Not

this life where it is true we have only met once, but of the past the past where you and I—"

She laughed, and her laughter gave him a sudden chill, s familiar were its scales. "That's terrific," she said, her voice brim ming with amusement. "*Très bon*, monsieur! That's the best on I've heard in a long time."

"Angelique—"

"Who?"

"I call you that because I know who you are and why yo are here."

Her eyes grew serious as they focused on his. "You know Barnabas, you've got me completely confused."

"Why have you come here?" he said.

"What? To Salem?"

"Yes, to begin with." She was exasperating.

"Well . . . I am doing research on medicinal practices of th late seventeenth century. This is a very unusual library. Most o the books are so rare they can't be removed from this room."

"And why are you studying the history of my family?"

For the first time something betraying uneasiness flickered across her face, and she looked away. Still, as she moved to close the books and gather up her notes, her voice was controlled.

"Look, I bought that old house and it belonged to these Collins people, you know, your family. So I'm curious about them Why wouldn't I be?"

"I would think you already know all you need to know."

She laughed. "Okay, I've gotten carried away—I'll admi it—with the reconstruction. It's become an obsession." She shuf fled notes into a limp velvet sack that was from some Middle-Eastern country, perhaps Afghanistan. It was heavily appliquéd with bells and sparkling beads embroidered over silken birds and flowers, and it jingled as she shifted it to accommodate her papers. He could feel her warm to her topic as though she had discussed this all before. "I've hunted all over for the materials and fabrics, the furniture . . . antique stores, junk shops. I want it to be just like it was."

"But, why?"

"Why?"

"It seems such a waste to recreate the crack in the mantel, the twenty layers of paint, the mold on the porch, and really my dear, let's be sensible, the coffin in the basement?"

"The what?"

Again he thought he caught something flicker across her face, if only for an instant, and her eyelashes fluttered in that old way before she regained composure.

"What are you talking about?" She was suddenly much more sober, and now he was certain she was lying.

"Let's end this charade. I know perfectly well why you came. And what's more, you know I know. I am not confounded by your cunning pretenses, your hippie disguise. I see through your painstaking efforts to delude my family, and I know you have rebuilt the Old House as a trap."

She spoke softly, with hesitation. "All right. I will tell you the truth. I am here because of my daughter—"

"Your daughter? A daughter no one has seen? Oh, come let us draw away this curtain of deceit and at least acknowledge what we both know. You have returned to Collinwood to torture me once again, and if you remain here, my life will be a living hell—"

"You know what? You're nuts." Her face hardened and all her warmth faded in an instant. She turned and, jerking her books together in a pile, gathered them to her breast. "I have no idea what you're talking about. But I do know I don't want to stand here any more and listen to this shit." Her eyes filled with tears. "Who do you think you are? You don't know a thing about me or my daughter. You have no idea."

"My dear, I know you well. Have you forgotten we were once lovers?"

Her face reddened and she flared. "Okay. This . . . joke has gone on long enough. Stay away from me." She turned and walked quickly towards the landing.

Helplessness gripped him, and he struggled to find a way to stop her.

"Angelique, wait—"

"Don't call me that! And don't come near me. Stay back or I'll scream for the cops." She raced for the stairs.

Barnabas stood looking after her, rigid, as though he had been slapped. He wanted to call her back, to go after her, but he was unable to move from the spot. Over and over again in his mind he saw her flee towards the balcony, her blue cape over her arm, her long skirt skimming the polished floor, her figure disappearing down the stairs. He was in a state of utter confusion. How could this have been the interview he had anticipated for months, the confrontation he had played over and over again in his mind in endless rehearsals and revisions?

Deep in his body the heat began to build. His hands quivered and trembled with tingling spasms, and the rush of blood bloomed in his limbs and flooded his face. He collapsed into a chair while his thoughts spun in slow swimming circles, and his eyes grew dim. What a dolt he was! What a blundering idiot! He had finally found a way to confront her and confound her with his logic, his knowledge of her secrets, his compelling threats. But he had only managed to antagonize her.

Slowly, the heat began to subside. He was stung by her rejection, that was true, and she had left him red-faced and embarrassed. But beneath the surface something else was stirring, something far more basic and terrifying. Angelique was his mortal enemy. There could be no one in the world towards whom he felt greater enmity. The sound of her voice, the cut of her gaze, her quick gestures, her volatile nature—all he hated and feared. But after looking into her eyes, he could only remember thinking two things: that this woman could not be the Angelique he knew, and that once again he was caught in her spell.

Eleven

Salem—1692

Five magistrates sat behind the bench in the meetinghouse and looked down at Miranda, who was so filled with loathing she shook the veil off her eyes and saw them for what they were. Five lace collars gleamed, and five white jabots hung stiff like knives against black robes. Five cruel faces leered at her, and at first glance she made out John Hathorne, the feared judge of witches, Bartholomew Gedney, Samuel Sewall, Jonathan Corwin and Amadeus Collins, the father of her benefactor. The second time she looked at them, she saw snakes curling at their lips and sliding through their long hair. Bartholomew Gedney had green snakes with forked tongues slithering from his mouth, and Samuel Sewall had eyes like baby snakes still in the egg, glossy and quivering. She took heart when Amadeus Collins placed his large soft hands upon the record book. But a huge snake slid out of it to the floor and began to move silently toward Miranda. She watched it crawl beneath her skirt.

Magistrate Gedney spoke first. "Miranda du Val, you are here before the General Court of Salem City, charged in the name of this commonwealth of not having the fear of God before your eyes nor in your heart, being seduced by the Devil and yielding to his instigations; and, to the wickedness of your own nature, about the beginning of October last in Salem Village, near the house of Reverend Whaples, that you did willfully murder his daughter by bewitching her, causing her to fall to her death, against the word of God and the laws of this jurisdiction, long since made published. What say you?"

"I am an innocent person," she replied. "I never had to do with witchcraft since I was born."

"Miranda du Val, you are now in the hands of Authority. Tell me now why you hurt this child."

"I have never hurt anyone."

"Who did?"

"I do not know sir. Pray give me leave to go to prayer."

The magistrates murmured among themselves, nodding after this remark. Then John Hathorne spoke, the twitching red serpent quivering on his tongue.

"Who is your God?"

"The God that made me."

"What is his name?"

"Jehovah."

"Do you know any other name?"

"God Almighty."

"Doth he tell you, that you pray to, that He is God Almighty?"

"What mean you sir? I do worship but the God who made me."

Now Attorney General Thomas Newton, an ancient man with a full beard of pus white lizards, leaned forward and spoke. "Can you read the scripture, child?"

"Aye, sir."

"Step forward and read this verse." He opened the great Bible and Miranda looked down at the page where his bony newt finger pointed and squirmed. She felt her heart thumping in her temples, but she spoke in a clear voice.

"If there arise among you a prophet, or a dreamer of dreams, and giveth a sign or a wonder—put to death, be it son, daughter, or wife of thy bosom."

"Art thou a dreamer of dreams, Miranda?"

"I am a servant girl, sir."

"Why did you frolic with the children in the woods?"

"We went with Tituba, sir."

"Tituba has confessed to witchcraft and repented. And the evidence reveals that if after quarreling or threatening a person, mischief do follow, or death thereof, there is great presumption against them that do quarrel. Do you not see these complain of you?"

Miranda turned and looked at the three evil-eyed girls: Betty, with her arm in a cloth sling, Abigail, and Mary. They had all testified against her to save themselves a whipping. On a bench behind the girls sat the ministers: the bereaved Reverend Whaples, father of the dead girl; Cotton Mather, son of Increase Mather; the unordained Deodat Larson; and Benajah Collins, who looked at her and shook his head sadly.

"The Lord shows his power to discover the guilty," she said.

"Did you not dance with these children and delight in ecstasies?" said John Hathorne. "And did not these delights invoke spirits which pushed these children toward the cliff? Confess now and you will be spared."

"I followed these children into the woods because I knew Tituba had promised them they would fly. I thought to save them from falling, but I could not."

"How might you save them? As God saves them?"

"As I might by blocking their fall."

"Did you not dance with these children? Give an answer.

They say there was a man whispering in your ear. What did he say to you?"

"I saw nobody."

"But did you not hear?"

"We must not believe all these distracted children say."

"Do you think to find mercy by aggravating your sins?"

"I have not sinned."

The magistrates gasped at this presumption and once more moved together in conference like black slugs on a piece of rotten squash. Then Magistrate Gedney spoke. "Miranda du Val you are suspected of having the Devil's mark, for it is thought when the Devil maketh his covenant he always leaves his mark behind him to know them for his own."

"A true thing. I have not a mark."

"Let the accused be examined for a Devil's mark or some sort of teat whereon the incubus might feed."

Miranda felt a hot flush rise from her stomach that reddened her face and neck.

"Goodwife Broughton and Goodwife Cable, come forward and perform the examination for the benefit of this Court."

As the women approached, Miranda grew panicked and cried out. "I have no mark, sir."

"Give glory to God and confess then."

"But I have naught to confess."

"Do you believe these children are bewitched?"

"They may for ought I know. I have no hand in it." She faltered, and then said, "It may be the Devil appeared in my form without my knowledge."

"Then the Devil will surely show himself. Proceed."

Sarah Cable was a mean-spirited young woman with no children. She hesitated before she came close. "Please sir, bind her hands, for when she moves them about, I feel I am pinched."

"Do you fear the witness, Goody Cable?"

"Aye sir."

"Know you that we can find no way to both bind her hands and remove her clothes. Be courageous, woman, and we will protect you."

Deodat Larson, a younger man with a gentler nature, grimaced at the thought of Miranda's humiliation. "Would it not be sensible to await the dunking? That shows the greater proof," he said.

Hathorne answered, "There be no more perfect evidence than the Devil's sign." He turned to the women, who pulled Miranda's cap from her hair. His eyes glittered. "Recall sometimes it's like a teat, sometimes but a blemish spot, sometimes where the flesh has sunken."

Miranda felt her skirt loosen and fall, her woolen petticoat and her pantaloons. Shame flowed over her like a fever as Goody Cable unrolled the dark stockings from her legs, and she stood before them in her cotton shift and shivered as they began their search. She despised them all so deeply it gave her strength. The men watched with their serpent eyes, and she could smell lust like the stench from a chamber pot rising off them. At last the women looked to the Court.

"Nothing, sir."

"Search further," said John Hathorne, and a newt leapt from his mouth. "The Devil intends nothing but our utter confusion, the reason being his malice towards all men." He paused, and added in a lower voice, "And his insatiable desire to have witches as his own." Miranda, who was now bared to him, held his gaze with a defiance she could not suppress, though centipedes coiled in his cheeks. Then he said, "Let the record show the accused sheds no tears."

"I only find the dirt and rough scratches on her hands and face from having languished in prison," said Goody Broughton. "Her body shows no unnatural marks."

"Have you searched everywhere?" Jonathan Corwin's voice

was hoarse. The women looked at one another and then cast down their eyes.

"Search further."

They lifted her arms and peered at her armpits, behind her ears, beneath her breasts, into the crack of her behind; and Goody Broughton knelt on the floor and, first checking to make certain that Miranda would not smite her, gazed upwards between her legs. As Miranda endured it all, a warm mist settled over her body, while John Hathorne's breath came in milky puffs. She could see creamy maggots oozing from his lips and wriggling on his jabot, and she smiled to herself to think of his lascivious dreams that night.

Now in the pit of the jail, she allowed herself to reflect on these things. After first telling her that she would be expected to pay for her trial, her food, and even the chains that bound her, and that the cost of these things would ensure her indenture for another year, were she to confess and be pardoned, they led her to the reeking dungeon and locked her in with the other disgraced and defenseless women accused of witchcraft. Emma Williams was there with a newborn babe, now grown sickly from the foul stench. Sarah Dorset had been jailed with her child of five years, a girl with terrified eyes.

"What shall you do?" they whispered.

"'Tis a fiendish ordeal, to be sure."

"Art thou the Devil's handmaiden, Miranda?"

"Have you carnal knowledge of his secret parts? Do they differ from other men's?"

"Hush, woman, this is a girl without a husband. What knows she of a man's parts?"

"What wilt thou do, Miranda? Wilt thou swim?"

"Yea, swim, that be best. Rise like a cork and let them think thee a witch. Then confess, and beg forgiveness."

Her voice was low. "If I confess, they will take my farm."

"Aye. But 'tis better than dying."

"There you are most grievously wrong," she said. "My life and my farm are one and the same."

"What will you do? If you sink, then surely you drown."

"How can one drown and live? One cannot."

"Can you not place rocks in your pockets?"

"Hide in the brambles."

"The water will be cold."

"'Tis painful to breathe in water. I believe the chest swells and bursts."

"Hush. You will frighten the child. Is it not difficult enough?"

"What will you do, Miranda?"

She did not answer them, but her heart held fast to a feeble, reckless plan, a plan she whispered to Andrew Merriweather when he was allowed one last visit before her ordeal. It was felt by the magistrates that he alone might convince her to confess.

The day was cold and the sun was dim behind streaks of clouds. All the color had drifted off the trees and their withering leaves hung limp and motionless. Miranda stood by the side of the pond and heard the words of the magistrate.

"I adjure thee, O vessel of water, by the Father and the Son and the Holy Ghost, and by the holy resurrection and by the tremendous day of judgment, and by the four evangelists, that if this woman is guilty of this crime, either by deed or by consent, let the water cast her out to float upon the stream, violently, and do thou O vessel, rid thyself of her evil forever more. For in a contract with the Devil she hath renounced her baptism. Hence the natural antipathy between her and holy water."

On the way down the bank, Miranda stumbled, then fell. Peter Clothier, the jailer, took her arm and lifted her to her feet.

Her hands were bound by the long rope which they would use to pull her up, lifeless and no longer breathing. Because they had removed her shoes, her skirts dragged the ground, and the sharp rocks tore the soles of her feet. Nevertheless, she held her head high and dared any of the townspeople to look her in the eye. A glowing red oval hovered in the back of her mind. She saw it clearly: a round reddish light in the murky darkness.

Michael Griswald had brought his battered skiff, and he was bent over the oars, keeping the boat near the shore with a gentle nudge now and then from the edge of a frayed blade. His eyes were a mossy green and his beard a reddish brown; he was a strong man and a farmer newly sprung from Scotland, whose deepest wish was to see an end to this madness. He longed to return to work his land in peace. Miranda was glad that he was her boatman; she knew he was reasonable, and she wondered for a moment whether she could have been happy as the wife of such a man. But he was God-fearing and loath to challenge the Elders. Like all the citizens of Salem, he feared the witch trials might come to his door.

Reverend Fowler began his intonation. "O Lord, sanctify the water in this pond. Give aid if she shall plunge into the water, being innocent, and, as Thou didst liberate the three youths from the fiery furnace and didst free Susanna from the false charge, so, O Lord, bring forth this woman safe and unharmed, after it be seen that she not float but fall into the depths and be embraced by the unblemished deep. But if she be guilty and presume to plunge in her body, the Devil hardening her heart, let Thy holy justice deign to declare it, and lift her to the surface, that Thy virtue may be manifest in her body and her soul be saved thereafter by penitence and confession. And if the guilty woman shall try to hide her sins by the use of herbs, or stones, or any magic, let thy right hand deign to bring it to no account. Through thy only begotten son, our Lord Jesus Christ, who dwelleth with thee."

Miranda looked back at the crowd. With their flowing robes they resembled a flock of huge crows fluttering and pressing together for some rare bounty of seed. Andrew was far off to one side and she glimpsed the dark fear in his eyes. When he caught her look, he nodded; then, as if he could bear the sight no longer, he turned, and she watched his tall figure cross over the stream and move towards his little house in the woods.

Her gaze wandered over to the rise that separated the stream from the pond. Once, years ago, a beaver had dammed the water, and now the high intervening hill stood thick with grasses. Near the close end of the barricade she could just make out a bulge that had once been the beaver's den.

Reverend Fowler gave the Benediction of the Water: "I bless thee, O creature of water, flowing from the stream and the hill beyond, by Him who summoned thee forth from the rock, and who changed thee into wine, that no wiles of the Devil or magic of men be able to separate thee from thy virtues as a medium of judgment; but mayest thou punish the vile and the wicked, and purify the innocent, through Him whom hidden things do not escape and who sent thee in the flood over the whole earth to destroy the wicked and who will yet come to judge the quick and the dead and the world without end. Amen."

And the congregation echoed, "Amen."

At Peter's urging, Miranda climbed into the boat, scraping her shin on the gunwale, and when the bottom dipped under her weight, she fell heavily against the side. The boat rocked beneath her as she tried to balance and, with her bound hands, to gather her skirts around her knees. Once again she looked to the old dam, gauging the distance. She could see it was too damaged to house a den. Winters and summers had come and gone and collapsed it in upon itself. She shivered, her feet cold from the water sloshing in the bottom of the skiff; her heavy petticoats clung to her ankles, and the skin of her face tightened from the sting in the air. She waited, focusing on the red dish orb she could see clearly behind her eyes, while her mind fell prey to direst dreads.

Endlessly, the Reverend droned on and she could hear but snatches of his words that fell on an empty heart, for she knew no God such as the one they spoke to, no jealous or vengeful God. As her chest rose and fell with the pain of her breathing, her eyes filled with hot tears. The only gods she knew were the spirits of the forest who spoke to her often when she was with them.

She tried to hear the words for the first time with her heart and not her mind.

"O God, pour down the virtue of thy benediction that this woman may be imbued with thy grace to detect diabolical and human fallacies, to confute their inventions and arguments, and to overcome their multiform arts."

Amen, she thought, Amen.

The last face Miranda saw was that of Judah Zachery. Anguish clouded his eyes. Drained of blood, his haggard visage loomed above his black coat like the mask of death.

"Let not the innocent, we beseech Thee, be unjustly condemned, or the guilty be able to delude those who seek the truth from Thee, who art the true Light, who sees in the shadowy darkness, and who makest our darkness light."

"Who sees in the shadowy darkness," she whispered. The boat bobbed in the shallows of the pond and nudged the mud near the shore. The congregation looked on in silence.

"O Thou who perceivest hidden things and knowest what is secret, show and declare this by Thy grace and make the knowledge of the truth manifest to us who believe in Thee."

"Who perceivest hidden things . . ."

Michael began to paddle slowly to the middle of the lake, and Miranda wondered if there was a prayer of her own she could speak, some invocation to the mysteries of the forest, but none came to her.

"Untie me, Michael, I beg of you."

"Nay, lassie, I canna do such," he said, but after a pause he added, "The knot be not tight. Lean back into the boat, and rub your wrists against the ribs." She did as he bid her but was unable to free herself, and she sat up once more, straight as a sapling.

"Wilt thou jump, child?" Michael's voice was low.

"Aye . . ."

She clung to the rope as the boat moved further and further from the dam. Her head was spinning and the thought of drowning came clearly into her mind, the breathing in of water, the pain of flooded lungs. Her heart pounded in her ears, and she shivered from the cold.

Looking back at the trees, strong sentinels lining the bank, she tried to draw their strength into her body. As she watched, they blurred to flaming clouds and began to vibrate. A breeze wafted over the water, fragrant with moss and mold. Faint at first, and tentative, the gusts grew increasingly forceful, gently thrusting the boat away from the shore. She leaned back against the bow once more and rubbed the knot with renewed vigor until she felt it loosen, and she was able to wrench one hand free. Grasping the rope, not speaking, not breathing, she stared into the water, seeing her murky form in the surface, and watched Michael's oars dip and swing, creasing over and over the mirror that held the sky.

Now the wind rose and she heard it moan. Tiny ripples fluted the surface of the water, and she looked back at the seething trees. They shuddered with a sudden blast that rocked the boat, caught the side like a sheet, and forced it towards the dam. Confused, Michael looked back at the townspeople for some sign, but they were dumbstruck as well by the sudden wind that blew grit in their faces and tossed their robes to sails. Miranda stood up in the boat, rocking it slightly, placed one foot on the gunwale, drew in one great gulp of air, and jumped.

With a thundering clap in her ears, she went straight to the bottom, and the icy cold rushed under her skirt. A shower of noisy bubbles tumbled over her head. She began to rise with the air still trapped in her clothes, and she struggled to free her skirts. Down, she must stay down. She doubled up, tore off the rope which snaked around her, and dug for the mud, found roots of trees she knew had been waiting there for years. But her lungs burned with the need for air and, although she forced herself to release only a few bubbles at a time, the pain grew unbearable and she knew she would suck in the murky water and that breath would be her last. She tried to swim towards the dark shape, darker than the surrounding gloom, but she could not bear the pain, and she clawed to the surface and gasped.

If they saw her, she did not know it, and if they shouted, "She rose! She is a witch!" she never heard their cries. She saw Michael's boat looming, and she reached for it for a moment until she could ease her aching lungs, saw his startled face staring down at her, and then she dove again, and swam, kicked, squirmed deeper into the twisted and tangled masses of sticks and trunks slimy with moss and algae. Her chest ached again with a pain like a vise. Frantically she searched the dark expanse for some opening, and she beseeched the trees so long in their grave of mud to give her a sign. Where is it? Where? Is it there still? Until in the blurred water she saw the dancing circle of light softly beckoning. Then all the roots and twisted branches opened for her, loosened and made a path, and she swam, her vision growing fainter, her chest splitting, through the brackish water, the weeds and rushes, towards one pale glimmering moon. Just before her mind went blank, her head broke through the jagged hole, and she gasped, and gasped again, clung to the twigs and ooze, and before she fell into a swoon, saw the ancient weaving, knew that she was hidden in the beaver's den, abandoned but still intact, and that she was saved.

As she hovered there, she saw in her mind's eye the confusion on the shore where the townspeople stared out in disbelief, Michael paddled wildly in a circle since the wind had died now and his boat was his to master. But nothing rose to the surface, not one lone bubble, until her skirt floated up like a dark wing. There were shouts of, "There! She is there!" but when Michael pulled it into the boat it was empty as a shroud.

Judah Zachery was dumfounded. Where had she gone? Murmurings around him hinted that they had made a mistake, that she was not a witch at all. But he alone knew better, he who still bore the burn from the cherrywood switch on his palm.

It was hours later, long after the chastened and penitent townspeople had returned to their homes, and a moon had risen and danced upon the lake that held the sky, that a shivering and dripping figure climbed out of the willows. Miranda, dark with mud and the lake's benediction, appeared like a phantom at Andrew's door.

Twelve

Boston—1971

As Barnabas sat pretending to drink his Turkish coffee in the warehouse of the Boston rug dealer, he could visualize the rocky hillsides, the dull yellow sand, the women in head scarves bent over the warps of their wooden looms. But, such colors! Surely autumn must have been their muse. Yet how could that have been possible in the treeless wilderness of the Iranian plateau?

Now that he was dealing in Persian carpets, Barnabas saw Maine's rolling hills reflected in the rugs he purchased. And the rugs themselves were like fields flowering with the patterns of the woodland. Here in this cavernous room, a king's ransom of Oriental carpets—some of which hung on the walls or lay piled on the gleaming hardwood floors in masses that rose to the ceiling—pulsed with the energy of the thousands of fingers which had woven them. They wafted odors of mothballs, sheep's wool, and dust.

He watched the two Iranian boys pull back the rugs from one pile for his inspection. One by one, they unfolded those rich designs that had made the Persians the rug weavers of sultans. Barnabas was excited. He had driven to a fine shop in Boston since, through serendipity, a business card had been left unexpectedly in his door. He had come to find a carpet, one that would be the perfect replacement for the fraud in Antoinette's drawing room. With every mile he traveled, he had become ever more convinced that he had found the precise means to make amends. How could she have chosen such an ordinary rug, so inconsistent with the flawlessness of her other selections? He was baffled by her blunder. However, it afforded him an excellent opportunity to set things right. If he could find her a Tabriz— one that was two hundred years old, worn but still lovely—he would present it to her as a gift. Already he was imagining the light in her eyes when she saw it.

He waited eagerly as the boys unfolded the rugs. Every so often a pattern made his heart swell with admiration, but he had not yet found the treasure he was seeking. Medallions and tiny birds clustered on the Shiraz, stylized dragons and deer played on the fields of the old Chinese. The curlicues and leaflets drew him into visions of delicate trees arching over a pond; he saw pale pieces of sky, a sprinkling of snow, the blue-black indigo of branches, and always the wine blood color of the background. Each rug was unique, like a dream.

Barnabas could see the boys were bored. Young and still in school, they worked at the shop just as they would have at a bazaar in Isphahan or Heriz. He assumed they were sons or nephews of the owner, brought to America to supplement their education. The rugs were heavy and Barnabas watched as the two leaned in, one at each corner, and lifted back a specimen, pulled it flat, and waited patiently until he shook his head. One boy was hefty, with a fleshy face and small eyes peering out from under a wedge of black hair. The other was more attractive, lithe, his eyes shadowed with some sort of pain. His chiseled cheekbones and carved lips bore the beauty of his ancestry, an ivory complexion dipped in ashes and mauve.

Had Barnabas been on the watch for victims, either might have served. He toyed with the old memory of pursuit, lingering until dark when the shop closed and he could venture out, a stealthy tracking along the alley behind the store where they would approach the necessary black Mercedes, the family car. Then one, perhaps the slender boy with delicate features, would remember something he had forgotten, a jacket or a phone number, and return to the back entrance where the bare bulb above the heavy steel door was burned out. While he hesitated, fumbling for the lock with his key, Barnabas would leap from out of the shadows, the cape fluttering over the white neck, the cry stifled in the throat, the panic and the ensuing struggle, and the slow release of resistance, as predator melded with prey and the life force flowed from one into the other.

"Have you found anything to your liking?" Nassar Khalili entered with a new pot of coffee. After setting the tray on a small inlaid table beside Barnabas's chair, he chose a place on the sofa and looked on.

"No, nothing," Barnabas answered. "I want a Tabriz, an old one, preferably worn to the nap, and blood red."

"And nothing like that has appeared?"

"Sadly, no."

"A calamity, to be sure." Nassar was small and neat. He wore wire spectacles that teetered on the end of his nose. His suit was cut flawlessly to his slender form, and gold cufflinks glimmered in his starched cuffs. Barnabas noticed with dismay that the rims of his own shirt sleeves were soiled, and he tugged on his jacket to hide them.

"What about your private collection?"

Nassar's eyes lit up. "Do you have a price?" Barnabas could tell that he was balancing in his merchant's mind the forfeit of one of his treasures against the lure of profit. Carpets that had been in the family for generations were kept in a back room and rarely shown. They were not for the uninitiated public whose banal remarks could be painful. These were the family jewels, rare and irreplaceable.

"Let's just say . . . the right rug . . ." Barnabas left the sentence unfinished.

"Perhaps a trade?"

"Show me what you have."

Barnabas prepared himself for the contest that was to follow. For dealers of this caliber, pleasure lay in negotiation. Barnabas knew from experience that buying a fine rug was a creative enterprise, one in which the dealer always held the upper hand. As the ultimate connoisseur, Nassar alone knew the true value of the rug. However, as a tradesman, he was so enamored of the trade, he might be tempted to sacrifice rather than not make a sale. That alone gave Barnabas a possible advantage.

Nassar leaned back and crossed his legs, allowing a well-polished wingtip to protrude from his perfectly pressed black trousers. He was swarthy, but his skin shone, and lustrous black hair curled at his ears and forehead. As he lifted the small cup to his thick lips, Barnabas saw his eyes narrow behind his glasses and his body tense, revealing both anticipation and wariness. Barnabas felt a peculiar thrill at finding himself the victim for a change.

"I have a rug of this type," he said, "but it is not for sale."

"Then I do not wish to see it. I would be heartbroken."

Nassar leaned over and whispered to one of his boys, and they left the room. An indigo Boukhara with scarlet medallions lay opened on the floor, and, squinting, Barnabas could see crimson leaves scattered on black mulch, florettes dancing on decay.

"Is the Boukhara red madder, or cochineal?" he asked innocently, although he knew the answer.

"Cochineal. Very rare. Not used these days with the onset of chemical dyes." .

"That's a beetle, isn't it?"

"No, no, not a beetle. Not at all. It's *dactylopius coccus,* a scale insect that sucks from a cactus. And only the unfortunate females are crushed to make the dye."

"Such a radiant hue, and from an insect. It's hard to believe." Barnabas was content as he sat back to listen, knowing he had loosened Nassar's lips.

"I myself, when I was a boy," said Nassar, "would carefully brush the insects from the cacti into a special container. It was my job. Seventy thousand tiny bugs to make one pound of dye. They were killed by exposure to heat or, of course, sunlight, then crushed. And after mixing with henna or saffron, there it is: carmine, crimson, orange, and lake."

"Far brighter than madder?"

"Yes, madder is a duller hue, without the vibrancy of cochineal, which is like new blood flowing from the vein."

Rug after rug was laid out on the floor. Emotions and responses were choreographed so that neither participant would appear to benefit from the transaction. Barnabas was aware that his knowledge of the rugs, their history and quality, recognition of the knots per square inch at a glance, all were indispensable tools of bartering. What's more, he would be expected to quibble and procrastinate when he saw the rug he wanted. Finally he rose up and began to pace the room, feigning impatience.

"Perhaps the carpet I want is the Ardebil, only in scarlet."

Nassar laughed. "The great carpet from the Ardebil mosque? Some say it is the finest carpet ever woven. For that you must travel to London. But, I applaud your taste. Do you know the inscription on the shield?" he asked.

Barnabas knew it well, but he shook his head.

Nassar rose to the bait. "It reads:

'I have no refuge in the world other than thy threshold.
There is no protection for me other than thy door.'"

The words moved Barnabas more than he expected. He grew thoughtful for a moment, then shrugged, "So, a Mahal, perhaps?"

"At least two hundred years old."

At that moment the boys returned with a large rug, rolled and tied. The intricacy of the weave was evident from the back, the tiny knots, the lush colors. Setting the roll on the floor, they pulled loose the strings and drew the rug into a folded rectangle. Then the boys walked to opposite corners and opened the carpet like a great book.

If Barnabas failed to gasp at what he saw it was only through rigid self-control. The carpet was beautiful. Florets and palmettos entwined on a field of scarlet were framed in no less than five brilliant borders. It was faded but still luminous; worn, but its delicacy intact. Most exquisite was the medallion, as brilliant as the rose window at Chartres, glowing, as if pieced together from sparkling pieces of jeweled glass. And marvel of marvels, from each end, twisting and curving in graceful arabesques, laden with tendrils of fluted ferns, heavy with lotus blossoms, lifting in its branches multitudes of tiny birds and peacocks, bloomed a majestic tree of life.

"And I believe, my friend," Nassar began quietly, "you have a prayer rug I have been coveting, silk, a Nain, in blue and white?"

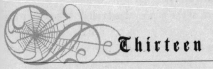

Thirteen

Collinsport—1971

$\mathscr{A}$ restive wind was tossing the trees as Barnabas, with David in the passenger seat, pulled the Bentley into the driveway in front of the Old House. The leaves rebounded, dancing in the air like giant snowflakes. There were no other cars in sight and Barnabas was both relieved and disappointed to find the place deserted. As anxious as he was to bestow his gift, he had fallen victim to embarrassment, suddenly conscious of the extravagance of his purchase. The carpet had come at a painful price; not only an exorbitant amount of money, but two of his finest specimens had been sacrificed to Nassar's shrewdness. Nevertheless, Barnabas had been determined to buy the carpet, and only now did he feel somewhat sheepish. He had already decided to say nothing of the cost to Antoinette and to insist that he had found the rug in an upstairs bedroom of Collinwood.

David helped him carry the heavy roll through the door and into the entrance. "I found the keys to the upstairs room on the key rack at home," David said, his voice lively with excitement. "Maybe one will fit the locked door."

"I don't think you should wander around," said Barnabas. "Here, help me move these chairs." David dragged the furniture to the edges of the room and watched as Barnabas pulled the string ties loose and unrolled the rug.

"You got this for Toni? Why?"

"A gesture of goodwill."

David looked down at the factory-made rug. "What's wrong with this one?"

"It's nothing but a cheap imitation."

"Yeah, but maybe she likes it."

"I don't know how she could. She's made every effort to rebuild the Old House to absolute perfection. The entire project is uncanny in its verisimilitude. Except for the carpet. The carpet was wrong, and I have remedied that oversight. I hope it will make her happy."

"I don't know," said David, reaching for a large globe of the earth that sat in the stand by the settee. Tossing it into the air, he began twirling it like a basketball on the end of his finger. "I don't know whether you should mess around with her decorating."

"David, if you drop that it will shatter. What makes you think she will be anything but pleased?"

"I just think it's a little pushy." He balanced the globe, spinning it faster, and sidestepped beneath it to keep it aloft.

"David, rugs are something I know. This way, I can make a contribution."

"Sure." David replaced the sphere unharmed and bounded for the stair. "I'm going to try my keys."

"They won't fit any more. The doors are all new," Barnabas called after him.

David's voice rang from the upstairs corridor. "I thought you said everything was exactly the same."

Barnabas lifted the new carpet over the old and worked at smoothing out the wrinkles. He replaced the chairs and coffee table and stood back to survey his handiwork. The intricate weave bloomed like an exquisite garden intertwined with the mirrored images of lotus blossoms, feathery fronds, and the flowering tree of life.

But he was not content. He felt slightly dejected as a result of his mild disagreement with David. He valued the closeness of their relationship which had developed during their trip to Salem, and already they had planned another journey to Mystic to see the old sailing ships. He realized how much he enjoyed himself in the role of David's guardian and benefactor, how much he craved the boy's banter, his unflagging good humor and enthusiasm.

Perhaps David's opinion had some merit. Perhaps it was presumptuous to have purchased another rug and discourteous to insinuate himself into Antoinette's life. Earlier that morning the search for the perfect carpet had seemed a fine idea, a generous invitation to friendship, even, he thought with growing unease, a strategy to turn her head. The night before the trip to Boston, he had lain awake with a vivid memory of her azure eyes flecked with fire, the tendrils of blond hair clinging to her neck, the soft rise of her breasts beneath the transparent cotton of her blouse. He had dared to dream, dallying with the fantasy of drawing her close, reaching for her supple body, the curve of her waist within his hand.

A harsh ringing of the iron clapper roused him from his reverie. A burst of wind from outside blew open the door and whisked a bundle of leaves through the opening. Quentin was standing in the shaft of sunlight that shone across the tiles. Dressed in faded jeans, camel cowboy boots, and a fringed leather jacket, he carried a bouquet of red roses. A paisley scarf hung loose at the neck of his shirt.

"Barnabas! What the hell are you doing here?"

"I might ask you the same question."

"I have an invitation." Quentin laughed easily. Heavy side-burns framed an angular face that hovered between handsome and sinister, an intelligent face, perceptive, bemused, exuding an almost jaded cynicism. "What about you?"

"David and I . . . were . . ."

"Aha! Just as I thought. You are trespassing, right?"

The flicker of irritation that rose inside Barnabas took him by surprise. It was not embarrassment as much as the offhand mention of an "invitation," and, of course, the flowers, that un-settled him. "And you? You say you are expected?"

"I have come to take Miss Harpignies to dinner. Is she around?"

"I haven't seen her."

"Then she is late. As usual."

Barnabas found himself annoyed to the point of rudeness. "To dinner," he repeated. "And, may I ask, are you in the habit of taking her to dinner?"

Quentin was over six feet, but he often lowered his head and glowered from under black brows. He shrugged. "We have be-come friends."

Barnabas was deeply chagrined. He blurted out, "How could you think to befriend her?"

A smile spread over Quentin's lips. The secret shared by the two men, who were both immortals, was rarely alluded to, but it always lay in waiting like a viper in a pit. Quentin owed his youthful splendor to a portrait which aged in his place, a portrait he kept hidden in a secret attic. He raised his eyebrows. "And why not?"

"You know as well as I do who she is."

"Who is she?"

"Angelique."

Quentin chuckled and shrugged. He gestured with the bou-quet as if it were a baton. "If she is, she does not know it. Some happy creatures are born again with no memory of their past lives. You and I are not so fortunate."

"You don't know that for certain. Angelique has always confounded us all with her duplicity. And you must be cognizant of the fact that, if she has returned, she has come for me."

Quentin turned away and moved to the secretary where a crystal decanter of brandy with four glasses adorned a silver tray. Laying the roses aside, he poured himself a drink. "Barnabas, I like you. I always have. But your egotism knows no limits. You are not the only man in her life."

"I am bound to her. You know she holds the key to centuries of misery. I am not speaking of a romantic intrigue, a fortnight of dalliance. I am speaking of lifetimes."

"Sorry. I don't see it that way at all. I find Antoinette charming. I see no trace of Angelique in her manner, and I think you might very well be mistaken." He sat in the wing chair and leaned back, his elegant body at ease. "At this moment she is Antoinette, and that is all I care about. I am attracted to her. And come now, who has more right to her? Think about it. She will fall in love with me. She will be deliriously happy, content and purring like a kitten. Whereas you will only betray her once again and ruin her life. Be a sport. Don't you think it might be my turn?"

Barnabas moved to the window. A dull ache spread across his chest. "You know if I find your painting I can destroy you."

"Destroy . . . destroy . . . Barnabas do you never tire of these dire threats? Really, my good man, there is more to life than one monster's power over another's. The truth is I am weary of this depraved existence. I am prepared to go at any time."

"You say that lightly, but when the moment arrives—"

"I'm not claiming I won't put up a fight. After all, I am only human." And he laughed, eyes dancing. "But tell me, in all honesty, aren't you also sick of it all?"

"You mean you haven't noticed?"

"Noticed what?"

"That I am cured."

Quentin snickered. "I thought you were looking a bit thick around the chops."

"No, truly, with the help of Dr. Hoffman, I have beaten the curse."

It was Quentin's turn to be stupefied. His smile vanished and he rose from the sofa. As he crossed to Barnabas, a wave of envy clouded his expression. "Impossible," he said. "I don't believe you."

"But it is true. You see, I am out in the daylight." He placed an arm across Quentin's shoulder and turned him to a small mirror beside the window. It gave them back images of themselves. Quentin was rakishly handsome and possessed a mysterious charisma, with something like an electrical charge that quickened his gaze, whereas Barnabas was sadly diminished, ruddy, slack-jawed. Bloodshot eyes looked out of a face where tiny broken capillaries of incipient roseola spread upwards to his temples and across his cheeks.

As soon as he saw the contrast, Barnabas was stabbed to the quick. He regretted his flash of grandiosity. He even sensed his rival's uncharacteristic sympathy as Quentin struggled for a remark that would be reassuring. "Well, old man," Quentin said finally, "I am staggered by your courage."

There was the sound of another car arriving and the unmistakably distinctive slamming of a Chevy door. Barnabas lifted the edge of the scarlet curtain, a perfect replica of the one hanging in the Old House for centuries, even to the moldy odor of the velvet and the dust on the fringe. Antoinette walked quickly across the gravel, her bobbing gait acutely familiar. She stopped when she saw the Bentley, a quizzical expression upon her face. But it was the behavior of the leaves that caught his attention, the carpet of leaves that lay on the drive. Swirling up in the wind, they cleared a path for her, and she walked through the masses on bare pavement.

When she opened the door, Barnabas froze in embarrassment. At once he realized that buying the carpet was an arrogant miscalculation, and he was completely at a loss. By now the impossibility of the situation overwhelmed him. He withdrew his handkerchief and blotted his brow, where sweat was glistening, and eased himself back into the gloom. He wanted to disappear, to merge into the paneling, to be sucked into the black hole of the fireplace.

She looked astonishing. Her blond hair hung close to her face and her eyelids were coated with black mascara which hooded her piercing blue eyes. Her dress was of cotton gauze, pale green, and sprinkled with vines. The skirt was split in the center and he caught glimpses of her long legs when she moved. Sleeves like scarves fluttered over her arms, and the bodice was shaped with a twist of fabric under her small breasts.

She saw the rug at once and exclaimed. "Oh, my God! Look at that!" Seeing Quentin, she gave him a teasing smile. "Did you?" Quentin shrugged and raised his hands, palms up, shaking his head. "Then where did it come from?" she asked.

Barnabas stepped out of the bay window. "I brought it, my dear." He hesitated. "As a gift."

"Barnabas!" she gasped, surprised at his sudden appearance.

"I thought you might like it," he said, struggling for words. "It's . . . one of a pair, two hundred years old . . . a twin for the one burned in the fire." He felt his knees buckling and he longed to sit. The nausea was rising and the core of his body flooding with heat. "I noticed the one you had chosen was not a good match."

She paused, then grimaced. "I should ask what you are doing here, but I guess with the house open all day to workmen, anyone is free to wander in and out."

"I never meant to intrude." A hopeless excuse.

She gave him a shrewd look that seemed to be sizing up his intentions, then she looked down at the carpet, the ferns and palmettos swirling around her feet, and said, "I suppose you are right. This one is much nicer."

Stung by her lack of enthusiasm, he realized in a flash that Antoinette, whoever she was, came from wealth. How else would she have been capable of purchasing the Old House? Gifts meant nothing to her, other than that they reeked of the giver. He could see her struggling with her response, weighing the memory of their last encounter, which had ended so badly, against this extravagant gesture. She sighed. "It's just that . . . I don't know. I do appreciate your generosity. But Jackie chose the other rug. The one that was here. She was insistent. I had to buy it even though, as you said, it wasn't right."

"Jackie?" Barnabas was at a loss.

"Don't get me wrong. She's been a big help with the restoration, at least until she had to go back in the hospital. Really wonderful. Going everywhere with me, tracking down paint, materials. She even found the chandelier and the clock. I have no idea how she did it. They are identical to the ones in the photos. But for some reason, she had to have that rug, and only that rug. She actually became a little manic."

"Who is Jackie?"

"Jacqueline. My daughter."

Quentin moved to take her arm. "We should go," he said. "We have a reservation."

"Sure," she said, and she smiled. She turned to Barnabas at the door. "I think I'd better keep the one I've got. Thanks anyway," she said. And they were gone.

Barnabas stood helplessly listening to the baffled beating of his heart. Oddly, he could sense her ferny aroma still in the room, the lingering scent of pine forest and tree sap.

Then from the upstairs corridor came a cry of alarm, a curse, and the sound of furniture crashing, then a door slamming. He heard David's hysterical voice.

"NO! Get away from me! Who the hell are you, you creep?"

Then another scream echoed through the hallway. Barnabas leapt for the stair but David was already catapulting down it, his eyes wide with fear, his face drained of color. The two collided at the landing then tumbled down the other set of stairs. David scrambled to his feet and, grabbing Barnabas by the coat sleeve, lunged for the door. "Come on! Run! Get in the car."

In seconds they were safe inside the vehicle with David looking back towards the house and screaming, "Start the engine! Hurry, do it, hurry!" Barnabas, propelled by David's frenzy, did as he was told, and with a screeching backwards motion, turned the car around and gunned for the highway.

After several minutes of driving down the road, during which David sat staring out the window and trembling all over, the boy finally groaned, "What . . . was that?"

"I have no idea," Barnabas answered. "Tell me what you saw."

David shook himself and sat up, then looked over at Barnabas with a bewildered expression. Feigning bravado, he gave a weak laugh, but his face was gray. He frowned and opened and closed his hands several times, as though checking to see if his fingers were broken. Then he began a tentative investigation of his features, touching his cheeks and his eyes.

"David? What did you see?"

David made a helpless gesture. "I don't know. It was dark up there, no lights, heavy curtains over the windows, and I was in that room—someone lives in that room you know, a girl—and the door opened and there was this . . . this *thing* . . . black and filthy and covered all over with dirt and grime and wet leaves. I saw some muddy work boots and a face, God . . . it was awful. The face was all decayed, ragged, the skin hanging off the bone."

"You must have been hallucinating."

"No, Barnabas, I swear I saw it."

"Thank God you're not hurt."

They rode for a short distance in silence. Gray light slipped between the trees, silvering the hood of the Bentley, and Barnabas watched the reflections of clouds fly across the mirrored surface like ghosts.

David spoke again. "Actually I had a funny feeling it—that thing—was looking for someone else, not me." After another moment he said, "The key worked. You know that? I went in the room and I saw . . . some clothes, a couple of blouses, and some shoes."

"Toni's, don't you think?"

"They were . . . like a teenager's. And there were some books, and a diary. I read a little bit of it. I know I shouldn't have done that. It was private. But I was curious. Then I heard a noise in the hallway and this . . . awful . . . hideous . . . *ghoul* came through the door."

"But who do you think it was?" Barnabas was beginning to panic.

"Jesus. I don't know. A walking corpse."

"Could it have been one of the workmen, drunk perhaps, and out of his mind?"

"Well, if it was, he was dead."

Slow comprehension crept over Barnabas like a flood of ants loose on his skin. He turned to look at David, whose hair was wild and cheeks flushed. A whistle escaped the boy's lips, and he shook his head. "God, Barnabas, that thing was scary."

"It's all right. We're safe. We'll be home soon."

Nervous and still frightened, David finally closed the door to his room, and Barnabas was able to leave the house. He was not certain whether he could find the place where he and Willie had buried the body of the workman, but he was going to try.

He parked and walked into the woods. A storm was working its way over the mountains and the wind was howling, then whistling through the empty branches of the oaks. Drifts of leaves were knee deep on the forest floor. His feet made crackling noises as he tromped through the papery mounds, and the barren limbs over his head tossed back and forth across a waning moon.

How could he have been so stupid? Tracing and retracing his steps, he cursed himself for his carelessness. He had followed Willie blindly, too tortured by the act they were perpetrating to remember where they had dug. The ground beneath the blinking moon was a lake of leaves, fluttering, heaving, like the back of a huge dragon whose hide twitched in its sleep.

Finally, he saw the lights of the hippie camp flickering in the distance. He knew finding the grave was impossible, and it was not really necessary. The leaves had claimed the burial pit, and he had done something unthinkable. He laughed bitterly to himself. How far he had fallen from the crafty resourcefulness of his old life. How reckless and senseless he had become. He had buried the undead victim of a vampire who had risen and walked again.

And now there were two.

Fourteen

Barnabas slogged towards the clearing. It was past nine o'clock. He thought of Antoinette returning after her dinner with Quentin, and of the defenseless hippies who could have no way of knowing the danger lurking in the forest. He wondered what means he had to warn them. The flower children living in tents beneath the trees were such easy pickings.

Once he heard footsteps and he jerked to a halt, listening with his faulty human ears, but he was unable to pinpoint the direction of the sound. He could hear only the last of the summer frogs croaking down by the stream and the cicada's insistent buzz. The sounds of the night were almost comforting, the insects and the toads, all frantic the season might end before they found a mate. An owl hooted the coming of snow.

The forest was burning itself out. Soon the hippies would depart and the clearing where meals were prepared, songs were sung, lovers embraced, would lie quiet once again under a still, cold blanket of stars. Deploring his diminished powers, Barnabas tried to listen beyond the wind rattling the leaves and beyond the whirring of insects, for the sound of a monster breathing.

He would be famished; his body squeezed raw with pain. No compassion would arrest his purpose, no mindfulness of age or sex, or of that spark brimming with small problems and large dreams, a spark to be abruptly extinguished in agony. He would feel only the hunger like no other—the hunger that drives starving wolves to carrion, jackals to the bones.

Nearing the camp, again he heard a sound, someone whispering under the rustle of the leaves, something murmuring and moaning. A hiss, and then a groan, and then another. Barnabas stopped, looked through the trunks, and saw a silver glade near the stream. The moonlight pierced the canopy and there were bright patches on the ground. Something was lying there, long and dark, almost buried in the leaves. It moved slightly. Barnabas recoiled in fear. In earlier days he would never have hesitated. He would have welcomed the chance to rid the world of another miserable soul. A swift thrust, a broken neck; and that would be the end. Feeling ridiculous, he picked up a large stick. Whatever it was seemed to be settling down for sleep. Perhaps he could catch it unawares.

He approached stealthily, but his footsteps in the leaves were like small explosions. The creature squirmed and rolled over. Barnabas raised the stick above his head in what he knew was an ill-advised show of strength. Gathering what was left of his nerve, he made every effort to convince himself that this act of courage was something other than a farce. But before he moved into the light, the dark shape split into two shadows, and two white faces stared at him. One was that of a young girl, flushed and sweating, her black hair a mass of tangles, her eyes huge and pale as slivers of the moon. The other face, flabbergasted and terrified, was David's.

Barnabas shrank back, praying he hadn't been seen, turned and headed back for the car. Shock and embarrassment for David drove thoughts of the campers from his mind. David was still so young! And he had left him at home, sleeping, he thought, less than an hour earlier. Alone with a girl! He reminded himself that they had been fully clothed. But they had been lying close to one another in the leaves, obviously caressing one another and kissing passionately. Her face was flushed. David must have crept out and come along the path by Widows' Hill. Surely he had been afraid. Either that, or he had forgotten all about the creature he saw in the upstairs room. So reckless! As Barnabas drove home, he imagined the monster stumbling upon the young lovers in the woods, and he felt physically ill.

Numb with indecision, Barnabas drove back to Collinwood, vaguely thinking he needed some means of defense. He parked the car and opened the door to the kitchen, then, in his nervousness, tripped on the sill and unintentionally slammed the screen. He heard voices in the drawing room: Elizabeth's droning, modulated vowels and over it, her daughter Carolyn's angry tirade.

"Fine. Think what you want. I'll do what I like, and you can't stop me."

"No, you will not. As long as you are living in this house, you will respect my wishes."

"Really, Mother. You are so old-fashioned."

"Now listen to me, young lady, you stay away from there. Your Uncle Roger would be furious if he found out."

"But why?"

"Those people are . . . why, they remind me of . . . what's his name? that Charles Manson and his cult."

"Great. Now you've turned into some kind of narrow-minded bigot!"

"I am only thinking of your welfare."

Barnabas entered the foyer and Elizabeth looked up. Her dark hair was loose around her shoulders and she was wearing her blue velvet robe with the lace collar. She had a brandy in her hand. He could tell at once that it was not her first.

"Tell her, Barnabas," said Carolyn. "They're really wonderful. They dance and play music and cook all their food outdoors on the fire. It's a wonderful way to live."

"And use our woods as their lavatory. Like savages."

"Oh, Mother . . ."

"Barnabas, please talk to Carolyn. I don't think it's safe for her to be around that gypsy encampment." Elizabeth held herself regally, but her face was strained with worry. Barnabas had a sudden vision of Carolyn in the monster's embrace, her mouth contorted in a terrified scream.

"Oh, Barnabas," said Carolyn, "you understand, don't you? I'm twenty-five years old, and I'm bored, and there's nowhere to go in town after dark but the Blue Whale. I sit in this miserable house every night and I never have any fun. We're ostracized by the community. They all think we're weird."

"Carolyn, that isn't true."

"It is, Mother, and you know it is. Why don't you want me to have any friends?" She turned to Barnabas. "You've met them, haven't you? Aren't they nice? I mean really, really sweet?"

Carolyn's long golden hair was tied back with a ribbon and her blue eyes, sparkling like amethysts in her pinched face, were glittering with tears. She was obviously quite agitated. Had she found a paramour among the love children as well? He could see her little teeth just slightly protruding from her thin mouth. Carolyn was spoiled, too dependent to pick up and leave this stifling environment and at least find some means of employment, some other life. She preferred to take shopping trips to Boston, play solitaire at home, and wallow in self-pity. But tears always upset him. Vampires could not cry.

He shrugged, feigning reflection. "Actually, I have not met the campers," he said. "I have only seen them from afar. They do, however, seem to be harmless." He realized he was trembling and leaned on the desk to steady himself. His hand brushed a wooden object, something like a toy or a puzzle, and he saw that it was an old stereopticon lying among scattered cards with paired pictures. "What have you got here?" he said in a dull voice.

"You see!" cried Carolyn. "You see how bored I am? I'm reduced to playing with some old thing I found in a drawer."

Barnabas leafed through the cards. "Any good ones?" he asked, making an effort to smile at her. He picked up the instrument thinking he remembered it vaguely. It was beautifully carved of walnut, with a curved eyepiece and a fluted handle. Turning it over he saw the date of the patent under the slender grip, 1903, and a frayed label which read, VIEW THE WORLD FROM YOUR EASY CHAIR.

"All the outdoor scenes are boring," Carolyn said. "But the Victorian ladies are so naughty. It makes you wonder who posed for the pictures."

The edge of the stereopticon was trimmed in scarlet velvet. Barnabas placed a card in the wire rack and drew the oval eyepiece with its two square lenses up to his eyes, but his hand shook so much that he had trouble focusing on the pictures. The Leaning Tower of Pisa and its cathedral sprang into view, resplendent in the sunshine, with the Appennine Mountains behind, all bathed in Italy's wonderful light. He allowed himself to visit the Taj Mahal, as well as the Tower of London, and enjoy a superb paddle wheeler on the Mississippi, all amazingly three dimensional, before he responded. "I think your mother is right," he said.

"Of course I'm right," said Elizabeth, a harsh timbre in her voice. "Roger has contacted the police. Just this morning. They have posted notices. If those . . . those derelicts don't leave, they're going to arrest them."

"But how can you throw people off someone else's property?" asked Carolyn.

"Oh, they are breaking all sorts of laws," answered her mother.

"David's been," she said quietly.

Elizabeth caught her breath. "No. You don't mean that."

Scheming little vixen, thought Barnabas, to tell on her cousin. She knows no shame. He looked away from the Great Wall of China to see Elizabeth's face, drained of color.

"He goes there all the time. He has a girlfriend."

"You can't be serious."

"Well, Mother, he is fifteen. You should be more worried if he didn't have one. You want us to both wear black and stay in the house our whole lives?"

Elizabeth reached for her pearls. "Where did it all go?" she said.

Carolyn rolled her eyes. "What's Uncle Roger's problem, anyway? Why can't he just let them be? They have to leave when it gets cold."

Barnabas put the Grand Canyon back in the box with the Parthenon. He was about to shut the cards away when he saw another set of paired photos: plump, fashionable ladies in extravagant bustle dresses lounging about in Victorian parlors. Selecting one, he slid it into the rack and peered into the eyepiece. The scene was so clear he might have been looking through a window. A woman in a black and white dress cleverly cut to accentuate her voluptuous figure stood in front of an arched doorway hung with an elaborate fringed curtain, beyond which stood a giant potted palm, and beyond that a woodland scene with a stream. The woman, who was very beautiful, and whose blond hair was piled high on her head in a Gibson Girl bouffant, stood beside a small library table in the center of the photo, holding a rose. A vase of roses on the table indicated that she was in the process of arranging a bouquet. The three dimensional effect of this card was quite remarkable. The woman was forward of and completely separate from the background, and the hand that held the rose leapt out of the frame. Barnabas noticed the rug on the floor. It was Persian, of course, and bore an uncanny resemblance to the one he had purchased for Antoinette. Tendrils and rosettes of the carpet encircled the flounces of the lady's skirt, and Barnabas spied a small black toe peeking out from under her hem. The woman looked demurely down at the flower. Sliding the picture back and forth on the rack, and trembling even more, Barnabas adjusted the focus to see her more clearly. As he did this, the woman appeared to jerk slightly forward, thrusting the flower towards him. A cold chill ran down the back of his neck. Only now did he look at her face, and instantly he recognized her.

It was at that moment that he realized the wooden handle of the stereopticon had grown warm to the touch. He released the contraption and it fell to the table.

"Barnabas, what is it?" asked Carolyn. She stared at him in surprise.

"Nothing. It's nothing," he said. "Please, listen to your mother. Don't wander in the woods. The hippies . . . it could be dangerous."

"Dangerous?" Her blue eyes pained him.

"Yes. They can't be trusted. They must be made to leave at once."

The telephone rang, which was a rarity at Collinwood, especially at such a late hour. Carolyn ran to answer it and Elizabeth gave Barnabas a look of gratitude. Carolyn returned. "It's for you," she said, her face in a pout.

He was surprised to hear Antoinette's voice on the other end of the line, especially since he had only just been looking at her image.

"I'm so glad I reached you," she said.

"What is it?"

"I wanted to let you know that Jackie saw that rug you gave us and she absolutely flipped. I've never seen her so excited."

"Really."

"She said it's the most beautiful carpet she has ever seen."

"Then you will be keeping it after all."

"If that's all right." There was a pause. "I'm sorry I was rude." Once again he was stunned by her sincerity, her lack of guile.

"Don't be silly."

"I am grateful to you. Nothing means more to me than her happiness. I was afraid she would be insulted, you see, since she had chosen the other one. But she actually lay down on the new carpet, stroked it with her fingers, and fell asleep."

He was curious. "Is she there now?"

"No, no, she's back at the camp."

His felt a pinch in his throat. He searched for some way to keep Antoinette on the line. "I see you have installed a telephone."

"Oh, no. I'm on a pay phone at the Blue Whale. I'm just about to leave."

"Oh . . ." Was she going to the woods? He was at a loss.

"You should come by for a visit sometime, if you like, and take a look at all the renovation I've done."

"Of course. That's very kind."

"Well . . . thanks again."

And he was left holding the receiver.

Later that evening when Barnabas parked on the road and stepped out of the car, strong gusts whipped the branches of the trees above his head. The whine of the wind built to a trembling crescendo, and tumbling leaves spun crazily in the air. As he walked towards the camp he drew his cape about him, feeling for the stake secreted in his coat pocket. Thinking it would offer some protection, he and Willie had cut and sharpened it in the basement, but now he felt foolish carrying it with him. Willie had been worried. "You don't need to go chase down a vampire tonight," he said.

Barnabas drew near, and he could hear the sound of a guitar and a plaintive voice singing,

> "Come all ye fair and tender maidens,
>   Be careful how ye court young men."

Smoke from the campfire wafted through the trees, acrid in the cold air.

> "They're like a star on a summer's morning;
>   They'll first appear, and then they're gone . . ."

When he reached the camp, Barnabas stood for a long moment, distressed by a peculiar sensation. It was as if he were seeing Paradise. The love children were gathered in a ring, some lying in the arms of others, some sitting on flat rocks or logs, while the singer played a soft accompaniment to a flute melody.

> "They'll tell to you . . . such lovin' stories.
>   Declare to you, their hearts are true."

The hippies, hugged by the fire's glow, were in a safe cocoon of golden light, while the dark forest lay just outside their circle like a gaping cavern.

> "Straight 'way they'll go, and court some other.
>   That's all the love they bear to you."

Loneliness gnawed a hollow in his breast; he ached to be embraced by a loving fellowship. But he was afraid he would be peculiar and ancient in their eyes, nothing but an old and foolish man.

As he entered the clearing, he saw the young faces reddened by the coals, their eyes focused on a speaker dressed in black who reclined on a blanket with his back to the path. Long ebony hair hung past his shoulders; his voice, whispery and nasal, floated over the song.

"Out there they got the madness. They got six million freeways, and smog, and cars and ugly women, and all the poison on TV, and insurance policies and taxes. Here we got music, a place to live, good hash, we got fantastic Owsley to trip on, and are we trippin'? Yeah." He leaned back, twisted his head in a circle to release his neck, and relaxed with a long sigh. His voice droned on. "We got nothin' to do but make love, and make music, while the angels sing. And children, the summer is almost over, but the family's got to stick together. The time has come to spread the young love. Just remember, so long as you've got the love in your heart, you'll never be alone. We've got to get clean of all the shit society has laid on us. We've got to forget who we were, so we can be ourselves. Don't fall for all the hype. See the beauty."

Barnabas walked into the clearing, keenly aware that he was interrupting the gathering. He saw Antoinette sitting on the other side of the fire with her guitar, her face glowing with a wild light. She smiled and waved in recognition. The speaker paused, turned on his hip, and looked up, his eyes pinpoints of flame.

"Hello, Barnabas," he said, "come join us." Barnabas was surprised to hear his name spoken until he recognized the carpenter, Jason Shaw, whom he had first seen at the Old House. But this charismatic individual was quite different from the man he remembered. His hair, no longer pulled into a ponytail, hung in a glossy curve on either side of his face, in the style of a medieval knight, shadowing his hollow cheekbones and hooding his glittering eyes. He rose and, obviously affected by some drug, swayed a little, his long hair swinging at his shoulders, and gripped Barnabas by one arm, pulled him towards the fire, and motioned him to sit.

"I'm sorry, I don't mean to intrude," Barnabas began, but Jason placed a finger over his lips and whispered, "We are all friends here. What's ours is yours, and you are welcome."

Then Antoinette came forward and took his hand, led him to her sleeping bag spread over a log, and pulled him down beside her. She eased her body close and whispered, "Jason is channeling Jesus. That's so cool, don't you think?" and she giggled softly.

Barnabas looked into her eyes and saw his own reflection, so huge were her pupils. "Here," she said, looking down at something in her hand, "there's one left." She touched her finger to her tongue and lifted up and kissed him softly. His head spun when he felt her lips. Her kiss left a bitter taste in his mouth, and he heard the wind moan in the trees. There was far-off thunder.

Barnabas watched Jason settle back on his pallet. In the firelight, his chiseled features were alabaster, his hair ebony. His crooked teeth were hidden beneath full, reddened lips, his voice a drawling monotone.

"You got to drop all the programs you got from society, all that garbage on TV. You know: you got to eat this, wear this, drive this, buy, buy, buy, and create all that poison that pollutes the land. We're not gonna listen to their lies. The boys in uniform, taught to hate gooks, taught to kill, their minds filled up with lies. We're gonna fill our minds with love, young love. Let the love come down like rain. This here's an enchanted place. We got the pure water, we got the little animals runnin' wild. You can hear the sound of the wind—"

One of the young men slapped a mosquito, and the slap was like a cap exploding.

"No, no, man," said Jason. "Please. Don't kill. Not a single living thing, not even a bug, man. Shit, they live here, too. It's their forest. We're the intruders. We're the strangers. So we got to blend in. We got to blend into the love."

Even as he spoke, a mosquito circled and landed on his arm. He waved it off, but it returned and hovered near his cheek. Gently, he fanned it away. The flower children were mesmerized. Everyone watched the mosquito as if it were an enchanted spirit. Finally it landed on the back of Jason's hand, and he pursed his lips and blew it off. He smiled all around, "See. It's so easy," he said. But the mosquito returned, floated in the air, and again it landed on his hand. This time he let it remain. Barnabas watched, as intrigued as the others, as the insect inserted its proboscis into Jason's flesh and began to drink.

"Where's the fear?" said Jason. "Where's the pain? Feelings, that's all they are, feelings that remind you you're alive."

Cramped and off-balance, Barnabas shifted on the log. "I'm sorry to interrupt your . . . congregation," he said. "But I've come here to tell all of you something important." There was grit in his mouth and the air felt thick.

Jason turned to look at him, the sliver of a frown etched between his eyebrows. Vague expressions of interest flickered across the faces of some in the group. Others seemed lost in a daze, drifting in their own fantasies.

Barnabas continued. "You must listen to me. I've come to warn you." The fire flashed as a log collapsed, and the wind blew the smoke in his direction. His eyes were stinging. "You should all pack up and leave as soon as possible," he said.

Jason shook his head and leaned over. He threw a stick on the fire. "This is our home," he said.

"But it's dangerous for you to stay."

"Why? You plan to set the pigs on us?"

"No," said Barnabas, startled by the insinuation. "It's nothing like that. The police have nothing to do with this."

"Then it's the Collins clan, wanting their land back, right? It's Toni's land, bro'. Right, hon?"

Toni gave a little shrug and smiled at Barnabas, watching for his reaction. The wind moaned again, and he thought he felt raindrops.

"And we made this." Jason swept his arm in a wide arc towards the fire ring, the tents and hammocks, the mirrors. "We put that flash in the trees." One of the boys laughed and mimicked the gesture, lifting his arm in the air. Then others did the same, until the whole band of hippies was making sweeping circles in the firelight, as if they were dancers in some ragged corps de ballet.

"If you must know," said Barnabas, weighing his words carefully, "I'm afraid there's a killer on the loose."

There was moment of silence.

Then Jason leapt up. "You bet your ass there is," he said, teetering. "More than one. The body killers and soul killers of the marketplace, the greedy ones that feed on the masses, eating them alive. Profit. That's all they live for. All the young love, all the young boys, programmed to be marines, to hate gooks and kill them with M-16s, like so many John Waynes. They make it look heroic, an All-American dude, a hero, dig? Just killin' and killin'. But the man on the cross, he just loved. He just submitted to the love. That's all his body carried was the love."

"Not just an ordinary killer. A monster, somewhere in these woods," Barnabas said. He felt Toni's grip on his arm tighten and he looked down at her. Her eyes were luminous.

Jason began to pace like a restless panther in a cage. "We know this monster," he said in a hoarse whisper.

Barnabas wondered if it could be true. "You've seen him?"

"He walks among us. He waits for us in the dark while we sleep."

"You're not afraid?"

"You got to look past the fear. You see, if I ever had a philosophy, it's *don't think*. The minute you think, you're divided in your mind. You start to look inside and it scares you what you see." He lifted his hand and stared at his wrist, turning it over and back. "You see the blood flowing in your veins. You hear your heart beat."

The guitar strummed a stronger rhythm and Barnabas could see the musician sitting just outside the circle of light, the girl with the flute resting against his knee. Jason came over to where Toni sat beside Barnabas and leaned into her. He cupped a hand under her neck and drew her mouth to his. His tongue slithered over her lips and prodded between her teeth. Barnabas looked away.

"What are you afraid of?" said Jason. "She's a woman. She's scared someone's gonna see her game. She hides behind her beauty. You know what I think, man? I think you're afraid of your own secret. But that's okay. Your fear is what helps you see who you are." Jason began to twirl slowly. Rain was falling now in light drops.

"Stoke the fire! Come on, man, stoke the fire." He pointed to a pile of sticks beside Barnabas, where an ax lay against some chopped logs. Barnabas rose, at first confused, and then realized he was meant to put some wood on the flames. But before he could reach for a piece of kindling, Jason grew impatient, lunged towards him, and pushed him aside. Then, with dexterous grace, he scooped up several logs and placed them with care, nudging each into a void where it would catch and flare. Even under the influence of the drug, his movements were fluid, his slender legs and arms like those of a gymnast.

The fire flashed and roared, and Barnabas could feel the heat rising within him, and frustration as well. A creature from another realm walked in the dark forest, perhaps as close as the ring of trees. Another was hunting now, flying under the moonlit clouds. And a third lay in waiting in his own body. He stood his hands hanging at his sides.

Jason moved easily to the music, his sinuous movements ap-ing the flute's high vibrato. He came close to Barnabas, swaying as he glared at him.

"The monster is in us all," he said. "Don't you think I see it in you?"

Barnabas was stunned to silence. In a low voice, more to himself than to anyone, he said, "Do you not fear the Undead?"

But Jason heard the words. "The Undead?" he said. "*We* are the undead. Aren't we, children? Because we will live forever. The young love will never die."

Delighted by the phrase "We are the undead," flung across the timbre of the guitar, several of the campers rose to their feet. Charmed by the sound, as though poetry clung to the words, as if some lyric to a song performed by a rock band from hell cap-tured their fancies, first one, then another, reached for a partner, laughed, staggered, all eager to dance. Bodies stooped and twirled, then nestled together, hips meshed, as sprays from the fire whirled in the air. It was a bonfire now, battling the raindrops coming down in a fine mist. The guitar player coaxed a hard rhythm from his instrument, and the flute whined a high, thin melody, as soft rain began to fall.

"We are the non-dead, we are the undead, and we shall never die," cried a girl and, reaching for a spent ember, brandished it aloft like a baton. When she saw the black on her hands, she laughed and smeared her face with the charcoal. The other dancers followed her lead and, delighted by her sooty mask, transformed themselves into cavorting minstrels, wide eyes peer-ing from faces streaked with pitch. Some ran into the forest and returned with armloads of leaves which they tossed into the air, and the leaves fell like ashes, clung to damp bodies and tangled hair. Where once there had been flower children, now garish

pparitions appeared, and they cried again and again, "We are
he Undead. We shall never die."

Barnabas knew he was witnessing a celebration as old as Di-
onysus, as innocent as child's play, and he was helpless to stop
hem, even though his body ached with anxiety. One girl drew
off her blouse, and another pulled a camisole over her head. Boys,
lready shirtless, tugged wet bodies into squirming embraces. He
could see only odd pieces of clothing on dancing shapes: a ruffled
kirt, a pair of fringed chaps, a soft, shimmering veil. A girl held
er arms high above her head and twirled like a gypsy, her dark
air falling down her back, her rounded breasts an adornment
beneath her beads, her crimson nipples like jewels. Feeling light-
headed, he sat back on a log and watched her. Beauty. All was
beauty. There was nothing more than this.

He envied the couples, their flying hair, their burnished skin.
Moving in shadow play around the fire, shifting between curtains
of raindrops, the bodies intertwined and fell apart, were indis-
tinguishable from one another, and he could see only jeans that
shaped a thigh, a garland of flowers, a spangled scarf, an ankle
bracelet jingling on a slender foot.

"Life is music. Life is love," someone cried out, and a chorus repeated the refrain to the throbbing guitar, "Life is love.
Life is light. We are the Undead." And someone giggled hys-
terically. Barnabas was caught between Puritan and voyeur, his
own debased existence somehow absolved by the scene. What's
more, his warnings had fallen on deaf ears.

Toni stood before him. She was still clothed, and her silhouette blotted the light from the fire. She leaned in and took his
hands. "Come and dance," she said, and tugged on his fingers,
laughing as he shrank back in embarrassment. Shadows of the
fire played across the clearing, and Barnabas thought he should
leave but he could not make himself. The smoke stung his eyes;
he squeezed them shut to ease the pain, and to his surprise, he

felt hot tears. When he opened them again, Jason was standing beside Toni, his pupils glowing as he stared down at her. Obviously, he had some claim on her. Still seated on the log, Barnabas watched Jason lift a hand and touch her cheek. She swayed slightly and seemed riveted, gazing into Jason's eyes for a long moment while the fire glowed between them. Then there was a bright streak of lightning and a far-off rumble. The rain fell gently now, tap-tapping on the leaves still clinging to the trees as if an invisible hand knocked on the forest door. Then another clap of thunder sent the campers scampering as they frantically unzipped flies and scrambled inside their canvas caves, and Jason, too, was gone. Antoinette turned to Barnabas, took his hand and said, "Come on." Somehow he got to his feet and followed her to her tent.

His first thought was that she was offering him a place out of the rain, but she reached for him and pulled him down beside her. He could not see her smile but he could feel its warmth in the closed space, and he breathed in her scent, vanilla and fern, mingled with the musk of her perspiration. He tasted the damp of her cheek against his mouth and, when she turned her lips to his, she was more liquid than flesh as she moved with amazing tenderness, nestled her body within the curve of his, and tugged his arms so that, haltingly, they embraced her. She did all this with such skill that he had a fleeting thought of harlots he had known and fed on in another life. She was all sweetness and, although he knew her eagerness was brought on by the drugs, he could not help but be aroused. It was natural to gather her to him when he felt her arms encircle his neck and her body spring against his. Confusion rioted in his brain. He forced himself to pull away but she shivered and pressed closer. Indecision, he thought, is the common state of man. How dimly he remembered the clear, cold reason of his vampire life. In his languorous state he was too weak to resist. She was deft, skilled, as free as water flowing in a stream. And then, amazingly, he wanted her. His hands swam over her urging her on. He could smell the balsam in her hair and the odor of the aging canvas above their heads as the rain drummed down on the tent. The sound was melodic, oddly soothing and mesmerizing. It was Angelique lying in his arms, her glow palpable and radiating like the heat from a stone left in the sun. Gently, she touched his cheek, his neck, his lips; then she curled to him, and he was struck with a sudden longing.

Not since those times when he had been forced by circumstances to go without blood for days could he recall a hunger such as this; and the anticipation of release after the ache of denial, when his breath was hot above the jugular just before he gave way and sank his fangs, rang in his body like a gong. As he gathered her to him, those same pangs of guilt made him hesitate. Angelique was his nemesis, and intimacy with her could only lead to disaster. He must desist. But reluctance flared like an ember, then dimmed, until it was a faint pinpoint of light, and in its place came a flood of emotion that could only be called gratitude. He fell from a great height into her arms.

He never knew when she removed her clothes, but when he finally held her against him, she was warmer than he had thought possible, supple and merging, and he pressed the thin film of her skin with his fingers, his tongue, his kisses, his teeth. He looked up to see her dark form, her hair wild in the faint light, her parted lips, her rapturous expression, and in that moment, he knew she loved him still. She let go his mouth, gasping, and whimpered as he buried his face in her neck. She moaned when she felt his breath, and then his teeth, her fingertips prodding the back of his shoulders, and she arched, presenting a fluttering pulse to his hunger. He was tempted, but it was all of her he wanted; and breathing with her was like coming back to life, as the rain pounded on the roof.

When he returned to his senses, he was lying near the opening of the tent, watching the faint light of dawn appear in the sky. Exhausted, but suffused with warmth, he lay staring at, but not seeing, a couple entwined on the ground. Antoinette roused to whisper, "Close the flap or the rain will come in."

He sat up to reach for the zipper and looked out. The rain still fell in bursts, and a bolt of lightning exposed the two near the blackened fire ring. The boy had the girl pinned beneath him, his hands pressed against her shoulders, her legs squeezed between his knees. His lovemaking seemed more brutal than necessary, and the girl tossed her head back and forth as though in pain. Barnabas felt Toni reach for him, but he could not look away from the couple. The boy's dark head and shoulders rose and fell as the girl struggled to pull free, and his movements were less those of a lover and more those of a beast who was rhythmically licking and feeding. Barnabas leaned out of the tent. Another bolt of lightning brightened the gloom. It was then he saw the torn overalls, the faded plaid beneath a coating of mud and leaves, and, to his horror, the heavy work boots. The girl's eyes, which moments earlier had appeared glazed with lust, were vacant. Blood oozed at her throat, and her limp body shuddered and collapsed as the dark creature raised his head, and then his shoulders, then lowered himself again to feed.

Jerking on his clothes, Barnabas jostled Toni and almost stepped on her when he ducked out of the tent, and she uttered a cry like a struck child. He could barely stand, and he was afraid he was going to be sick. Uncertain of what he should do, his heart beating wildly, his brain blurred, he looked around in helpless bewilderment. He could barely make out the pair on the ground, but he staggered towards where they lay. When lightning flared again, he saw the glinting blade of the ax by the woodpile. In desperation, he jerked it up. The wooden handle was wrapped with tape and the tool weighty in his hand. The odor of blood came to him now, and for the first time in centuries the smell repulsed him. His fingers closed on the grip and he took another clumsy step. Oblivious, the creature rose up, then fell against the girl with one more thrust of its head.

Barnabas thought he might pass out. There was a roar in his ears, and beneath it he could hear the sucking sounds of the beast. Forcing himself to breathe, Barnabas edged towards the monster, and—his body shot through with panic—he came behind it, stood with legs apart, and raised the ax above his head. *Deep,* he thought. *It must go deep. He is stronger than I am.* Barely able to make it out, he aimed for a space between the straps of the overalls. *It must reach the heart.* And, with a shudder, he swung with all his strength and let it fly. There was a sickening thud, and a grunt. The monster sprawled on the girl, his legs rigid, his arms flat, and a slow black stain oozed beside the blade and spread over the back of his shirt.

Barnabas stood panting, waiting, numbly conscious of some of the campers sneaking out of their tents. Daylight glimmered and dull shadows flickered over the clearing. Breathing hard, shaking his head to clear it, Barnabas backed away.

The creature did not move. It lay covering the girl, its face against her neck. Her glassy eyes stared over its head into the dim light. Barnabas cast about again for some new weapon. The stake—where was it now? He must have dropped it by the rock where he had been sitting. Keeping an eye on the fallen creature, he felt around in the dirt by the fire ring, rummaged under his cape, patted the wet ground, but his hand closed on a tent pole and, after several jerks, he pulled it loose. The creature was still. Desperate now, he knew he must have the stake to finish it off and he kept searching. He crept nearer to Toni's tent, scouring the ground, and back towards the fire, shuffling with his shoes, but the sharpened stick he needed had disappeared.

And so he stood panting, feeling slightly ridiculous, the tent pole in his hand, like a primitive hunter at the cave of a dying bear. His heart slowed its ricocheting in his chest, and his breathing grew less ragged. All was quiet but the pattering of the rain.

The monster shuddered and groaned, then hunched to its knees. It raised its torso until it was a dark hulk, the ax protruding from its back like a pump handle. It swayed, then turned, and lurching as though blind, lumbered forward. Again, a flash of lightning lit its face, smeared with the girl's blood, and flesh was hanging from a naked skull. But it was the eyes that gave it away. They were hollows of madness. This, Barnabas thought bitterly—remembering the hippies' song—this is the Undead. In that split second of brightness, he saw maggots crawling from its empty eye sockets, and the ruin of its mouth, a hole with no lips, only black ooze and teeth protruding from the bone. It came as though automated, its movements clumsy and heavy, and exuded the stench of rotted fish, as phlegm bubbled up from its insides in a guttural wheeze.

Barnabas looked furtively around for Jason, or one of the hippies. Stupidly, he spoke to the creature. His voice was harsh and helpless in his ears. "Stay back! Don't come nearer." He jammed the tent stake against a rock, sharpened end pointing outward, desperately hoping the thing would fall upon it. But before he could make it fast, the flimsy rod went flying and the fiend reached for Barnabas, took hold of him, and knocked him to the ground. He gasped as it crawled up him, its breath reeking of offal. Barnabas cried out, and pushed against it, struggled with all his strength, his hands batting the air, clawing at the dirt, digging into the leaves, where, miraculously, they came upon the stake and his fingers closed around it. The creature rose up, and Barnabas froze in an agony of fear knowing it would fall upon his face and feed. With a mighty heave, he jerked the sharpened shaft between them, and jammed the stake into its chest, pierced it as it fell. But the ribs snapped, and his hands plunged into slime.

In his dream, the weight was gone, and the putrid odor was replaced by a fragrance of ferns and hemlocks. Fingers as soft as petals stroked his face, and he whispered Antoinette's name. He must have tried to rise because he fell back hard, and the wind was knocked out of him. For a moment he couldn't breathe, and he panicked, certain he would die from lack of air. Smothered by a fog, drowning in an airless cave, he was suffocated by a soft gauze, filmy and diaphanous, but strong as steel. He thought he would never be able to breathe, and would surely perish, when he felt the sharp teeth pierce his neck, and air rushed into his throat as blood rushed from his veins.

When Barnabas awoke, he was wrapped in a sleeping bag and lying in Toni's tent. He could smell what must have been his own vomit. She was bathing his face with a rag, and he heard her wring the cloth out in a basin and felt the coolness against his skin. He jerked, and shuddered, and sat up, spilling some of the water and knocking her aside.

"Where is it? I must stop it—"

"No, he's gone," Toni whispered. "Sh-h-h-h, it's okay. Don't worry. He's dead." She was amazingly calm.

He fell back and looked into her face. She no longer seemed drugged, and her smile reminded him once more of Angelique when he had first met her. But he knew he had only dreamed it was she. He opened his mouth to speak, but no words came. Toni leaned close to him and said in a hushed voice, "A couple of the guys dragged him out of the clearing and up the path towards the cliff. A few minutes later, after everyone came back to the camp, Jackie showed up. She was very upset."

"Upset?"

"Yeah, sh-h-h-h. She's asleep." She looked across his body and nodded. Only then did Barnabas realize Jackie lay beside him, her face hidden by black hair tumbling over the top of her sleeping bag. He could hear her breathing softly. Toni whispered, "She said she saw what she thought was a wild beast running through the woods, and you know she is fearless. She followed his trail into the trees. But then he ran towards the cliff, and she saw him standing on the ledge, his shape against the moon, teetering there, and before she could get to him, he fell, all the way down on the rocks. She said he just sort of exploded, you know, on the sand, and the waves washed him away like he was driftwood."

"She chased him?"

Toni nodded, grimacing. "Crazy, huh? She saw him fall."

"So . . . he's gone."

"Yeah, he's dead. Some vagrant, I guess, wandered into our camp. And everyone knows it was you who fought him and drove him away. We are all so grateful to you."

"You think it was a vagrant?"

"Well, we all dropped acid. We could have imagined anything, right?" She shrugged and wrung the rag again, hard, as though keeping herself distracted.

"What happened to the girl he was . . . ?"

"Someone went and called an ambulance and they came and took her to the hospital."

"Is she alive?"

"She was barely breathing." Toni sighed and looked out of the tent. The morning light shone on her skin and her eyelashes fluttered against her cheeks. His hunger for her was fresh, but with Jackie there he was reluctant to embrace her. He wondered how long it would be before he had the strength to love er again. Possibly his term in the natural world would soon be nished. He reached for her hand, but she pulled away, and fted the pan of water.

"I should pitch this out," she said. She gave a little laugh, ooked over at him, and shook her head. She seemed embarrassed. Last night was wild," she said, and flashed him a sheepish grin efore she crawled out of the tent.

Barnabas lay thinking of the chaos of the night, the turnoil of ecstasy and terror. But his memory of Antoinette was lear. He searched for words that would express his gratitude nd his great joy. When she returned, she sat beside him and ulled her knees up, her arms encircling them. He took one of er hands, kissed it, and whispered, "You are so beautiful."

She smiled. "You should sleep," she said. "He bit you pretty ad on the neck. I'll be back in a little while." She nodded towards Jackie. "Try not to wake her." Jackie's breathing was barely udible, faint and even, the sleep of a child. The nightmare had lready faded from her thoughts, whereas vivid images kept flying through his brain.

Antoinette was right; he needed to rest more than anything. He needed sleep. His body ached with a pain deep in his bones, nd a weakness that left him limp with something close to delirium. He was not certain he could stand. He lay thinking of her ast remark, that he had been bitten. He remembered the monster alling on him. What was the creature that attacked him? What ad the workman become? A vampire? A ghoul? Then he remembered the dream. By the time his fingers found the two puncture wounds, his heart was pounding again. He forced himself to endure the sting as he traced each wound, circling, pressing down. Both were uniquely round, and deep.

We all resist fate, he thought. Even when it comes crashing owards us like a meteor out of the cosmos, we duck, or swerve, or dive underground. But our fate is the inevitable result of choices we have made, dreamed and juggled, and held close to our hearts.

Fate could become a celebration, something to be embraced, but when he had willed himself back to mortality, had he chosen a fate that was not his true path? Now, after suffering the day-to-day desperation that is the human condition, the dumb show, the helplessness, did he not see with stunning clarity what he was, who he was meant to be? Was he destined to remain a vampire, cold at heart, calculating, but with the power to shape his world? Or was this new love the answer? And was it worth it in the end?

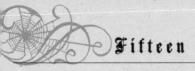

Fifteen

Driving back to Collinwood, Barnabas was preoccupied with thoughts of Antoinette, and now he questioned the wisdom of his night with her. Even though he was certain she had been the instigator, nevertheless he had responded. Was the grip of the past never to tire of tormenting him? Or was he simply the hapless victim of another human frailty, susceptible to sexual desire, weak and easily compromised, incapable of making wise decisions.

Speaking with her in the library at Salem, buying her the expensive carpet, seeing her leave for dinner with Quentin, all these scenes had created a tempest in his brain. And then to become the sudden object of her affections, even though she was compromised by hallucinogens, was too confusing. His head felt waterlogged, and a thick mass throbbed in his sinuses.

He endeavored to comprehend his options. The intimacy—bliss—he had missed for hundreds of years was now his to

explore and command. For the first time since the cure bega
his body was alive, truly alive, with sensations of euphoria. H
missed her already. Not to be ignored, however, was the ver
real threat of a demon hovering on the sidelines, a creature—
he knew only too well—without conscience, without pity. Eve
if the vampire's ghoulish creation were gone, there was still th
greater threat of the vampire himself, an individual with nothir
but contempt for emotions such as the ones pulsing in his hear
a fiend apart, distant and cold, a monster who must, at all cost
be destroyed.

And was he both? Was it possible that he housed both i
his being?

Julia entered his room carrying her medical case. She flung
on the table by the window and turned to look at Barnaba
He could feel her frenetic energy when she moved.

"I know I have missed one of my shots," he said.

"Yes. Without your medication, you might revert."

"I am aware of that."

"Or the discomfort will be much worse."

He sighed and lay back on the bed. He found himself sta
ing at a large print on the wall, a reproduction of a Turner—th
painting of a ship in a storm at sea. He wished himself far awa

"But that's not what I have come to speak to you about
Julia said, her mood softening. Barnabas shifted his gaze t
look up at her. She was less attractive than he had ever seen he
gaunt and sallow-skinned. Her auburn hair was unkempt, an
he was surprised to see gray at the roots. He had a queasy fee
ing.

"What is it?" he asked.

She raised a hand to her brow and rubbed her temple. "Th
is so difficult for me."

"Please," he said, with effort, "tell me what is on your mind

His encouragement seemed to renew her resolve. She drew
erself up with a sigh. "Months ago you proposed marriage."

Ah, that was it. Marriage once again.

Julia continued in her halting voice. "Although I knew the
roblems were formidable, I consented. I have always loved you.
inding a cure for you has given meaning to my life."

"Julia, I have always said you are a brilliant physician."

She sat on the bed and placed her hand over his. Her voice
rew gentle. "You once suggested we go to Martinique. To search
r a new elixir. But I feel a reluctance in you, perhaps a change
f heart."

Uncanny, he thought, that on this night of all nights, she
ould bring up these intimate concerns. How the urge for sur-
val fuels us all, from the lowly mosquito to the undying brute.
his woman, whom he knew as intimately as he knew anyone,
as still a stranger to his feelings. Until this moment, she had
ontinued to ignore the obvious strain between them. And as
rateful as he felt, as much as he might feel he should, he could
ot love her.

"Barnabas, what do you intend to do?"

She waited while silence settled in the room. For some rea-
on the misery she felt only left him weary. For an instant he
rifted off, then woke with a start, to find her still there looking
t him. He strove for compassion. "Julia," he said, "I know, with-
ut your help, I have no hope of a natural life."

"But I have told you I'm certain that the cure will be suc-
essful, and the injections will no longer be necessary."

"Perhaps, my dear, that is so. But perhaps it is not so. I may
e forced to rely on you for many years."

"And I will care for you—with all my heart."

He looked at her face in the light of the bedside lamp. Com-
ared to the freshness of Antoinette's beauty, her angular features
ere worn and drawn, and she exuded a musty odor, perhaps
rom cigarettes. He could see her gaunt figure beneath her skirt,

her bony hips and sunken chest. Sensing her distress, he felt
flutter of sympathy. She would be as faithful as the rising su
as loyal as a soldier to his captain. The problem was these consid
erations no longer awakened his energies. Her sacrifices arouse
guilt, even a sense of despair, and no matter how deeply he du
he could not unearth that noble determination required to re
spond to her plea.

"Julia," he said, "I will be eternally grateful to you. Mo
than anything, I longed for the human existence stolen from n
so long ago. But time has changed everything. I am no long
that young soldier in New England, nor can I ever be. I am
vampire."

"Barnabas, don't—"

"I can't continue to allow you to use your own blood. I ca
see it is making you ill. My God, I might as well have draine
you in the old way."

She smiled sadly, then waved her hand in a gesture of dis
missal. "It's just that they became suspicious . . . at the clinic . .
asking questions. Don't worry. I'll be fine."

"But my heart aches for you. Julia, listen to me." She lifte
her gaze. He could see the tiny capillaries in her eyes, the dul
ing of her irises. As difficult as it would be for her, this was th
time to tell her the truth, the truth which would, if nothin
else, free him from her custody. He set his teeth and again stare
at the ceiling.

"I have been bitten again," he said.

He heard her catch her breath.

"And this time I intend to let it stay." A charge of exciteme
flowed through him as he spoke.

Her face went gray. "But that's impossible—let me see
Rising and moving to him, she leaned in and turned back hi
collar. "Where?" she said. "There is nothing there. Where wer
you bitten?"

Barnabas felt for the wound. To his amazement, it wa

healed. The skin was smooth to his touch. Had he imagined it? "But, I thought . . ." He floundered in confusion. "I meant to say . . ."

"What?"

"I want to stop the injections."

She sucked the edge of one lip, then rose, turned her back, and walked unsteadily to the table. She opened her valise.

"Did you hear what I said?"

"What makes you think you can stop?"

"As you just pointed out, without the elixir I will simply return to my vampire life."

She lifted her hands in a limp gesture, her fingers spread, then rubbed them upon her skirt as if to remove a stain. Slowly, she shook her head.

"Julia . . . ?"

"When we embarked on the cure, I think we may have relinquished that possibility, since . . . well, since I never expected it to arise."

"What do you mean? What about the power of the curse?"

She turned to him. "Barnabas, you . . . you cannot go back. Without the injections you might revert, that is so, but then again, you might not."

"But you have hounded me, always saying that I would."

"I know, but—but I have never done this before. I'm really not sure what would happen if you stopped the medication."

He stared at her in disbelief. Never had he thought he would want to reverse her machinations. But he had always believed the possibility was there. He had allowed her to meddle in his destiny.

"Then what would happen?"

"You could die."

"That can't be true! You say these things to bind me to you. In the end you are like everyone else."

She flinched at the insult but she said nothing, and a new

wave of guilt rose in his heart while shadows upon shadows fell across his mind. He watched in a stupor as she reached in her valise and removed the hypodermic. Outside the window a wind moaned in the trees, and heavy branches brushed against the casement. Julia's movements were quick, and Barnabas heard the familiar clicking sounds of the elixir being drawn into the vial. Dumbly he submitted to the needle. Julia sat in the chair opposite the bed. The glow from the lamp cast a cold, round circle of empty light upon the carpet between them. Barnabas stared at it as though it might catch fire. But it remained flat and lifeless.

Then Julia did something he had never seen her do. She wept. At first he only glimpsed redness in her eyes, and his heart sank; but then she put her face in her hands and her shoulders shook with sobs. He thought in a flash of the thousands of human men who found themselves in this predicament, humbled by a weeping woman. The enlightenment and sophistication of two hundred years shrank in this moment to a condition of desperation and helplessness.

"Come now, you mustn't cry," he said. His voice seemed very far away. His shoulders hunched, and his body felt sluggish. He could barely lift his head. Shame flooded him, but he felt he must free himself of her presence, even if it required a lie. "How could you think otherwise? We will marry. And we will try to be happy." A wistful smile broke across her face. Quickly, he took her hand. "Let me rest," he said. "We will speak of these things in the morning."

She looked at him, her faced bathed in melancholy, and after a long moment she said, "No, you are right, Barnabas. I have been manipulative and controlling. I will not pester you any more. From now on, I will respect your wishes. That was the last injection I will give you."

He was stunned.

She rose and moved to the table. "Whatever will come, will come."

Numbly he watched as she replaced the needle in her medical case and snapped it shut. She walked to the door and left his room without looking back, just as he felt the heat rise in his core and the pain begin.

Sixteen

The next morning Barnabas rose before dawn and let himself out the back kitchen door. Dire dreams had plagued his sleep, and his skin itched as if he had been chewed all through the night by lice. The air was cold and clear, and a quarter moon lay on its back just above the trees.

He had with him a hammer and a stake. He had decided he would track the vampire, even in his mortal state. His plan was to wait until daylight was near, and try to catch a glimpse of it on its way to its lair. He knew what its habits would be: stealth, wariness, gnawing hollowness if it had gone hungry, a throbbing in its veins if it had fed. It must hunt the woods behind Collinwood, or the docks at Collinsport, just as he had done. And somewhere it must sleep. He thought perhaps a cave deep in the woods.

Longing for Antoinette had now reached a crescendo of torture. Her spell had wrapped itself around his heart, and he floundered in a miasma of self-doubt and feelings of worthlessness. His first worry was the difference in their ages. She must be, he had decided, thirty-five or so, in the bloom of womanly beauty, and he—now that his aging had begun, and tormented him more every day—was much older. He remembered her in the drawing room of the Old House, standing on the carpet he had bought for her, surrounded by autumn colors, the glittering birds and vines, the branches of the tree of life. She was there in her apple green dress, the most vivid color in the room, dazzling, incandescent, with her ferny odor, her turquoise eyes, her flirtatious smile, her golden hair lit by the sun streaming in the window. A few days earlier he had only one desire, to destroy her by any means possible; and now he could only wonder at his abandonment to the ache in his breast.

He lifted his hands and stared at the veins, the horrid brown freckles, the crepy skin. As a severed limb still aches with phantom pain, a face grown haggard still holds a shadow of that once bright visage of youth. This morning he had searched for his own vanished beauty hidden in the mirror. Should he go to her? Would she come to him? What joy it would be if he were to wake to find her in his arms, or even standing by his window, looking over at him, the curtains softly flowing at her back, the moon over one shoulder.

He was in the woods again, incapable of staying away, trudging through what he now thought of as Antoinette's forest, drinking in the beauty surrounding him with a ravenous hunger for all things alive. He looked up at the trees, their arms aloft like giant dancers, black branches exposing pieces of the gray sky. He stumbled over roots clutching the earth with gnarled fingers. He drew in delights that had eluded him until now, newly revealed to the eyes of a lover, to a soul so filled with wonder it gave him pain. It was as though every tree, every leaf, were perfectly created. He stared at the carpet of fallen leaves at his feet and he was amazed, as he had been by her body, by the colors: rose, chartreuse, vermilion, chocolate, and ruby red, and by the infinite shapes: oval, jagged, knife blade, star, arrowhead, and heart.

He heard for the first time all the bird calls: harsh chirps and whistles, insistent repetitive kissing sounds, little chirrups, clicks, and smacks. He saw creepers crawling over smaller trees, their tendrils woven into branches, merging and clinging, living in symbiotic union. And he gazed up at the white trunks of birches with dappled canopies of glittering coins lit by the sun. Such wealth! As though from some palace in the sky, Olympia's treasure had spilled forth.

He was consumed with an exuberant passion of such intensity he thought his body would break in half. He had a vision of their life together, a fantasy he wanted more than anything: he, entirely human, strong, and filled with a man's desires, his body sprung with the brash optimism of his lost youth, raw with bravado and recklessness, savoring the riotous sense of conquest. Why had she come so easily? So brimming with eagerness. He had never expected that. Perhaps—could it be? He dared to hope he still retained some of his former charm, the allure and mystery that had sustained him through the centuries. And another, more desperate hope lay deeper in his consciousness. If she should be his old enemy, even though she had no memory of it, she loved him still. If she could be nudged into remembering—through gentle and persuasive affection, rather than malevolence or suspicion then—of all miracles this would be the most magical—perhaps she could lift the curse—the insidious curse that had made him a vampire—and set him free.

He was renewed with reckless determination, and to his surprise, he was filled with tenderness for the flower children and their camp. A demon threatened them all: the peaceful clearing called Paradise; the young lovers, David and Jacqueline, with all the world before them; and, most of all, his Antoinette. None lived more sufficient to this particular task than he. He who had lived almost two hundred years in this guise could not allow himself to be dismayed or frightened by a fledgling monster, afraid to show its face, and—Barnabas suddenly thought—new to the breed.

After some time he reached the Old House, and he decided, before he went further, to make another visit to the basement. The deserted halls of his old mansion whispered a welcome. Odors of aging varnish, musty velvets, and charred candlewicks assailed his nostrils. It could easily have been a hundred years ago. Once again he was astonished by the restoration, eerie and familiar in its perfection. The stairs to the secret room creaked from his step in the same complaining manner.

He was surprised to see that his coffin was open. It had been pushed to one corner of the room, and the top propped back by a fire tong. The satin lining was ripped out and only the bare boards remained. Someone was refurbishing his casket. He laughed out loud—a hollow, bitter laugh that echoed to the back walls of his old sanctuary. Who would do such a thing? The padding had been serviceable enough, the delicate quilting even comfortable. He was dumfounded by the absurdity, but he knew his feelings were ridiculous. It was a sign from the world of mankind. Julia had been wise when she said that he had no other alternative but to remain as he was. Even the trappings of his immortality had been destroyed.

The blue lining, he noticed, had not been discarded, but had been used as a wrap cloth. It encased an object on the floor, something large and flat. He walked over and tugged at the fabric. The familiar texture, so sheer, so easily snagged, sent shivers across his skin. Underneath was a painting of an ancient man with a visage so demonic Barnabas pulled back in disgust. The technique was astonishing. The hair was matted gray fur that grew from the temples and sprouted wild above pointed ears. The mouth was elongated, and the nose canine. It was less a man than a wolf-like creature, but dressed as a man in a threadbare morning coat, with an ascot that was torn and flecked with saliva. The eyes were bloodshot, and so keen they could have been alive and staring, and the slather that dripped from the teeth glistened as though, if one were to touch it, it would respond with moisture. Although he had never seen it, Barnabas realized with a jolt what it must be. It was Quentin's hidden portrait, the one object he could not live without, the painting that held the werewolf's dark secret in check.

They never spoke of it, but he and Quentin both knew the other's fate was cursed. Both immortals, they had always maintained the pretense that everything was normal, respecting one another's secret. Quentin had been away for years. His return was something of a mystery. Until now. This portrait in Antoinette's basement, in her possession, was even more of an enigma. In spite of his new feelings, once again suspicion of her flooded through him, leaving him feeling ill. How could she have come by it, and did Quentin know it was here? Was she storing it for him, or had she stolen it? Perhaps this was why Quentin was pursuing her. Had Barnabas still been a vampire, he would have been tempted to whisk the portrait away to some hiding place of his own. Imagine what power it would afford him over his old rival! Such control would allow him to manipulate the entire Collins family.

Long he stood staring at the painting, weighing his options. If he took it, he would have to find some place to hide it, and his car was back at Collinwood. Perhaps if he could reach the graveyard under cover of dawn, he might secrete it away in the family mausoleum. Seizing the cloth, he wrapped the picture as it had been, and lifted it with both bands. Cumbersome as it was, he was able to climb the stair and move towards the door. His fingers cramped with the weight, and pausing in the drawing room to rest them, he turned to look at the carpet.

Early morning sunlight pierced a single pane of the front casement and cast a golden shaft across the floor. The carpet was exquisite, more beautiful than he had remembered. It seemed less faded, the colors richer and exceedingly vibrant. The vines and tendrils curled among flowers opening to the morning dew, and the birds appeared poised to lift into the air. Unable to resist, Barnabas leaned the painting against the back of a chair and approached the rug. More than anything, the crimson color of the background delighted him. Kneeling, he smoothed the rich velvet, but, to his surprise, the texture of the wool was slick and warm, and exhaled a bitter metallic odor. Puzzled, Barnabas looked at his hand. His palm was coated with red dye. Had Antoinette painted the rug? Now the moisture was seeping into his trousers where he knelt. Bewildered, he felt the rug again, fingering the damp fibers and the soggy nap. He drew back in disgust. The carpet was saturated with blood.

At that moment he heard muffled sounds from the second floor, a dry shuffling, a creak, a resounding thump, and then a heavy, heaving sigh as though the house was despondent, settling on its melancholy bones. He walked hesitantly to the bottom of the stair, dismayed to see his shoes tracking blood on the floor, but when he placed his foot on the first tread, he was struck with a blast of air so cold it chilled him through and through. He seized the painting and fled.

Once in the woods again, he trudged towards the cemetery, dragging the painting through the leaves. Shuddering he considered abandoning his quest and returning to the hippie camp. His mind was a blur. His night with Antoinette had awakened unfamiliar desires, and he hungered for her in a manner he found disturbing. Not only had she offered him happiness, she had given comfort, escape from torment. This was the human joy he had missed for so long. He tried to ease his anxiety by reliving every moment: the silk of her skin, the lushness of her form, her gentle movements. Even though he had been delirious with joy, he could remember vivid instants when she had touched him, and a pleasure so intense he throbbed again to think of it. And her gifts had been bestowed without guile, as though she savored his happiness. She required nothing more from him than acquiescence. The Angelique of his past, whose desperate jealousy drove her passions, whose insatiable greed entangled him with guilt, seemed to be no more. He visualized crawling into Toni's tent. She would be warm with sleep, merging, welcoming.

This time he would not let her go.

They would live together. He imagined them in the dining room of the Old House, reminiscing over a glass of wine, after a delicious meal of venison, perhaps pâté, succulent pork, spiced apples, or pheasant with roasted potatoes and tiny peas. He was suddenly aware of other needs stirring, and he laughed out loud at his new human hungers. What a fool he had been not to realize that this was his one great love, the love of his life. He had been blind with Angelique, but now with Antoinette he would make amends. He would give her all he had denied her, and devote his life to making her happy. Immortality seemed a fair price for bliss such as this.

A white rectangle flickered on a trunk ahead, and Barnabas stopped to look at it. NOTICE TO VACATE was barely legible in the predawn light. Roger had made good his threat to call the Sheriff, convincing him to force the hippies to move. There were code numbers of violations and Barnabas was able to read "fires in non-designated areas" and "inadequate toilet facilities." His body sagged with regret, but he was relieved the campers would have to move. They were such vulnerable prey.

He turned away from the camp and, still lugging his heavy load, followed the leaf-strewn path towards Widows' Hill, curious to see where the monster had fallen. When he reached the cliff, he stood for a long moment looking down at the waves crashing on the rocks, the white foam in the glint of dawn. He thought of his beloved Josette. Her last moments had been here. A tortured mind, frantic with grief, had sought its peace on those boulders. He, or what he had become, drove her to it.

Barnabas shivered, holding fast to the painting which swayed against the wind from the sea. Icy blasts cut through his jacket, and he gathered his cape around him. He seemed to see, as if in a mirage, an island or mirroring cliff that rose from the great deep on the other side of a chasm. The opposite shore beckoned, a distant dream where he could join his Josette, hold her startling body in his arms and gaze into the eyes he had loved, eyes like dark pools, full of wonder. Even his new love for Antoinette could not dim the force of her memory.

The path led under the great hundred-year-old oaks to the graveyard where the tombstones floated like small rafts in a sea of leaves. For the first time since his cure he could sense the ghosts, restless spirits wandering about, longing for contact. The fallen leaves were so thick, they came to his knees and clung to his clothes, but this time he was determined to ignore them. After searching for a mausoleum to serve as a hiding place for the painting, he finally found a low vault with a rotted door. He managed to slip the square frame inside. It would do until he could find a more suitable spot.

Then at the far end of the cemetery he saw a whirlwind of leaves rise into a body and flail about like a dancing idiot, arms and legs akimbo; and he thought it was a living creature before it dissolved and fell back to earth. His imagination was plaguing him again. He began his hunt for some sign of the vampire. He felt certain he would smell its odor, hear the velvet silence of its breathing. In the next few days he intended to follow every whim, however irrational or impulsive, in pursuit of his new nemesis. In this cemetery alone were several structures that would be ideal lairs for a living corpse to go undetected during the day. Each of these that allowed entrance he searched but found them empty. Slogging between the tombstones, through hidden briars, his shoes sucking up mud, he shivered with the sensation that, were he to fall, the leaves would bury him. Some fiend governed their piles; some insidious scheme lay in their drifts.

He shook off such absurd conjectures, concentrating on his hunt until he heard the wind moan like something trapped and, under a scarlet maple, the dancing fiend rose up again.

This time it drew nearer and assumed the form of a corporeal mass, thick and fluttering. Barnabas stepped backwards, his hand on a tombstone, and feeling panicky turned to move away, but tripped, and fell into the sunken rectangle of an ancient grave. A gust of wind blasted the bundle on top of him, filled his mouth and nostrils, and blinded his eyes. He floundered like a helpless swimmer in an avalanche, terrified and choking, and unable to breathe. Like stinging furies with vicious beaks and claws, the leaves descended, forcing him down into the grave. He batted and heaved against the smothering heap as it wrestled him. Sharp stems prodded his ears and dug at his tongue, but when he grappled with the dark cloud, his hands only found tumbling debris. Afraid to open his eyes, his throat clogged with ash, he thought, *what a ridiculous way to die.* Pinwheeling both arms, he jabbed the pile over and over, until the reeling air dissolved in an explosion of rubbish, and he lurched to his feet. Dry leaves fell from his body as he shook and panted with terror, certain he had been marked for death.

He turned to flee, but when he reached the gate to the cemetery, he heard footsteps on the path, and he stopped, peering into the gloom, anticipating another attacking flurry. Someone, or something, was moving through the trees. He tried to still his trembling. Perhaps the hippies were awake at this hour, pursuing some mischief around the graves.

But the forest was deathly still. Rays of misty sunlight streamed through branches and small patches of sky shimmered, but morning birdsong had stopped, and he could hear not even the scurrying of woodland creatures, nor the whisper of a breeze. And yet, someone was walking through the dry leaves and coming his way.

He grit his teeth and moved towards the sound. Far down

he path he saw the figure of a girl. She wore a long cape that
railed the ground, and dark hair fell over her shoulders. She
eemed oblivious to his presence, and continued towards him
leep in thought. As she drew closer he noticed her small hands
lasped together below her waist and a white cap of ruffled cot-
on on her head. Her lips moved as though she spoke to herself,
or prayed, and only when she drew very near did she look up
and allow her eyes to meet his. He had never seen such eyes.
They were of an icy blue, almost white, and the pupils were very
dark. Her wild hair, which was in masses of black curls, tumbled about her face, and the force of her gaze so startled him
he could not breathe. Pale blue eyes she had, and cold as ice. As
she drew close to him, she nodded her head slightly and said in
a low voice, "Good morning, Reverend." Then she passed him
by. He caught a whiff of pine and hemlock.

She turned, and walking back to her, touched her lightly on
he arm. "Who are you, my dear?" he said. "What is your name?"

She paused and lifted her eyes to his. Her gaze sent a shiver
down his spine. "Why, good sir, you know me. I am called Miranda," she said. "Miranda du Val."

Seventeen

Salem—1692

For days Miranda lay sick in Andrew's bed. A fever bough sweat and she squirmed in the clutch of nightmares. Finally, on the third morning, she woke to a memory instead o a dream. She remembered the day when she had thought in he mind to go to the woods and find this Black Man, the one sh would be accused of serving, the one whose book she was cer tain to have signed. The only books she ever signed were Judah Zachery's lessons, where she was obliged to make sums to the tune of switches. If she was meant to be the handmaiden to thi vile perpetrator, then his home must be in thickets and briars deep in impenetrable wilderness, and the Wampanoags woul know his tracks.

It was past midnight before the house was deadly still, and Goody Collins snoring away. Only then could she climb ou her casement and duck behind the barn. Time being precious and dawn but a few hours hence, she flew. Clouds hung low and there was no moon, and if she had been seen, she would have been taken for a night hawk, or her winged shape an owl's slow beating shadow.

The Wampanoag camp was easy to find from above; she spotted the fires, and the wigwams scattered among the trees. They had removed since her last visit, as was their way, and now had built a great campground by the river for dances coming into season. So astonished were the warriors by a girl appearing out of the dark, they gathered in arms to face her, and when she asked to see Metacomet they only said, "He is dead."

"Tell him it is his daughter, Silver Bird."

"The great sachem's severed head hangs in the meetinghouse at Plymouth for many years now."

"Then take me to his body."

"His body was cut into four quarters and placed in the trees for the ravens."

"Then take me to his wigwam, and be done with it."

In awe of her obstinacy, they ran to do her bidding and woke Metacomet, who was glad to see her, and invited her into his hut. He lay on his favorite bearskin and smoked his long pipe, watching her every movement and nodding his approval every now and then, while she built the fire and ground the maize. She had brought honey, tobacco, and three wild duck eggs hidden in her skirts. She warmed a bowl of gruel which she offered to him, and he drank it greedily, his dark skin aglow in the firelight, a sleepy feather hanging from his braid. With his knife he had cut a thin line under each eye and down each cheek; the scars were the abiding tracks of his tears.

Although she feared the dawn, Miranda knew she must be patient. It would never do to broach any subject before preliminaries had been sufficiently discharged. Metacomet, like all Indians—and more than ever now that he was thought to be dead—had few worldly desires, and as a result, an abundance of time. This was opposed to the Puritans who must always be busy at some task, convinced that indolence invites sinful thoughts.

Finally, after Metacomet filled his pipe a second time and leaned back against a deerskin pillow, she spoke.

"These people of Salem, who, as you know, call themselves Christians, have a great fear of a Black Man who dwells in the forest with the wild animals."

Metacomet nodded as though he understood perfectly. "I have been wondering," he said. "How does he live? Who feeds him?"

"He is a savage spirit."

"Ahhh-h-h, I see. Wily and transparent."

"Yes. An apt description of someone else I know. Why do you hide yourself away when your people need their great sachem more than ever?"

Metacomet rose and went for his pouch decorated with porcupine quills, the one he had kept since she was a child. His legs were bowed and his body stiff with great age and many tattoos. "My father, Massasoit, gave the settlers their first feast. In deference to their English ways, as you know, he named his sons English names. My brother, William and I, King Phillip." He returned to the bearskin and sat with his legs crossed. "It broke him to see such giftgiving and tokens of respect turn to bitterness and betrayal. At first the Puritans asked and bought. Now they only take." He opened the pouch and took out the tobacco. With great care, he filled his pipe. "I do not remember the story but the mothers tell it like this. When I was surrounded in the swamp, muskets on all sides, I chose life over honor. I placed my necklace of bear teeth and dewclaws around the neck of another fallen warrior and ran away."

"So it is his head that hangs in Plymouth?"

"I wish I had chosen one better looking, as it is his head they spit at, and point to, and say King Phillip was a doleful great naked dirty beast." And he laughed merrily, she thought, until she glimpsed the bitter tears in his eyes. "I can no longer lead, Little Bird. Like the squaw sachem of the Naumkeag who sold her land, that is your town of Salem, to the English. I sold the air I breathe. I am not a sachem, but a dead man, and this is my penance, to remain invisible." He lay back again and found a comfortable spot in the thick fur. "Now tell me of this Black Man."

"They say he entices naive women to sign his great book, and in return he promises them those things they desire."

"Yes, this is true of women. The squaws never tire of skins, or rare shells to make beads, or difficult-to-find herbs for cooking and healing. And always a new wigwam." He chuckled, his bronze skin crinkling like dead leaves. "This Black Man grants wishes, bestows gifts, strong children?"

Miranda was confused. "No. For those things they pray to God."

"Ah yes, the God they would have us worship in our dancing."

"You know of Him?"

"Those who speak in their meetinghouse have come to us and I admire them for their courage, for we could knock them on the head. But they are determined to persuade us that their God lives somewhere, not in the sun and the stars and the rain, but in another part of the sky, the empty part."

"Yes, the God of all creation."

"They tell a story of a man and a woman and a snake, about a tree of knowledge. You know this story?"

"Of course."

"It is a very interesting story. We like it very much. There is a man eating an apple the woman gave him, and that is the beginning of mischief in the world. This makes sense. Then the first warrior, named Christ, is obliged to repair this wickedness with miracles and suffering. One of our warriors agreed it was foolish to eat apples which were bored through with worms. It is much better to crush them into cider."

"So you were persuaded by the story?"

"Yes, and we thanked them for coming so far to tell us stories they have heard from their mothers. In return, we told them a story, the story of two brothers who are starving, a favorite of mine. You know this story?"

"Tell it me."

Metacomet took a puff from his pipe and leaned back, preparing to expound. "Two braves were hungry and they feared death would come soon. Then at last the brothers tracked and killed a deer; they did this. They built a fire to broil a piece of the hindquarter. Just as they were ready to eat, a beautiful woman came down from the clouds and sat on a hill behind them. They said to one another, 'It is a spirit that has smelled our broiling venison. We should offer some to her.' They cooked the tongue and gave it to her; this they did. She liked the taste very much and said to them, 'I will reward you for your kindness. Return to this spot in fourteen moons and you will see what I have brought you.' In fourteen moons they returned to that spot and were surprised to find maize growing where her right hand had touched the ground, and kidney beans where her left hand had touched the ground, and where her backside had sat on the hillside, they found tobacco. These are the crops that from our ancient times our people have cultivated to great advantage."

"How did the Puritans like your story?"

Metacomet laughed so hard his body shook all over. "They did not like it."

"Why?"

"They say to us." Metacomet drew himself up in imitation of the Reverend and spoke in a self-righteous tone. "'We have told you sacred truths, and you have given us fables and falsehoods.'" Metacomet laughed again. "I reminded them they were forgetting the rules of common civility. 'We believed your story,' I said. 'Why do you refuse to believe ours?'"

Miranda smiled. "They are afraid of the Devil," she said.

"I think the Puritans worship a jealous and demanding God. Do not make the same mistake, Sisika. Do not choose as your god someone who serves your narrow vision of the truth. I would be happy if a great warrior in the sky, someone very like myself, cared for my people and gave answers to all the mysteries. Someone I could smoke a pipe with by the fire and discuss the ruling of the world. That would make me happy. But there is no big strong warrior like this. We Wampanoags would not be so vain to imagine one. The Great Spirit is neither man nor woman, neither beast nor human, nor smoke, nor water, nor air. But when you stand in the forest among the great trees, if you watch a stag lift his head from the stream, or see the partridge disappear into the brush, when you hear the eagle's call, then you tremble. The Great Spirit is there, in the breeze that makes a small tongue of every leaf and blade of grass, whispering of earth's bounty and asking nothing in return."

Miranda grew serious. "Is there a story of a Black Man?"

Metacomet shook his head. "We have only the stories and songs remembered by our mothers."

"Have you seen a Black Man in the forest?"

Metacomet thought for a moment. Then he took a long drag from his pipe, and, as he blew the smoke into the air between them, he looked deep into Miranda's eyes. "This Black Man is not in the forest," he said. "He lives among you. In Salem Town."

Because she feared discovery, Miranda began to find ways to hide her whereabouts. She searched the deep forest for the secrets of concealment, and when she heard the snake's whisper in the leaves before she saw it, she gathered birch leaves—heart-shaped, ratchet-edged—into her skirt, and placed the tip of one leaf over the stem of the next, and secured it with a thorn from the Devil's Walking Stick. In this way she wove a long green snake a hundred feet in length, and she laid it gently in the

stream. Fastening it to a dipping willow branch to give it mo
tion, she cast a spell of invisibility. The green snake meandere
down through little rills and curled around rocks, and Mirand
hoped it would keep them safe, she and her Andrew.

Next, she saw the yellow eyes of a raccoon before she coul
find his shape, and so she gathered golden dandelions now i
season and made tight nosegays which she stuck in every hol
low in the rocks, every cavity in the ground, whether it be th
opening to an animal's den or simply the way the rain flowed
The bright bouquets stole the light from the sun and shone lik
tiny lamps all through the night.

Finally, because the trees writhed in the wind, she made si
lent trees of rock. Andrew came to watch, now curious, and sh
needed his strength to move the largest boulders. With levers an
prying poles, they rolled the stones into position and she built to
tems, adding rock over rock in decreasing size until she reache
the top, and there she placed a tiny pebble. Together, she an
Andrew built these guardians alongside every path or game trail
and they were powerful and kept her invisible.

In this way, they lived in peace. During the daylight hours
Andrew hunted and brought home rabbit and quail, at time
a beaver or a duck. She scouted furtively for wild grains, acorns
or berries; her days with the Wampanoags still in her memory
she knew how to live in the forest. She swept the floor of An
drew's hut until it hardened to a shine, wove cattail rushes fo
rugs, mended the roof beam with thick grass mats, sewed pine
needle pillows, and saw life as it could be.

Still, her restlessness grew. It was stifling to remain hidden
and to live in fear. If someone from the village wandered down
their path, she drew inside the hut, heart pounding, and breathed
a silent prayer to the stone trees, the tiny suns, the green snake, to

eflect curiosity, to quell suspicion. Andrew nailed slats over the windows so that she could keep watch but not be seen.

The days were full of toil, but the nights were dreary. She had thought Andrew loved her, but he feared her as well, not understanding her, he who was fearless. Once, he told her, and the story was well known in the village, he had crawled inside the body of a bear, to retrieve the liver and the heart. He could stalk a moose or trap a black fox, but there was timidity in him. Once she caught him looking at her as they sat by the fire.

"What is it, Andrew?"

"Have you bewitched me, as well?" he said.

And she went to him and held his face to her breast.

Andrew was obliged to go to town for bullets, tin, and a little honey, among other necessities. While there, he kept his head down and spoke to no one; but he listened to the gossip and returned with the news.

"Goody Olcott is in the stocks."

"Not her head?"

"Aye, and her hands, her big hindquarters wagging in the air."

"What is her crime?"

"She flaunted a red scarf on the Sabbath."

"What other news is there?"

"Charges brought forth in the meetinghouse."

"More hangings?"

He nodded gravely. "As I walked home by way of Gallows Hill, I saw three poor souls dangling, their necks broken, their shoes thrust out of their skirts."

Often the charges were vague: Worms found in the cow dung. Milk soured before it turned to butter in the churn. A cow bloated and died. Cherries shriveled before they ripened. Tightly woven baskets loosened and came unraveled. Paper caught fire

in the stove where no paper had been. A woman's hair fell out
Another woman grew a goiter the size of a squash.

Other times they spoke in sober tones of more baleful signs

Two dogs were tried and hung for witchcraft. Shingles blew
off the roofs. The child at her slate forgot her sums. A lamp
filled with soot. Mold grew on the bread, green and feathery
Doors flew open, locked doors. The cover of the soup kettle went
missing.

Some happenings were beyond comprehension.

A young mother's milk turned to tar in her breast. A mirror
showed someone it was not. A dead bird was found in the pig's
trough. A green worm in a kitten's nostril. The cow's hooves
grew soft. A lamb born with two heads. Rats ate a newborn
baby laid in the cradle. The moon turned blood red and disap
peared.

"Cotton Mather has come from Boston to judge the pro
ceedings," Andrew told her. "His father has written a great book
that reveals the methods for discovering witches." He gave her
a sly look as he said these words, and she felt uncomfortable un
der his gaze.

"You mean he can decipher who has signed the Devil's book?"
She hoped he found her statement as absurd as it was meant. But
Andrew retained his sour, expressionless tone.

"He puts great store in spectral evidence."

Suddenly she knew he was taunting her, in his own way
He could never be quick or devious, but there was some poison
in him that made him unkind.

"Spectral evidence . . . what is that?"

"When the girls cry out, they point to a woman in the
dock, insist they are pinched by her, or they say they see a little
yellow bird in the minister's hat."

"What is the little bird?"

"That would be her tormenting spirit. If the accused turns
her head to the side, they are obliged to turn their heads also

And if she sucks in her cheeks or wrings her hands, they do the same, as if bewitched."

"But they do it for sport, surely."

"Would that it were sport, lass. It is deadly serious. All Betty Parris must say is she saw the figure of Rebecca Nurse or Martha Corey standing over her bed in the night, and they are arrested as witches."

He looked at her again in that same suspicious manner, but she ignored him and went to heat the water for the bedpan. As she stirred the coals beneath the pot she felt his eyes on her.

Because they were not married, they did not lie together. Andrew gave Miranda the pine needle mattress and he slept on a blanket by the hearth, his back to her. She would wake at night and see his form in front of the fire, his tall shoulders and his narrow hips, a man in the shape of a plow. She watched him breathe. Why did he not reach for her, and she so close, a few feet across the room? Was he unmoved by desire? Was one moment of rude forcing in the wood to be her only adventure? She thought better of chastising him and said nothing. Nor did she make another spell.

Instead she hoed and reaped his small garden, telling herself what a clever man he was to plant beans where they could climb the tall stalks of corn, and squash plants to cover the ground in between, shading the roots from the sun with their broad leaves. She prepared a new plot for fall seed with a plow Andrew made for her from the shoulder of a deer. She made hominy cakes from the maize they grew, and searched for wild artichokes and mushrooms under rotted logs. Why did he not reach for her?

Finally the day came when she fastened her bodice and it was tighter than the day before. She thought perhaps it was the wild apples she had stewed, but her breasts were tender and her monthly bleeding had stopped.

When Andrew noticed the swelling about her waist, he grew more sullen. Never talkative, now when they crouched by the fire at night, he did not speak a word to her. She tried to reassure herself that his nature was to be stubborn and mute, that in two months, when she came of age, the banns would be published. There would be shame and banishment, but her deepest hope was that they could escape to her farm. Perhaps, if they proved themselves to be God-fearing people, church-going and devout, they would be drawn again into the fold. Still, Andrew's silence frightened her. He sat by the fire with his eyes aflame and unblinking and his jaw set, and thought his cold, invisible thoughts, while she secreted away the fear in her heart.

One day when rain threatened, he did not go to the forest, and she set an early meal of stewed rabbit before him in a new clay dish. She banked the fire, scraped the last of the roots, and went to the stream for water. She saw the trees had turned the color of blood. They were all one; the brilliant leaves, the bushes and briars, the forest floor, even the light reflected on the trunks was a blazing scarlet. She saw the crimson shimmer in the stream, and she stopped to watch the water change from carmine to silver blue to black, and to listen to the jeering voice of the rapids. The green leaf snake had come unraveled. Time to make another. She climbed to the top of the hill to watch the sun disappear, but it was cheerless behind the haze, like a waning moon.

She returned to fold the quilts, her heart beating a new rhythm, quick and hard. What do the magistrates fear, she thought, and how does the Reverend chill their bones to the marrow? How to strike back at the quivering air which has taken the form, in their cowardly minds, of imps and demons? Always evil is kept stewing, lies waiting, like a pot simmering on the hearth, and there is nothing that is not cause for fear: the Indian who walks silently, the Indian whose dark skin gleams with sweat, the Indian who possesses his own arrows. One must also fear the cripple, and the clairvoyant child, the orphan, or the woman no longer of childbearing age, the scold, the complainer, the woman who is widowed, or the woman who is too beautiful.

Fear is a clenched hand around a cold and narrow heart, a poison in the blood, a lethargy in the limbs. What did Metacomet say to her? The day a man turns his back on knowledge, he becomes fear's fool. For the Puritans, fear demanded they find the truth. But knowledge shows no truths, only the eternal unfolding mystery. He often said of the Puritans, "We wondered how people so inept could ever be a danger to us."

Such was the darkness of the day, Miranda hurried to gather the blankets off the rope where she had hung them to air. In the cabin Andrew was lighting the fire while she waited for the sun to drop beneath the rim of the world. At first the wind was only an encumbrance, whipping the sheets on the line, insistent gusts that lifted her skirts as if she were a kite poised to fly. When she felt herself rising, she reached for the sapling where the sheet was tied, but the tree pulled away and she slipped from the earth's grasp. Loose on an errant breeze, she swayed and looked down, swung on the air, rose up, floated, tethered to the rope of the wind. What had the girls said when they flapped their puny arms? *Whist Whist.* Hair flying, body arched, she pressed her skirt in front but it flew up in back like a bell, and the air leaf-fluttered beside her cheeks. She was drawn into a vortex, like the deer driven into the pen, coming from a wide place driven into a small place where they could so easily be killed, and the pinpoint of the vortex for her was her farm.

In minutes she was looking down from a great height at her father's house—its rosy sides and gray roof, a beaver dam rebuilt stronger than before, the widening pond reflecting the sky, and a lone figure behind the plow in her field of flax. It was Benajah Collins hard at work on her land.

The following morning the stones came. At first they were only a few, falling like hail, a delight to the children who ran to collect them like wild goose eggs out of the grass. But those were only her tears. That afternoon Andrew returned from the town with strange news. Commonly taciturn, he was brimming with talk.

"Calamity has befallen Salem Village," he said. "It is raining stones."

"Hail, most likely."

"No, this is a true thing. Benajah Collins, his wife, Esther, and their three children: the boy Peter, the girl Mercy, and Authority, the baby, guests and servants, all were seated by the fire when they heard a great clattering noise on the roof."

"Stars falling . . ."

"Benajah ran out to investigate and saw nothing other than the bright moonlight; but his new gate was torn from its hinges. When he turned to seek refuge within his own walls, his back was pelted with small boulders."

"I can only think his wife served him a poor dinner."

"Why will you not listen? Within the house stones flew about, and a hand reached in the window and tossed stones into the room. The children shrieked. Stones fell out of the sky and, flying about, broke the window glass, forcing out the bars, the lead and the harps. Stones pelted down the chimney and fell into the fire, then flew out red hot and struck the pewterware and sent the brass candlesticks crashing to the floor. Esther was screaming. The poor woman snatched up her children and ran down to the cellar where the walls were thick. But that room was infected as well. Stones dislodged themselves from the foundation and flew through the air like birds. Rocks fell from the ceiling and she was struck many times whilst she hovered over her children to protect them."

"Is his the only house?"

"No, the stones are falling in the fields, laying waste the rye. The town is a cauldron of fear. They say 'tis witchcraft."

"Then it must be that."

Andrew jerked up, his eyes yellow with distrust. She won-

...dered what he saw when he looked at her. He rose and paced the cabin, hunched over, his heat filling the air with mist. His bushy hair flew out from his head and his red beard bristled. He had been shamed back into silence, but it was a brooding hush that felt ready to explode. A new fear rose in her heart, and yet she managed to speak gently.

"The stones are far from here, are they not?"

"The stones are troubling, but not the worst of it."

"What is the worst of it?"

He paced, and was silent. When he found his voice, it was harsh, and his hazel eyes, when he looked at her, had shrunk to cinders. His face grew dark and he nodded to her thickening waist.

"At first I believed you were growing plump on apples, Miranda. But your ankles and wrists are thin."

She let the air bottled up in her chest escape in a long sigh. "I thought you would never speak of it."

"I see you have new life in you," he said.

She smiled shyly. "Yes."

"Dost thou expect me to raise another man's child?"

Her eyes widened. "The child is yours, Andrew. How could you think otherwise?"

"Nay. It cannot be mine. Do not lay the blame on me."

"How can you say such a thing? Five months after that terrible night."

"Because I have never touched thee."

A hot wave rose up in her. Her words tumbled out. "The night I brought the cake. The night before you left on the raid against the Naumkeag. You followed me into the woods, and there, in the dark—in the storm—"

"Nay, lass, I never did." When he stood, he so filled the space with his bulk and his odor of bear grease and leather, she felt squeezed into a corner.

"It was you, Andrew. And only you."

"I did not leave the cabin."

"Yes, Andrew. You caught me on the path and pulled me down into the leaves. Don't deny it. There is no need to be ashamed. I was glad on it. You hurt me but I gave myself to you. wanted to marry, and I wanted to bind you to me. You were violent, but the fault was not yours. I can only admit this shameful thing to you now. There was a spell in the cake. One you could no have resisted."

"There was a spell, that I know. After you left, my body was on fire for you. I thought I would go mad. I told the farmers to leave without me for all I could think was I would search for you in the forest, and find you, and—" He drew in his breath with a hiss. "I bid the youngest boy, Richard Brazier, to hang back since he was too inexperienced to soldier, being but eleven years By then, I was mad and feverish. I told him I suffered from fit and begged him to tie my hands to the table leg that I might no endanger myself. This he did, and put my coat and musket out of reach, on the other side of my door. All night I bucked on the floor, and suffered the torments of Hell, but I could not loosen the knots. Morning came and I was somewhat recovered. Richard came to release me and I went to fetch my things, only to find my coat missing."

"Stolen?"

"Aye."

"By whom?"

"That secret was revealed to me many weeks later. I found my skins in the bottom of his cart. It was the schoolteacher, Judah Zachery."

Miranda washed her collar and bonnet and hung them in the sun. She pulled them flat as they dried to press them and give them starch. She brushed the mud from the bottom of her cape and carefully cleaned her shoes. Then, setting her teeth and stiffening her body, she bathed in the stream. Shivering in the cold water, she looked up at her trees, wondering whether she would see them again. The oaks reached out to hold the sky like a great basin in their arms. Their trunks were moss painted, the bark deeply crevassed. Their majesty made her bold; their beauty made her weep. A bird repeated a musical call, over and over, and his fluting brought on deep melancholy. Beside the stream, a fallen monster from the previous year had begun to decay and was now trimmed with ruffles of mushrooms and lace of lichen. Hordes of ants crawled feverishly in and out of the sawdust.

Drawing on her woolen dress, she cupped her hand over her swollen stomach. There were flutterings now of the vile thing she carried. Were its feet cloven, its face shriveled like a bat's? She would rid herself of it this very day were it not for the protection it afforded. In Salem Town, a woman with child, though she were condemned, could not be put to death before she delivered. The Puritans valued every child as a gift from God, made in His glorious image. But this one was not one of those.

Andrew had clung to his sullen ways, but he had not forced her to leave. He still brought her food and allowed her to clean and cook his meals, thereby feeding herself. She thought long and hard over telling him her plan. If he tried to stop her, they would argue, and those tenuous ties they still enjoyed would be broken. If he followed after to protect her, he might come to harm in the village. She waited until the morning she was prepared to depart.

"Andrew, I mean to go to Salem Town and show myself, proving their trial was a farce. My farm belongs to me. My father cleared the land and built the house. I will appeal to the magistrates for justice, and that my unlawful sentence be annulled."

"Nay, lass, they will arrest you. 'Tis hysteria now in Salem Town."

"But there must be among the populace some who are still pure of heart. I floated not, and I lived."

"There are none left who will not say witchcraft." His eyes were full of worry for her and she was surprised.

"That may come to pass. And it may not."

He stood for a long moment staring at her. "You are a pretty sight, Miranda," he said, "with your fresh collar and white cap like wings beside your eyes." She reached for his arm and laid her hand upon it.

"Do not think on the child, Andrew. It will not come into the world alive."

"I cannot tell you what to do, Miranda." He loomed over her but did not touch her. "God be with thee." She stopped and turned back to him.

"I have been happy here," she said. And they both went out the door, going their separate ways.

When she walked into the town, Miranda saw boulders of all sizes scattered in the barnyards, branches broken from trees, carts smashed, roof beams splintered, even a goat lying dead by the road. At first she was not noticed, as the townsfolk were all enthralled with the cataclysm, clearing out sheds and searching for cattle lost to fright and broken fences. It was the children who believed they were seeing an apparition and cried out and ran to their mothers.

"Miranda du Val has returned from the dunking!"

Wives came to their broken windows to look out. Husbands came from their barns. Miranda went first to Goody Collins to look in on her old home. Esther was sweeping glass. Her newframed house listed like a beached ship. When Miranda appeared at her hearth, she too believed she saw a phantom. She stopped her sweeping and stared, a stupid look on her round face. Her children ran to her skirts.

"Why, girl, is it really you?"

"Aye, 'tis I."

"And are you . . . surely you must be poorly."

"No. I am well. Where is the Reverend?" Goody Collins's face clouded over; she shook off her clinging children, and went to lift the baby although it was not crying.

"He is away."

"Sowing my land?"

The woman flared with resentment. "Why what else could we do? We thought you were lost, and since we have provided for you all these years, the farm seemed rightly ours."

"But it is not. The food you gave me—I worked for it, did I not?"

"The land lay fallow!"

"Tell him I have returned to claim what is mine."

When Miranda reached the meetinghouse word had gone before, but they were unbelieving until they saw her walk through the door. The hall was crowded with spectators and another pitiful specimen was in the dock, bewildered and begging for justice. The girls cried out as if in terrible pain and rolled on the floor. The woman—Miranda saw it was poor Sarah Good—wept, wrung her hands, pleaded for mercy. She was a pauper and often begged for food and lodging for herself and her two sickly children. The judges, cold and unmoving as statues, looked up when Miranda made her way through the throng. John Hathorne was the first to speak.

"Miranda du Val," he said pleasantly, as if she had appeared at his home as a guest. "What brings you before this tribunal?"

"I have come to tell you that I have met the Black Man in the forest." There was a murmur all around, agitated and suspicious. "And I am here to give you his name."

The reaction was one of nervous laughter and disdain.

Distrustful whispers buzzed and even the naughty girls grew quietly curious. Mercy Lewis sat on the floor where she had been crawling and stared with her mouth hanging open.

There was a new personage Miranda had not seen who possessed a powerful countenance, and who leaned forward to look at her carefully. This must be Increase Mather, she thought. He wore a thick curly wig of snow white hair brushed to a gloss which betrayed his vanity, as did his fine linens. He had a long nose, an obsequious mouth, and a double chin stuffed into his collar. After studying her with his pink-rimmed eyes, he turned to John Hathorne. "Be this the woman who disappeared after the dunking?" The judge nodded, as mystified as all the rest to see her standing there.

"An army of devils is horribly broke in upon Salem," he said. "If you know of this Black Man, say it now."

She lowered her head for a moment and waited until the room had quieted. Then she met his eye. "First I must have your pledge. I ask assurance that I will be spared the rigors of examination, and be allowed to go and live on my farm, with no unjust grievances against me, and with my record cleared of guilt." Another murmur rose up, both horrified and wondrous, that a mere girl could speak with such conviction in the presence of a powerful judiciary. But John Hathorne was not to be deluded. "Tell us what you have to say, Miranda, and we will decide those matters. Witchcraft is a serious change and there must be proof. Come forward and reveal to us what you know. Then, if we are satisfied, you shall have your freedom."

"I have heard it has rained stones in Salem Village," she said.

"The dwellings of good people are filled with the doleful shrieks of their children and servants."

"And inflicted considerable damage on all the houses and fields."

"A most dreadful calamity," said Amadeus Collins.

"And this rain of stones bodes witchcraft, does it not?"

"The most despicable sort. We are tormented by invisible hands and torture preternatural."

"Is there in the village a house untouched?"

Again a murmur rose up, and many shook their heads as if to say the storm afflicted them all alike.

"Is there a garden spared?"

All responded in the negative. But a woman in the crowd rose to her feet and shouted out in a raw voice as though her knowledge had bought her considerable grief, "Judah Zachery's house stands unblemished."

There was a gasp from the crowd. "Is this a true thing?" asked Amadeus Collins; his eyes protruded, and his mouth puckered in uneasiness. He looked somewhat disappointed to hear this news.

"Go and see that his window panes be whole and hollyhocks standing in his plot," said Miranda.

"No stones?" repeated the stupefied Amadeus to the bleating woman.

"None. There is a perimeter of stones on all sides as though they had been removed by an unseen hand." The crowd jostled to get a look at her, and several men in the back of the meetinghouse ran out, determined to investigate.

Judge Collins leaned forward and said, "If we discover truth in your statements, Miranda, this is damning proof. Have you anything else to reveal?"

She paused, then spoke in a soft voice. "I hesitate to utter words that will be injurious to the decency of these proceedings."

"Go on girl, we will hear it all."

"As you know, I have attended the schoolhouse for many years and Judah Zachery has been my teacher. Often he has beat me and misused me, tortured me terribly, and forced me to sit in his dark closet, for his way of punishment was confinement, sometimes for hours at a time."

"Perhaps these penalties were deserved."

"That may be so. However, in his closet I have seen, stored under clothes and shoes and broken slates, books he brought from England. Required to remain sometimes the entire day in the darkness, I became curious, and as my eyes found some small source of light, I began to examine these books which were both traitorous and blasphemous."

Reverend Mather looked horrified. "What sort of books?"

"Why, books of the most heinous illustrations: human anatomy depicting the parts of bodies, both male and female, drawings of sexual intercourse, pastoral and theatrical scenes of dancing and demonizing the Lord, mathematical treatises theorizing the journeys of the stars and stories disputing the history of Creation, one which determines that we are not the children of God but instead the descendants of jungle creatures, baboons and chimpanzees." At these words there was a new clamor, and Miranda was obliged to speak above the din. "There is a book you had best keep at the ready, once you have made your search. It displays drawings and designs of mechanical objects: a crossbow, a catapult, a camera obscura, and something you might have special use for: a Halifax Gibbet for severing heads. Judah Zachery is no ordinary witch."

Now Judge Hathorne leaned forward on his chair. "Why have you only now come to us with this news, Miranda? Wittingly or unwittingly you have done Satan's bidding."

"This is a true thing. I have kept silent wittingly."

"And what excuse have you? The penalty for your sins is death."

"I have been under his dominance, sir. He is a despicable wizard, a disciple of Lucifer, and he has fiendish powers to possess and destroy. He is the leader of a coven that has rendezvous with the Devil."

The tumult in the courtroom had now reached a crescendo and Amadeus spoke, his voice a sibilant screech, "And that one book, the one where those who sell their souls are obliged to sign away their lives for all eternity. Is that book in his closet as well, Miranda?"

Now it was Miranda's turn to approach the judge's bench. She stepped forward until her hands rested on the polished wood, and said in a voice filled with rancor. "Aye. It is there." The courtroom exploded in consternation. Mary Walcott and Abigail Williams screamed and fell to the floor spouting gibberish, but they were paid no attention.

"And have you signed that dreadful book?"

"He forced me to do it."

The hubbub grew and Miranda lifted her voice above the bewildered cries. "And one more thing will you find, this the most damning of all. In a box at the back of the closet, under the switches, he has hidden the Devil's mask!"

"A mask?" cried the astonished Reverend.

"A mask of gold, encrusted with jewels."

This revelation released the greatest reaction of all, and the meetinghouse rang with hysterical shouts as Sheriff Corwin was sent for, and he and several men of the town went forth to search Judah Zachery's secret closet. Amadeus alone still sat in the judge's seat and looked down on Miranda. He was not pleased with these new revelations, any more than he was pleased to see the rightful owner of his son's new farm standing before him alive and determined. She could read the aggravation in his eyes.

"Will you testify before this Court against this man? And will you swear that he has abused you in these ways?"

Miranda took a deep breath and said, "I cannot."

Amadeus rose up incensed, but she thought, secretly pleased as well. "Then it is you who will be in the dock. For books and masks and stones do not a witch make. Only the testimony of the poor victim who is afflicted."

"If I look into his eyes, he will render me helpless."

"The tribunal shall forbid him to look at you," said Cotton Mather.

"But he will hurt me grievously."

"It is your Christian duty. You have nothing to fear. You stand in the protective cloak of the Almighty. Have you signed Judah Zachery's book?"

"Yes—"

"Then you will testify," said Amadeus, "or rot in Hell."

She saw that he was now fully contentious and she said one more time. "If he look at me, I will go blind."

"Then we shall cover his eyes."

Cotton Mather spoke to her in a calm voice. "For there shall arise false Christs, and false Prophets, and shall show great signs and wonders, they shall deceive the very elect. You must testify, Miranda, for the sake of us all."

The gibbet that was erected outside the prison door was so clumsy and ill-made, Miranda wondered whether it would serve. The blade was but a beaten plowshare, hardened and sharpened in the coals. She forced herself to disassemble the contraption in her mind rather than to look upon the prisoner, for she feared his evil eye. Instead she observed there was a sole beam holding the contraption erect, very much as an easel would hold a painting. To this beam the rope to loose the blade was tied. Two upright posts held the axe, and on top of the plate was a mass of lead weighing at the very least one hundred pounds.

This being the first beheading anywhere near Salem, there was a great crowd gathered, some sober, some fearful, and others festive as though making their way to a fair. Entertainment was a scarce commodity. Two young boys standing beside Miranda jested with one another.

"Do you wish to see if the eyes blink? Stand near the basket."

"It bodes life lingering in the head after the body is severed."

"I will watch the legs, to see whether they make to run away. My father killed a chicken with an axe, and it ran headless around the hen yard, the neck spurting blood." They laughed until they saw her staring at them, and they withdrew in shame.

"Wish I were at the rope," whispered one. "'Tis a mighty axe."

"I heard of a time when the severed head bounced into the basket and out again whereupon it clapped its teeth upon a woman's apron and would not leave go."

"Was it the apron of his accuser?"

"Aye, and the teeth were like a trap."

With this horrible image alive in her mind, Miranda moved away. The memory of her testimony was a fresh recollection. The Sheriff had placed a hood over Judah's face, but she was still able to see the rounded shape of his bald head under the knitted wool and his contemptible chin protruding, the cords of his neck sprung tight. He was padlocked to the bar with chains on both hands, but he shook the courtroom when he roared like a lion, "She lies! She lies!"

Judah's head was not covered when he was led from the prison door. His hands were bound, but he swiveled about searching the crowd for Miranda. When he saw her, his face grew black with rage and he sent a shaft from his eye that seared her like a brand. A dark cloud hung on his brow, his jowls were deeply creased; and his pugnacious nose and turned up chin, his bald pate glistening in the sun, his tangled black mane about his neck, all gave his countenance a furious demeanor. But it was the cast of his eye that was like a poisoned arrow to her flesh.

The crowd pressed forward the better to witness the act, and some muttered complaint at being thrust aside. Judah was pushed and jostled to the gibbet and forced to kneel. Miranda placed a hand on her belly and felt the child move.

Reverend Hathorne read the sentence. "Judah Zachery, thou art here accused and found guilty of not having the fear of God before thine eyes, of having entertained familiarity with Satan, the great enemy of God and mankind, and by his help hast acted, and also hast come to the knowledge of secrets in a preternatural way, beyond the ordinary course of nature, to the grief and great affliction of several members of this commonwealth, for which, according to the law of God and the established law of this colony, thou deservest to die."

Miranda shuddered at the words, which also had been read out before the hanging of eleven innocent souls. She wanted it to be over and done with. Judah glared at her and shouted, "Do what you will. You are miserly hypocrites who would not know the truth if it stood blushing before you."

Judge Hathorne droned on. "Let it be a solemn warning and awakening to all of us that are before the Lord at this time, of these direful operations of Satan which the holy God hath permitted in the midst of us. The Lord doth terrible things amongst us, by lengthening the chain of the roaring lion in an extraordinary manner, so the Devil is come down in great wrath, endeavoring to set up his kingdom and wreaking torments on the bodies and minds among us."

"God is dead!" cried Judah. The Reverend raised his voice.

"Let us then return and repent, tear our hearts not our garments. Who can tell if the Lord will return in mercy unto us? Let us repent of every sin that hath been committed, and labor to practice every duty which hath been neglected."

"Sinners!" cried Judah. "The greatest sinner stands in your midst." Once again he glared at Miranda.

"And when we are humbled, then we shall assuredly find that the kingly power of our Lord and Savior shall be magnified in delivering his poor sheep and lambs out of the jaws, and paws, of the roaring lion. And the Lord sayeth to Satan"—he turned to Judah with wrath and condemnation in his gaze—"the Lord rebuke thee!"

The masked executioner took hold of Judah's hair at the back and pulled it up, the better to expose the neck, and drew his head to the block. Judah struggled, and before he was in position, rose up again in fury and sang out, "You cannot kill me. My death will not last! Take heed! Take heed! You will live to regret this day!"

The Sheriff jerked him forward and he slumped over the block, his bound wrists springing up behind his back in one last supplication, and he drew one final breath through his shuddering limbs even as the rope was sprung and the axe plummeted. Blood spurted and coated the blade. The head toppled into the basket. There was a moment of silence before a shout went up and the inquisitive boys leaned in to see what life remained there. But no sooner had they looked, than they drew back.

"It blinks!" cried one. "It speaks!" wailed another. Sheriff Corwin thrust them aside in disgust and reached for Judah's black locks. He lifted the face to the crowd to display the grisly mass, and as they all stared, confounded and transfixed, Miranda's worst fears came to pass. The face grimaced and the eyes opened and fixed on her. The mouth moved, and although no sound came out, the lips clearly shaped her name for all to see. Sheriff Corwin leaned in to listen to its whisper and then his eyes fell on her, as did the crowd's, who one by one turned to look in her direction. Amadeus Collins mounted the platform and stood towering over the populace. His hands were clasped in front of his hassock, and his face was grim.

"What did the head say?" cried a man from the back of the crowd. "Tell us what it said."

Amadeus pointed an accusing finger. "The head hath spoken after death, a miraculous and pitiful damnation. It said, 'She lies!' and again, 'She lies!' She is the witch! And now an angry God will descend upon us all!"

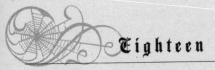

Eighteen

Collinwood—1971

That afternoon at Collinwood, Barnabas became aware of how much he missed David. Nothing afforded him more pleasure than the young man's company. He climbed the stairs and walked down the hall to David's room. The door was closed and he knocked, but there being no answer, he turned the knob and looked inside. There was a blast of cool air, and he was surprised to see the boy sitting on his window ledge. Barnabas knew, from David's vantage point, he could see the vast lawn and the great oaks that marched to the cliffs. Beyond that lay the sea.

"David?"

The boy turned and revealed a face contorted in anguish. His features were drawn like those of a very old man, and the flesh was puffy around his bloodshot eyes.

"Oh, my dear boy, what is it?" Barnabas said. David shook his head and turned again toward the sea. Barnabas stopped before he drew too close. "Come, David," he said. "Come down from there."

David gripped both sides of the casement and looked down. "Why?"

"Why? Because you could fall, and die before you have lived." He hoped his tone was lighthearted, but he felt a wave of compassion. David had no one to turn to if he were in despair. His father was unsympathetic, his aunt out of touch, and his poor mother gone, probably dead.

"Maybe I want to fall," said David. Barnabas suppressed a desire to laugh. But David leaned further out. The window was thirty feet above the ground, and Barnabas remembered a silly tradition: boys were given rooms in towers to make them more virile.

"David, come back inside and tell me what is troubling you." Still, the boy did not respond. Stealthily Barnabas moved to where he too could look down to the paving of the courtyard.

David made a choking sound in his throat. "Barnabas," he said, "have you ever been in love?"

"Yes, of course, I have been in love. Is that what has you so upset?" The girl he was kissing in the woods, thought Barnabas in amazement.

"Was it so painful?" Hot tears fell on Barnabas's hand where it rested on the sill next to David's.

Barnabas considered the question. "It is that. Yes. Usually."

"I love her so much, and she told me she did too."

"Then, what is the problem?"

"Now she won't have anything to do with me. She won't even speak to me." David shuddered again and leaned forward. His body swayed out.

Barnabas glanced down again, and feeling dizzy, took hold of David's hand. "That sounds serious," he said.

"Why did she change?"

"I don't know. I'm sure it has nothing to do with you, or anything you did. Where did you meet this girl?"

After a long sigh, David said in a whisper, "At the camp."

Ah, thought Barnabas, one of the hippie girls has seduced a young man for the fun of it. It seemed a cruel trick.

"Two nights ago," David continued, "she fed me soup in her tent. She's so beautiful. She said it was a potion to steal my heart, but it looked like some kind of broth. She said it was made from roots and dew and, I don't know, ferns and flower petals. I drank it, and it tasted like soup. It was pretty good. Barnabas is there such a thing as a love potion?"

"Of course not." The pavement beneath them whirled.

"Well, something has happened to me. She sang songs to me, funny songs I'd never heard, about knights and kings, and girls whose lovers murdered them, and then she—" David stumbled on his words, "and then we went for a walk, and lay down by the stream and—and she—she let me kiss her."

She certainly did, thought Barnabas, but he said gently, "What is wrong with a kiss or two? It seems harmless enough."

"The next morning she wouldn't have anything to do with me."

"La belle dame sans merci," Barnabas said softly, almost to himself.

David turned to him. "What's that?"

"A girl in a famous poem by Keats. You are not the first man to be so misused. Nor will you be the last." Gently he held the boy's arm and tried to draw him back from the ledge. But David clung to the window frame.

"How does the poem go?"

Barnabas thought a minute. "*I met a lady in the meads, full beautiful, a fairy's child; her hair was long, her foot was light, and her eyes were wild.*"

"That's her," said David.

"Then you must realize these feelings are not uncommon. Young girls can be heartless. You must not let it make you so unhappy. Please David, come back inside and I will tell you the rest of the story. You are frightening me, sitting out here like this."

Reluctantly, David crawled in and went to his bed. The boy was still in pajamas, and his sleep odor filled the room. He lay down while Barnabas closed the window and settled in a chair, blocking the way back outside.

"Tell it," said David.

"I can't remember it all," said Barnabas. "*And there I shut her wild wild eyes—so kissed to sleep.*'"

"I kissed her a lot," said David. "What else? Say some more."

"Oh, I don't remember," said Barnabas. "The poet has a dream that all the warriors come with starving eyes and gaping mouths, all the others who have loved her, and . . . '*death-pale were they all. They cried—"La belle Dame sans merci hath thee in thrall!"*'"

David lay still, thinking, and Barnabas mused on the tenderness of young love, those rare moments which never return again in a lifetime.

"Is this girl one of the hippies?" he asked.

"No." David sighed again, then looked over at Barnabas with an expression so pitiful that he instantly regretted having taken David's misery so lightly.

The hollows of the boy's face were drawn against his skull. He spoke slowly. "Remember when we went to the Old House to deliver that rug?"

"Of course."

"And I went upstairs to look in a room that was locked, right before I saw that weird man who looked like he was dead?"

"Yes. You said a girl lived there."

"I had already met her at the camp."

"You saw her clothes."

"And I read from her journal. I shouldn't have. I was prying."

"What did it say? Do you remember?"

"That this was not her time. That she had lived before, in the New England colonies, in the seventeenth century. That she really belonged there."

"Interesting."

"That's not all. She said she had a child, and that she was tried as a witch and hung."

"Perhaps she wants to become a writer."

"I know, that's what I thought too, at first. You've guessed who she is, haven't you?"

"No—"

"Toni's daughter. Jacqueline."

Barnabas rose to his feet and began to pace the room. He was surprised at the feeling of unease that stirred in his stomach. "Hasn't she been in Windcliff?" he said.

"Yeah. She took a lot of drugs. Messed herself up."

"Well, that explains her hallucinations, doesn't it?"

David sat up and wrapped his arms around his chest. Again, he moaned. "Oh, God. Barnabas, I don't know what to do."

"David it's difficult for you to believe, but this suffering will pass."

"I told you. I love her. More than anything in the world. I can't sleep. I can't eat. I can't think of anything else but her. I hardly know her and I don't understand why I feel this way. It's like she put a spell on me. And she's cruel. No one in my life has ever treated me like this. She's cold as ice, won't let me near her. Won't let me touch her. She looks at me like I'm some kind of worm."

"She'll come back around."

"No. She said she never wanted to see me again."

Barnabas closed his eyes and pictured the scene. The fairy child leaning over David, feeding him, singing to him. His heart ached for his nephew more than it ever had for himself.

He sat on the bed, and placing a comforting arm around David'
shoulders, drew the boy to him.

"She's young," he said. "She doesn't know herself yet. You'
a fine boy. She'll come to love you again, I feel certain. And yc
must try to be a man. Don't let her see you weeping in this mar
ner. She might abuse the power she has over you."

"But that's exactly how I feel, Barnabas. That she has som
kind of power over me."

"Nonsense. None other than you grant her. Promise m
you won't do anything rash. No woman is worth it."

Tears came into David's eyes again and he trembled. Barr
abas was struck by the boy's pallor. His lips were whiter tha
his skin and there was no color in his cheek.

"Don't worry," he said. "Many more girls will come int
your life. Some day you'll look back on all this and laugh."

David sighed and shook his head. "She gave me a story sh
wrote," he said. "Would you like to see it?"

"Very much."

"It's there. On the dresser."

Barnabas walked over to where a small sheet of paper wa
lying on top of a bureau. The text was written with a fountai
pen in cursive handwriting. He began to read, but after the firs
lines, he was forced to grab his wrist to keep the hand that hel
the paper from shaking.

Miranda

There was once a witch girl who lived as a child with the Indians in the forest. Birds sang to her when she passed and trees
let down their branches. She was as beautiful as the rising
sun, her hair black as raven's feathers, and her skin like the
falling snow. Her eyes were like two silver minnows in a pool.
Because she was a witch, she could fly at will, and she sometimes slept in the branches of the trees who protected her.

More than anyone or anything she loved the farm her father had cleared for her in the forest. Young as she was, she whitewashed the boards of the farmhouse and planted a field with rye, dragging a plow roped to her own slender waist. She cleaned the pasture spring of winter weeds so the woodland animals might come to her meadow and drink.

When the time came and Miranda turned eighteen, she was ready to move to her farm with her young husband and child. But the greedy merchants in the town wanted her land. They offered to buy her farm for a goodly sum, but she always refused them. At first they argued that her indenture was not over and she must remain in service. Then they claimed the writing in the book of property was not clear, her name illegible. They called her disrespectful when she argued with them. And they looked on her with disapproval every time she missed a Sunday meeting.

And so they set upon her and called her "witch." She pleaded her innocence, saying she had never harmed a living soul, but they were deaf to her supplications. The harvest had been ruined by an early frost. One woman had buried five babies at birth. A man's cow had bloated and died screaming. They said the girl was to blame, that she was a witch. She was tried by the magistrates and sentenced to be hanged.

Her mother was heart-anguished and offered to die in her place. But the townspeople cast the mother into chains. Her lover tried to free her but he was shot by the townspeople and buried without a coffin in a shallow grave. Death was the taste on their tongues.

The girl was placed in the cart and carried to the Hanging Place. As she rode to the gallows, Miranda was given her wee babe to suckle one more time. It fretted and would not be comforted. On the platform she produced a hidden blade and with it slit the child's throat. Raising its bloody corpse above the heads of the people, she cursed the families of those who had condemned her. "Thou shalt have blood to drink," she cried, "for all eternity."

Barnabas dropped the paper on the dresser as though it we aflame. The heat began in his core and rose as far as his finge tips. He struggled to breathe. And all this time he knew he mu maintain an outward calm. "I think she is talented," he said, "an she will make a good writer." He turned and looked at Davi The boy's beseeching gaze held his, their eyes locked, and a spa of understanding passed between them.

"I have seen her," he said. "This morning early, near th graveyard. She called me Reverend."

David frowned. "And was she beautiful?"

"Very beautiful, but her eyes were frightening."

He heard a car in the drive beneath the window and looke to see who it could be. Red and blue lights circled on the hoo It was the local Collinsport police.

Nineteen

oger stood in the foyer red-faced with annoyance. He was smartly dressed in a chestnut suede morning jacket and brocaded vest, but his blue eyes blazed and his upper lip quivered. "These questions are preposterous," he said to the two policemen who stood just inside the door. Barnabas hesitated on the landing.

"If I understand you correctly, Mr. Collins, you don't know anything about the girl who died," said one policeman.

"I sold the property to that woman, Antoinette Harpignies. I've never wanted to have anything to do with her or what went on there. I told Sheriff Patterson weeks ago to clear away those degenerates. It was your responsibility."

"We put up notices. Today's the day they have to be out."

"Then you are a day late and a dollar short."

"Yes sir, Mr. Collins."

"I also asked my cousin, who has had several opportunities,

to convince them to leave, but he has repeatedly neglected to do so. I never wanted a hippie camp anywhere near Collinwood. In my opinion, the family name has been denigrated."

"Can you explain the fact that the victim was mauled by some kind of animal?"

"Probably a satanic ritual. That's exactly what I mean. These people are not civilized."

"So you think it was them who did it."

"Absolutely. Really, officer, you don't believe there are still wild beasts in the forest outside of Collinsport."

"Her neck was—if you'll excuse the expression—ripped to shreds."

"And that was what killed her?"

"Yeah. She bled to death."

Barnabas clung to the banister.

"Well, I have only one thing to say to you, officer. You have my express permission to bulldoze the camp and send those sociopaths somewhere else. My sister can't sleep at night for fear they'll burglarize us, looking for something to steal to pay for their drug habits."

It was time to intervene, but Barnabas stopped when he heard the policeman say, "I'm afraid, Mr. Collins, it's not that simple. This is a murder charge here. There's been a violent death. It's not enough to clear the rabble out and be finished with them. We'll have to do a thorough investigation."

"I find the entire situation," said Roger, "deeply abhorrent."

Barnabas continued down the stairs and joined the trio in the foyer. "Good day, officers," he said.

"Barnabas," said Roger, "there's been an unfortunate accident. On the property next door. A girl has been murdered."

"I'm aware of the accident, Roger. I was with Antoinette when she called the ambulance."

Roger's face blanched. "You?"

"It was a transient, an unknown vagrant, who attacked the

irl. The campers had nothing to do with him. They were all errified. I'm sorry to hear that she did not survive."

"And she's not the only one," said the other police officer, who had been quiet until now. "Something very suspicious washed up on the beach this morning. We found some human emains. There's some real hanky-panky going on around here, nd we mean to get to the bottom of it."

"Horrible," said Roger, turning away.

"But why do you suspect the campers?" asked Barnabas. "I'm ure they are innocent. They simply wanted to spend the summer iving in the woods, close to nature. Isn't that their right? You nake unfortunate accusations when you suggest satanic rituals, Roger. You have no proof of such a thing."

Roger's gaze was cold. "I cannot believe that you of all people would defend them, Barnabas," he said.

The first officer spoke up. "What we were looking at here was health violations, and unlawful assembly."

"But they are not staging any kind of protest—"

"Wait a minute. Let me finish. Anytime a group of more han ten persons gathers together they need a permit."

Barnabas knew the policeman was bluffing. He threw his hands in the air. "That's small town despotism," he scoffed. "They were camped on private property with the permission of the owner. It's perfectly legal."

"We have tourists on the weekends," offered Roger. "It's an economic situation as much as anything."

"Yeah, the camp is a big eyesore," said the officer, looking weary. "We know they've had illegal drugs on the premises, but we've been hoping they would take off before there was any trouble. I've even had some words with that guy who's their leader. He out and out told me they wouldn't leave. That's contempt of a court order. But all that is beside the point now. Someone is dead."

"Why didn't you act sooner?" said Roger, his temper rising. "Then none of this would have happened."

"All right. Calm down, Mr. Collins. The sheriff has just dis
patched a team over there to clear them out," said the policeman

Barnabas looked up in surprise. "Clear them out? I don
think that's necessary."

"The sheriff has already given the order. By this evening ther
won't be anything left." The officer looked smug. "The men will b
using new riot control tactics. They've only just taken a trainin;
program. Six weeks, very intensive."

"Tactics? What tactics? You can't be serious."

"Just let any one of them resist and they'll be in some rea
trouble. Every one of them will go to jail."

"Now, just a minute," said Barnabas. "You'll not use violenc
of any kind. Roger, say something." But Roger only drew himsel
up in disdain. Barnabas turned back to the policeman. "I won'
allow you to employ precipitous methods that are uncalled for
and could injure innocent people—"

"Cousin Barnabas?"

David appeared at the landing. His face was ashen. "Jacki
is at the camp. They won't hurt her, will they?"

There was a vicious wind in the trees. Black branches un-
dulated violently as though enraged, hurling debris into th
air. Barnabas's hands gripped the wheel of the Bentley as he sped
down the road with David beside him. The campers would be
completely unprepared for this invasion. As soon as Barnabas
pulled up behind several patrol wagons and parked, he saw the
fire in the woods.

Quickly exiting the Bentley, he approached a policeman inside a squad car who was shouting into a two-way radio. Forcing
himself to appear calm, he leaned over and said, "Excuse me, sir,
are you the officer responsible for this action?"

The heavyset cop looked up and muttered quickly, "Yeah.
Captain Brady here."

"Captain Brady, this is not necessary. These young people re not involved in any wrongdoing."

The captain spoke into his popping radio. "Hold on a min- te," then turned to Barnabas. "Who are you?"

"Barnabas Collins. I live just down the road. I know the eople camping out on this property, and I can assure you, they re quite peaceful."

"Oh, yeah? We ran into a lot of resistance," said the police- nan.

"Well, what would you do? They must all be terrified."

"All I know, Mr., uh, Collins, is we got a wounded officer." Ie pushed the toggle on his radio and Barnabas heard it crackle, They . . . rounded up . . . three . . ."

Seeing it was useless, Barnabas turned and jogged towards he lights of the camp, David at his heels. Two policemen bur- lened with riot gear brushed past him, knocking Barnabas off alance, and ran ahead. Even before he arrived at the clearing, he eard cries, curses, and sounds of scuffling, and the first thing e saw when he broke through the trees was a huge bonfire and hree naked boys handcuffed together in the clearing.

"Oh no," cried David. "They're burning everything!"

Canisters lay on the ground spewing yellow smoke. Hys- erical campers ran about coughing, grabbing belongings: books, soup pot, a torn shawl. One girl stood helplessly, her arms anging at her sides, tears streaming down her face. Police in ;as masks threw objects on the flames and entire tents were lragged across the clearing and pitched on the fire like giant noths. The mirrors on the trees flashed brilliant shards of light as ungent smoke exploded and the fire bristled, consuming ham- nocks, sleeping bags, the makeshift tables, even wildflower bou- quets. Barnabas ran for Toni's tent, which was still intact, and stooped to look inside. The sleeping bag was crumpled in a cor- ner. Her clothes and Jackie's, as well as other belongings, were strewn about, but the women were nowhere in sight. He caught a glimpse of Toni's Afghani sack in the back beneath a blanket.

"David," he called. "Over here."

The boy appeared, his face reddened. "They're wrecking i all," he said. "Do something."

"Here, take these things and put them in the car." Eyes stinging, Barnabas crawled back out of the tent, but before he could rise to his feet, something bright and luminous caught his eye. Trays of spilled beads, all the brilliant colors, flashed in the dirt.

The cops carrying objects to the fire seemed to be deformed creatures with heavily padded elbows and knees, their thick belts bristling with chains, stun guns, clubs, and bulging holsters. Their heads were encased in masks that transformed them into giant anteaters, round snouts hanging from leather contraptions, and wide insect-eye visors. Barnabas saw a girl he recognized, Chastity, run to the fire and, risking the flames, scramble forwards to retrieve her notebook. One of the snub-nosed creatures struck her in the shoulder with his club.

Barnabas was galvanized into action. "Hey! What are you doing?" The cop lifted his baton again. "Stop that! Are you insane?" He lunged for the man, jerked him backwards, seized his shoulder in a vise grip, and ripped the mask from his astonished face.

"She hasn't—what are you? Some kind of beast?" He thrust the policeman away with such savagery the man rolled to the ground. He was leaning over to lift Charity to her feet when a heavy boot connected with his gut. The air in his lungs exploded and he collapsed in the dirt. Colored beads spun under his eyes, and his mouth filled with grit. Shaking his head to clear it, he turned and, through a blurred haze, saw a girl run towards the trees with her guitar. An elephantine monster caught up with her, grabbed the instrument, swung it, and splintered it against a tree trunk. It exploded with a dissonant chord of sound.

Barnabas pulled himself up on all fours; there was a sharp

pain in his side, and he gasped for breath. The fire was spitting sparks and reeked of burning cloth. Balloons of flame rose into the air. Through bleary eyes he saw another cop push a young woman towards the dark of the forest. He was fumbling with his belt. Barnabas squinted in recognition, and caught a glimpse of her terrified face before he saw her fall. It was Carolyn!

What happened next was an outburst of fury. One moment Barnabas was straining to rise, the next he was behind the cop with one hand on the back of the gas mask. His fingers dug in the straps and he jerked the man off his feet. He heard the crunch of a shattered nose as the cop collapsed in a heap. He turned to see a policeman coming for him with a club raised over his head, but in a flash the man was on the ground. Barnabas knelt on his chest with one hand on the top of the mask and the other gripping the bulky collar. Rage fueling strength, he ripped open the jacket and exposed the jugular. He leaned in for the kill. Only a look of horror through the goggles stopped him. Releasing the cop with a shudder, he rose to his feet and saw another policeman standing in front of the fire with his pistol drawn.

"Stop right there, buddy," he said. "You're under arrest."

Barnabas blinked. "Put that away," he said, panting. "I'm not the criminal here."

"Get your hands in the air."

Barnabas hesitated, confused as to his next move. The bullets would not be silver. He took a step toward the policeman.

"Halt. Or I'll shoot."

Barnabas lurched for the weapon. The gun fired. Rocked by the impact of the bullet, he staggered back, and swayed on his feet, but only for the briefest moment of comprehension. He was not invulnerable. Wrath filled his body and exploded into his limbs. He raised his fist, struck the cop's hand, and the gun flew from his shattered fingers. Suddenly everything was quiet. He knew he was hit, but he could not feel the wound. The police in the clearing stood aghast, all watching Barnabas, who turned slowly, daring them to move. Slowly, he pulled the keys from the belt of the fallen policeman and unlocked the naked boys. Then he reached for Carolyn, drew Charity to her feet, and turned to the others. "Come with me," he said. "You'll be safe." And he led them toward the road.

Looking around for David, he spotted him coming from the forest with another armload of papers and books. "I got all Toni's stuff," called the boy as he headed for the Bentley. Barnabas fumbled beneath his cape where he was bleeding, and he felt a slight twinge. He was about to follow David when he saw Jason standing in the line of handcuffed hippies and walked over to him.

"What happened?" he said. "Have the police lost their minds? What did you do?"

Jason's eyes blazed with hatred. "Son of a bitch," he said, and he spat on the ground at Barnabas's feet. "You'll be sorry you did this. They got nothin' on me and as soon as I'm out, I'm coming back, and the Collinses with their high-and-mighty patrician shit better watch their backs."

"Wait a minute. I had nothing to do with this. I came to stop it."

Jason leaned in until his face was close to Barnabas and said in a whisper, "I know what you are. I knew as soon as I saw you. You're a phony. Nothin' but a big pretender." A policeman pulled Jason toward the paddy wagon and Barnabas hesitated.

"Just a minute. If you'd give me a chance to explain, you'll see we are on the same side here—"

"Save it, buddy."

"I am sorry this happened."

Jason's eyes glittered with tears. "They busted up Little Chris's guitar, man, threw it in the fire. Why'd they have to do that? Sally's flute. Busted in half. Yeah. Think about it. Why?"

"I don't know."

"Lemme ask you something. What did we ever do to you?"

"Jason, I—"

"Those jerk-off cops. They pulled the girls out of the tents, wouldn't even let them get dressed. An' then they handcuffed them so they could look at 'em naked."

"I—I never meant for this to happen."

Jason leaned in to Barnabas and whispered in his ear. "Start lockin' your doors and windows, man, 'cause I'm comin' back."

David was standing at his side. "Where's Jackie?" he said. "Where's Toni?"

"He-e-e-y-y-y, Bro," said Jason, his eyes softening. "Whatta you doin' here?"

"Where's Jackie?"

"So, what about it? Are you with us or against us?"

"Jason, please, just tell me . . ."

"Toni's not here," he said. "If she had been, she'd of told the cops to go fuck themselves."

"So, they're okay?"

"She went to Salem, see. Said she was going to some meeting. So she missed it, man. She missed the whole party." He looked at David, his eyes shining. "You know what they did? Asshole cops. They shot a hole in the pickle barrel."

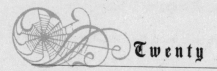

Twenty

On the highway to Salem, Barnabas tried to calm the tempest swirling in his brain. His newfound strength must mean only one thing. He was reverting. His body felt light and powerful for the first time in months. However, he was wounded—not badly, just enough to give cause for worry. The bullet had pierced his side but only a silver bullet could stop a vampire. On the other hand, could his real wound mean the cure was nearly complète?

David would not stop talking. He was still young and idealistic, Barnabas thought, not yet cynical enough to realize that good and evil were far from definable. But he was having difficulty listening to David's tirade. He was thinking of Jason, his red-rimmed eyes, his cruel taunts. Something about him was odd.

"Why didn't they give them a chance?" David said. "I know

there was a court order, but winter was coming. They would have left soon."

"A girl died," said Barnabas, wondering now whether he should return to Collinwood and to Julia's room to have her dress his wound—not drive to Salem tonight. But more than anything, he longed to see Antoinette. And it was only right that she be told her property had been invaded and that she was headed for a legal battle. He intended to offer his help.

"But they didn't kill her."

"The police thought the hippies were responsible," Barnabas said. He opened and closed his fingers on the wheel, feeling them bend and tighten. Was it his imagination, or were his hands more flexible?

"But they weren't," said David. "They were just as scared as anyone else. Jackie knew about the thing that killed the girl."

"No, I don't think so."

"You know what she said it was? A zombie. It was in Toni's service or something."

Barnabas jammed his foot against the gas pedal.

"What's going on?" said David. "Slow down."

"What—?"

"You're going ninety miles an hour."

Disoriented, his head spinning, Barnabas stared at the speedometer. He floundered for the brake. The Bentley slowed and hummed more softly. Gripping the steering wheel, he felt a storm of emotions. Were they both suspect? Mother and daughter? Antoinette had seemed so sincere when she told him she had called an ambulance and they had taken the girl to the hospital. Or had he imagined it?

He found it difficult to speak. "Jackie told you this?"

"Jackie told me her mother was a witch."

Of course, of course. With anguish, he recalled her sweet abandon. A lie. All a lie. "David . . . are you sure?"

"Well, that's what she said. But I think she makes things up to scare me."

Contempt for Antoinette rose once again in his heart, and shame for his own absurd culpability. Now he wanted to punish her, to force her to succumb to his desires. As he sped down the dark road, he became aroused with the thought of holding her, hearing her moan. The muscles in his arms became rigid. He gripped the steering wheel with such fury he heard it crack.

"Barnabas, what are you doing?"

"It's . . . I . . ."

"What are you doing to the steering wheel?"

"Oh, how stupid of me." He strained to relax. It was essential that he drive carefully, if only for the safety of the boy. In his lap, David still held papers rescued from Toni's tent, and he was looking through them. "Maybe you should put all that in the glove compartment," he said, in what he hoped was a lighter tone, "so it won't get lost." But David had already opened a file that contained several letters.

"Look at this," he said. "It's Jackie's medical report."

"I think that is private," said Barnabas.

David was poring over one of the pages, hungry for some information that would explain his sweetheart's behavior.

"This is really weird. Do you want to hear this?"

Barnabas looked through the windshield at the dark night. It had begun to rain and in the headlights beads of water danced on the asphalt. "It's going to be a long drive," he said.

David began to read.

"'October twenty-five, 1971. Dear Mrs. Harpignies: This letter should serve to recall the phone conversation we had at 7:03 A.M. This morning the fourth floor nurse, Miss Fluentino, advised me that in making her rounds she discovered your daughter, Jacqueline, was not in her room. She also informed me that she had provided you with a key to the exterior/interior door, since you are in the habit of visiting your daughter late at night.

She assured me that she trusted you implicitly, and that she counted upon you to respect the security of the locked floor. As you know, patients the staff feels may be a danger to others are kept on this floor.'

"So that's why she was at the camp," said David. "Toni sprung her."

"What else does it say?"

"'Although we are not a prison, apparently the guard was patrolling an outside area when you came to the facility and, without our consent, removed your daughter from the grounds. I regret to inform you that Windcliff Sanitarium can no longer assume responsibility for Jacqueline. In the event that you wish to return her to the hospital, a meeting to decide her status as a patient will have to be arranged and the senior staff of the sanitarium will be required to be present. This can be initiated only under my recommendation.

"'As we have discussed in our numerous conferences here in my office, I have misgivings as to Jacqueline's prognosis. I must reiterate that she is, in my opinion, incapable of living on her own, and she is a potential threat to others as well as to herself. After the episode with the rat, I am certain she belongs in a locked facility where she can be cared for and observed.

"'I hope you will reconsider your impetuous and misguided decision to remove your daughter from the sanitarium. Yours very truly, Kenneth Solares, M.D., Ph.D.'

"Wow," said David. "It's a lot more serious than I thought."

"You had no idea she was so ill?" said Barnabas.

"Well, I thought she was mean, but I didn't think she was crazy. And then at other times she was so kind and beautiful." He extracted another document and once more began to read.

"'September seventeen, 1971. Dear Miss Harpignies: This is an interim report on the psychiatric care we have provided for your daughter, Jacqueline. We have already discussed her case with you on several occasions, and this letter only serves as a brief compilation of the steps we have taken in her rehabilitation.

"'One. Hypnosis: Jacqueline responds well to hypnotic suggestion and answers questions readily. She continues to claim that she lived in Salem, Massachusetts, in 1692 or thereabouts, and that her real name is Miranda du Val. She describes her life there in rich detail, and is willing to talk for hours in the voice, accent, and character of this particular individual.

"'Two. Psychotherapy: Jacqueline is sullen and unresponsive in therapy. She is either silent or belligerent in group sessions. She displays contempt for other members in the group as well as for her therapist, and will only answer questions when it pleases her. Her answers, when she supplies them, are nonsensical and bizarre.

"'Three. Diagnosis: A diagnosis of schizophrenia presents itself since she displays the traditional symptoms: preoccupation with one or more systematized delusions, or frequent auditory hallucinations related to a single theme. She also evidences unfocused anxiety, anger, argumentativeness, and a predilection for violence. There is either a formal quality or an extreme intensity in her interpersonal reactions. However, neither lithium nor valium has resulted in a positive response. Thorazine (chlorpromazine) is administered daily, and although it has a calming effect, it results in catatonic indifference and severe loss of personality.'

"Heavy. Really heavy," said David and kept reading. "Listen."

"'October three, 1971. Report of Jacqueline Harpignies. ECT: After much serious consideration, the psychiatric staff at Windcliff Sanitarium made the decision to pursue B-lateral Electroconvulsive Therapy in the case of the above patient.'

"What's that?" said David.

Barnabas thought a moment. "I think it's Shock Treatment."

"Oh no . . ."

"'Disclaimer: As with other somatic therapies in psychiatry, we still do not know the mechanism by which ECT exerts its therapeutic effects. It is considered in many channels to be obsolete—in fact much like a treatment from the dark ages—and in those same areas it is postulated that irreparable brain damage may result. More often, however, the treatment results in a rather miraculous cure. Although punitive superegos can require repeated shocks of 110 volts for appeasement, the usual dose is seventy to one hundred volts at an amperage of 200 milliamperes. Since paranoid schizophrenia involves unknown biological abnormalities of the brain, it is theorized that when administered with care, these electrical assaults rearrange brain chemistry for the better.'

"Barnabas . . . I can't believe they would do that to her.

"'Result: The first treatment was thought to be successful, and Jacqueline appeared to be a more subdued and cooperative patient. The positive changes, however, were short-lived. Three nights after the first treatment, Jacqueline became hysterical and beat the walls of her room in an effort to escape until her hands bled. Consequently, she had to be restrained. The second and third treatments have only served to increase her hysteria. Her resistance to the third treatment was sobering to the staff and the physician in charge. In a full report recorded by the orderly on duty, she braced both hands against the door in an effort to keep herself out of the room, screamed, struggled violently, and had to be dragged to the table. It has been noted in various studies on ECT that this is not unusual, as the fear of the treatment intensifies after each session. It is thought that patients begin to dread what they imagine, and describe, as an agonizing experience of the self being shattered to bits. However, in Jacqueline's case, the risk seems less objectionable than for her to remain in her present state. Jacqueline is scheduled for five more regimens.'"

Barnabas looked at David. He had gone pale. Then he continued in a quiet voice.

"'Analysis: In Jacqueline's case we have observed that she suffers from racing or uncontrollable thoughts, sometimes talks to herself, evidences paranoia, hallucinations, and delusions. She overemphasizes the connectedness of words, objects, and sounds in a non-linear, quasi-poetic manner. Consequently, her thinking seems dominated by metaphors. In our experience, if the patient's horizons are allowed to expand too far, there will be serious consequences. If not controlled these uncurbed cognitive processes can become disabling. Fortunately, modern medicines and other forms of treatment remain available.'"

Barnabas and David were quiet for a few moments, absorbing this new information. David sighed and stared out the window into the rain, now flashing in sheets, spattering the pavement before the headlights.

"I still don't believe it," he said. "She didn't seem that bad. Doctors can be wrong, can't they?"

"They can indeed, and often are. Like everyone else, they have their own agendas."

"What does that mean?"

"Oh, they latch on to special cases to prove their expertise. They become entranced with their own brilliance. They can become so obsessed with the illness of a certain patient—and finding the cure—they lose all sympathy for his suffering."

"I wish I could see her," David said, with another long sigh. He turned to Barnabas. "I still love her," he said simply. He shuffled the papers again, then hesitated at another small page. Barnabas glanced over and saw that it was a handwritten note. After David read it to himself, he let out a mournful sound like a hurt animal.

"What? What is it?"

"It's a letter from Jackie, to her mother."

Dear Mommy,

Why won't you come get me? You said you would come. The walls of my prison drip blood. There are rats under my bed and the baby cries all night long. I am chained to walls that drip blood. They tortured me on the rack. They wanted to kill me but I survived. It was horrible. It hurt so bad. Please don't let them do it again. Are they going to hang me? I am not a witch. Why do they say I am a witch? They made me sit in a circle with the girls who testify lies against me and call me names. They say I have bewitched them. I know they would kill me if they could. Please come for me. I want to help you with the beautiful old house so we can all live there together forever and ever.

I love you,
Jackie

Rain fell in a steady downpour. Fat drops spattered the windshield and the great Bentley wipers swept them away. Barnabas could feel David weeping silently.

Unlike the night of their first visit, the streets of Salem were dark and empty. Only a few cars roamed the shadows, and the rain flashed to needles in the pale spheres of the streetlights and drummed on the roof of the car.

"We don't have any idea where they are, do we?" said David. "They could be anywhere."

"Shall we just get a room and look in the morning?"

"Yeah, everyone's in bed."

David was asleep when Barnabas crept down the stairs of the B&B and out into the stormy night. It was past midnight. His wound ached with a dull throb and he favored his right side when he moved. He longed to lie down, but he remembered something, and he didn't want to miss the opportunity if he was right.

Driving through Salem, he once again became lost in the labyrinthine one-way streets. Moving slowly, but with a sense of inevitability, he searched for Antoinette's truck, and just past the Witch and Pirate Museums he found it. The Chevy pickup was parked several spaces beyond the entrance. Barnabas drew up to the curb, killed his engine, and reached in the back seat for his cape. Drawing its folds about him, he climbed, with some effort, to the sidewalk. Approaching the carved oak doorway, and the copper plate on which was engraved in small letters, Witch Education Bureau, he noticed a damp slip of paper which read SÉANCE, midnight tonight.

After a moment's hesitation, in which the rain beat down on his back, Barnabas placed a hand on the iron handle, turned it slowly, and heard the bolt click. The door opened silently. At first he could see nothing inside the room but a red glow. A heavy odor of incense filled his nostrils and a dozen candles flickered in the gloom. A flash of lightning illuminated the arched gothic window on the back wall, exposing its tracery, and he saw a large circular table with a dozen or so black-robed individuals seated around it, their heads bowed. The table and its ring of worshipers seemed to float over a blood red carpet on the heavily polished floor. Coming from somewhere in the circle was the deep reverberation of an incantation.

"Once again we call upon the great powers locked in the shifting firmament, trapped in the membranes of memory. Take us back to this very spot, two hundred and eighty years ago, to Salem at its founding, to a simpler and purer time, that this woman and her daughter may search the far horizons of their past. The Salem we seek surrounds us now, its ghosts and its spirits. We call on those who lived then to come for us. Lead us, embrace us."

How ridiculous, thought Barnabas. The idea of going back in time was possible, but the words chosen to enact the spell were sadly lacking in originality. His eyes becoming accustomed to the dark, Barnabas moved forward and glimpsed on the huge table various objects from earlier times. They must have been borrowed from the historical dioramas in the Peabody Essex Museum. He recognized a child's cradle, an oil lamp, an iron kettle, and a milk bucket. He was musing on their inadequacy to the task when he spotted Antoinette seated on the far side, her golden hair covered by her blue cloak. She was concentrating so deeply on the incantation her mouth quivered and tears dampened her cheeks. As he drew nearer, she lifted her eyes, and he saw in them a look of such profound relief, his doubts about her vanished in an instant.

"Barnabas . . ." said Toni softly. "Come join us. Help us."

It was then he saw Jacqueline, her mother's hand clasped tightly in her own, and her pale eyes gleaming, like two tiny moons. Her stare pierced him to the bone. It was a look of recognition and contempt, and had he not known she was but a child, he would have said—a look of evil.

At first a natural reticence restrained him, but Toni's expression was impossible to ignore. She was asking for his assistance, and of course he would help her, if only to console her when this misguided séance failed. Drawn by nothing more than a need to be close to her, he rounded the table. The circle shifted to make room, and he slid in beside her, wincing from the pain in his side as he took her hand.

A man dressed in a black hood with slits for eyes—some sort of high priest, Barnabas assumed—took hold of Barnabas's other hand and resumed his invocation. "We see before us objects from another time. Let those who employed these things in their daily lives come for us. Oh, men and women of Salem, hear our plea." Barnabas cringed at the hackneyed syntax. All he could see by the greenish glow of the oil lamp—a clay pipe, a tankard with the face of the Devil embossed on its side, a bottle with what appeared to be finger bones, a clump of eagle feathers, a starched collar and a lace cap, a curled gray wig, a judge's gavel, and a very old and well-worn Bible—these seemed feeble implements for such inordinately difficult alchemy. Barnabas looked at the other circle members. He thought he recognized the two young waiters from the restaurant who had served him and David. All had their eyes tightly shut and hands clasped with knuckles turned white. The pitch of the intonation rose. "Turn back the pages of time to when these objects were in use. Draw forth the molecules of their material memory. Only a paper-thin membrane separates us from the living townspeople who moved in these rooms, sat at this very table which served as the judges' bench of iniquity, those self-righteous perpetrators of fiendish fabrications who passed woeful sentences on their neighbors. They are with us now, seated beside us, Bartholomew Gedney, Jonathan Corwin, John Hathorne, Samuel Sewall, and Amadeus Collins, who in their infinite wisdom and cruelty sent this child to her death." The priest's voice screeched and he seemed possessed. "Find the opening. Take them under the wing of time, fly them back into darkness!"

At that moment, out of the corner of his eye, Barnabas saw Jacqueline rise, still holding fast to her mother and neighbor, but her body was rigid as though in pain, and spasms traveled through her frame. She threw back her head and screamed.

The huge table shuddered and the great gothic window flared as if from a falling meteor. Lightning careened behind them, and thunder exploded and shook the building. Barnabas thought the window had shattered, for the room was drenched with a light so blinding he shielded his own eyes, and his head pitched forward on the table. He rose and instinctively he reached for Antoinette, drew her to him, and stood with her body molded to his. They hovered in a disembodied mist—rain blowing through the opening. It was bitter cold, and he wrapped his cape around her shivering form, as thunder cracked again and streaks of blue and silver light flew past. Then, to his dismay, he began to lose his grip on her; first her body and then her skirt shifted in his hands, and some unseen power wrenched her from his grasp.

Twenty-one

Salem—1692

"Why are your eyes silver?"

Miranda looked up at the smudged face of the seven-year-old child who was curled beside her in the corner of her jail cell, and, as it was bitter cold, tried to pull her skirts around them both, her shawl over their shoulders.

"From the moon," she said. Her chains chafed her ankles, now raw with open sores, and she moved gingerly that they might not bleed again. She knew she was gravely ill. A fetid vapor hung in the air like wisps of oily smoke, for there was still waste in the center of the cell; the jailer had not come for the bucket. Sickly and weak, Little Dorcas nestled into her, and Miranda thought she must die; but the child said every day she wanted to live to see the baby born. She was an orphaned girl accused of witchcraft, her mother already hanged. Damn them! May they all burn in the very Hell their zealotry envisions. God in Heaven, may it be for them.

She mourned that she had no roots or herbs to save those who were ill, and although she was able with laying on hands to aid a few, all her feckless spells were lost to her now. There was no help for it in a dungeon where even the rocks oozed a sour grease, and the floor was slimy with mold. Though the women made every attempt to use the chamber pot, those few with chains, like Miranda, were so burdened they could not manage it. If not for the cold, the stench would have killed them all, that and the fleas and the rats that came every night. And if they did manage to sleep, they woke bitten. Unrecognizable now, one from the other, shapeless gray shades, they wept, moaned pitiably, embraced for meager comfort, and when the jailer came with their gruel, roused themselves to beg for a new trial.

From where Miranda lay, she could see one small window. Without bars or panes, it allowed a glimpse of the dawn and then the day, a slowly changing spectrum from pale rose of morning, to glittering black when the frigid night settled over them again. At times the sun caught an angle that bestowed gentle warmth for an hour or so. But the harsh light revealed the grime on the faces of the inmates: the tortured grimaces of those gone mad with grief, or the deathly stupor on the masks of those who had abandoned hope. Some nights the moon drifted across the little window, and they were able to count their days by its changing shape. This night it had a bulge on one side, a melon moon, glowing brightly in a sky with no clouds.

In the outer room where George Locker, the constable, kept watch, visitors often stopped by, curious about the inmates; but then none looked into the cells, as they were driven back by the foul odor. There were no locked doors, for even the unchained accepted their fate like penned sheep. Where would they go? Not to the forest they feared more than death itself, nor upon the road where they would be ridden down and shot. Newcomers talked in hushed tones, were incredulous, whispered among themselves, and bought George's beer, for he had opened a tavern on the premises; sometimes they challenged him to a game of chess. Did they play for the souls of the prisoners, Miranda wondered?

Some poor women made every effort to keep themselves clean, having to choose between drinking and washing with the grimy cup of water they were given once a day. Those losing faith began to scream in the night and, after first praying to Lord Jesus, began to curse the God forsaking them.

Word came that Andrew had appeared with his musket and stormed the meetinghouse demanding his wife—that was what he called her. He was fired upon and driven away. A body of men organized to assist the constable was sent to burn his hut, destroying all that he had. Defense of a witch was cause for suspicion, but for once they stopped short of arresting an innocent man, perhaps out of fear for their own hides. He must have fought all six of them with his great heart bursting, and in the end he fled to the forest, banished from Salem, never to return in this lifetime.

A yeoman friend to George brought news that Judge Sewall had argued eloquently for Miranda's release, saying that she had healing powers, had often saved the lives of animals, or treated young children. Increase Mather took an interest in her case and she was to be examined again, but Amadeus Collins insisted her healing arts were nothing less than witchcraft. She had two months before the birth, and in that time by some miracle, she might win a reprieve.

Only the baby, bastard that it was, kept her from the gallows. She cupped her hands around the bulge in her stomach and was warmed by the small fire. But she was failing fast. Whatever little she had to eat was not enough to feed them both, and the child took the necessary portion. She knew something was wrong in her body, tearing at her, a tiny knee or elbow; and she was so thin she could feel its shape with her hand: the rounded back, the fluttering tail, for the little beaver in her belly clawed and dug.

There had been no hangings for weeks, and every day another prisoner was released. Fine ladies had been called out, and there was the mistake. The fashionable wife of the new governor, Sir William Phips, had been named by the foolish girls, now emboldened to the point of absurdity; and she had come in her finery to see the prison, incensed that her person would be tainted with this terror. She had not even reached the door before the stench assailed her delicate nostrils, and she withdrew enraged.

Miranda grew weaker and drifted in and out of sleep. Voices jarred her consciousness, but they gave her little hope.

"Nathaniel Saltonstall has resigned against the proceedings."

"More than a hundred still imprisoned."

"Increase Mather has asked his son Cotton Mather to forbear. No more spectral evidence is to be allowed."

"They are saying those from Andover were innocent."

"Abigail Hobbes has incriminated her own father!"

"Sheriff Corwin grows rich on jailer's fees and confiscated property."

"God help us all for we are innocent."

Her limbs ached from lying on the stone floor, and her body was like a paper package with the loose bones no longer attached to one another. Because of the grime on her skin, she imagined she was a piece of the wall, one of the stones embedded in the cement, and she thought if someone were to come for her, they would find only a reeking boulder or a pile of discarded rags.

Dorcas often sang to her in a bright voice, hoping to soothe them both with stories from her young childhood set to mournful melodies.

"An earthly nourris sits and sings,
And low she sings by lily wein,
Saying little ken I my bairn's father,
Far less the land where he dwells in."

"What song is that?" Miranda asked, although she shivered when she saw the child's blazing eyes.

"It is a song my mother sang to me, of a woman who married a silkie and had his baby."

"Did she love her child?"

"Aye, but the great seal came in the night and took him away." Dorcas had a voice like chimes, bell-like and pure. All the shadows in the cell held their breaths and listened when she sang.

> *"And he has tain a purse of gold*
> *And he ha' placed it on her knee*
> *Saying give to me my little young son*
> *And take thee up thy nourris fee."*

Miranda wondered whether Judah Zachery would have come for his child, and if it truly was the child of the Devil. Would he have paid her a paltry price and taken it away to raise in the manner of his breed?

"Did she let go her baby?"

"Aye, she was bound to do so, for she was a nourris."

"Ah, I see. Sing, Dorcas."

> *"And he came one night to her bed feet,*
> *And a grumbly guest I'm sure was he*
> *Saying Here am I thy bairn's father*
> *Although I be not com-e-ly."*

Miranda closed her eyes and dreamed of the young seal swimming the foam with his father. And she thought of Andrew's very human jealousy as Dorcas sang in her mournful voice.

> *"And ye shall marry a gunner good*
> *A fine ship's gunner I'm sure he'll be.*

And the very first shot that ere he shoots
Will kill both my young son and me."

Perhaps Andrew would have killed the child, she thought, one day in the forest, mistaking him for a deer. "'Tis a strange song," she said. "Did your mother sing many?"

"Aye, too many for her own good. Her own mother, my old grandmama, came from Scotland and taught her the ballads. And then, when I was little, she taught them to me. But singing, except for the dull hymns in church, is heresy. They called her a witch and for that they hanged her. I will sing them anyway, since I am a witch, and I don't care what they say. She was like you, Miranda, kept in prison until her wee babe was born. I saw it—so small and sick, like a little doll. Will your babe die too?"

"Pray let me rest."

"Why do you have light eyes?"

Miranda roused herself to answer. "The Indians told me the moon was caught in the branches of a tall tree, and little slices slid into my face."

Dorcas snuggled closer to her and looked up at her with a curious searching gaze. So hungry was the child for love, she began in her small way to care for Miranda. She bathed her ankles, seeping now with pus, using the water she was given to drink; and she tore rags from her shabby dress to pad the iron rings. When Dorcas slept, and Miranda woke to look for the moon, she sometimes gazed down on the girl's small limbs, and wept in her heart—loving her as her own child—for she was helpless to love the child she carried, a little brown beaver with long claws and beady eyes, scratching and biting, making her ill.

"Have you seen the witch's teat on my finger?" Dorcas said once. "See. There it is. The witches suck on it at night."

Miranda inspected a red sore as small as a freckle at the base of the child's knuckle. "I think it is only a flea bite, Dorcas."

"No, it's a witch's sign. We are witches both, you and I, and worship the Devil."

"You must not believe that. We are not witches."

"But I have only to look at that matron there," she pointed to a moaning woman seated against the wall, "and she will be tormented. I have not to come near her but I can bite her, and leave a circle of teeth marks on her hand."

Miranda's heart grew heavy. "Why have you been sentenced, Dorcas? Was it for singing?"

"I had a doll my Mother made for me, with a green dress. They called it a poppet. They said I stuck it with pins, but that I never did. I would not stick my dolly what I loved with all my heart."

One night the child shrieked in her sleep, and George Locker looked in with a swinging lantern and a grizzled face.

"Quiet that little beast," he said.

Miranda knew she was losing her strength when the moon's lunatic face peered in the window and grinned. With so little means to move about, her limbs grew rigid, and Dorcas helped her sit, holding her steady, and rubbed her legs with her small hands. "May I have a taste of your milk when it comes? I won't take what goes to the baby."

Miranda watched the moon waver and change, shrinking to a sliver almost invisible with the green-dark orb in its arms. And then it was a fish wriggling in phosphorous seas, and then the snout of a dog. Once it became a fine boat, and she felt herself glide from the grimy shell of her body, and float clean and white up to the shining frigate in the sky, where she stretched beneath the fluttering silks and breathed the pure air of the heavens. Each night the moon grew larger until one night it was enormous, and when she saw it, she thought it was not a solid thing, but a huge hole in a sky surrounded by black and forbidding water. The golden aperture beckoned to her, and she swam towards it, through a thicket of tangled limbs, the wreckage of

Salem, the houses collapsed back into fallen trees still strewn on the ground. She kicked and struggled toward the light, towards leafy boughs that reached for her, enfolded her, and wrapped her in their sticky arms.

Miranda woke to find all the water of the sea was beneath her. Dorcas's eyes were dark with worry. "The child is coming," she whispered.

"No, no." At first she could only howl in silence, a wrenching sob she tried to smother. "Not yet," but she was swimming in wetness under her body, between her legs, and a pain like a knife sliced deep inside her, doubling her up. Her legs jerked into the air, and she cried out, then hugged her knees to her stomach and said, "Not yet. Oh God, if there is a God, don't let it come so soon."

Dorcas was stroking her, caressing her hair, crooning another song in her ear, when the pain came again, precise, insistent, like a huge wave that shuddered and shook the secret den where the small creatures waited, eyes bright. She clung to Dorcas, rolled over and moaned. She opened her eyes and saw Dorcas's face streaked with tears, and fear rising off her like steam.

Women gathered around, crooning and murmuring.

"Would we had a piece of groaning cake."

"Ask the jailer for a draught of his beer."

"The agony of childbirth is God's punishment of Eve, for her evil ways."

Miranda struggled to rise, but she was helpless to move, and a new pain hammered her to the ground as though huge rocks were rolling over her body. Through her daze she heard a woman's sure voice speaking with George Locker.

"But I am her mother. I've come a long way. You have to let me in."

The lady was as gentle as an angel when she leaned over Miranda, bathed her face, gave her water to drink, took her hand and pressed it to her lips. Her golden hair fell in shining locks free from her cap, and her blue eyes were smiling and kind. She held her as no one had ever held her, with great tenderness.

"I've come to help you," she said.

Dorcas looked with wide eyes. "Can you make it stop? She doesn't want it to come yet."

The lady kissed her face. "Darlin' you'll be all right. Don't be afraid." She pulled her close. "When you were born, it was hard. But I've always loved you so much. You are my treasure."

"But my mother is dead."

"No," she said. "I am here." She leaned into her and whispered in her ear, "I won't let you die."

When the pain came again, and she lay moaning, the lady went to the jailer.

"Send for a midwife, can't you?"

"Alas, there be no midwife in Salem Town. Goody Nurse was the midwife, and she was hanged this past month for murdering newborns."

"Isn't there a doctor? Someone who can come?"

"Look at her. Too weak to bring forth, and the child too early."

"Never mind. You can help. Unlock those chains and bring me a blanket and some water. Go on. Don't stand there like a fool!"

Miranda was swimming now, following the webbed feet, the undulating paddle, in among the branches; but the opening was too narrow, and then she was caught, squeezed from all sides, and once again the pain seared her lungs. She should never have come this way; it was too dark, and there was no way out. The underwater trees betrayed her, were killing her surely, sucking her in tighter, pressing on her body; and enormous bear-like creatures tugged her into the mesh, trapped her arms and legs until she could no longer breathe, twisted and wove her as a part of their den.

Dorcas whispered, "There's the head," and the lady leaned in and kissed her and said, "It's here, darling. Have you got anything left? Can you push?" She doubled up her knees, tore her limbs loose, broke free, and swam towards a silver moon caught in the branches of a great tree, which sighed and released it and flung it into the sky.

When the afterbirth gushed out, Miranda opened her eyes and saw a golden-haired angel holding the baby with Dorcas by her shoulder, staring down at the child. From somewhere the lady produced a little knife and cut the pulsing cord. She wrapped the child in her blue shawl, but it made no sound. There were whispers, "At least it's a boy. Less chance it will be called a witch."

"It doesn't cry."

"It breathes."

"It's too small. It will not live."

"Still, it breathes."

Miranda, lying in a stupor, took less notice of the child than she did the knife. It had an ivory handle. One shaking hand reached out, her fingers closed around it, and she pulled it under her clothes. The blade was hot against her skin.

Twenty-two

Barnabas woke to find himself lying on the sand of a small inlet. Two fishermen drew their flat-bottomed skiff, trailing a large net laden with flashing fish, onto the shore, the slapping tide at their feet. Another boat bobbed at anchor in the shallows, and a third appeared abandoned on the beach. The coastline was rocky and, except for the fishermen, deserted, but across the lagoon was a town with some trees and a dozen or so imposing houses, flat-sided, two-storied, with pitched roofs, their neat, unpainted surfaces reflecting the light of dawn. He wondered whether he had come alone.

Hearing a sound behind him, he turned and saw a wagon approaching pulled by an emaciated white ox with curved horns. A scruffy young man sat astride the cart, hunched over, his hands on the reins. He waited until the cart was alongside and it lurched to a stop. The man hollered down to him.

"Going to Salem Town, sir? Come along if you like." He

nodded to the space beside him, and Barnabas reached for the rail. When he bounded up for the platform, Barnabas remembered his wound. He could feel stiffness in his side, but there was no pain.

It was like a dream. Now he sat atop a roughly made wagon, looking down at the muddy back of a bony animal, and beside a man whose hand-sewn garments of coarse woolen cloth and deerskin spoke of another era. The man, whose face was ruddy from the sun, glanced curiously at his elegant cape.

"Come from Boston, have ye? To witness the execution?"

Barnabas nodded, relieved to have found himself in the company of someone both jovial and imperceptive.

"'Tis a sorry sight to be sure. Two full days and the poor fellow can but call out, 'More weight!'"

Barnabas frowned and nodded to express some commiseration, although he was helpless to know for what. He hoped to glean some evidence of the news in the town from his companion, so he would not appear to be an intruder in their midst.

"It was I, John de Rich, who gave the damning testimony," said the driver, sucking at his gums and slapping the reins on the ox's rickety back. "I knew full well he was entertaining a hoard of them. When he told me he wanted some planters for he was going to have a feast, I followed after. This I told the Court. There appeared a great number of witches in the field, and Giles Cory did give the sacrament to them all in great heresy."

Barnabas remembered the story of Giles Cory, a farmer falsely accused of witchcraft, and was astonished that he was at this moment facing the man's accuser. "But did you really see such a thing?" he asked.

"Why he is a wizard!" John cried, his mouth hanging open and revealing but three stained teeth. "I did not partake of his offering though he did torment and affect me grievously!"

"And you remember this day quite clearly. It is not imagined?" said Barnabas again.

"To be certain," said John.

"Is it his execution we are to witness?"

"Perhaps it is past by now," said John, shaking his head, but now eyeing Barnabas with some trepidation. "Yesterday I had needs to return to my mowing. But three days he had lasted!"

Barnabas decided the clarifying information would surely be forthcoming and kept silent.

"What is thy surname, good sir?" asked John abruptly. Barnabas hesitated, then thought there could be no harm in telling the truth. "Barnabas Collins."

"Collins? A family hereabouts. Why Amadeus Collins is a judge of these woeful proceedings, and Benajah Collins is his son. You are a Boston relation, I presume?"

Barnabas nodded once more, hoping that this was a positive position for him to choose. But John sat back in the cart with a look of horror.

"Dost not thee accuse me, for I have not born false witness. Giles Cory urged the girl Mercy Lewis to write in his book, beating her and hurting her!" Becoming extremely agitated, the driver leaned into Barnabas and spoke so close to his face that he could smell the man's foul breath. "I tell thee, there appeared to her a man in a winding sheet who told her Giles Cory had murdered him by pressing him with his feet. They found the man bruised to death, having clodders of blood about his heart!"

"And where is this infamous Giles Cory?" asked Barnabas, although he was afraid that now he had guessed.

John nodded and urged his poor beast forward. "He lies ahead—suffering greatly from"—he was careful in his pronunciation—"Peine forte et dure."

"Hanging?"

For the first time the driver looked at him in puzzlement. "Why no, sir. He cannot be hanged, if he be not tried. And he cannot be tried, if he do not plead. He pleadeth not, and suffers to be pressed for standing mute."

"But you said there was to be a trial." Was he now taking a chance appearing so ignorant?

"Aye. As soon as Cory pleads, or dies, the girl is to be sentenced. Miranda du Val. She has delivered her child and will be hanged."

Barnabas was startled by the name. So that was why he was here. And where was Antoinette?

As they drew near the town Barnabas looked towards the houses. They were two-storied, square in shape, and he remembered the architectural style was called saltbox, with few leaded windows, stone foundations, and a slight overhang. The roofs met the walls precisely, without frivolous embellishment, as was the nature of the Puritans. Beyond the town was a wide expanse of what must have been meadow, and past that he saw a forest that touched the sky. Never had he known there were such trees in the world. Some of them were fifty, a hundred, two hundred feet tall with great branches that arched to the heavens, or stretched far out over the earth.

Then from beyond the houses he heard a cry of such heart-rending anguish his muscles seized. He thanked the driver, and they both disembarked from the wagon. Walking in that direction, he saw yards with chickens, a cow or goat, and small gardens. Through the gray buildings he could make out what seemed to be an open square where a few trees had been left standing, lindens with pale yellow leaves.

A crowd was gathered, and Barnabas hastened to pull his cape about him so as to appear unobtrusive, but he need not have bothered. The attention of the crowd was focused on a pile of stones heaped upon a flat wooden platform, and beneath that was stretched the suffering prisoner. His face was swollen, and as red as a tomato, and his eyes were protruding from his head like boiled eggs. It was he who was screaming.

Surrounded by the people of Salem Town, Barnabas felt slighty ill. Their heavy clothes reeked of wood-smoke, barnyard manure, and sweat. Each person was dulled by a patina of filth, an unwashed grayness on the hands and face. He noticed that ragged bits of linen served as collars, and mended tears and missing buttons were the rule. Hair was long and untidy, scarcely combed. A palpable stench of suspicion hung in the atmosphere, as though a storm approached, and obliterated all conscious awareness. The crowd pressed against him in a stupor of prayerful devotion, subjugated to God's angry and inexorable will, and Barnabas knew he was confronting the grim forces of intolerance.

Red-faced and ballooned, the suffering man spat the grim water back into the cup and gurgled in a voice more filled with grit than air, "More weight!" When another stone was added to the pile, the poor man's tongue burst from his mouth. A constable in a helmet stepped up upon the boards, and with the tip of his cane, forced the man's tongue back between the parched lips. The victim's two exposed hands, thick with the last of the pumped blood, opened and clawed the air, his eyes bulged as if they would leap from his face, and he cried, "Damn you! Damn you all! I curse you, Salem!" and died.

The populace surrounding Barnabas seemed to sigh as one, and mutterings could be heard over the general hum. The towns-folk, moving within their dark cloud of prayer, drifted toward a small frame building facing the square. There, gray-branched lindens towered and swayed over pools of yellow leaves. Barnabas turned back to see the stones being rolled off the dead man's body, which had been flattened to half its thickness. He shivered with the thought of the bones and organs joined together. He smelled the stench of death.

Swept along by the mass of townspeople, Barnabas was shoved into a building and up a narrow stairway to a wooden balcony. From there he could look down into the courtroom. It was as though he were in the midst of a pack of wolves, starved for some scrap of meat laid out before them. Two women leaned ut over the railing, their matted hair creeping from their caps. A man with a stovepipe hat stood on the bench to peer over his eighbors, and a strong youth in a leather jerkin raised a child o his shoulders. Barnabas found a seat with a long line of vomen on either side of him, their hands folded primly on dark ool skirts, nodding in their winged caps like pigeons with red-immed eyes.

The scene below could have been a performance at any the-ter, the stage set for drama, the dour judges behind the bench vith their glossy wigs, starched collars, and black robes. There vas a chorus of young girls, perhaps twelve of them, crowded n a bench to one side, who were crying piteously and grabbing t their necks and faces as though pierced by instruments of orture.

The girl in the witness stand was filthy. Barnabas imagined he must have been dragged from some dungeon, for her clothes vere rags, her face covered with soot, and only her eyes, white vith defiance, stared out. She held a small package in her lap, vrapped in a blue shawl he thought was oddly familiar. He saw tiny fist protrude from the folds and realized it was an in-ant.

She lifted a corner of her hem and wiped her cheeks. Then he sat straight and held herself in such a way Barnabas had a leeting sense that she was not an unfortunate, but a queen. She rojected a guileless truth, earnestness and purity of heart, and eauty of spirit. To think she could be called a witch, even by uch a misguided populace as this, was incomprehensible. When he girls cried out there was a bird in the rafters, she never linched, but looked up with the congregation with a kindred uriosity, and Barnabas saw her face for the first time, her un-orgettable silver blue eyes, as pale as the dawn sky. The locks of air that hung at her neck were raven, her fragile features shone orth, and he was astonished to see that the girl was identical to David's beloved Jacqueline.

At that moment a blond-haired woman rose from the bench of chained prisoners. "I want to speak for the accused," she said in a clear voice that sent a shiver through him. It was Antoinette. She wore her sky blue cloak, that seemed to fit the style of early New England, and it brightened her azure eyes. Her face was flushed and her hair a tangled fall of golden curls. Never had she looked so beautiful. A hush fell, and even the terrorized girls grew still. Barnabas could feel the awe in the room.

"Woman, your place is in the prisoners' box," cried the judge. "You have not been called. You stand before the Court of Oyer and Terminer, and you stand in contempt."

"I only want you to consider my offer."

"What gives you a claim on our attentions?" he said. "Who are you?"

"I am the girl's mother," said Antoinette. The crowd gasped as if with one breath.

"Surely you are mad. Take the woman away," said another more pompous judge, with a wave of his hand. "Place her in the dungeon until we can question her further." Antoinette raised her finger and pointed at Miranda.

"I'm telling you that the girl is my daughter." Not a bench creaked or a cricket chirped, so silent was the room. But after a stunned moment the judge said sternly, "Nonsense. Her mother is dead, killed long ago. She is an orphan raised by Indians until Benajah and Esther Collins provided her keep. And she has proven most ungrateful, I might add."

"I wish to take her place." Barnabas felt his heart lurch. There was a tremor in the room as the words she had spoken were repeated over and over, and the judges stared down at her with absolute incredulity.

"Impossible."

Now the murmuring rose in pitch and several in the congregation tried to obtain a better view of the speaker. Whispers of "Who can she be?" were audible, and the girls began to moan. Bewildered, Barnabas pushed past the other seated parishioners, and hurried down the stair. How had she managed to get herself imprisoned? What Antoinette was intent on doing was dangerous. A séance allowed one to tread the pages of history, but it was foolish to meddle with what was written there. He entered the lower chamber in time to see one of the judges questioning the prisoner.

"Miranda du Val, you are accused by six of the bewitched as the author of their miseries, and you are accused by eight of the confessing witches for monstrous deeds, the least of which is flying, which could not be done without diabolical assistance, and which irrefutably fixes the character of a witch. Evidence and argument, as well as credible eyewitnesses, have attested to thy satanism in this debauched town. What say you?"

The girl spoke in a sure voice. "I have given you the identity of the Satan you seek. And you have turned my testimony against me."

One man rose from a chair beside the judge's bench and looked at the girl. Barnabas wondered whether he was the famous Cotton Mather, renowned for his writings on religion and witchcraft. He wore a monstrous, curly white wig, square in shape, as if it had been kept in a box when it was not on the head of its owner, and it protruded from the sides of his face.

"Judah Zachery has been beheaded, as you well know, after your testimony," he said in a reasonable tone, as though he had the right to question the prisoner. "His head hangs in Plymouth, along with the head of King Phillip, and his body is buried in a tomb many miles from here. Thus should all traitors to the commonwealth be exposed and shamed for the terrorized and devout to gaze upon with wonder. With his head so far from his body, can his power still be at work?"

"I cannot say. But I would not be amazed, for he was the Devil."

At this moment the girls began to moan, and one rose to

her feet and pointed at Miranda, her eyes blazing, "Hang her!" she screamed. A fairly large girl with an ample bosom began to crawl about the floor and bark like a dog, making a spectacle of herself. Many in the meeting stood to see the performance. Two young girls fell to the floor and writhed, twisting their bodies into contortions that seemed impossible without their backs breaking, as though they were tied neck to heels. An older girl with curly hair clawed at her face until it was streaked with blood, and another dark-haired child screamed while staring at Miranda, "A black pig! Why dost thou plague me?" All the girls were writhing in fits, gnashing their teeth and rending their hair in a veritable display of lunacy, all the time making the most piteous cries and saying they were struck with blows, their bellies were cracked, they were cut with knives, and they could bear it no longer.

The congregation watched spellbound, as did Barnabas, who could never have imagined such a display of playacting. But just as he was feeling the severest contempt, a girl vomited up a ball of green slime which turned out to be a living rat. Another drew out her tongue until it was a foot in length. And a third stepped forwards and with a cry of "Witch! Thou shan't choke me!" grabbed for her own throat, and, as her eyes fell back, her head twisted on her neck, and he thought it spun around and around in a blur like a top.

Many of the parishioners fell to their knees in prayer. Others screeched in hysteria. The judge cried out over the din, "Do you not see these that thou bedevilist? I beg you stop at once, before they are destroyed."

Miranda, who had been watching impassively, turned to the board of judges and said simply, "Why do you not fall down in fits when I look at you?"

The judge's face grew red. "Do you not hurt these children?"

"I do not."

"Who doth?"

"Why, Judah Zachery."

"And did you sign his book?"

She sighed with a gesture of resignation. "We all signed a book as we were forced to do, as we were tortured to do, a false book we believed was his record of attendance. Know ye not who he was? He was the schoolteacher." She turned and looked at the girls writhing on the floor. "Think on it. These were all his unhappy pupils, as was I."

"And you are saying it was he who bewitched them? And still doth bewitch them?"

"I do. And, if he is the Devil, he has surely confounded you all. He could not have asked for a greater victory, for he has set you all on your perverted business in these trials. You who struggle to drive him out, only draw him in with greater fury."

The judges huddled into a conference, and now Barnabas was convinced that the acting interrogator was the famous philosopher from Boston. They spoke among themselves, the racket made by the girls now somewhat diminished, and several times they looked over at Miranda. Unable at this point not to be concerned about her future, he wondered whether her artless defense had won her pardon. Finally, the judge spoke to her again.

"If we find thee innocent and set thee free, where wilt thou go? Thy time with the Collins family has been severely undermined by thy actions."

"I ask only that you let me live on my farm. The house is the one built by my father."

Another judge rose rapidly to his feet. He possessed a stern visage, cold blue eyes, and a patrician manner. He reminded him of someone but Barnabas could not remember who, until he realized the man bore an uncanny resemblance to his own cousin, Roger Collins.

"Miranda du Val," he said, "answer now before this court

and these proceedings. Art thou a witch? Confess now, and you will be spared."

She hesitated. "What will become of me?"

"Confess!"

"Banishment?"

"But not death—"

She paused and looked out over those who waited for her decision, their faces alert with expectation. Barnabas could see her pale eyes, like moonbeams, as she searched the crowd; and for one brief second her gaze fell on him, and he caught his breath. Then for the first time, she looked down and frowned. From where he stood, Barnabas could see her profile, and for a moment he could almost swear she was Jacqueline, with her delicate nose, her soft mouth, her high cheeks, and the grace with which she held her neck and shoulders. She lifted her head. "I have only fled the Devil. I have been unjustly accused," she said. "Hang me if you must. The sin shall be upon your souls."

"Then accordingly you must be sentenced! 'Thou shalt not suffer a witch to live!'"

Antoinette cried out again. "Wait! What difference does it make who you hang? You want to find someone guilty. You want to see someone die. Then take out your revenge on me."

The gavel fell again and again over the din of the crowd, and the judge cried, "Woman, bite thy tongue. You are accused as well, and will be tried, and you only implicate yourself with this ranting."

"Then sentence me. You will have your witch on the gallows, and all your hatred and fear will be placated. What's more you won't wake up one morning with guilt in your hearts and vomit on your pillow because—"

"Silence, woman!"

"—because you murdered a girl as innocent as the newborn baby in her arms. She has suffered. And she has done nothing wrong. Let her live, I beg you." And she stopped, out of breath.

The judge with the large wig looked down at Miranda. "Is this woman your mother?" he asked.

"I do not know her," answered the girl, who now seemed ready to faint. "But if my mother lived, I would have it be her."

"Set her free, and take me," Antoinette cried desperately.

But the judges seemed not to hear her. They rose as soldiers and marched down from the bench and out of the meetinghouse door.

Barnabas was determined to change the verdict, if only to help save Antoinette. He had the arguments of history on his side, and the Salem Witch Trials had long ago been exposed as nothing but religious mania. While searching for one of the judges in the crowd, he saw Cotton Mather leaving the courtroom by the back entrance.

"Sir, if you please, I must stop you for a moment."

Mather looked up in surprise. "Are you from these parts?"

Barnabas fished for an answer. "No, I come from the North, from the territory of Maine. But I am . . . originally from England."

"And are you a member of the legal profession? By your elegant haberdashery I can only assume you to be a man of some means." He patted his own fine black waistcoat and fingered his lace collar, as though inviting a compliment in return.

"I . . . hold a position of importance in the . . . analysis of the law."

"Ah, a magistrate? A philosopher?" Mather seemed pleased to meet one of his profession.

"You could say that, in my way, I determine the fate of other men. I am a judge—of sorts—as was your father, Increase Mather, I believe."

"You know of my family?"

Barnabas realized that he had struck home. He now had the man's full attention. "I have read both your writings. Your illustrious father founded a university, did he not?"

Mather nodded, displaying some pride. "Harvard. The first college in the commonwealth. And I attended those halls as well, following in his footsteps."

"As you do at these proceedings."

"Yes, although I regret to say my father has proven inadequate to the awesome responsibilities of prosecuting witchcraft. I am afraid he now falters in his histrionics, and wavers in his doctrines." Other parishioners walked past them and several stopped to look back but then turned and moved on. "What is your purpose in addressing me, good sir. I must proceed to the hanging."

"To say that I believe in my heart the girl is innocent."

Cotton Mather looked surprised. "Miranda du Val? But her diabolical nature has been proved by damning evidence. The girls have all witnessed her evil at work, and the slave, Tituba—who has confessed and been pardoned—saw her fly. Fly, my good man! Take to the air! What's more, a severed head spoke her name." He made a motion as if to say that was the end of the conversation, but Barnabas persisted.

"Seemed to speak her name. Who heard it?"

"Amadeus Collins. One of the judges."

"A severed head speak?"

Mather turned back to him. "Miraculous, I agree, but such are the diabolical wonders of the invisible world."

At these words Barnabas realized he was dealing not only with a man of superior intellect, but also profound faith. If he was going to convince him of his misguided direction, he would need a powerful argument.

"I was at the meetinghouse just now and saw the hearing. I overheard several townspeople say that Amadeus Collins seeks to obtain her property for his son. Surely his motives are suspect."

"He is the most respected of judges! Come, sir, walk this way." He moved forward and Barnabas hurried beside him, pressing his point.

"And the foolish hysterics of children? How can you put faith in their antics? I defy you to take any one of them aside, threaten her with severe punishment, and she will say whatever you ask her to say. And later she will admit it was all for sport." Mather stopped, and drew himself up in anger.

"Sport? Call ye these dreadful machinations sport?"

"I'm only saying that you have it in your power to put an end to this madness. Before you make another terrible mistake."

Mather's cheeks flushed in obvious annoyance and he spat out his words. "I shall hold you ignorant and downright impudent if you dare to assert the nonexistence of witches. These afflicted children present doleful evidence."

"But haven't some admitted they did it in jest? And don't some of the girls say, 'She said it,' and then, 'No, *she* said it.' Has it occurred to you they love their theatrics, and the attention of the town has gone to their heads?" Mather shook his wig, and began to walk once more, waving Barnabas away.

"Only think," said Barnabas to his back, "what if you are wrong!"

"Wrong?" He stopped and glared. "God would never allow the Devil to use innocent persons to condemn others." Mather looked hard at Barnabas. Then he collected himself as though at the pulpit, ready to deliver a sermon. His voice became melodious. "My good man, hear me well. I know not why you have chosen to accost me, or where you find your reasoning, but I have seen with my own eyes these effects of cruel and bloody witchcraft, the flying of demons, and poor children driven to despair. I have seen atheism and blasphemy, and many who run distracted with terrors. I have visited the homes of God-fearing families, and seen their tortured children. It would have broke a heart of stone to see them."

Now other townspeople gathered: an old man, and a woman with a child. They listened with fear in their eyes, and looked to Mather as though he alone could save them. Antoinette moved by with the other prisoners, disappointment written on her face.

"Sometimes they would be deaf, sometimes dumb, sometimes blind, their jaws out of joint, their necks broken, their heads twisted around, as you saw today in the meeting. Untold and wondrous things! Some claim to be in a red hot oven, others lying under freezing water. One rested upon an invisible spit, run into his mouth, and out his foot, and he screaming, and groaning as though he were put to the fire and roasted, and then crying out that knives were cutting him. And more, much more, beyond imagination. I will never use one grain of patience with any man that shall impose upon me a denial of devils or witches. And I say to you an army of devils is broken in upon us! The Last Judgment is at hand! And it is we who must lead the charge against the Devil's legions!"

"Have you spoken with your father, Increase Mather?"

Again Mather puffed himself up. "I speak to a Higher Father!"

"But what of the fact that your father has rescinded his treatise on witchcraft, that he no longer believes spectral evidence is valid. He now challenges his previous position."

Mather's face darkened. "He is no longer a soldier of the Lord. When we began this battle, he carried sword and shield against the lion, and he was victorious. But he drew back his legions before he found the Black Man. The battle was only half over."

At this moment Barnabas began to despair. "And you see no irony in the fact that these unhappy people came to the New World to escape religious oppression? Only to find themselves even more fearful for the fate of their souls?"

Mather seemed to have thought long and hard about this question. "It is true. The fervor and faith of those who landed on these shores was implacable." He warmed to this topic. "But having inherited this great banner of the Lord's grace, our children grow soft before our eyes, desire only property and earthly power. Why?" Barnabas was at a loss, and the judge thundered out his own answer. "Because the Devil has followed us over the water! Satan is the great conspirator laboring to overthrow the Kingdom of Christ. He knows we ask ourselves each day what we must do to be saved, and for that he despises us. He fears our piety, for he knows in the end it will mean the final destruction of his heinous kingdom. And just as Jesus pointed to Judas at the last supper, Christ knows full well how many devils there are in his church."

Barnabas laughed bitterly. "Yes, at first there were two. Now there are nineteen hanged and hundreds in prison. Why are there suddenly so many? If you let these girls go on, soon we shall all be devils and witches!"

Mather's wig had gone slightly askew during his tirade and he raised both hands to settle it back on his head. Then he smiled. "You argue well, I must say. It is something of a pleasure to spar with you." The judge leaned in to deliver one more attack. "Good sir. Salem will not endure without a stalwart leader of men at her helm. One who knows the truth and is willing to fight for it. Don't you think it pains me to see those poor specters hanging from the gallows? But I shall leave no stroke unstruck that may bring men from the power of Satan unto God. There are devils and witches, I assure you, nightbirds that appear when the light of the gospel shines forth."

"Just one more thing," Barnabas said to Mather out of

desperation. "Of all these deaths, even Rebecca Nurse's, do you regret any?"

"All were found guilty."

"Have you made any errors in these proceedings? Would you do anything differently? Do you repent any of it?"

The man held himself like a statue. "Absolutely nothing. God has spoken through me, and I will not weaken. I need no man's permission, nor my earthly father's blessing. I have set myself to countermine the whole plot of the Devil against New England. God has made me his emissary, and we shall be victorious."

"And what of the Indians?" he said. "Are they all devils as well?"

If Mather was irritated he did not show it. "Some may be saved. But in the wigwams of Indians where they have their pagan powwows, they raise up masters in the shape of bears and snakes and fires. And what is it these monsters love to do? In the homes of Christians? I leave it to you."

Now most of the townspeople had walked ahead. Mather stopped and turned to Barnabas. "I will only tell you that this Miranda du Val you defend was raised by the Wampanoag. They gave her a name, Sooleawa Sisika, which I believe means Silver Bird, and they called her Tree-Flyer, because, as absurd as it seems, they said she talked to the trees when she flew through them." He moved away, for he had seen the other judges and wished to walk with them.

Barnabas was stunned, and suddenly understood why—if Jacqueline were truly possessed by Miranda—the leaves around Collinwood had bedeviled him for weeks. Tree-Flyer! At that moment, Mather called back.

"Do you intend to continue on to Gallows Hill?"

Barnabas offered to accompany him, although he knew now changing the course of history was all but impossible. A séance carried one into a dream where the heart reaches out in desperation, but the body cannot follow. Now he must find a way to free Antoinette and take her back to the present. He followed the procession of dark figures, strung out in twos and threes, and he thought of those words said when Death was at the head of the caravan. *And in a long line he shall lead them.*

They tried to take the infant from Miranda, but she held on so tightly they would be obliged to rip it in half to tear it from her grasp. Even though she put it to her breast, it did not suck, and it did not cry. There were whispers that it was deformed, a Devil's child, further proof, which now they did not need. She was a witch for all to see. Someone would catch it when she dropped it, a devout parishioner who would raise it in a pious home.

As the wagon moved slowly up the road on the way to Gallows Hill, Miranda failed to notice the trees dropped the last of their leaves as she rode past, bare branches clawing the sky. She was mulling over her sinful plan, for the knife with the ivory handle was still secreted in her dress. Even the child of a demon was murder. She shook the bundle gently, opened her shift, saw its dark eyes, touched its cheek, and taking her nipple between her fingers, nudged the wee mouth. It thrust out its fists to keep from falling and she took heart as she saw its face shrink to a grimace and she thought it might cry. Again she tried, and weak as it was, it first jerked its head back and forth, then finally caught her and began to suck.

Something rushed into her heart. Perhaps if she humbled herself one time, they would free her. The golden lady had pleaded for her; might she not plead for herself? The cart rocked gently and the child held on. If only they would let her live, she would go to her farm alone, raise her babe in the Indian way, teach him the lessons of the forest. She might share with him the mockingbird's whistle, the smell of wild oats, the bear's hidden shadow. She might cheat him of his Devil's ancestry, and perhaps they could fly together.

They reached the scaffold, and she saw standing beneath the empty noose a tiny form in a white winding sheet. That was the sign. The baby's mouth had gone limp, and when she looked down, the child's face was smooth and untroubled. Miranda stared amazed and unblinking at a stillness so complete, the light extinguished, and was settled at last on what she would do.

They unlocked her shackles and pulled her from the cart, keeping a tight grip on her arms. She held herself erect, perhaps for the first time aware of her comeliness, and was careful not to trip on the makeshift stair. Peter Clothier, who had been her beatman, was now her hangman; what dismal occupations fell his way, she thought. Once more he tried to take the child, but looking over his shoulder, caught the eye of Amadeus Collins who slowly shook his head.

"Hang them both," he said under his breath.

Then, like a fine plumed bird, out of the crowd flew the woman with yellow hair, dragging her chains. She sprang against the edge of the platform, arms outstretched, and turned to the astonished congregation. "No, no, please, you mustn't do this. She is the purest among you, as innocent as the babe in her arms. Please, I beg you, don't take her. Before you do something terribly wrong, take me instead."

With impatient movements, the constable pulled the woman back, and held her while she stood trembling, her eyes bright with tears. Reverend Collins shook his head and said in a disdainful tone, "Observe, the accused has no shame! Here stands a poor afflicted victim of this scheming witch who tortures another in her final moments. Surely Hell is her home!"

A flock of blackbirds careened across the sky, hundreds in flight, turning this way and that on the wind as one wave, before they settled, noisy and fluttering, in the bare branches of the great hanging tree, leafing it once more. Somewhere Miranda knew she must find her voice. Already the noose was settled on her shoulders, the trap poised to spring.

Peter looked to her. "Wilt thou say a prayer, Miranda?" When she nodded, he stood back and bowed his head. A faint breeze lifted the edge of her skirt and caressed her hair; the sky darkened, the blackbirds quivered, and in the circle of the forest, the great trees bowed down. At first she spoke softly, clutching her dead child to her breast.

"People of Salem. I do not doubt there are among you disciples true of heart, who hold to their faith, and love God. I bless these, and wish them well." She looked down at Antoinette. "One has shown me love."

She drew a breath and spoke with greater strength. "But there are also those who have shouted 'Witchcraft,' whispered it, and shunned it, and searched it out, only to find it smoldering in their own hearts. Because you know truly you have never seen witches, at this, the moment of my death, I say to you, look within. Have you not tortured innocents, with no proof other than hearsay? In your hearts you know these girls lie villainously. Again and again you have cried 'Witch!' but you have not seen one. You have cried 'Witchcraft!' but in truth you have seen it not. I say to you, since you have so lusted for it, watch carefully, for you shall see it now!"

When she raised up the child, its swaddling fell from its body and it was perfectly formed. "I curse this town, and all those who have driven this madness. Most fixedly, I curse the Collins family who took my farm but will find no happiness there. The fields are poisoned and the stream a bog of snakes. And those who take my life shall never prosper, shall never know happiness, but will have blood to drink for all eternity!"

The knife flashed, and before they could stop her, she had

opened the little corpse. Without a beating heart to speed the pulse, the blood oozed slowly, spreading over her hand and down her arm, until at last she lifted the child above her head and cried, "Behold, my baptism!" and, as the blood flowed over her face, coating her in liquid crimson, she cried once more, "May my death be the last!" before the trap fell, and the noose sprang for her unquiet life.

Twenty-three

Salem—1971

Barnabas lifted his head from the table and peered into the dark. At first he did not know where he was, but Antoinette was still at his side and, when she saw him, she fell against his shoulder with a harsh sob. Relieved to find them back where the séance had begun, he held her and said softly, "It's over. We're safe." All the other participants were still in a trance, hands clasped, eyes closed. One by one they came back to consciousness and looked around vaguely disoriented. All but Jacqueline. He thought she had disappeared, but he saw her standing by the shattered window, the cold wind lifting her hair and ruffling her long skirt. The storm had passed and faint moonlight etched a silver outline around her silhouette. Something about her demeanor astonished him. She seemed older, melancholy and yet serene, wrapped in solitude. Her hands were folded in front of her, she held her body erect, and a faint smile played upon her lips. A shiver crept along his spine. And yet what he saw was not evil, only magical. Her black hair fell in a tangled mass about her face and her eyes were bright with tears; and there was something about the folds of her skirt: they floated and swayed, barely touching the ground. He held his breath thinking she had been changed during the séance, transformed, but she finally walked to the table, and she was still the young girl he remembered. She seemed frightened and lost; but then, when she saw her mother, her face flooded with an expression of profound relief. She went into her arms with a cry and they embraced and kissed cheeks and lips, and Antoinette rocked her daughter, both of them weeping. Jacqueline let go of the object she had been holding so tightly in her hand and it clattered onto the table. It was a small knife with an ivory handle and it was stained with blood.

🔴avid was still sleeping when Barnabas returned, hardly any time having passed in this world while he was away. The boy lay on his side breathing through his mouth, one hand hanging off the bed, his dark hair tussled over his smooth brow, his lashes soft upon his cheek. The other hand had tugged the quilt up under his chin as though he had been cold while sleeping, and he seemed unusually pale, his skin almost transparent, his lips a faint pink. His head was turned to the side and the jugular fluttered in his neck.

Barnabas could only assume Julia's warnings had been meant to frighten him and keep him within her control. Except for his wound, which had begun to throb, he felt better than he had in months—vigorous, more youthful. The spasms of heat had subsided and his vitality had returned. If he were now completely human, would he need another shot?

The boy stirred, and Barnabas drew back before he opened his eyes.

"Barnabas," he said, "where were you?" He threw off the

bedclothes and sat up, stretched his arms over his head, and yawned. "I woke up in the middle of the night and you were gone. Your bed wasn't even slept in."

"Yes, I know. I went back out, and I found Antoinette."

"How?"

"I drove around until I saw her truck. She was . . . she was inside a bar with some friends."

"Did you tell her everything that happened?"

"She's returning to Collinsport right away."

"What about Jackie? Was she with her?"

Barnabas sensed how deeply pleasurable it was for David to say his sweetheart's name, and, at the same time, the anxiety she aroused in him. He decided not to tell David the truth. "No, she wasn't there. I think Toni left her in her room at the Old House."

"So, she's safe."

"I think for now, yes."

David was silent. Barnabas found it impossible to explain his foray into the past. Already it seemed a dream. However, he now had one new responsibility over which he had no choice. He must find some means of ending David's association with Jacqueline. She was unpredictable—perhaps enchanted—and surely dangerous. Sensitive to the difficulties in admonishing a belligerent teenager, he waited until they were on the road back to Collinsport, and only then did he attempt to draw the boy into a conversation that he hoped David would not find threatening.

"Did you—had you, any idea your friend Jackie was so deeply troubled?"

"Yeah, well, I knew there was something wrong with her."

"But you didn't suspect it was schizophrenia before you read those reports, did you?"

"I don't know. She's so changeable. I thought she liked me, I mean, I thought it was me she wanted, but now I'm not so sure. When I was with her, she would act excited and happy, and then she would get grumpy. But even when we were together, I always had the feeling that she was waiting for someone or something else. You know, like that feeling you get when you're at a party and talking to someone, but they don't look at you. They're always looking over your shoulder."

"Yes, I know that feeling."

"She would let me kiss her and hold her just the way you would expect a girlfriend to do, but I could tell; I mean, I sometimes thought I wasn't the one she loved."

There was a pause. The only sound was the hum of the engine as they drove through a dense forest. The sun had chased away the dark clouds and the whole world was glistening; every leaf glittered with a diamond droplet, the pavement shone, and the sky was a painful blue.

"Did she ever tell you anything about her childhood?" asked Barnabas.

"Well, one weird thing. Toni was stoned on acid when she was born."

"Oh . . . ?"

"The stuff was brand new, and they were experimenting. They thought, I don't know, it seems so crazy today, but they thought it would make the baby be born easier. It came from ergot, a mold on rye, and I guess women used to take ergot to speed up childbirth."

"Yes. Aldous Huxley even said he witnessed the moment of his own conception."

"When he took LSD?"

"He said he had a moment of transcendence when he realized that love is the fundamental cosmic truth."

"That's cool."

"What else did Jackie tell you?"

"She said she was really an unhappy kid until she met some Glitter girls in junior high. Back then they weren't so weird looking. Just black clothes and white make-up. Red lipstick. But still, a couple of them pretended to be vampires, and they—I don't know, she said they drank each other's blood."

"How disgusting."

"And they did a lot of LSD and mescaline, mushrooms, shot up stuff. I guess she got really wild, and Toni put her in Windcliff."

"Poor child. And we know what happened there."

They sped down the highway past magnificent forests radiant with fall color; Barnabas was struck by a reappearance of the earth's majesty, as though the trees were chords played in a sweeping symphony of light.

David was silent. Barnabas settled into his comfortable cushioning and became newly aware of the luxurious appointments of his car—the supple leather, the lavish use of chrome, the claret tint of the burl paneling. He looked over at the boy, who was gazing out the window at the landscape flying by in a blur of crimson and magenta. He wanted to reach over and take David's hand, but he realized the boy was now too old for a display of affection—at least of that nature.

"Let me ask you something," he said. "Now that you know so much about Jackie, do you still want to be with her?"

David sighed. "I still love her."

"Why?"

"She reminds me of myself," he said, and then after a pause, "She's lonely."

"Does it occur to you that she might harm you in some way?"

"What? More than she already has?"

"No, I don't mean breaking your heart." He hesitated. "I mean in some physical way."

"But she's just a girl. I'm a lot stronger than she is."

"Would you be willing to consider my opinion?"

"I don't know. What is it?"

"I think she might become violent. That's what it said in the report, didn't it?"

"Yeah. . . ."

"I think you should stay away from her, David."

"Don't tell me to do that, Barnabas. I can't."

"Then I may be forced to tell your father."

David looked at Barnabas in surprise. "You wouldn't do that, would you? You're my friend."

"If I thought it would keep you safe."

"He'd send me to Exeter. He's been threatening a military academy for years. This would be all the excuse he needed."

"But if you thought she was someone who was evil? . . . I mean, do you really trust her?"

"She's— I don't know— I told you, it's like she's bewitched me. I know that sounds silly, but no matter how she treats me or how angry or hurt I get, if she wants me with her, all she has to do is ask. I haven't any control over myself."

Barnabas waited, then said, "It sounds like military school would be the solution."

"This is stupid. This whole conversation! You can't make me do anything. Neither can my father. You have no idea how it feels to be in love."

"As hard as it may be for you to believe, I do. It's agony. But I am only thinking of your welfare. I am afraid you are in danger. And if I have to do something drastic to stop you, I will."

"Oh, yeah? Okay. You're right." David's voice was flat with indifference. "Sure, Barnabas, whatever you say. I'll stay away from her."

For the rest of the drive David sat with his earplugs inserted, listening to his cassette player, the tinny sound of rock 'n' roll music leaking into the interior of the car. He refused to speak again. Barnabas hoped he had made some progress, but he feared he had only alienated the boy. Perhaps Antoinette would know what to do. As they drove into Collinsport, he searched the streets for her truck. He was anxious to see her, to be alone with her, to see her smile, to simply enjoy her company, but he was worried about her reaction to the question he planned to ask. It was clear to him now what he intended to do, and the thought thrilled him with expectation.

When he and David arrived back at Collinwood, Barnabas found Willie waiting for him near the back door, agitated and stuttering. "Barnabas, where have you been? Someone's been creeping around the house. I-I saw him behind Rose Cottage last night around midnight, and . . . and then again up on the first floor parapet looking in a window. Then I-I saw him up on the roof, near the tower."

"Did you call the police?"

"Elizabeth did. But after the raid on the camp, they didn't even want to come. It's like they've got some grudge against the Collinses."

"Why in the world?"

"Their excuse was—they said all the hippies were kept in the Collinsport jail until yesterday afternoon. And then some of them were released, but they—they put most of them on a bus and took them to Portland, to County. A lot of officers on duty had to go with them, and no one was back yet. When a police car showed up, it was close to midnight, and—and whoever was roaming around was gone. What if he comes back tonight?"

"Tell Elizabeth she need not worry. I'll be happy to keep watch. Doesn't Roger have a pistol?"

"Yeah, and there's a shotgun too, one that stays in the downstairs closet."

"Good. Make sure that is loaded as well. If you see anything, call the police."

"Where are you going?"

"I have an errand in town."

"But, Barnabas—"

"I'll be back before nightfall."

Jason had kept his promise, Barnabas was certain. Some how he had escaped the clutches of the police and returned t seek revenge on the Collins family. But there was something els that stirred his deepest suspicions, something he had ignored until now. He remembered the carpenter's lithe movements, hi effortless grace, his glittering eyes, his cunning behavior at th camp. And where had he disappeared to when the ghoul attacke the girl? He had fled, either to avoid suspicion or because h knew the monster, and had sent it into their midst for his ow purposes—angry, perhaps, over Barnabas's tryst with Antoi nette. Of course! Had he still been his old self, Barnabas woul have recognized another of his clan instantly. How miserabl unperceptive was the human mind.

The drive back into Collinsport was more difficult than h had expected. His heart beat like a hammer and anticipatio made his stomach churn. More than once his vision clouded an dizziness bedeviled him. Until now, he had harbored a fleetin hope that he might finally be cured. But for some reason a fo filled his brain. His wound was much worse. It throbbed wit pain, and he felt flushed and feverish.

Antoinette's pickup truck was parked outside the Blue Whale She was sitting alone at a table near the back, sipping a glas of wine, and listening to a young girl on stage singing a mournfu folk song. Even though his heart jumped when he saw her, Barn abas lingered a moment to look at her. She wore a sapphire jacke embroidered around the collar with leaves and flowers. Tendrils o her yellow hair fell softly over her brow and clung to her neck. H made in that instant an inescapable decision. From this momen on, she would be the woman he loved.

The girl singing had a fine voice, and he heard the lyrics a if they were meant for him.

"My love and I did to the church go,
　With bride and bride maidens they made a fine show,
　And I followed last that she might never know,
　For she'd gain to be wed to another."

"Antoinette?"

She looked up with a start, her face aglow in the lamplight, but when she recognized Barnabas, she frowned almost as if she had been expecting someone else. He was dismayed to see what he thought was disappointment darkening her eyes, but in her way, she tried to cover this, and she smiled rather sheepishly, her expression acknowledging all they had experienced in the last few hours, or days.

"May I sit down?"

"Oh, sure."

She looked tired. Her mascara was smudged and her eyes had dark circles beneath them. But the eyes were the same, those hypnotic azure eyes, changing from pale turquoise to mossy green, with the dark rings around the irises. He was mesmerized.

"I had to see you," he said, thrilled with new energy in spite of the pain in his side. "As soon as I got back. Have you recovered?"

She did not meet his gaze. Instead, she looked down at her hands, looked up at him quickly, then looked away.

"How is Jackie?"

"Better. She's got some of her little girl back." She shrugged, sighed, then fingered the stem of her glass. "I couldn't save her." Her eyes filled with tears. "It's over."

"No, my dear. It's just beginning." He took her hands. She frowned.

"Toni, I have to tell you something. I was very moved by what I saw in Salem." She flinched and turned her head to look towards the door. "Your unselfishness, your sacrifice—" He stopped himself, but only for a moment, before he blundered heedlessly into his topic. "Are you certain you have no memory of a woman named Angelique?"

She gave an exasperated little laugh and shook her head.

"But I do," he said with sudden eagerness. "I remember her well. As I have tried to tell you before. We've known one another, you and I, in the past."

She stared at him without expression. "How could that be?"

"Doesn't it strike you as odd that we alone shared such a miraculous experience? If the séance was possible, then anything is possible. Is it not?"

"I don't know. I really don't want to think about it. It was a nightmare."

"Of course. I agree absolutely. That is why I've come to tell you what's past is past forever. I've come to offer you all the help you need."

"Thanks."

Her nonchalance annoyed him, and at the same time the words of the song penetrated his consciousness.

> *"My love and I sat down to dine*
> *And she sat down beside me and poured out the wine*
> *And I drank to the lass who should ha' been mine,*
> *For she's gain to be wed to another."*

He looked at his beloved. She wore no lipstick and her full lips were pale and slightly lined. Her hands, which he now held in his own, bore ragged nails and the veins were prominent.

"Toni, listen to me. I want to spend more time with you."

She seemed to be making an effort to be polite. "But, why?"

He hesitated, unsure of how to begin. "Did the night we spent together, in your tent, did you—" and suddenly he knew that if she were in love with him, it would be obvious, and there would be no need to say anything at all. "Were you glad?" he asked finally.

She seemed to sense his distress. She laughed lightly and squeezed his fingers. "Drugs are funny," she said. "They take away inhibitions, and all the social codes seem ridiculous. The strongest urge is to experience life in all its forms, to abandon yourself to love. Who with is not so important."

"You're saying I could have been anybody." The bones in his chest felt pinched.

"Well, not anybody. Not Jason. I seem to remember he was pissing me off."

Barnabas felt the muscles in his neck and shoulders tighten and burn with little spasms of pain. Still he blundered on. "But that night in the tent with you was for me a—a journey to paradise."

She laughed. "Don't forget. I gave you some too."

"Some what?"

She frowned again. "Half a tab." She pulled a small crevice between her eyebrows. Again he was bewildered by her jarringly modern demeanor, so different from Angelique's, so lacking in nuance or duplicity. He didn't know what to say to that, but for some desperate reason he found he could not stop himself from making every effort to reach her.

"I fell in love with you that night. I long to spend my life, no—eternity, with you. And you may not know it, you may not be aware of it, but you have somewhere inside you, the power—"

"Barnabas, stop." A lock of hair fell in front of her eyes and she drew one hand away and brushed the curl back and tucked it behind her ear. For the first time since he had begun to speak to her she looked deeply into his eyes.

"I understand now what you are trying to say." She took a breath and sighed. "I'm so sorry. But I really have no interest in a relationship with you. I don't love you. I could never love you.

You're not at all what I'm looking for. You're a perfectly nice man
but you're far too intense. I feel somehow that you have som
kind of deep dark history that I really don't want to know about

"But—since the séance—you don't think we share some
thing in common?"

"Yeah, and it makes you mysterious, I guess, but also kin
of heavy." Now she looked again towards the door and Barn
abas was forced to admit to himself she was expecting someone
She turned back to him and blushed slightly. "I like—well ac
tually I'm ashamed to say this—but I like guys who are not s
into me. Younger guys—you know? I've always run after boy
who ride bikes, or play music, or, I don't know, join crazy cults
Our night in the tent was great, but, really, not something to—
well, to take too seriously."

"Maybe you haven't heard me, Antoinette. I'm asking you t
marry me. I'm a wealthy man. I can offer you a house in London
another in the Caribbean"—He was beginning to feel as though
he were sinking down into a deep well—"every pleasure, ever
luxury. And my undying devotion to your happiness—"

"But I don't want to get married. I wasn't married to Jack
ie's father. Listen, Barnabas. I'm really not the girl for you. I'n
sorry. But isn't it better that I tell you now, than for me to lead
you on? That would be really cruel."

It was as if the singer had leaned in too close to the micro
phone and her plaintive voice wailed its way into his brain.

> *"I met an old man, who ask-ed o' me,*
>   *'How many strawberries grow in the salt sea?'*
>   *And I answered him, with a tear in my e'e*
>   *'How many ships sail . . . in the forest?'"*

Barnabas rose, shaking, and knocked over his chair. "Then
my dear, I will say good evening." And he walked with as much
assurance as he could muster out of the bar.

It wasn't until he was safe inside the Bentley that he allowed himself the luxury of despair. He clutched the steering wheel, laid his head upon the cool varnished wood, and trembled. The darkness within the car, the cold and loneliness, was reminiscent of the hours he had known in his casket before falling asleep, cursed to bestiality and isolation. It was not too late. He must return to Collinwood, and to Julia.

As he started the engine and pulled out of his parking place, easing alongside the window of the Blue Whale, he could not resist slowing down to see whether he could catch a glimpse of Antoinette one last time. She was still seated at the same table, but someone was with her now. Her expression was animated, and her face luminous with emotion. Her eyes sparkled and she seemed to be laughing and crying at the same time, completely absorbed in the conversation. More than once she grasped his hands, her cheeks flushed with warmth and excitement. The man leaned in and took her face and kissed her deeply, and Barnabas could see the elegant cut of his coat, his long lean body, his thick dark hair, and graceful hands. It was Quentin Collins who had won her heart.

Twenty-four

He was driving too fast and was oblivious to the speedometer easing around the dial. Humbled by what was now a bitter irony—he had convinced himself that she loved him, as he loved her—Barnabas focused on the one method of relieving the mortification gnawing at his insides like a hungry rat.

He careened recklessly at the bend in the road nearest the cemetery, blasting into a mound of sodden debris before he turned off the ignition. He struggled from the car, and hurried toward the graveyard gate. The bare trees were calm, their stillness eerie, and the full moon was fattening, a cruel round disc hovering on the horizon. This time his sense of direction did not fail him, and he went directly to the mausoleum with its sagging door where he had hidden Quentin's painting. There it was tucked behind the iron grate, sleeping with the dead.

His wound throbbed and carrying the canvas was difficult but Barnabas dragged himself slowly up the path toward Wid-

ws' Hill. When he reached the precipice, he stopped and looked
own. Moonlit foam rose and dissolved in never ceasing lines
f rolling surf, as it had since time's beginning. The waves crashed
n the rocks and the wind from the sea knocked him off balance.
Barnabas drew the painting to the edge. Rancor pulsed through
is body and the thrill of revenge produced a rush of euphoria.
He would destroy Quentin forever, his true image smashed into
its on the sand. Barnabas imagined the painting cartwheeling,
overing in the air, then dashing, torn and splintered, against
he rocks. The werewolf would be released on the rampage, and
Quentin would grow venal and repulsive, his soul no longer hidden, his urbane features deformed by a wolf's snout. Barnabas
aughed, his jealousy kindled to rage, and he rejoiced in the vi-
ion. She would not love him now.

The saucer moon danced and played a wicked game of hide-
and-seek in the low-lying clouds. Barnabas teetered at the edge,
his entangled fantasies torn between past and present. Where did
his own body hover? Somewhere between the inevitable infirmi-
ies of aging, and the loneliness of immortality. Was this why he
had felt such a thrill from his new life? Or was it his returning
ampire powers? He walked a tightrope over an abyss.

After the séance, Antoinette had clung to him and wept as
he consoled her. Holding her had rent him with happiness and
awe. She had been willing to sacrifice herself; she would have
died for her child. Where does such love come from? Does the
heart possess such courage? Once more, he looked down at
he rocks in the churning foam. His beloved Josette . . . here she
had leapt to her death, driven mad by a vision of the monster he
was to become. What agonies must have tormented her final moments? Just as Quentin would transform before Toni's eyes, grow
monstrous, and she would—she would—

Suddenly the image of Antoinette in the embrace of the
werewolf flashed across his inner consciousness like a film flickering in a broken projector. Again and again he saw her face:

her uncomprehending panic, her eyes wide with fear. She di
not deserve cruelty such as that. She deserved happiness, how
ever brief—with Quentin.

After Barnabas had replaced the painting in the crypt, h
stopped to look at his reflection in the car window. His breat
misted the pane and his image blurred, a ghost in a shroud
until the damp slowly receded and he saw his face in the nigh
Dark eyes looked out of a skull. What was he? Human or de
mon?

With his foot heavy on the accelerator, and his mind fum
bling over his own stupidity, Barnabas tortured himsel
with thoughts of the vampire. The Bentley blasted past mounds o
leaves sodden from the rain; and was just topping the hill abov
Collinwood when he saw beyond the trees a spilling of phospho
rescence, an explosion of fractured crystals, and then a fluorescen
haze. The full moon bloomed forth and teetered on the tops of th
trees. Glancing away from the road, he drank in Diana and he
chariot, the goddess he had worshiped for centuries. The tug wa
still there, as powerful as ever.

He fought back despair. Two miseries joined to tormen
him—anguish over Antoinette; and his wound, which now
pulsed continually and flared like a burning brand in his sid
as though it were a physical replica of his heartbreak. He though
back on the afternoon when he had first met Jason. A vampire
could not bear the sunlight, that was true; but his daytime ap
pearance could be easily explained away by something as simpl
as his dark sunglasses. There were vampires who were not dis
turbed by sunlight—unfortunately he was not one of those—jus
as some Nosferatu were immune to the power of crosses. Jason'
capacity to charm his listeners as he had done around the camp
fire, his magnetism, and even his seductive manner with Antoi
nette, had seemed remarkable, and what better masquerade coul

e have chosen than to pose as a belligerent hippie, luring his
trusting flock to their deaths. Barnabas recalled the young man's
supple masculinity; that alone should have betrayed uncanny
powers. Vile trickery! He had somehow eluded Barnabas's in-
stincts, dulled as they were by human naïveté. The perfection of
the Old House's restoration would have been incomprehensible
had it not been wrought by a master carpenter with diabolical
assistance. The business card of the Boston rug dealer tucked in
the door to his shop had led him to replace an unsuitable carpet,
intentionally laid out on the floor of the drawing room to trap
him. The same scheme determined the placement of his casket,
set there to lure him to his inevitable demise. Of course: a new
vampire would demand control over his territory. It all made perfect sense, and he had allowed this whipstart of a diabolis, this
newly birthed monster, reckless and unskilled, bereft of judgment and experience, to threaten his domain. The realization
that this lowlife ruffian was now intent on destroying his family
clouded Barnabas's brain with fury. He thrust down on the accelerator, and the Bentley leapt forwards like some great pri-
mordial beast devouring the road.

Shards of moonlight streaked the hood, and for a moment
Barnabas thought the moon might come through the windshield.
Larger and larger it swelled until it filled the glass, and only then
did he realize his vision was dangerously blurred as spasms of brilliance exploded in his brain. The car lifted slightly, then rocked,
and Barnabas was forced to steer blind, the road obliterated by
bright light; and he clung to the wheel in a glowing vacuum, until
he finally remembered to brake. The car jerked horribly, lurched,
then bucked across the road, rolled and crashed with a sickening
shudder into a ditch.

When he opened his eyes he had no idea how long he had
been unconscious. The car was on its side, the engine still running, and he reached for the key. The motor died in a tinny
gasp. Numb with pain, Barnabas crawled to the side of the road

and staggered to his feet. The lights of Collinwood flickered in th
distance and the moonlight drenched the surroundings as thoug
it were a day without color. It was imperative that he reach Juli
before it was too late. How could he have thought it would be pos
sible to continue on without her?

Now that he was out in the night, he became conscious of th
bite in the air, the cold against his cheek, and the voices of thou
sands of frogs keening in the ditches where water pooled from th
gutters. The buzzing seemed to be inside his brain. Lurchin,
spasmodically, he staggered up the drive and around to the fron
of the house. The great Tudor mansion loomed up over its wid
lawn, its turrets and chimneys silhouetted against the silver sky
The pale blue light behind the tall leaded windows of the drawin,
room beckoned, and he felt renewed affection for the place, a
though it no longer mocked him for his time there. The hous
seemed instead to belong to him, a gift from the centuries, and
although he labored up to the door, his side burning, he felt al
most refreshed by thoughts of those he loved. He would sacrific
it all for David, and for Julia, for Elizabeth, Roger, and Carolyn
even for Antoinette, although the thought of her flooded hin
with melancholy. He had loved her, and loved her still. Because o
her, he had tasted life again.

Just as he reached for the door, a flash of movement caught hi
eye, and he thought something passed over the lawn towards th
cliffs. He followed it, then lost sight of what he was pursuing. Th
sound of the sea rose to his ears and he stopped, leaned forwar
with his hands on his knees, gasping for breath. The poundin,
convinced him that he must be near the cliffs until he heard the
booming behind his eardrums and knew it was his own heart
empty of blood, rushing and sucking like the sea against a barren
shore. Rising up within him was the horror of his life, bereft of
purpose. He could not fail now.

The moon was higher, and the great oaks surrounding Colinwood stood silent and forbidding, their twisted branches reaching into a sky silver with light. Something reared up just ahead, the running figure of a man, and Barnabas dared to think it was Jason fleeing him. He rushed forward only to lose his quarry once more. He began to think his feverish mind was inventing a mirage, when he stumbled, and almost fell, across the body of a man who had collapsed on his face in the grass. Summoning strength, Barnabas turned the body over only to hear a shriek.

"No! No, Please! Don't!" A pair of bulging eyes looked up at him. "Barnabas? That you?" Willie's great relief at seeing his friend and master was palpable even in the dark. "Barnabas—he's there, a murderer—prowling around—I had to get out of there!"

"Willie, are you hurt?"

"Yeah, but I'm okay, just—Barnabas, you got to stop him, he's got a knife and crawling around on the roof—"

Barnabas probed under Willie's coat and pulled his hand away when he felt the moist blood through his shirt. Was this what he needed? He leaned in, his eye drawn to a small patch of skin under Willie's collar. But Willie sensed something strange and stuttered, "Barnabas, please, what are you doing? Don't please, not me." He pushed feebly against Barnabas's chest but the cape lifted and fell over the two of them, and Barnabas's breath was hot over the jugular, as with a moan he sank his teeth.

He could not even break the skin.

He tasted Willie's sweat, smelled both their odors, and knew, finally, that he was not a vampire, but a man, and he was dying. Faintly, he heard Willie whimper, "Please, Barnabas, he's got a knife and he's going room to room—trying to kill everyone in the family—"

Barnabas pulled away and looked back toward the house. The main tower thrust into the sky, and a light from the room he knew to be David's flickered as though candles burned within.

The front portal was a rectangle of warm, inviting light. He could make out patches of ivy crawling up the walls and see, in the moonlight, the long porch with its balustrade of carved posts. Willie panted beneath him, quivering, and Barnabas looked down at his servant, who wheezed, "Don't Barnabas, don't, please—" Again he raised up, searching for some sign. The moonlight illuminated surfaces of slate, the roof's deep pitch; and he traced the long horizontal ridge with its nine protruding chimneys, down across the slanted ceiling of the ballroom, then back again to the great tower, up to the widow's walk, and across to the lightning rod on the ridge. All was familiar and still.

Then he saw something that made him hunch to his feet and break into a run. Above the front entrance, where the half-timbered trim of the three dormers glowed in the moonlight, he could just make out the figure of a man. There on the topmost ridge, where the lightning rod was attached, stood Jason, his body dark against the moon.

He is waiting for me, thought Barnabas, and his only fear was that he could not manage to climb the roof before the killer fled. Breathing heavily, he plunged back across the lawn, and reached the edge of the porch. Was he gone? No, he was still there, glaring down with savage eyes. Jason stood erect, as though soldiering his post, his arms at his sides, and the shank of the knife shining in the moonlight. The drugs had taken their toll and, in his lust for revenge, Jason had gone mad.

Dragging himself through the front portico and up the staircase, Barnabas groped the long hallway, desperate to discover some opening to the roof. Finally he found an unlatched tower window near David's room, and climbed out. The pitch of the roof was treacherous, and he dug his feet against the shingles, teetering, and walked the narrow peak like a rope dancer, steep sides falling away, his cape billowing like a dark wing. In his old life, this would have been child's play, but he struggled to stay balanced and forgot his pain and weariness as he pushed forward.

Each time he looked to where Jason stood—certain by now he would have disappeared—he was revitalized to see him still there, watching him advance, daring him to proceed, his eyes lit by a flame of insanity. Moonlight silvered the back of his head and his high cheek, and it caught the glint of his knife, stained with blood.

Barnabas fought anxiety. Was he too drained by his months as a human to clash with one so much more powerful? A gust of wind buffeted them both, and Barnabas rocked, then lurched; his cape flew out like a sail, he found his balance and took another step. His heart throbbed in his chest like a drum of doom.

Finally Barnabas gained the cross ridge, and he stood behind Jason, who turned, ready to unleash all his power. He was faintly aware that, against the moonlit sky, they made a macabre pair, two assailants poised on a high roof's ridge, each primed for the kill. Just before Barnabas reached his quarry, the wind gusted, and Jason spun slowly all the way around like a weathervane. Barnabas drew back when Jason's rigid figure turned, and then returned, as though he were searching for another attacker, until, convinced that there was only one advancing, stopped to face him. Barnabas crouched, ready to leap, and weighed his options, while Jason, with a diabolical grin on his face, challenged him to make the first move. Then Jason pivoted again, but this time too stiffly, too mechanically. Barnabas was baffled until he saw, to his horror, that the man was not moving on his own, but was stuck—skewered on the lightning rod thrust up through his entire body, its point protruding from the top of his head!

What had seemed shadows of menace, from far off, were rivulets of gore seeping onto his cheeks. And on his neck, two gaping holes oozed with blood. Now the wind took him and turned him slowly once more, making him its plaything, and he returned to Barnabas and met him glazed eye to eye, speared by a lightning rod, hanging helplessly with his knife still in his hand.

Barnabas drew back. The dead man stared at him with all the evil in his nature now displayed in a macabre countenance: the diabolical grin, the eyes glazed with hate. Who could have done this? If Jason was not the vampire, then who could it be? Who would have had the strength or the agility to walk this peak with its steep shingles falling away three stories above the ground, lift a man of Jason's size, and impale him on a pole?

Instantly Barnabas thought of his family, of David, alone in his room, and the others still exposed to unimagined terrors. He crossed the ridge, scaled the curved walls, and found himself within the mansion, pacing the hall, stealthily opening every door. To his relief, Carolyn slept blissfully, her golden hair silkening her pillow, her lips curved in a smile. Elizabeth stirred when he looked in, her sleep troubled, and he glanced around the shadows of her boudoir. Silently he leaned under her canopy to make certain she was alone and checked in her closet. His search only heightened his anxiety. Becoming more afraid every minute, he entered Roger's room, but drew back at a strange sound. Roger's snore was as aristocratic as his other pronouncements, a sonorous snuffle. Safe. All were safe. Hearing a noise at the top of the stair, Barnabas wheeled.

Carrying a flashlight, Willie labored towards the landing, breathing heavily. "Barnabas," he said, "You seen anything yet?" His pale face appeared above the glare.

"I am on my way to Julia's room. Fetch Roger's gun. Be careful not to wake the house." Willie turned reluctantly, but Barnabas stopped him. "Wait. Bring—instead—a stake and a hammer."

"Why?"

"We no longer seek a prowler, Willie. I should have warned you. Jason, the prowler you saw, is dead, and there—there is a vampire—"

"Another one?"

"There were deep punctures in Jason's neck."

"Oh jeeze, Barnabas, this is crazy. What's happenin' around here?"

Outside of David's room, Barnabas hesitated, conscious of his failing strength, fearful of what he would find. With quivering fingers, he pushed against the door. The room was gleaming with candlelight, and shadows danced on the walls. There was a soft sound of crooning, and the faint odor of blood. Something inside Barnabas collapsed as all his hope gave way. David lay stretched out on his bed, his head hidden by a dark and shaggy hulk that rocked and keened. It was Jackie, leaning over him, her white arms wrapped around him, and her dark, luxurious hair falling forward and obscuring both their faces. She dipped her shoulders again and again, and sang in soft tones, the words unintelligible, as she rocked, encircling David, and pulled him to her.

Barnabas staggered into the room, his labored breathing betraying his presence. She lifted her head and looked at him, her eyes two stars, and just as he had feared, her lips were red with blood. With the boy lying over her lap she was like a painting of a Pieta, the folds of her robe flowing to the ground.

"You," he whispered. "My God. It was you all along."

"Why are you here?" she said in a voice that was more a growl.

"Jacqueline, what have you done?"

"I?"

"Is he—is David dead?"

She shook her head, and Barnabas saw in a flash the child beneath the demon he had imagined, her delicate face and flushed cheek, and her amazing eyes like minnows in a pool. She pulled David closer and answered in a meeker tone, gentle and innocent.

"No, he is hurt. He has cuts. I am only kissing them."

His mind blurred. Was she a changeling, or something possessed? "Kissing them?"

"To heal them," she said simply, as if it were perfectly obvious. She was a demon and she had gone mad as well. Barnabas moved closer, ready to grab her and pull her away; then David moaned and shuddered slightly. There was dried blood on his neck, but he was alive.

"What is this ghastly deed?" Barnabas asked her again, reaching for the table to lean on. He thought he might black out.

"I told you. Jason cut him. I'm kissing them away."

He took another step, and her face grew dark. Her eyes flashed like knives. "What are you doing?"

"He needs help—a doctor— Surely you will let me take him—Jackie—what have you done to him?"

She drew up and placed her hand on David's cheek. "I have saved his life," she said. Then she looked hard at Barnabas. "And he is the only Collins worth saving."

"What—how? Who are you?"

"You know who I am. I am Miranda du Val."

"And are you—my God—are you a vampire?"

"No, Barnabas. I am a witch."

Candlelight warmed her face, and David's as well, for the boy was sleeping peaceably again. Both were flushed as though they had just made love. They were so beautiful, the two of them, radiant in youth's perfection, their childish features caressed by the flames, it was difficult to imagine any evil about them. He reached again, but the steel in her gaze stopped him.

"Stay back," she said, and her flinty eyes glittered. "Leave me here to care for him."

"I can't leave him with you, Jacqueline. Don't you know that?"

"But he is in no danger. You were the one I came to destroy."

"To destroy me?"

Her face grew hard, her voice bitter. "I hounded you. I

trapped you with a phony carpet, and you took the bait. I bit you in my mother's tent. Even a vampire's bite is easy to fake. I followed you and I tormented you. Didn't you know the leaves were meant to kill you? And they would have the next time."

"But, why?"

"Because I carry the curse."

The room was tilting. *The curse, the curse,* the words buzzed in his brain like the inside of a hive. The curse had begun in Salem, and she was the witch who cursed them, the witch reborn as Angelique, and now Jacqueline. The sins of his ancestors were always to be his heritage, and he had only added to the legacy. He would never escape. He stared at her in astonishment, slowly shaking his head, and put his hand over his eyes to blot out her face.

She spoke in a gentler tone. "But you needn't worry any more, Barnabas. I have changed. You and my mother came to help me. She was willing to give her life for mine. I have been taught love. And so, you are free. I don't want you any more." The flames from the candles spun in dizzying circles and flared behind his eyeballs. "She came to save me, don't you see? And now I have saved David. You can go free."

Free? Could he trust her? He should make a move, do something, but he felt helpless. From far away he heard her voice. "But you had better take care of what is wrong with you," she said. "Because I think you are dying."

Julia! A doctor devoted to the Collins family. She would know what to do. He heaved down the corridor until he found her door, and now he knew for certain that the time he had remaining was nearly over. He could feel his strength draining away. His burst of vigor had been but a final flare in a dying fire. No wonder he was no threat to the witch girl. His days without blood had taken their toll. Like a fool, he had ignored his dependence on the elixir for too long. A gunshot injury he had thought was nothing was infecting his entire body. His heart was beating too slowly, too faintly, hovering on the edge of silence. The floor reeled, and the walls closed in on him, then sprang back. He had no control over his legs; his arms dangled at his sides. The only sound he could hear was his own panting, and the white light flashed and hissed like a revolving beacon inside his head.

He found Julia's door and fell into her room.

A single bedside lamp cast an eerie glow on the rug and across her bed which lay smooth and unslept in. He looked around for her in desperation, and was about to run back out, then saw her medical case on the table in front of the window. It gaped open, and all the contents were spilled, the vials broken, the capsules of elixir drained, the hypodermic needles shattered. With a deep groan, he leaned against the table, and stared at the discarded instruments. All were ruined. Who could have done such a thing? Whatever wanted him dead had attacked Julia as well. Could the monster have killed her? Had Jason come before—or Jackie? He sagged with exhaustion. Outside the window, the oak branches hung thick and still. Barnabas stared into the dark and wept empty vampire tears.

A thud from the hall outside dragged him to the doorway. He clung to the portal, praying it was Julia, that she would appear and save him; but it was only Willie tiptoeing down the corridor, a flashlight in one hand, a stake and hammer under his arm. The whites of his eyes shifted back and forth in the dark.

Barnabas could barely speak. "Willie, have you seen Julia?"

"Ain't she in her room?"

"No, I'm afraid something dreadful has happened to her."

"Well, I did see something, the vampire—whatever it is— Barnabas I don't want to track down another—"

"Where?"

"Going down into the basement." He jerked the light, and Barnabas felt its glare. "Jeeze, Barnabas. What happened to you? You look awful."

"I'll be all right once I find Julia. Willie, all the medication has been destroyed—"

"And that's why you—well, maybe she has some more hidden away—"

Willie's face loomed like a Halloween mask. Barnabas closed his eyes and listened for his heart. It was slowing; he was growing weaker. There were long seconds between each beat, and each one shook his frame. What was happening to him? Julia would know. What if she were dead—killed by Jason—or the demon loose in the house? And all because of his blundering.

"Willie, come here. Let me lean on you." Willie eyed Barnabas suspiciously. "Don't worry, I won't hurt you. I need you."

They descended the stair to the foyer, Barnabas's arm slung over Willie's shoulders. Barnabas shuffled like a sleepwalker, staring out of unseeing eyes. The familiar corridors, the wallpaper, the pattern of the carpet shifted and crawled as if alive. Were worms already feeding behind his eyes? When they reached the landing to the basement stairs, he swayed and nearly toppled into the gloom. Willie caught him and pulled him back.

"Barnabas, you sure you want to go down there?"

"We must."

"But what'll we do if we find something?"

Barnabas reached for the hammer and stake.

The basement was cavernous and emitted the odor of damp concrete and earth. Beneath the huge hand-hewn joists on which the great house rested were dark caves where the beams lay on the stone foundation. Hidden cubicles were stuffed with cardboard boxes of clothes and books. Willie reached for the single bulb hanging from a cord, and pulled the string. The light, which swung slowly, altered the shadows, but failed to diminish them. Spiders' webs hung from the plumbing pipes overhead, and conduit snaked up the walls. Old chests, a battered electric fan, an air conditioner turned on its side, a steel safe with the accusing eye of one combination dial, all stood like squat soldiers guarding their territory. In the center of the basement, posing as their general, a rectangular forced-air heater, covered with dust, towered ten feet high.

Willie cast the beam of the flashlight into corners and behind crates, muttering, "There ain't nothin' here. Can't we go back upstairs?" In truth, Barnabas could hear nothing, nor sniff the unmistakable odor of his breed.

An area with a cement floor and a rusty drain served as the house laundry, and, beside an ironing board with a badly burnt cloth top stood a washing machine and dryer. They glimmered an almost ghostly white until Barnabas noticed a narrow window through which a pale light gleamed. It was dawn. Once more the vampire would escape with the day, flee to some cave of comfort, and slip from their grasp.

The pilot light of the furnace clicked, and the gas jets exploded with a violent whoosh! Willie grabbed for Barnabas like a frightened child. "I got to get out of here. I got to take a leak."

"No, Willie, wait. Don't leave me."

As it began to heat, the furnace pinged and hummed with a deep roar. Reluctantly Barnabas turned to the stair. He would search further, through all the first floor rooms. A wave of weariness washed over him. He must hold on. He must do this one last thing before the white light returned and seared his brain. He knew he was dying. Was that what had worried Julia? That he would grow weaker and weaker and one day—what fatal irony! To finally become human only to succumb so quickly to the final human destiny.

Following Willie, he began his lethargic climb when he spotted, tucked beneath the stair, a door without a doorknob.

"Wait, Willie—what is that?" There was only a keyhole and the door appeared latched from inside. "That door. Break it open."

"Barnabas, there ain't nothin' in there—"

"Do as I say!"

"Okay, okay, hold on—" Willie cast the beam about for some tool, but finding none for the purpose, he sighed and set the flashlight on the floor. He stepped back and threw his weight against the panel. The splintered portal gaped open, and a golden light spilled out.

The room was a crypt. Tall iron candelabras hung with dripping tapers cast a honeyed light within the chamber. Bouquets of lilies—masses of snowy trumpets tinged with coral—emanated an exotic aroma. And there in the center of the room—there it lay—at last. The casket was large, wide enough for two. Barnabas noticed with a flicker of envy that his adversary's choice was elegant indeed. It gleamed—a polished ebony—and its curves were sumptuous. "I think—we have found our vampire," he said.

"Who do you think it is?" Willie whispered.

Determined to end his quest, summoning all his strength and fighting a wave of dizziness, he grasped the stake tightly in his left hand and hefted the mallet.

"Open the casket. And stand back."

For once, Willie obeyed. Perhaps he was curious as well, eager to end the uncertainty. Barnabas poised, knees shaking, legs apart, and the shaft raised at the ready. Slowly, Willie lifted the lid. It did not creak as Banabas's had always done—that old musical whine. Instead, it rose with a sigh.

Willie jumped out of the way and Barnabas lunged forwards but he heard Willie's footsteps slapping on the stair. "I can't watch it! Not her!"

When he saw what lay inside the coffin, he slowly lowered his tools.

Julia lay on a bed of saffron satin, her hands crossed over her breast. A single lily caught between her fingers had drooped slightly and scattered its crimson pollen on her gown. Her face was carved ivory, with deep shadows, and her skin a translucent amber hue. Her hair was once again a vibrant auburn, and her high cheekbones flared beneath cinnamon lashes. He wondered at her body, every voluptuous curve visible beneath the silken robe. She was beautiful.

He fumbled with the stake. He must release her. The vampire who had bitten her must not be allowed to damn her to the life he had known. He placed the point above her heart and pressed it into the flesh. He hesitated for an instant, then he raised the hammer, but his shaking hands could not perform the deed.

He collapsed on her body, shuddering with guilt. He was a villain. She had sacrificed everything for him; and he had shunned her, treated her with contempt, and something even worse, indifference. If he had only stayed near her, protected her, and loved her, this would never have happened. Was there no atonement possible, no penance he could perform? He raised his head and gazed at her still face. He touched her cheek. Slowly he began to stroke her limbs. She was warm and pliable even in death. He leaned in, and kissed her, softly, as he should have done in life. He gathered her to him, pressing her close, and held her against him, his head on her heart.

For many minutes he lay there, aware of a steady beat. She would rise again. He breathed words, his lips against her lips, "Julia, I am dying. Is that not punishment enough?"

The flames of the candles flickered as he set the stake once more. "Forgive me," he whispered, and, summoning resolve, raised the hammer. With all his power, he struck. At that moment, her brown eyes flared; and her hand swept up and caught his wrist on the downward blow.

"Barnabas—" she whispered. He stared at her aghast and shrank away. She was beautiful no longer, but a terrifying apparition. The rims of her eyes and her inner nostrils leaked red, and her soft lips parted to reveal her fangs, sharp and descended.

He jerked his hand from her grasp and heaved the mallet, jamming the stake between her ribs.

"I must—forgive me, I must—I cannot let you—my God, how you must despise me!" He closed his eyes and struck.

The next thing he knew, he was flying across the room. He slammed into the wall and fell in a broken heap on the floor. Rolling over with a groan, he swooned. When he opened his eyes she was standing before him, her face gleaming, her dress falling in amber folds. "I could never despise you, Barnabas," she said.

He could barely speak. "Julia . . . you . . . a vampire?"

"You hadn't guessed? The needles. I became contaminated when I mixed my blood with yours. I struggled so long, much too long, to keep you human—to keep us both human—" She took a step toward him. She was regal, her copper hair, her topaz eyes aflame.

"But—you were always such a cautious physician—"

"Yes. I became careless, I suppose. Or perhaps, all this time, I have had an unconscious desire to join you in your world." She moved closer, and he was astonished again by her beauty. Her skin was luminous, her body fluid and rippling like the muscles of a cat. But something in her mood frightened him. He drew back against the wall.

"Julia. David is hurt. Badly hurt. You are his doctor. That girl is possessed—mad—we have to help him."

She laughed, a guttural laugh that played the lower scales. "Why is it, Barnabas, you only think of others when you are in danger?" He tried to rise but fell back with a cry, pain shooting through his body.

"But . . . David—"

"The children have no need of us," she said. "Jackie will save him, for, as you must know by now, that is her gift. She has astonishing powers. I was forced to fight her, as well, to keep you alive. It weakened me—"

"And I was so ungrateful." He sagged against the wall, then muttered, "Something terrible, Julia—the medicine—the vials are all broken—the elixir—"

"There is no more elixir."

"Your great discovery?"

"How could I make the formula, once I had become infected? My blood was tainted."

Realization flooded his brain. "Then it was you in the wood?"

"Yes." Her voice was like chimes. "The workman was my first victim. I knew nothing other than I needed blood. But when I saw that you were going to track the vampire, I tried to frighten you so that you would not find me out. I needed time. . . ."

"But . . . your bite did not change me back. . . ."

"No—" She floated above him, smiling.

"Why?" Feeble panic flickered in his body.

"Fate plays its tricks. The cure was successful. You became human at last, whereas I—"

He could smell the lilies, their pungent perfume. He was desperate to keep her away. "But the workman became—?"

"Jackie's doing, not mine. She pulled him out of the leaves and made him her slave. But that is all over now." Her eyes blazed, coral, then vermilion, flames flickering in the irises. "I have been waiting for you." Her copper hair flared from her head as she raised her arm and swept the chamber. "I have made the preparations for our wedding."

He closed his eyes. "It's too late. You warned me—and you were right. And now . . . I'm . . . Julia, I'm old . . . and I'm dying."

She sank beside him and he was dazzled by her smile, her eager expression, her flaming eyes, which were hypnotizing him now, and a cruelty in her curled lips that he could never have imagined in his gentle Julia.

"I can make you young again," she said.

She placed one hand on his shoulder and another on his

forehead and pushed him down, twisting his body, arching his neck. Her teeth gleamed and her eyes were glowing coils as she whispered, "I have a new cure."

He floundered and heaved up, but he was helpless under her grip. She lowered, and too soon he felt the exquisite pain when she pierced his neck, hovered there for a moment, then lowered her body to his, enveloping him in her embrace. He moaned as she began to drink. Many times he had imagined his victims' terror, but never had he dreamed it would be like this: the utter helplessness, the limbs like water, the paralyzed will. This is the fate I deserve, he thought, as his mind dimmed: to die as I have lived. The swirling lights in his brain faded slowly like pale flames until extinguished by a breath. He reached his arms around her and abandoned himself to her power.

Darkness fell over his thoughts. He was tossed into black waters, caught by a wave, swung back, then dashed against a reef, seized in eddies and swirling sea grass, until he was plucked up again, sucked out to sea then smashed on the rocks. He died, and died again, each time picked up and swept out to sea, then flung against some unforgiving beach, his heart shuddering, as what blood he had wound its way through his veins, and she—Julia!—drained him until he was an empty shell. His heart beat its last muffled drumming, once, twice, and then silence.

He would have smiled had his face been more than a lifeless mask. He had always wondered if, when death finally came, he would be there to see it. Whether he would show courage or cowardice. But now it no longer mattered. He floated on a sea tide of darkness, drifted against a soft shore, and lay still, abandoned and alone. Then something reached for him and drew him onto the sand.

He opened his eyes and, through glazed vision, saw Julia on her knees beside him. She smiled and spoke low. "This, finally, is our wedding night." Reaching up to her own neck, her nails like knives, she sliced her throat. Blood oozed, and she whispered, "Come fly with me," and came down in a rush, falling lightly against him, and he found her and drank in a swoon, thinking he must be dreaming after death, that this, too, was death's cruel trick, until slowly, warmth returned; his long channels filled, as a dry riverbed in a rain shower, and his heart began to beat once again.

David and Jacqueline had spent the day exploring the eighteenth-century buildings at Mystic Seaport. Flushed with excitement, they burst into the sitting room of the old Randall's Ordinary.

"Barnabas you missed it!" cried David. "Where have you been all day?"

"I've been here with Julia," he answered. She reached for his hand and smiled.

"We saw a neat-o sailmaking loft with huge pieces of canvas and old awls and needles," said David. "I tried to sew with one of the needles and I could barely push it through the cloth!"

"Really?"

"And we saw a rope-twisting demonstration," said Jackie. "They stood a block away from each other and twisted four strands into a rope, just like magic."

"There's a machine shop with enormous gears and huge leather pulleys to drive the saws and lathes."

"And Ye Old Apothecary with soaps and herbs!"

"You have had fun," said Julia.

"And beautiful schooners! Square-rigged sailing vessels. You have to come and see them."

Julia smiled at the two teenagers brimming with merriment, and Barnabas noticed how handsome she looked this evening. Her clear skin shone and her eyes were lustrous. She was all of a coppery auburn color.

"Will you come with us to see the boats?" said David to Barnabas. "I know you will love them."

"Of course. Is it nearly dark outside?"

"It doesn't matter," said Jackie. "Somehow they are even more mysterious when you can pretend they are only in port for one night."

"One of them is called the *Joseph Conrad*," said David. "He wrote a book called *Heart of Darkness*, and I have even read it."

Jackie smacked him on the arm. "You are such a nerd. Always studying." And she laughed, her minnow eyes dancing.

As the four walked along the docks in the moonlight, David and Jacqueline argued about the *Joseph Conrad*, whether it was a brigantine or a barque, and which sail was the top gallant. Barnabas and Julia walked hand in hand, their bodies elegant and powerful. The trail of the moon played on the water, and the masts of the fine old schooner rose against the sky and tipped slowly back and forth. Her heavy sails were gathered under her spars, and her decks were cluttered with the tools of seafaring. It was possible to imagine she was a working square-rigger with her vats for rending whale oil, her great black anchor, and its rope the thickness of a man's arm. The heavy lines squeaked as they pulled against belaying pins thrust deep in the pinrails, and the ship shuddered and creaked as though it longed for the sea.

The four climbed on the deck. Julia stood against the stays, her slender body taut and graceful, and gazed out at the water. Barnabas leaned into the binnacle, fascinated by the compass still floating under the glass. David climbed the rigging to the crow's nest and waved to those below, his bare arms silvered by the moon. Jacqueline walked to the bow and leaned over the bow-sprit. Her hand gently grazed the carved figurehead of a woman whose flowing robes and tumbling hair suggested that she was flying into the wind. Her face was serene and, folded among her billowing garments, were the wings of an angel.

Epilogue

The day Benajah Collins took up residence in the house built by Miranda's father, the forest stood one hundred yards beyond the beaver pond. Later that evening, he and his wife and his children, six in number, failed to notice the patient cedars lined up along the bank. Little Peter, rising early and eager to investigate his new swimming hole, was ankle deep in mud before he saw black snakes wriggling around his toes. He ran to tell his mother, but she paid him no heed, as she was preparing the noonday meal, and had her hands in flour. She found, however, almost all her kindling was spent and the fire in the grate gone to ashes. She called to her oldest son Edward, a strapping lad of fourteen, to fetch some firewood. Gathering up her colicky baby, she went to the window to look out.

The trees, which had stood at a reasonable distance the night before, seemed much closer this morning, but she told herself, as she soothed the whimpering child, and scolded another whining at her skirts, that she must have been mistaken; what with the difficulty of unloading all her possessions from the cart, she had not been observant. She chastised herself for this fault.

She was at her sink washing the baby's soiled rags when she looked out and saw the trees on the other side of the yard, but once again she simply shrugged, and, irritated at what she perceived to be sinful laziness, went to wake her husband, who had fallen asleep in his chair. After dinner, to which no Edward returned, leaving her more annoyed than worried, she gathered the bowls in the sink. She was scrubbing the bread pan when the room grew dark, and this time she knew something had changed. The trees were at her window, blotting out the sun, and branches were scraping and clawing at the opposite side of the glass.

Some said later the Naumkeag had cut the trees and hidden behind their trunks. Others wrote, years afterwards, in scientific journals, explanations of how the trees themselves had attacked the hapless family. Physicists expounded their truths with mathematical formulae, and preachers invoked the Biblical Wonders of an Invisible World. Stories, as is so often true in these cases, varied as well, in their description of what was found. Some said an odd piece of clothing or a child's wooden toy. But the usual report was nothing.

etacomet took Miranda to the lake beyond the great valley, a place she had longed to visit ever since she was a child. He launched his birch bark canoe and they paddled until they reached the center, where they drifted. The still surface of the water was like a bolt of silk stretched on a giant loom. She could see to the bottom—a dark world.

Around the edge of the lake the trees made one unbroken line. Snow lay scattered in the shadows along the shore. The branches were bare but shone with a rosy aurora. She knew if she were to look at any twig, she would see the new growth, and the red buds ready to uncurl.

"Metacomet, look. The trees are rose-colored as the dawn."

He smiled at her and nodded. "Death is only a season," he said.

As the canoe slid forward, she trailed her hand in the water, and it left a shining path.

"We will all live again?"

"And again. Perhaps, the next time, you will be born of water."

"I remember the raid on our village when I was a child, all the deaths."

He looked a little sad and pursed his lips.

"I remember when you pulled us up on your horse, my mother and me, and carried us off to the Wampanoag settlement. It was you, wasn't it? I saw your bear claw necklace."

"That was the second time your mother was there with us."

"When was the first?"

"She came once, before you were born, searching for the Black Man."

"Why?"

"She was wanting a child and had waited many years. She thought he might grant her wish."

"Where did she find the courage to wander into the forest?"

"I don't know, but she found our camp."

"Did she find the Black Man?"

"She found me."

Miranda turned to Metacomet. "You have always called me daughter, but I thought—is this true?"

"To the best of my memory."

She was silent.

The lake stretched on forever, the trees on either side, until the water met the sky.

"Oh, your stories of creation," she said at last, lying back in the canoe to look up at the clouds. "Tell me of the Great Spirit."

Metacomet looked ahead and pulled one time with his paddle—dip, dip and swing. His face was lined like dried leaves, and the tracks of his two scars were his long tears.

"Cautantowwit made a man and a woman of stone, but he didn't like it, so he broke it into many pieces and made another man and woman of a tree. Of the core and the bark that clings to it. This he did. The trees therefore are the fountains of mankind. The souls of all our ancestors live in the trees. When you fly, Sisika, you fly among the souls."

She thought for a long time. "You are only saying that to make me happy."

"It is a good story."

The canoe drifted until it was a spot far off on the water.

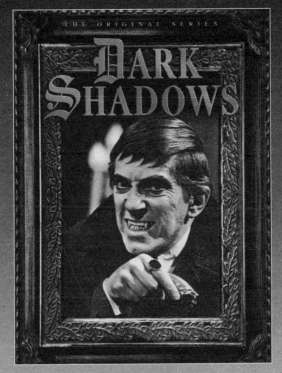